Lesbian Romance (4 Books in 1)

True Erotic Sex Stories, EXPLICIT DIRTY HOT NOVELS FOR LESBIAN

Explicit Erotic Sex Stories

Aubree Mislead Isabel

Prohibited companions Sapphic experiences.

Recently, Isabel has been confounded about her sentiments towards Aubree, a beautiful blonde young lady with a strange past who lives across the road, a lot to the dismay of Isabel's folks who detest their little girl partner with Aubree. Will Isabel be a similar consistent young lady she has consistently been, or will things begin to change for her from this point forward?

All characters and occasions in this story are anecdotal, and any closeness to genuine people living or dead is unplanned and accidental. Just characters matured 18-years and more seasoned are in any sexual circumstances. Kindly appreciate this parody show story 'Aubree Leads Isabel Astray.'

***

"It's alright Isabel, we as a whole slip by into wrongdoing some of the time. It's the way we gain from our wrongdoing that Our Lord gives most consideration to."

IsabelSamara tuned in to her dad's expressions, the Reverend Larry Samara, and concluded it was simpler to apologize. "I'm extremely grieved," she said.

The wrongdoing 18-year-old Isabel had carried out on this fine and bright October morning - unexpectedly warm for North Carolina for this season was to take a piece of toast before Reverend Samara could pray.

"I realize you are Isabel," Reverend Samara guaranteed his little girl. He grinned at her. "What's more, what better approach to assuage our Lord than to say Grace now?"

Isabel, her mom Helen Samara and Isabel's more youthful sibling Peter brought down their heads. Simultaneously, the Reverend Samara prayed, closing by saying 'So be it,' and the family started to have their morning meal.

"I trespassed myself this week," Reverend Samara said to his girl. "I was driving as it were the point at which another driver cut before me, and I utilized a word that is just suitable for a water catchment. Presently terrible driving from an individual driver can be exceptionally bothering. However, it was no reason at all for me to utilize such appalling language."

"I trespassed to yesterday," said Mrs. Samara. "At the store this week, the clerk gave me a nickel a lot in the change. I understood as I was getting in the vehicle, and I considered simply heading out. Yet, at that point, I reconsidered it and returned the nickel to the store."

Isabel saw her folks. Her dad Larry was a tall and dainty man with a bare head, put something aside for a ring of white hair around the edge, and all over, he wore glasses. Helen Samara had light earthy-colored hair and held a portion of her attractive features from her more youthful years, even though she consistently looked stressed somewhat. Isabel tried not to feign exacerbation and couldn't accept how her God-dreading guardians were worried about such minor offenses.

A year more youthful than her, Peter supported the first occasion when that early daytime saying to his sister, "Isabel, did you realize that daily on Venus is longer than a year?"

Isabel consistently cooperated to be amiable. "Indeed, it's extremely intriguing, right?"

"What's more, did you realize that Venus turns west to east, not east to west?" Peter inquired.

"Indeed, that would be bizarre to see, wouldn't it?" said Isabel. "Envision remaining on Venus watching the sun come up preposterous skyline?"

Peter shot his more established sister a curious look. "That would be senseless. You'd be standing by excessively long for one, and Venus is shrouded in mists, so you were unable to see the sun at any rate. Did you realize that Uranus turns on its hub sideways? For what reason do you think Venus and Uranus turn so uniquely in contrast to different planets?"

Isabel had no clue, yet Reverend Samara did. "This is because when God made the universe, He concluded that the planet Venus would turn west to east and the planet Uranus would turn sideways."

Peter acknowledged this undoubtedly, at that point, asked his sister, "Did you realize that some of Jupiter and Saturn's moons are greater than the planets Mercury and Pluto? There are Ganymede and Titan ..."

Isabel, as was frequently the case, allowed her sibling's words just to pass her by. Isabel knew about Peter's fixation on the Solar System, which had possibly expanded as of late when John Glenn had circled the Earth the earlier year when the Russians and the Americans had placed satellites into space. President Kennedy had declared designs to put a man on the moon before the decade was done. The youngster considered her more youthful sibling as he had issues, yet it was difficult to pinpoint precisely these issues.

Since youth, Peter had battled with making companions and essential coordination, just as having a fixation on schedules and continually doing things a specific way. He knew the nearby transport schedules off inside and out and could tell immediately if any number was an indivisible number, so clearly, it was canny. However, he had never dominated riding a bike. He would either be removed with different children, assault them with realities about subjects that lone intrigued him, or would make a decent attempt to be companions, pushing different children away or driving them to menace and mocking him. He appeared to have little idea of proper conduct. He had an irritating propensity - presently, fortunately, got rid of - of thumping on the restroom entryway when Isabel was

5

in there, sharing realities on space and space investigation with his more seasoned sister through the entryway when all she needed was security.

Peter at last quit bothering Isabel with something about Halley's Comet - about how he was unable to hold on to see it regardless of its appearance not coming for an additional 23 years. Sadly for Isabel, Reverend Samara utilized the break-in discussion to raise his number one subject - sin.

"Discussing how we as a whole trespassed in minor manners this week has made me think about the manners in which our Lord works," said Reverend Samara. "The awful driver out and about, an excess of progress at the store, and the impulse to eat before imploring were all God's method of testing our confidence and resolve. He places numerous tests in our lives each day, just to perceive how individuals from His rush responds notwithstanding allurement."

"Along these lines, terrible things are generally tested by God?" Isabel asked her dad.

"Not all, more genuine things are crafted by hazier powers," said Reverend Samara. "Take gay people, the weird men who cruise all over to schools and jungle gyms endeavoring to draw kids into their vehicles with candy. Homosexuality is such a cursed thing, such wrongdoing that dim powers must craft it. On the off chance that solitary gay people looked for the Lord's Word and confidence through petition, they would be relieved; however, clearly, they decide not to and toward the end will endure the results. Be that as it may, some different occasions are a bigger test by God, for example, for us having the Clayton family move in across the road."

Isabel again smothered a moan. Given how her folks detested the Clayton family since their appearance in the late spring of 1961, one could expect that they were extremely troublesome, meddlesome. Upsetting neighbors, who made a lot of commotion, let canines wander indiscriminately, or bark at throughout the hours, or permitted their property to deteriorate into filthiness, pulling in rodents, mice, cockroaches, and different nuisances to the zone. In any case, the Clayton family - comprising the dad Ben, his kid twin girl and child Aubree and Brad and their cousin Chip - like Aubree and Brad likewise matured 18 - hushed up, wonderful and kept their home and nursery slick and very much kept up.

"Ben Clayton is a great representation of what's up with present-day culture today," said Reverend Samara. "The man should be a Roman Catholic - not that he and the children at any point go to Mass - but he permits his family to play sport on a Sunday."

Isabel recalled when she had gotten back from chapel the past Sunday. Mr. Clayton, Aubree, Brad, and Chip were inactively throwing a football around their front nursery while having a break from painting outside their home. Isabel thought this scarcely established game, yet her folks were frightened by the scene.

"Furthermore, if that family should be Catholic, where are the spouse and mother?" Reverend Samara asked challengingly.

Isabel herself didn't know of the response to this inquiry. She went to secondary school with Aubree, Brad, and Chip however had never heard the twins talk about their mom nor Chip discuss an auntie. Isabel wasn't going to go up and request one from them as it wasn't any of her concern; however, she had estimated that perhaps Mrs. Clayton had kicked the bucket at young age kids so annoyed with her passing that they never discussed her.

"Maybe Mrs. Clayton passed on?" Isabel recommended it to her dad.

"One may believe that however both your mom and I have heard Mr. Clayton allude to his better half not as his 'late spouse' but rather as his 'ex.' You understand what that implies, isn't that right? The man is a Catholic who is separated. God expected union with being a joining among man and lady just to be isolated by death; however, some way or another, Ben Clayton assumes that separation is worthy. Yet, what would you be able to anticipate from a man who permits his youngsters to sit in front of the TV programs where teens dance to take care of business, sees no issue with his child taking his better half to the drive-in and his girl not exclusively to go out on dates with unrespectable young men however wear those awful new smaller than usual skirts that publicize things that ought never to be available to be purchased? Where does Aubree discover such improper garments?"

"Aubree makes some part memories work at a shop," Isabel chipped in.

"You appear to be very amicable with Aubree," remarked Reverend Samara.

"Actually, no, not actually," said Isabel. "We're simply in a significant number of similar classes at school."

"You might have tricked me," said Reverend Samara. "Only fourteen days before, you visited her at the Clayton house, and the week before that, she came here to see you." Reverend and Mrs. Samara took a gander at Isabel, looking for additional clarification from the teen.

There was an apparent clarification for this, and Isabel explained. "Aubree was away debilitated from school with a cold for two days, so I took her analytics task home to her. What's more, I had a similar cold the prior week - recall that I was wiped out and off school - so Aubree took my topography task to class to hand it in so I wouldn't lose marks for turning it in late."

"Indeed, I surmise those are sensible clarifications," said Reverend Samara. "However, Isabel, I don't need you are connecting with Aubree Clayton anything else than you need to; she is a terrible impact similar to her sibling Brad. You additionally avoid Chip. That kid was shipped off live with his uncle as his mom and father couldn't handle him appropriately."

"They've generally been pleasant to me," Isabel called attention to.

"They seem decent because that is the way they bait blameless young ladies like yourself of the Lord's way and into transgression with enticements. We shouldn't connect with them in any case, with them being Roman Catholics."

"Father, the President, is a Roman Catholic," Isabel advertised.

"Indeed, and the Lord had some arrangement with this that neither you nor I could start to comprehend," said Reverend Samara. "The Lord in his insight made us unique, yet while He needs us to be open-minded toward one another, His will is for us not to turn out to be excessively recognizable."

"Thus, I shouldn't be companions with Roman Catholics?" Isabel inquired.

"You ought to be courteous and aware; however, stay away," said Reverend Samara. "It's not simply Roman Catholics. There are numerous fine Jewish individuals; however, do we go to a place of worship? No, we don't. What's more, it is something very similar with different Christians. Negroes have their holy places. Tomorrow, would it be advisable for me to miss our administration at our congregation and take you, your mom, and your sibling to a Negro church? No, we would feel awkward there, and the Negroes would likewise feel awkward. It would be equivalent to on the off chance that we went to a

9

congregation for Chinamen. We should regard the Negroes and the Chinamen and their temples, yet it isn't important for God's will for Whites, Negroes, and Chinamen to revere Him together."

"Your dad is correct, Isabel," stated Mrs. Samara, seeing the baffled look all over.

"Indeed, he is," Isabel said. Regularly it was simpler to concur with her folks if she did. Times were changing, yet her mom and father and a large number of their companions were not, sticking to the past with an iron hold.

"Presently, discussing church, we would be wise to hurry up; there's a ton to do toward the beginning of today for the fete," said Reverend Samara.

Isabel again smothered a murmur. A congregation fete, an incredible inverse of fun. Not that Isabel nor her sibling Peter had some good times at any rate. A good time for Peter was finding out about the Solar System in books from the library, so he had a great time in his unusual way. Notwithstanding, Isabel thought they were fun because typical young people like current music, spending time with companions, going out to see the films, and moving, things her folks disliked. In this manner, she was prohibited from.

Isabel was an image of pretty flawlessness with her long, dull earthy colored hair, wonderful earthy colored eyes, and sweet doll-like face. This Saturday morning, her thin figure was attired in a pink dress - somewhat old-fashioned, however, which actually looked great on her - and she had tied her hair back into a pig tail with pink lace. Part of the explanation Isabel didn't have similar degrees of fun a beautiful adolescent young lady of her age may typically encounter was obviously because she was the Reverend's girl and her life carefully controlled, yet this was by all account not the only explanation. Regardless of whether Isabel had more tolerant guardians, she would have thought that it was hard and, on account of certain exercises like moving, difficult to appreciate large numbers of the things her companions did.

Putting two hands on the table, Isabel gradually propelled herself out of her seat. An easygoing spectator seeing the young lady from her right-hand side may have essentially thought she had some kind of back injury. It was just when Isabel's left leg materialized and one saw the metal support that she wore on that appendage that it was obvious what caused the young lady her versatility issues.

As a kid, Isabel had consistently felt terrible that she was acceptable at sports and games, while her sibling Peter battled with the rudiments of coordination, not even ready to tie his shoes when he began grade school. Isabel wanted that there was not such a dissimilarity between their capacities. Her folks appointed their child's battles as some test from God. However, Isabel felt awful about it. At that point, along came the mid-year of 1954, and Isabel was so excited about going to day camp, interestingly. It was a Christian Bible camp. However, there were many other outside exercises and bunches of different children to play and mess around with. The then eight-year-old Isabel checked until the camp showed up and wanted that the late spring would last more, and she didn't need to get back to class in radiant September, yet rather in October when the fall climate was beginning to change.

The camp's initial three days were the great summer get-away Isabel had expected, yet on the fourth day, Isabel was alarmed when she caught seasonal influenza. At any rate, Isabel thought it was a portion of seasonal influenza. Isabel before long thought that it was wasn't as she deteriorated the following day, enduring a serious cerebral pain and neck solidness, and nearly before she knew it, Isabel lay incapacitated in the polio ward of the youngsters' medical clinic, the wiped out and panicked young lady contemplating whether she would even endure not to mention walk once more. Isabel spent the whole summer in the clinic recuperating from the loss of motion, sobbing well into the night numerous evenings, and wishing her mom was there to comfort her. However, her folks could just see her from behind glass because of the isolate systems to forestall the spread of the sickness, and Peter was permitted not even close to the emergency clinic, not that it would have been any use for a kid so youthful to see his sister in that state.

At the point when Isabel, at last, escaped clinic, it was mid-October, and she lamented her desire that she could have an additional month off school for the mid-year. Isabel likewise painfully lamented making the wish that there was less distinction among her and her sibling's actual capacity, as upon her re-visitation of school, she battled up the front strides on supports with her legs in supports.

Over the long run, Isabel's correct leg got back to its typical capacity, and she had the option to get around without bolsters; however, her left leg, while always failing to wilt like the appendages of some polio casualties, never recuperated appropriately from her sickness and remained too feeble to even think about supporting her enough, so she would have to wear a support on this appendage forever. The support she presently utilized as a youthful grown-up was far lighter and less revolting than the leg supports she had worn as a youngster, yet to Isabel, it advised her that she was injured and consistently would be. That and her awful back gave her discontinuous issues, another tradition of her youth soured by the scourge of poliomyelitis.

Isabel's back was causing her torment toward the beginning of today. The young lady advanced gradually up the steps to her room, grasping the unique rail introduced to assist her with her versatility issues. There were different rails around the house introduced for her, one in the shower so she would not lose her equilibrium in there and another close to the restroom so Isabel could plunk down on it at that point stand up again gotten done without hardly lifting a finger. Isabel was thankful that these rails were introduced as they helped her, particularly when she wasn't wearing her support, yet she wished she could walk typically, and the rails weren't there in any way.

Gathering her handbag, Isabel advanced back to the first floor and assisted her with mothering wash and dry the morning meal dishes; at that point, she left to the front nursery to find some early morning beams of the warm sun before they left for the congregation fete.

With her folks talking about the Clayton family such a lot of that morning, Isabel's consideration quickly went to the house across the street. The four individuals from the said family were busy working in their nursery. The front nursery contained deciduous trees that were presently losing their leaves in the fall, and Ben Clayton was on the rooftop guaranteeing they were cleared from his drains.

Isabel took a gander at the attractive, tough man with a good build as he ran his hands through his light earthy-colored hair and kept working. He was such a great deal more youthful than her folks - Isabel speculated he was matured in his mid to late 30s - thus a lot cooler as well, even though Isabel consistently ended up feeling awful about reasoning this. Despite her folks' hatred for the man, Isabel appreciated him as Aubree and Brad had disclosed to her that their dad had been granted the Medal of Honor for grit when serving in the European lobby during the Second World War. Isabel had referenced this to her dad, yet the Reverend Samara was pretentious of the thought, saying that Ben Clayton appeared to be too youthful to even think about having served in the Second World War and that Aubree and Brad seemed like such a child who delighted in telling fanciful stories.

Isabel's folks, nonetheless, couldn't question that Ben Clayton's flow occupation was as a circuit repairman, and his van was right now stopped external the carport. His electrical contracting business ran in association with two other conflict veterans, which appeared to be fruitful.

Brad was cutting the grass, and like his dad, the youngster had the great looks of an early showing icon, even though his hair was dull earthy colored contrasted with Ben's light earthy colored hair. The fit and solid Brad was in the school football crew, and he dated Susie Jones, one of the team promoters. Isabel frequently heard her folks speaking disapprovingly about how short Susie's team promoter skirts were the point at which the young lady visited her beau, and there was nothing left but to stifle her weariness at the perpetual devout way of talking from her folks.

Chip, who had red hair and a light complexion, was pruning support, and Isabel consistently felt so befuddled when everyone said what an awful child he was. Valid, Chip lived with his uncle and cousins instead of his folks, Ben's more established sister Jane, her significant other Donny, and Chip's 16-year-old sister Katie. There was some discussion of past issues with Chip; however, whatever had occurred in the past had never been revealed. Isabel contemplated that this was not an issue for any other person outside the Clayton family.

Isabel wasn't in numerous classes with Chip; however, it unquestionably didn't appear at school if he was troublesome. Chip was truly centered around swimming and was an individual from the young men's swimming club and reassuring his colleagues. When he completed his training, he would remain by the side of the pool, watching different young men eagerly and giving a shout-out to them. He was likewise so pleasant to Luke Simpson, a kid who since from the get-go in grade school had been the brunt of numerous jokes and the objective of each harasser in school, derided and despised as a 'mom's kid' and a 'sissy.'

When they were matured, around ten, Luke's mom would here and there drop Luke at the Samara house to invest some energy with Isabel, as she was one of only a handful few children in his group who was pleasant to him. In any case, while the more youthful Isabel was, in fact, pleasant to him and felt frustrated about Luke getting prodded, she now and again felt uncomfortable with him and uncertain of what to think about him. Luke would glance in her wardrobe and respect her dresses, skirts, shirts, and other female extras like her hair strips, saying how lovely these garments were and how fortunate Isabel had the chance to wear them. He adored a progression of books Isabel preferred, despite how they were composed for young ladies. He even loved the fancy purple curtains that covered the windows of Isabel's room, saying he wished he could have draperies like this in his room. Yet, his folks would make certain to say no. He, at that point, needed to brush Isabel's hair, tying it up in twists with strips, before brushing them out and fixing her hair into another style.

The polio-influenced Isabel hated being disparaged, cossetted, and coddled because of her undeniable condition. She had from the start felt that Luke was making a decent attempt to be pleasant and was just claiming to like young ladies' things, that he would like to be outside going around playing young men's games, something she couldn't do any longer, and she turned out to be very aggravated. In any case, noticing Luke more, plainly, he enjoyed these things.

Isabel tracked down this truly confounding, and as they got more established, she discovered different things about him that were comparably unusual. In middle school, Luke had grumbled to her finally about doing woodwork, metalwork, and mechanical workshop with the young men. He said he wanted to be cooking, sewing, and composing with her and different young ladies. This was simply absolutely particular. Young men did woodwork, metalwork, and mechanical workshop, while young ladies did cooking, sewing, and composing. That was the status quo and consistently would be.

At that point, when Chip moved to town and was selected at the secondary school, he and Luke positively appeared to discover an association, and the two hung out, strolling together to and from school and going out places toward the end of the week. Isabel thought it somewhat abnormal from the outset; typically, folks liked to hang out together in a gathering, not one on one with one another, but rather Luke appeared to be cheerful and had made a genuine male companion finally. Furthermore, Chip was a particularly decent person who becomes friends with the kid who was criticized by most of his schoolmates. How is it possible that anybody would say Chip was a problematic kid?

Isabel's folks regularly opposed Aubree's scaled-down skirts; anyway, toward the beginning of today, as she was raking up leaves and grass clippings, she wore an old shirt and pants. Be that as it may, in any event, when Aubree turned out to be wearing pants Reverend, and Mrs. Samara would say that they were excessively close and improper. What's more, the earlier week when Aubree wore to class a dress with a swing-style skirt that descended to her knees, Isabel's folks said that the top piece of the dress showed excessively a very remarkable piece of Aubree's body that was simply intended to take care of children. Not that Aubree had a child, but rather given a portion of the terrible remarks Isabel had caught wind of Aubree, it appeared to be that the two grown-ups and young people imagined that parenthood would show up as soon as possible for Aubree.

Isabel looked across the street as Aubree raked leaves into a heap and twisted around to get them, the daylight reflecting off the youngster's long, straight light hair as she did as such. Despite her folks' dissatisfaction with regards to Aubree, Isabel truly preferred her. Aubree was generally so pleasant to her and dealt with her like, dislike some poor, disabled young lady who was wiped out as a youngster. Aubree was so excellent, effortless, and exquisite, her figure as wonderful as her staggering great looks, the feature of which was Aubree's enormous blue eyes. She was shrewd as well; on the whole, the classes Isabel imparted to Aubree, her beautiful blonde schoolmate, consistently got passing marks.

As of late, be that as it may, Isabel had been exceptionally befuddled about her sentiments towards Aubree. Indeed, she loved Aubree and delighted in conversing with her, yet of late, her feelings had taken Isabel to places she never been to. At whatever point Aubree showed up, be it at home or in school or some place out in the open, Isabel's genuinely excited. This inclination possibly multiplied when Aubree addressed her or grinned at her. She regularly wound up feeling winded, reddening, and uncertain of what to say when Aubree was near. Regardless of whether the two young ladies traded a straightforward hi, Isabel would frequently stress a while later that she had said the hello off-base, that she appeared to be excessively over-energized and looked senseless. On different occasions, Isabel stressed that her hello to Aubree was excessively firm, excessively formal, or pompous and seemed inconsiderate.

Some different things happening as of late bothered Isabel significantly more. Aubree had been wearing one of her small-scale skirts at school only two days prior, which Isabel needed to concede left Aubree no place for mistake. At the point when Aubree had twisted around to get her pen, her skirt had ridden up, showing Isabel the white cotton underwear Aubree was wearing. Inside her ladylike private region, Isabel had felt shivering sensations from her vagina and herself getting sodden between her legs. Isabel disclosed to herself this was crazy. Under her dress, she wore a couple of white cotton undies simply equivalent to Aubree's undies. However, she was unable to get the picture of Aubree's clothing crazy the entire day.

Isabel couldn't work out what was befalling herself of late. She had pulverized previously, yet just obviously on folks, the two young men she knew and some male entertainers and artists. Furthermore, Billy, the child of Fred and Betty, who was companions of her folks from the chapel, had a pound a mile wide on her, not that Isabel was complementary to his conspicuous sentiments towards her. Isabel imagined that Aubree's sibling and father were decent-looking, yet for reasons unknown, Aubree energized her quite a lot more. Isabel thought now and again; perhaps she was going off the deep end. She was unable to like a young lady; it was incomprehensible.

Aubree completed the process of raking across the street and placed the leaves and clippings into the rubbish when she pivoted to see Isabel remaining in her front nursery.

Isabel felt the sensations of stress in the pit of her stomach that maybe Aubree thought she was gazing at her, yet the young lady was assuaged when Aubree gave her a well-disposed grin and a wave. "Hey, Isabel."

Isabel returned the grin and wave. "Hello there, Aubree," she said, trusting that she sounded typical and not very excessively energized. On the other hand, possibly she sounded excessively contemptuous? Again, Isabel ended up over-breaking down the least complex things she said around Aubree.

"It's a decent day today for your congregation fete," Aubree noticed.

"No doubt, it is," said Isabel. "We're having such a pleasant climate this week." At least she was right on that. The other week she had remarked to Aubree as they strolled to Geography on Monday that the climate toward the end of the week had been pleasant, a sensible comment aside from that Raleigh had encountered steady, hefty downpour the entirety of Saturday, Sunday, and it was all the while pouring on Monday, leaving Isabel feeling an idiot.

Brad wrapped up trimming the grass and killed the cutter. He went to see his cohort remaining across the street and gave her a wave and grin like his sister had done. "Hello there, Isabel," he called.

"Hello there, Brad," Isabel called, absolutely calm with the attractive youngster, yet generally so apprehensive with his lovely sister.

Chip moreover amicably welcomed Isabel before Ben Clayton descended from his rooftop and said, "All in all, would you say you are anticipating your congregation fete today Isabel?"

18

The teen gestured. "I presume."

"The children and I, when we've wrapped up here, we'll go down and look at it for ourselves," said Ben.

Isabel felt energy rising inside her. Aubree would have been there; she was going to the congregation fete. Before she could stop herself, Isabel exclaimed, "You're coming today? That is so swelled!"

Ben Clayton giggled great-naturedly. "You appear to be cheerful about that, Isabel. Theory, you're not difficult to please."

"I um - ah - simply trust you like it," said Isabel, becoming flushed somewhat.

Ben investigated Isabel's shoulders at the three figures who had risen out of the front entryway. "Morning Reverend, Mrs. Samara, Peter," he said, waving to them across the road.

Isabel's dad put on his most devout articulation. "Good day, Mr. Clayton."

"I was trying to say to youthful Isabel here that the children and I will tag along to your congregation fete today," said Ben.

Isabel could see her dad, and less significantly, her mom was not satisfied by this news yet needed to keep a considerate façade. "That is decent; I trust you like it," offered the Reverend Samara.

"I'm certain we will," said Ben.

"I will check whether they have any books about the close planetary system at the book slow down," said Peter to the Clayton family. "Hello Aubree, do you understand what the farthest planet from the sun is?"

Aubree was consistently amenable and tolerating Peter and his bizarre ways. "That would be Pluto," she said.

"Do you realize what amount of time it requires for Pluto to circumvent the sun?" Peter needed to know.
Aubree grinned and shrugged. "You have me there."

"200 and 47 years," answered Peter.

"Goodness, that is quite a while. I don't think I'd prefer to live on Pluto," said Aubree.

Peter gave her a bewildered look. "You were unable to live on Pluto. It's excessively cold. Did you realize Mercury is truly hot in the day, yet around evening time, it gets truly cold there ..."

"OK, OK, I feel that is sufficient fun science realities today, Peter," said Reverend Samara. "We would do well to take action; we would prefer not to be late setting up."

"I'll see you later then, Isabel," said Aubree.

"Indeed, see you at that point," said Isabel as she followed her folks and sibling to the vehicle. She frequently felt reluctant strolling in a gathering of individuals, even her close family; concerning clear reasons, she could not stroll as quickly as every other person and regularly thought all she was doing was easing back everyone down. Isabel moved her throbbing once again into the rear of the vehicle close to Peter and considered what fun realities about space her sibling would barrage her with as their dad headed to the chapel.

*

Isabel would have favored that her sibling had bothered her with 1,000,000 unique things about space. Peter's quietness in the vehicle trip permitted Reverend Samara to address Isabel in his stooping, devout route about the perils of not tuning in to his recommendation and partner with the neighbors across the road. Isabel was happy when they showed up at the chapel, yet even that gave no genuine getaway as she needed to go with her folks and sibling. They were strolling towards the congregation when Amos came approaching them, obviously in some condition of frenzy. "Reverend, Reverend, thank heavens you're here. We truly need your assistance."

Amos was a white-haired, hairy man who matured in his mid-60s and one of Reverend Samara's most committed devotees, holding tight every expression of Reverend Samara's messages every Sunday, even though the substance of the said lessons shifted pretty much nothing. Aside from the Sunday best suit he wore to the chapel, Amos consistently wore a check shirt, overalls, and boots regardless of what season it was, and this was how he was dressed today.

"What is by all accounts the issue, Amos?" Reverend Samara asked smoothly.

"It's horrible, Reverend," said Amos, a man who has been able to over-perform any circumstance. "Me and Fred and Billy are attempting to complete the electrical things, and the wires continue to blow. It's dreadful; we don't have a clue what to do; we're so happy you're here ..."

"It's alright, Amos, I'll come over and investigate," said the Reverend Samara with great certainty, his significant other and youngsters following. Isabel didn't feel similar certainty as her dad in his capacities to figure everything out. Reverend Samara was a congregation serve, never an electrical expert, and the possibility of Amos, Fred, and Billy - none of whom were electrical workers for hire either nor showed a lot of skill all in all - chipping away at electrical sort things filled the teen with great anxiety.

Isabel was not an electrical expert either, but rather one look at what Amos, Fred, and Billy had got up to astonished her. It resembled the three men who had perused a book on electrical security and afterward done the direct inverse. A progression of short electrical lines joined ran from the congregation, a twofold connector toward the end. Appended to this twofold connector was another electrical rope and another twofold connector, from which ran two more expansion leads and toward the finish of this? All the more twofold connectors from which ran more augmentation leads.

"Last time the wire blew, there was a humming clamor from the meter box," Fred prompted Reverend Samara.

"Maybe there's a free association some place?" proposed Reverend Samara, twisting down to take a gander at the tangled wreck of electrical leads.

"Father, perhaps you shouldn't ..." Isabel started. However, her dad cut her off, receiving his formal belittling tone with his little girl.

"Isabel, please, wouldn't you be able to see I'm occupied here?"

Seeing that Peter was going to stroll over to perceive what their dad was doing, Isabel's defensive older sibling impulses went to the front, and she held out her arm to stop him. She would not like to lose her dad and sibling to electric shock simultaneously. Isabel held well back. As she was the just one wearing a metal leg support, she would be generally powerless against getting shocked if something turned out badly here.

Isabel took a gander at where Amos and Fred stood, their countenances loaded up with profound respect for the Reverend, certain he would fix the issue for them. Fred and his better half Betty - who was no place to be seen and on the off chance that she had any sense she would have moved far away from the electrical wellbeing bad dream her significant other and child had assisted the blundering Amos with making - were in a like manner large fanatics of the chapel and unfailing in their participation.

However, while he was a God-dreading man who read the book of scriptures and went to chapel however much as could reasonably be expected, Fred appeared to battle with two of the lethal sins. One was voracity, the man more than 400 pounds and getting greater every year. Isabel didn't know how much these new satellites circled the Earth could see, yet believed that any American or Russian satellite disregarding Raleigh could get Fred's picture as an oddity. His subsequent sin appeared fairly incidentally to be pride, with the butterball-shaped man demanding wearing garments made for a perilously overweight man, his colossal stomach looming over pants that would not attach as expected.

Fred's child Billy could imitate his dad, and at 19 years old, he was at that point fat. Dissimilar to his dad Billy moved clear of the wreck of electrical lines and connectors, not because he dreaded electric shock but since the object of his expressions of warmth in Isabel had shown up.

"Howdy Isabel!" the excessively eager Billy hollered out notwithstanding the reality she was only a couple feet from him, giving Isabel a major wave.

"Howdy Billy," Isabel answered in a more nonpartisan tone.

"You look exceptionally thin today, Isabel."

Isabel realized that Billy was not the most honed instrument in the chest, and this was really implied as a commendation, so she was considerate in her answer. "Much thanks to you, Billy."

"Also, your pink dress sure is pretty."

"Once more, thank you, Billy."

"I believed that Samara dress you wore to chapel last Sunday was genuine pretty as well," said Billy. "Samara suits you. Furthermore, that is acceptable because Samaria is your last name."

Isabel again kept up her courteous position and grinned benevolently. All discussions with Billy went fairly like this; she just needed to smile and bear it. He was never going to ask her out, not that she would consent to date, at any rate, however on the off chance that Billy circumvented town wearing a sweater that announced 'I like IsabelSamara,' it couldn't be more clear that he enjoyed her. He generally sat near her as conceivable in the ch. Then the other week, when he approached the Samara house for lunch with his folks and the Samara family, it resembled his most prominent dream had been acknowledged - he was in a similar house where IsabelSamara resided.

Billy appeared to have a great preference for the Samaras' back garden, investing a great deal of energy out there. When she acquired the clothing soon after that, Isabel asked why Billy loved their back garden to such an extent. As the young person unpegged her underwear from the line and put them in the container, she checked out the nursery at the bloom beds yet couldn't see anything exceptionally compelling. Maybe Billy was all the more a cultivating lover than she was?

Isabel felt a twinge of torment from her inconvenient back and frowned in uneasiness, gripping the influenced zone with a tormented appearance on her beautiful face. Billy saw and looked concerned. "Does your back hurt?"

This appeared to be darned self-evident; yet again, Isabel was considerate. "Indeed, it does a piece."

"A few days ago, I rested clever, and my back was somewhat sensitive when I woke up," noticed Billy. "So I know exactly how you feel."

Billy didn't have a clue how Isabel felt given that not at all like her, he hadn't had polio as a youngster; yet again, Isabel was pleasant in her nonpartisan answer. "Terrible backs aren't loads of fun."

Before Billy could say anything additional, his dad addressed him. "Billy, go over yonder and watch that twofold connector toward the end." Fred highlighted there was one more length of additional rope lay, the end some place far away."

"Sure, Dad," said Billy, following the electrical line to look at one more twofold connector, Isabel shaking her head hopelessly.

"At the point when Billy's watched that, would I be able to turn on the force once more?" Amos inquired.

"Whatever you do, don't turn on the force," came another male voice out of the way.

Isabel and every other person went to see Ben Clayton strolling forward, with Aubree, Brad, and Chip behind him, Brad clasping hands with his sweetheart Susie. Aubree had changed out of her work garments, and to the awfulness of Reverend Samara, was wearing a tight blue sweater that highlighted her breasts and a coordinating with smaller than expected skirt that flaunted her long legs. The Reverend Samara's consideration at that point changed from Aubree to her dad.

"Would I be able to assist you with something there, Mr. Clayton?" Reverend Samara inquired.

"It would appear that you're having a couple of issues with the wiring there, Reverend," noticed Ben.

"Only a couple minor hiccups," Reverend Samara guaranteed Ben.

"No doubt, wires have blown multiple times," Billy chipped in.

Ben investigated the handicraft of Amos, Fred, and Billy, and he grinned. "So Reverend, your name is Larry, right?"

Reverend Samara gestured, not certain of what the man was discussing. "That is right, Mr. Clayton."

Once more, Ben Clayton grinned a well-meaning grin. "All things considered, in case you're Larry, this person should be Curly." Ben showed Fred. "What's more, this person here should be Moe." Ben demonstrated Amos, at that point, took a gander at Billy. "Not very sure of the youthful person over yonder. Is it safe to say that he is Shemp? Joe Besser? Wavy Joe, perhaps?"

Billy, as frequently was the case, missed the joke. "I'm Billy."

"Do you have some point that you wish to make Mr. Clayton?" Reverend Samara asked, offended by his detested neighbor alluding to him and three individuals from his congregation as the Three Stooges, a satire act Samara had never discovered interesting.

"Just that you can't run outside power out that way," said Ben. "You need particular electrical hardware and someone qualified as an electrical technician to set it up."

"Indeed, thank you for the guidance, Mr. Clayton," said Reverend Samara pompously.

"I additionally accept that as an authorized electrical worker for hire, there is a type of law in North Carolina that having seen this, I am legitimately committed to ending it." Ben demonstrated the horrible organization of augmentation leads and twofold connectors.

"Mr. Clayton, may I advise you that you and your family are not individuals from this congregation?" Reverend Samara inquired.

"Valid, I'm not an individual from your congregation, but rather what I do have in the rear of my van is the electrical hardware you need for this to run your outer force securely today," said Ben. "What's more, I am a certified circuit repairman, and setting this up will take me ten minutes, fifteen, and no more." Ben took his keys and threw them to his child. "Brad, bring the van around for me."

"Will do, Dad," said Brad, getting the keys and going to recover his dad's van.

"Presently, let me get this unplugged. I can't leave this briefly more," said Ben, starting to unplug the leads and twofold connectors.

"Mr. Clayton, on the off chance that you give me a receipt for this, I'll ensure you get a check straight away," said Reverend Samara.

Again Ben grinned. "No, no installment vital. Realizing I halted you or another person getting shocked or your congregation torching today is installment enough."

"I don't have the foggiest idea what to say; however, thank you," said the Reverend Samara.

"Much obliged to you is all I need to hear," said Ben, as Brad showed up with the van and Ben set to work.

The youngsters stood close by watching, except Peter, who scrambled toward the book stand, expecting to get more writing on the nearby planetary group. Brad stood clasping hands with Susie, while Chip remained on his opposite side until a youthful male voice, somewhat stuttering, called out. "Hello, Chip!"

Chip turned, and a charmed, practically fantastic look came over the young fellow's face as Luke came into focus. "Goodness, hello there Luke, how are you?" Chip asked, making a scramble to where his companion stood.

"Great, it's a particularly lovely morning," said Luke. "Would you like to accompany me to expressions of the human experience and specialties slow down? I'm attempting to track down an ideal present for my Grandmother's birthday."

"Without a doubt, it sounds swell," said Chip. He went to different young people. "I'll see you somewhat later."

"See you later, Chip," said Aubree, Brad, Susie, and Isabel as one. As Chip and Luke left together, Billy excessively diverted by Isabel to offer a reaction.

"Along these lines, I was considering seeing that new Rock Hudson film around evening time," said Chip. "Might you want to tag along and see it?"

"I love any film with Rock Hudson in it, so that is an unmistakable yes," said Luke.

The two young fellows left too far to hear, and Isabel again ended up perplexed by Luke and Chip's dynamic, yet contemplated as she was a young lady, she was unable to realize how young men's psyches functioned. Maybe Chip and Luke expected to meet two decent young ladies at the film? That appeared well and good, given young ladies regularly went places two by two.

This left Brad and Susie clasping hands, Billy unfit to keep his eyes off Isabel and Isabel herself, respecting how incredible Aubree glanced in her smaller than usual skirt and sweater, so current, so modern, thus excellent. She felt a square close to her lovely blonde neighbor as the two young ladies discussed school while Aubree's dad polished off the electrical work needed to run the fete's outside power and forestalling either a fire or a few passings by electric shock.

Close by, the Reverend Samara stood, detesting the way that a man he hated such a lot of had made him look something of a blockhead while making all the difference. He likewise cast disliking looks at the man's adolescent little girl, Aubree's small skirt pulling in a considerable amount of consideration.

*

In his endless shrewdness, God had not given the endowment of understanding bookkeeping to the Reverend Larry Samara. The man discovered things, for example, money receipts diaries, money installments diaries, general diaries, records, charges, and acknowledges as muddled as the projects used to send rockets into space. Reverend

Samara saving the books for his congregation was out. Helen Samara was similarly as confused with bookkeeping and accounting matters, so she was out as well.

Luckily, God had given Reverend and Mrs. Samara a girl with a characteristic capacity in bookkeeping and, like this, a readymade clerk for the congregation. With the goal that Saturday evening, Isabel sat at home checking out the cash made at the congregation fete and recording it in the diary. Typically Isabel wouldn't fret doing the congregation books, as she was mulling over a task as a bookkeeper after school and school, and her dad gave her a modest quantity of cash for her accounting abilities. Anyway, it wasn't equivalent to having a legitimate occupation like Aubree had at the shop. However, working low maintenance work as a server or in retail would not have been simple for Isabel to be on her feet the entire day.

This Saturday evening, Isabel felt like she was the solitary teen not having some good times. Peter sat perusing his new book about the nearby planetary group bought at the book stand, so he was having a great time. The more youthful individuals from the Clayton family went out to have a good time across the street. Chip and Luke headed out to see their film, Brad took Susie to the drive-in, and Aubree went out on a twofold date with a companion who didn't go to their school, the companion's beau, and another person.

Sunday wasn't fun by the same token. Isabel battled to remain conscious during her dad's long lesson in chapel about the good falling guidelines in the public eye in 1963 that could just outrage the Lord. A portion of this was brought about by current styles, like tight pants and smaller than normal skirts, yet more huge was present-day music. The much-dreaded rock and roll didn't appear to be going anyplace, and Elvis Presley was currently out of the military and making new music, yet films as well. Lamentably, rock and move as of late had been joined by other wicked tunes, for example, surf music from California and Negro gatherings from the urban communities in the North like Detroit. Far more awful was the music from England that was presently getting famous across the Atlantic and which presented exceptionally grave perils to youngsters who tuned in to it.

Individuals consistently griped about Mondays. However, Isabel didn't care about it much - at any rate, it wasn't Sunday, and she wasn't in the chapel. It was consistently Tuesday, she discovered troublesomely.

Like the vast majority who had experienced the bad dream of having polio as a kid, Isabel had a wide scope of feelings regarding the matter. She pondered it consistently, which was clear as a component of her morning schedule, included putting on her leg support.

One of the principal considerations she had was the secret of how she got polio in any case. The late spring of 1954 wasn't pretty much as terrible as some different years in the mid-1950s for polio. Isabel wasn't the lone child in Raleigh to endure that destiny that year, yet none of her companions, cousins, or kids at chapel back at home gotten the infection, nor did any of the different children at the day camp she was going to when she became sick. So the riddle of where she got it from was rarely addressed.

There was likewise the lament. The following year, the Salk immunization was idealized. Thus, numerous children were vaccinated that. Before that decade's over, polio was uncommon. If solitary Isabel had figured out how to keep away from the sickness for that last year, everything would have been fine.

Isabel frequently contemplated that things might have been far more terrible. She had recovered the utilization of her correct leg, and the way that this leg was OK empowered her to drive a programmed vehicle, an accomplishment she invested heavily in. While in the clinic, she had stayed away from the iron lung, a possibility that froze her. Also, her ailment changed certain individuals' perspectives from the congregation, who believed that polio just influenced terrible families and awful children. When the Reverend's little girl caught it, many changed their tune straight away and started to give to associations like March of Dimes.

In the nine years that had passed by since, Isabel had needed to manage various responses by individuals to her condition, some of which were not pleasant. As a young lady, Isabel had gone with her mom to see the specialist for standard registration. Isabel didn't know whether the specialist essentially completed rearward in his clinical school for bedside way or whether he was simply absolutely barbarous. However, he disclosed obtusely to Mrs. Samara that Isabel, albeit normally thin, was not, at this point a 'typical kid' however an 'injured kid,' and as such, she should never be permitted to eat any treat food as she would get fatter faster than ordinary children. One mother had requested her children to avoid Isabel in the recreation center one day after seeing the leg support she wore, telling the children 'they would wind up injured like that wiped out the young lady as well' on the off chance that they went too close to her even though her sickness lay four years in the past at that point. A financial aspects instructor in middle school would criticize Isabel and give her late slips since she was late to his group, regardless of how she needed to walk some separation from her last class and essentially couldn't make it there on schedule. Furthermore, only two years prior, a young man had gone up to Isabel and inquired whether she had cerebral palsy, to the loathsomeness and shame of the kid's mom.

For the most part, however, individuals were benevolent to her. She had both female and male companions at school and the chapel. At school, young men regularly elected to help her convey things, and Isabel often felt regretful about it. She was by all accounts not the only child in her year influenced by polio; there were another kid and another young lady named Nora who had versatility issues more regrettable than Isabel, however no one at any point elected to help them. Individuals felt that young men should help themselves, and Nora was an overweight young lady plain in looks.

Humble Isabel never considered herself pretty, yet heard it enough from a wide range of individuals to realize that others thought of her like this. In one event, Isabel had twelve young men all attempting to help her move things around in her storage, while Nora limped along battling with her big books and might have been imperceptible. Some other time, Isabel and Nora were in a similar class when the alarm sounded like a drill feature, not that the children realized it was a drill. Young men rushed to Isabel's work area to assist her with getting time, while Nora was left to fight for herself and most likely would have met her end in an open fire.

Isabel consistently made an honest effort to evade self-centeredness and the 'why me?' demeanor. There were others influenced by polio far more terrible than her and who use wheelchairs. For example, others who were disabled in alternate manners served in World War II or Korea or individuals harmed in mishaps. Anyway, there was one time every week when she generally felt angry and desirous. On Tuesday mornings, every one of the young ladies had exercise center class, and Isabel was relegated to the school library to examine.

More than everything else, Isabel yearned to be out there with them going around. However, she was unable to be. It irritated her when different young ladies griped about doing rec center class in sweltering, chilly, wet, or breezy climates. Isabel would have been glad to do a rec center class on days more than 100 degrees, freezing days with hefty snow and cold breezes, or driving precipitation. Isabel had not contracted childish loss of motion or had made a full recovery; she would most likely be among the young ladies whining about hostile climate and exercise center class harmonizing. In any case, she didn't, obviously, so she was stuck in the library dealing with her analytics schoolwork while different young ladies did rec center.

The hands-on check-in at the library appeared to turn more slowly than at any other time as Isabel investigated her math task and the teen's head started to gesture in the peaceful and stodgy climate when a youthful female voice behind her made her hop conscious. "Hello, Isabel."

Pivoting, Isabel saw the thin figure of Aubree strolling towards her conveying her topography reading material and a record, Aubree as was frequently the case wearing a sweater and a tiny scale skirt. Isabel felt her heart begin to race, and her palms get sweat-soaked as Aubree moved closer. "Goodness howdy, Aubree," she said.

"Did I wake you up there?" Aubree asked, a grin all over, chuckling in her voice.

"No, um indeed, perhaps a little," conceded Isabel.

"Resting during study time, I don't know, young woman," snickered Aubree. She demonstrated the extra seat close to Isabel. "You don't care either way if I go along with you?"

"Actually, no, not under any condition," said Isabel, befuddled why Aubree was there when regularly she would be in exercise center class. "What befell rec center?"

"I received in return today since I'm reviled," said Aubree as she sat down.

"Reviled?" asked Isabel.

"No doubt, the revile, I have my period," said Aubree. "Haven't you heard that articulation previously?"

"Indeed, more than once," said Isabel. "Apologies, I didn't have the foggiest idea ..."

"Well, I'm not going to go to class wearing a sign around my neck to promote it," chuckled Aubree, however. Her grin disappeared as a feminine spasm went through her uterus, and she scoured her difficult mid-region.

"Are you alright?" Isabel inquired.

" I simply need to suck it up," said Aubree. "I'll rest with a heated water bottle when I return home. I can comprehend why they consider the period the revile."

Isabel could comprehend it as well, given how much agony she was in from feminine issues when it was her time. "I have it to anticipate one week from now," she said.

Aubree looked across at the contiguous table where two young men from the senior class were contemplating and the two young ladies with uneasy articulations. "Indeed, young men, Isabel and I are both 18-year-old young ladies, and we get periods consistently, and we're discussing it. Is there such an issue with that?"

The two young men hurriedly gathered their books and papers and dashed to another table far, far away, and Aubree chuckled and shook her head. "Young men and periods, I don't have a clue. They're frightened by them. However, they aren't the ones who get periods. Like my sibling and cousin, Brad and Chip appear to be frightened by me at regular intervals. Psyche you, I need to concede I can get somewhat valuable when it's my time. Avoiding me is likely the protected choice on the off chance that you end up being male."

Isabel chuckled and contemplated her dad. During her last period, Isabel had been perched on her bed with a high temp water bottle on her stomach to facilitate her feminine spasms when her dad nonchalantly meandered in, inquiring as to whether she had seen his extra glasses. When he saw what wasn't right with his girl Reverend Samara, generally a man with a lot to say unexpectedly turned into all silenced and didn't have the foggiest idea how to assemble a sentence, murmuring that his glasses were likely in the lounge and how pleasant the climate was, before turning and practically running the ground floor. "They would coexist with my Dad. If he knows it's that time for me, he never appears to realize what to do or say when I'm near."

"Normal," chuckled Aubree, as she set to deal with her Geography task, her guide graphs immaculate, and Isabel wanted to be intrigued.

"Your guides are great. I like how you've caught the geology."

"Much appreciated, Isabel," grinned Aubree. She looked at Isabel's math schoolwork. "You've addressed inquiry 9. I was unable to make head nor tail of it."

"It wasn't the least demanding," said Isabel. "I was significant to say; it was great of your Dad to fix the electrical issues at the fete. That was a horrible what those folks were doing."

"Better believe it, it was," said Aubree. "Father is truly cautious with power. Well, in his profession, he must be. One slip-up and, you know." Aubree stopped briefly and said faintly, "However, Dad's just committed one truly genuine error in his life."

"Sorry?" Isabel inquired.

Aubree, out of nowhere, looked uneasy. "Gracious nothing, simply conversing with myself, simply fail to remember I said that, alright?"

"OK," said Isabel, rapidly failing to remember what Aubree had said as they kept on concentrating together. Isabel half-expected to see the harsh, going bald figure of her dad to show up in the entryway of the school's library and reprove her for a partner with Aubree once more; obviously, he didn't.

The examination period passed rapidly for the two young ladies. They had English together next, so they set off for class together, talking cheerfully yet with Isabel again, half-anticipating that her disapproving father should appear. The two young ladies sat down in English close to one another, and Isabel wanted to see Aubree discretely change her clean belt through her smaller than normal skirt and undies.

Regardless of the way that she went through six days every month managing sterile belts that would not remain agreeable as they held cumbersome clean cushions set up inside her undies, Isabel thought that it was difficult to envision that the delightful blonde Aubree had similar ladylike issues she did each time she had her period. Aubree appeared to be wonderful to such an extent that she would be somehow over the issues that influenced conventional ladies. Notwithstanding realizing it was ludicrous, Isabel couldn't exactly accept that the ideal Aubree really discharged, yet clearly, she did; the young lady had said as much herself.

Something comparable happened the extremely following day when Aubree and Isabel strolled together to the first-period Geography and halted at the young ladies' room. As Isabel sat in the restroom in one of the slows down behind a shut and bolted entryway, her dress hitched up around her abdomen and her white cotton undies down around her lower legs; she thought that it was difficult to accept that in the following slow down Aubree in like manner was perched on the restroom with her skirt raised and her undies around her lower legs. At the point when Isabel went after the tissue, she heard the sound of Aubree loosening up tissue from the move in her slowdown and got herself again distrusting that the dazzling blonde excellence utilized tissue. At the point when the two teens completed, flushed the latrines, opened a lot of the entryways, and arose, remaining at the sinks to wash their hands, Isabel saw Aubree change her undies through her scaled-down skirt. Once more, Isabel got herself incapable of accepting that ideal Aubree had aggravations with awkward underwear as such an issue appeared underneath a young lady so superb inside and out.

All that Thursday, Isabel circumvented feeling like she was skimming on a cloud, the pictures of Aubree's lovely face and ideal body in her imagination. She adored how Aubree talked, how Aubree strolled, and essentially all that Aubree did. That evening at home, Isabel had changed into her long blue night robe with clean undies under and stood shoeless in the washroom brushing her teeth before bed, wishing Aubree was remaining next to her brushing her teeth, and they were going to have a sleepover. Be that as it may, the basic idea of Aubree having a sleepover with their adolescent girl would be sufficient to send Mrs. Samara into apprehensive stun and put Reverend Samara in the clinic with a coronary failure.

Flushing out her toothbrush, Isabel held the washroom rails that were there to help her when similar to the case now, she wasn't wearing her leg support. The young lady moved gradually out of the washroom and down the corridor, again grasping the rail there then into her room, moving cautiously into bed and getting under the covers. Flipping off the light, the young person's lovely earthy-colored eyes vacillated as she shut her eyes and rested very quickly. Continuously so charming when snoozing, Isabel was significantly prettier this evening as Aubree entered her fantasies, and she grinned in her rest.

*

Friday was a quite swell day as well, and Isabel was in for amazement at noon. As the young lady paid for her lunch at the cafeteria, she searched for her companions from the chapel she typically ate with. However, they more likely than not been deferred as they were no place to be seen. At that point, Isabel heard a recognizable female voice, "Hello Isabel, come and sit with us on the off chance that you like."

Pivoting, Isabel saw Aubree finding a seat at her table with a portion of her companions, Brad and his sweetheart Susie and a part of her companions there as well. Chip wasn't with his cousins; he and Luke were having lunch together at another table a brief distance away as they generally did.

"Much obliged, are you certain it's OK?" Isabel inquired.

Aubree giggled. "It's OK. Please finished."

"OK, expresses gratitude toward Aubree," said Isabel, advancing over to Aubree's table and plunking down with Aubree, Brad, and their companions.

While having lunch with Aubree, Brad, and their companions, Isabel felt extremely eager to be sitting with the cool children, however strange as well. They were generally a similar age, and indeed some more youthful than her, given Isabel was one of the oldest in her year bunch civility of a September birthday; however, Isabel felt like they were undergrads as they appeared to be such a great deal more established than her. Isabel additionally felt apprehensive, stressing that she would either say excessively, say nearly nothing and appear to be impolite, or say some unacceptable thing and look moronic. In any case, she had another valid justification for being apprehensive as well. A considerable amount of the understudies at this school went to her dad's congregation, and their folks realized Isabel's folks. The news that Isabel was a partner with Aubree and Brad Clayton could discover its way back to her folks before long. At that point, Isabel saw the understudy who could go about as the immediate connect to convey this data directly back to her folks as her more youthful sibling Peter.

Isabel held her breath hanging tight for him to ponder over and begin posing 1,000,000 inquiries or welcome himself to eat with them, giving everyone 1,000,000 fun realities about space. In any case, Peter was in one of his universes today and didn't appear to try and notice his more seasoned sister even though he strolled by simply an issue of feet from her.

Not interestingly, Isabel considered the bizarre way that her sibling saw the world. One night a while prior, when their folks were out, Isabel had got up to get a glass of water and was sure about her capacity to get the ground floor and back up without her polio support as she had done it ordinarily previously. Shockingly on this event, she was pompous, misconceived a stage, and took a tumble, hitting her head on the flight of stairs and lying dazed with her back going into a fit. At that point, Peter arose out of his room to get a glass of water, venturing over his sister with a happy hi, careless about how she was in torment and required help.

At the point when the mid-day break was over, Isabel and Aubree advanced toward math. "Did you see that the Smith's up the street have effectively put out their Halloween embellishments?" Aubree asked conversationally.

"Better believe it, I saw that toward the beginning of today," said Isabel. "We don't do Halloween in our home; Mum and Dad don't support it."

"We don't do it either," said Aubree. "I've generally thought it was somewhat imbecilic. You advise kids not to converse with or take candy from outsiders. Afterward, one night every year, you send them out going house to house asking for candy to houses to acknowledge candy from individuals they don't have the foggiest idea. That is insane."

Isabel giggled. "No doubt, it is somewhat. One thing about Halloween is that it advises you that colder time of year is just about here."

"Also, November is the most exceedingly terrible month," said Aubree.

"November?" asked Isabel.

"Better believe it, November is generally cold and wet, and nothing intriguing at any point occurs."

"What might be said about Thanksgiving?"

"We don't do that either," said Aubree. "Primarily because each of the four of us is miserable cooks, and on the off chance that we go to Uncle Donny and Aunt Jane's, she and Chip simply end up belligerence. I never loved Thanksgiving as a child. It is possible that I generally felt frustrated about the turkeys. However, November is a nothing month. That is to say, if someone asks us in 10, 20, or 30 years what we did in November 1963, I bet we will not recollect."

Isabel thought it was adorable that the more youthful Aubree felt so pitiful for the turkeys, and she unquestionably concurred that November was a dull kind of month climate savvy. Anyway, she had no ideal opportunity to think any further as an excessively energized youthful male voice brought through the hallways. "Hello there, Isabel!"

At that point, Isabel seized first to see the fat type of Billy waving at her, at that point surging toward her, the tremendous type of his dad Fred behind the scenes. Fred had a business as a painter, and Billy was learning the exchange. The two men's sturdy casings were clad in overalls; however, if Fred asked why his business was not making as large a benefit as it ought to have, he just needed to see his child's overalls which were shrouded in huge amounts of dried paint of an assortment of tones, paint that presumably ought to have wound up on roofs, dividers or entryways.

With a colossal smile on his full moon face, Billy hurried up to the object of his warm gestures. She could feel everyone taking a gander at her, and Isabel reddened likewise. "Hi Billy," the humiliated young lady advertised.

"Are you at secondary school today?" Billy asked, unfit to contain his hunger at seeing the young lady he cherished to such an extent.

As usual, Isabel was pleasant, notwithstanding the craziness of the inquiry she was posed. "Indeed, truth be told."

"We're here to paint a portion of the homerooms," said Billy.

"I accumulated that," said Isabel.

Billy, his a great look on his fat face at that point, said, "So Isabel, do you have your period?"

"Pardon me?" the stunned and humiliated Isabel asked, embarrassed that different understudies had heard this and were presently gazing straight toward her.

"Apologies, I mean what period do you have straightaway?" the blundering Billy inquired.

Isabel inhaled somewhat simpler. She ought to have realized Billy had phrased a straightforward inquiry wrong instead of asking her a generally close to home and unseemly inquiry. She questioned Billy had any idea of the monthly cycle in any case, given that he just had a more established sibling who was somewhere close to Billy and their dad on the weight scale. "Math."

"Is that math?" Billy inquired.

Isabel gestured. "Indeed."

"On the off chance that you need assistance with your occasions tables, I can assist you with that," Billy chipped in.

The always amiable Isabel again figured out how to evade mockery in her reaction. "Much thanks to you Billy, I'll let you know. Unfortunately, I need to go now; I would prefer not to be late for class. I'll see you later."

"See you in the chapel on Sunday, Isabel; I can hardly wait to see you at that point!" He gave the leaving Isabel a tremendous wave, a monstrous smile all over.

The reddening Isabel advanced toward her group with Aubree alongside her and different understudies taking a gander at her. Billy, as normal, stood watching her with a lovesick, empty smile on his tubby face.

As Isabel sat down in math, Aubree, who had the following work area to her, hung over and giggled. "This may come as somewhat of an amazement to you, Isabel, yet I think Billy likes you."

Isabel recoiled and reddened much more. "It's that self-evident, right?"

Aubree gestured. "For Billy's situation, without a doubt so. Billy doesn't seem like the most discreet individual I've at any point met. However, as a rule, you can generally tell on the off chance that someone likes another person."

*

Isabel spent a significant part of the Friday evening considering Aubree's remark about continually having the option to check whether one individual likes someone else. The young lady stressed over it an incredible arrangement. HowIsabel considered Aubree felt a lot like the sensation of really liking a kid. Imagine a scenario in which Aubree thought Isabel liked her. Would Aubree be vexed and presently don't have any desire to be companions? Also, why did Aubree utilize the word individual, as opposed to young lady or fellow? Is it safe to say that she was at that point mindful of how Isabel was battling with her emotions towards her?

Lying in bed that evening, Isabel attempted to put a more philosophical perspective on her musings. Aubree had just utilized the word individually as it was easier than saying a young lady likes a person or a young lady liking a person. Furthermore, Isabel contemplated that she was unable to like Aubree. Isabel enjoyed young men like everything young ladies did. She regularly contemplated how incredible it is to go out on a legitimate date with a kid. Not that she had been asked out on the town yet. Young men were a lot mindful that she was the Minister's little girl, and because she was concerned with her left leg, her limits as a sweetheart were self-evident. In any case, there was consistently the expectation that a kid other than Billy would favor her and ask her out one day.

Furthermore, Isabel consistently visualized that one day she would get hitched - to a man clearly - and have youngsters. In this manner, she was unable to like Aubree, and along these lines, there was nothing for Aubree to see. Feeling somewhat looser, Isabel floated off to rest.

Isabel went through the end of the week considering Aubree from multiple points of view. Even though she attempted to reveal to herself that jealousy was terrible and evil, Isabel couldn't resist the opportunity to feel desirous of Aubree. On a Saturday morning, she saw Aubree get into the old vehicle that she, Brad, and Chip shared and drive to her low maintenance work at the shop. Isabel remained at home assisting with the housework and did the books for her dad's congregation.

On a Saturday evening, Isabel read her novel in English. She watched from her window as across the street as a similar young fellow Aubree had gone on a twofold date with the earlier end of the week this time drove up to the house to take Aubree out on a one on one date, presumably someplace fun like the drive-in from which Isabel was taboo. Isabel wished she was out on the town like her fabulous blonde colleague and neighbor. However, this wasn't going to occur. The youngster took a gander at her leg support, lamenting that the lone person who unmistakably needed to ask her out she wouldn't think about dating in 1,000,000 years.

Sunday as consistently was church and her dad's standard exhausting message. Aubree, wearing a sweater and pedal-pusher style pants, was outside again raking up fall leaves with her family, and she gave the Samara family a well-disposed wave as Reverend Samara turned around down the carport. Isabel was the simplest one to return Aubree's neighborly motion, and her folks gave her such a glare it resembled she had been found drinking liquor or smoking cigarettes, not that she could do all things considered. As she battled to remain alert in the chapel, Isabel thought how fortunate Aubree was not enduring being exhausted to the place of craziness each Sunday morning.

Monday and Tuesday were not Isabel at her best, but rather then the young lady was not at her best precisely a month already nor a month before that, etc. Isabel consistently felt disturbed and anxious when her period was expected and rushed to lose control or upset during her time. On Tuesday, she ended up sitting in the library, considering while different young ladies did rec center, and this time there was no well-disposed Aubree to sit with her. By this stage, Aubree's period had gone for an additional couple of weeks. Isabel felt like she was the lone young lady in a school near or having her period, even though she knew on the theory of probability that this wasn't the situation.

During the evening, Isabel felt like she had smashed a full pool of water before the teen's time frame showed up late on Tuesday evening. Following a generally restless night with serious feminine issues, Isabel sat in bed with a boiling water bottle on her stomach on Wednesday morning before her mom advised her to get a rush on or she would be behind schedule for school.

Isabel wished she might have gone home and relaxed school debilitated, however as this was her period as opposed to a real sickness, no chance was she permitted to, regardless of how much agony she was in. Isabel's back, acceptable since the Saturday of the congregation fete, started to inconvenience her to exacerbate the situation. Isabel needed to endure squeezes and swelling and her sterile belt slipping on inauspicious occasions throughout the day. What's more, as was regularly the situation when it was that time, Isabel started to encounter issues with her stomach-related framework, and her looseness of the bowels issue made her make successive visits to the young ladies' washroom during the day. As though she needed more issues with her vagina today, presently, she had issues with another piece of her body a brief distance away.

While Isabel consistently had heavy periods, today was particularly terrible for her. When school completed for the day, Isabel visited the young ladies' room and changed her cushion. Regularly she conveyed sufficient ladylike cleanliness items to last her during that time with one cushion left finished; however, today, her stream had been hefty to the point that she was down to her last protector. Joining the new napkin to her clean belt and changing it so it was agreeable between her legs, Isabel pulled up her white underwear at that point, smoothed down the lemon-shaded dress she was wearing. Isabel flushed the latrine and arose out of the slowdown, the young person washing her hands before changing her white sewed coat and leaving the restroom, Isabel making it without a moment to spare to get the transport home.

The transport ride home was not an agreeable one for Isabel, who was again annoyed by her excruciating uterus and awful back. This exacerbated everything with an uncooperative clean belt and a napkin that kept packing up between her legs. Partially through the excursion, Isabel wanted to pee even though she had just been as of late, and not long after, she felt the call of nature from her stomach-related framework, this inclination deteriorating and more terrible with every moment that passed.

Isabel was soothed when the transport contacted her stop, and she cleared her path for her home as quickly as possible. She would be returning home to a vacant house, as her folks were out and Peter was at science club after school. This was a moderately new thing in Peter's life, and Reverend and Mrs. Samara trusted that the science club would assist their child with associating different youngsters. Isabel also trusted that Peter would make companions more effectively; however, having driven down to the school to get her sibling from science club one evening, she had her questions. It was a case by and by Peter discussing his inclinations to different young men in the club, the greater part of whom appeared to be apathetic and faking interest just to be amenable.

Her more youthful sibling's battles to make companions were not at the cutting edge of Isabel's psyche right now, nonetheless. All the youngster knew was that she expected to get inside the house and the restroom quickly. Venturing into the travel bag, she conveyed to class for her home key; Isabel stopped with apprehension where it was no place to be seen. However, the troubled Isabel scrounged through the handbag could discover nothing and shake her head when it neglected to turn up.

"Dang it," the young person murmured. Isabel was not the most coordinated individual at whatever point she was on her period, and the young lady had gone out essential sitting on her bedside table that morning. Still, there was a simple arrangement. Isabel would go to a neighbors' home and request to utilize their restroom.

When no one addressed Isabel's thump on the house's entryway to one side of the Samara home, Isabel went to the house on the right side, and again no one was home. Isabel looked across the way to the Clayton house. Her folks wouldn't affirm her going there. However, she had a washroom crisis, and they were out, at any rate, so what they didn't know wouldn't hurt them. These hypotheses anyway stayed disputable, as none of Ben, Aubree, Brad, or Chip were home. Isabel attempted different houses in the road. However, karma was not running in her direction, and no one was home there by the same token. The inexorably urgent young person attempted another house; however, the older woman who lived there was going hard of hearing and had her TV turned up so loud she could not hear Isabel thumping.

The baffled Isabel, at that point, thought about another arrangement. The transport ran by here, all she needed to do was get it to the library, and she could utilize the restroom there. By and by, notwithstanding, karma was not running Isabel's direction, and she was barely past the point where it is possible to get the necessary transport. She waved and called to the driver to attempt to stand out for him, and if she had the option to run, she might have gotten it, yet the driver neglected to see her, and Isabel was left abandoned at the bus station.

Isabel examined what she planned to do straightaway, folding her legs, trying to diminish her desire to move quickly. At that point, her beautiful earthy-colored eyes got a recognizable vehicle driving down the road - Ben Clayton's van - and she moaned in alleviation. Her issue was just about finished. Isabel rushed across to the Clayton house as the van maneuvered into the carport, and each of the four individuals from the Clayton family moved out.

Aubree, today attired in a smaller Samara than a normal skirt and coordinating with a Samara sweater, was the first to see Isabel and turned, seeing the appearance of desperation on her schoolmate's face. "Hello Isabel, is everything alright?"

"Hello Aubree, not actually. I'm bolted out of my home, and I truly need to go to the restroom. Could I, if it's not too much trouble, utilize your washroom?" Isabel's feeling of distress was clear by her demeanor and stance.

Aubree looked suspicious and shook her head. "Well, I don't think about that." Seeing the awfulness all over, Aubree halted her kidding and snickered. "You can come directly in. We'd scarcely say no, would we?"

"Much thanks to you so much," said the hugely eased Isabel as she strolled forward as quick as possible. As Isabel drew level with Aubree in any case, the beautiful blonde held back with a look of consternation all over. Ben Clayton also took a gander at Isabel and, like his high school little girl held back with a concerned articulation, at that point, he went to his child and nephew.

"Brad, Chip, we should proceed to move that bureau as I said before," Ben said, quickly crowding his child and nephew into the house and letting Aubree be with Isabel.

"Is everything alright?" Isabel asked, worried by the responses of Aubree and her dad.

"Um, Isabel, I would prefer not to humiliate you, yet you need to investigate the rear of your dress."

Isabel turned her neck to see, and the youngster's beautiful face loaded up with ghastliness at sight. Her lemon dress showed a big, dull red mess over her base, and she could see that a portion of her feminine blood had likewise spilled onto her white coat. Effectively passionate from it being that time in her month-to-month cycle, the humiliated Isabel quickly burst into tears.

"Hello, it's OK," said Aubree reassuringly, putting her arms around the wailing Isabel and discretely turning her. Hence, her back was towards the Clayton house, and her situation not noticeable to passers-by.

"Sorry," Isabel wailed, destroys streaming her face.

"What's to be grieved about?" asked Aubree, venturing into her handbag and recovering tissues, which she gave to Isabel to wipe her eyes.

"I can't accept that this occurred," cried Isabel.

"It's alright, Isabel; I think this happens to each lady on Earth in any event once in the course of her life. I realize it needs to be. We should get you inside, and we'll set everything straight."

Isabel gestured, and Aubree again gave the upset young lady a consoling embrace; before taking her inside, Aubree strolling behind Isabel, so her period issue was not obvious to any other person. The two young ladies went higher up, and Aubree said, "You said you expected to go to the restroom, so while you're in there, I'll get you some perfect garments for when you've wrapped up. I'm somewhat taller than you, yet we can wear each other's garments on the off chance we need. Do you have any pads?"

Her tears dying down a piece now, Isabel shook her head. "Actually, no, not with me. I have some at home. However, I'm bolted out, so I can't get to them ..."

"I'll get you one of mine," said Aubree, driving Isabel into her room and taking a sterile napkin from her cabinet, which she gave to Isabel alongside a little earthy colored paper sack.

"Much appreciated," said Isabel as she cleaned her eyes. "I can't work out what occurred; I changed my cushion not long before leaving school."

"Possibly it was flawed?" Aubree proposed. "It occurs. It resembles you purchase twelve apples from the store; they all look the equivalent. However, 11 are OK, and one is spoiled inside? Or, on the other hand, an auto plant may produce 100 vehicles no different either way, 99 are okay, and vehicle 100 is a lemon?"

"Likely," Isabel concurred, the young lady hopeless that she must be the person who wound up with the damaged, clean napkin.

Aubree drove Isabel to a storeroom and gave her a washcloth and a red towel. "Give me a yell when you've completed, and I'll pass you my garments through the entryway."

Isabel gestured and strolled across the foyer to the restroom, shutting and bolting the washroom entryway behind her. As she strolled towards the restroom and put down the seat, Isabel held back, seeing no tissue on the move holder, simply an unfilled cardboard cylinder. With no other tissue rolls noticeable on the storage or in the washroom, the humiliated and baffled Isabel needed to turn and open the restroom entryway.

"Is everything alright?" Aubree asked, shocked to see Isabel arise so rapidly.

The becoming flushed, Isabel shook her head, feeling bashful and hesitant. "Aubree, there's no tissue."

Aubree snickered somewhat and shook her head. "Today isn't your day, is it Isabel?"

"No." Isabel could see just misery.

Aubree strolled back to the wardrobe and recovered another move of bathroom tissue. "Welcome to my reality, Isabel. The solitary young lady living with three people, I'm the one in particular who appears to realize how to change a move of bathroom tissue, and I've lost tally of the occasions I've gone in there and tracked down there's no bathroom tissue by any means or one sheet left on the roll."

"That should be irritating," said Isabel. Imparting a washroom to her sibling was irritating sufficient given Peter appeared to have some profound situated good issue with cleaning up toothpaste he had spilled all over, yet Aubree's circumstance sounded seriously disappointing.

"Better believe it, it very well may be," Aubree concurred. "The other week, I woke up, was still half sleeping, and almost plunked down on the latrine before I looked and acknowledged I had no tissue." The lovely blonde gave Isabel the new move of bathroom tissue.

"Much obliged, Aubree," said Isabel. She took the tissue roll and got back to the restroom, fitting it onto the move holder before lifting her dress and pulling down her underwear and afterward her clean belt and cushion. Aubree had said about it not being Isabel's day was right, as the youngster encountered the dissatisfaction of getting first her undies and afterward her clean belt on her leg support as she pulled them down before plunking down on the restroom.

Isabel was in the restroom for near ten minutes, managing her annoyed stomach before she at last wrapped up. Isabel stood up and flushed the restroom and washed and dried herself with the fabric and towel Aubree had to give. At that point, she changed her clean cushion, trusting that the one Aubree had given her worked before relegating the deficient cushion to the paper pack for removal.

"I'm done," Isabel called after washing her hands.

Aubree's voice reacted. "Alright, open the entryway, and I'll pass you my garments and a pail to put your dress, coat, underwear, and the material and towel in. I'll take them to the ground floor and put them in to drench."

"Much appreciated, Aubree," said Isabel, the young person opening the entryway and Aubree giving her the garments and container.

"I'll do the humiliating outing to the garbage bin all young ladies need to accomplish for seven days consistently," said Aubree.

"Once more, thank you," said Isabel, giving Aubree the paper sack.

Isabel went to close the restroom entryway yet held back as she saw that one of the garments things Aubree had given her was a smaller blue than a normal skirt. "Um, Aubree, this is a smaller than expected skirt," she said.

"Indeed, it is a little skirt," said Aubree. "What's more, you'll look extraordinary in it."

Isabel reddened. "Aubree, I can't wear a smaller than normal skirt."

"It is safe to say that you are a kid, Isabel? In which case, there is something genuinely wrong given what has occurred here this evening."

"No, no, it isn't so much that it's simply I can't wear a smaller than normal skirt with um, you know, this ..." Isabel demonstrated her leg support.

Aubree gave Isabel a consoling grin. "Isabel, when you wear slacks or pants or a dress like today, individuals can see your support at any rate. It's not something to be humiliated or unsure about."

"Indeed, however my folks ..." Isabel contemplated what her mom and father would say if they saw her wearing a scaled-down skirt and one of Aubree's small skirts at that.

"I don't see your folks anyplace around, isn't that right?" Aubree asked, checking out the passage with an entertained demeanor all over. "In any case, you have a valid justification for wearing it. Would they incline toward you to stroll around in your dress with an excellent red stain at the back?"

"I surmise not, however ..." the apprehensive Isabel started before Aubree cut her off.

"Isabel, on the off chance that you need, I'll disclose everything to your mom when she returns home."

"You'd do that?" Isabel was profoundly stressed over clarifying the garments she was wearing to her folks; however, on the off chance that Aubree addressed her mom, it wouldn't be so awful.

"We're companions, right? Companions help one another."

Isabel got back to the restroom and shut the entryway, eliminating her smudged dress and underwear and setting them in the pail alongside her coat. Presently wearing just her white bra, Isabel's anxious fingers got Aubree's spotless, white cotton undies. She could hardly imagine how she was taking care of Aubree Clayton's undies, significantly less going to wear them herself. The youngster disclosed to herself not to be idiotic; they were simply undies equivalent to what she wore each day yet couldn't resist the opportunity to feel abnormally energized as she ventured her exposed feet into Aubree's underwear and pulled them up, changing them. Hence, they were agreeable and covered her clean wear accurately.

Putting on the pullover and sweater Aubree had loaned to her were more ordinary, yet as Isabel put on and attached Aubree's small skirt, Isabel couldn't accept that she was wearing this piece of clothing. She took a gander at her legs and, as she had done on many occasions in the past, wished her left leg was liberated from the support, yet Aubree was correct. Regardless of what garments Isabel wore, she harmed left leg was self-evident, so Isabel shouldn't feel reluctant about wearing the little skirt. Shoved these emotions to the side, Isabel's brain floated onto her different worries about wearing the skirt, coerce that she was misbehaving by wearing such a piece of clothing. Again Isabel contemplated what Aubree had said, that Isabel was doing nothing incorrectly. All she had done was acquire some garments off Aubree to wear in a crisis circumstance. It didn't care for Isabel had taken cash from her folks, bought a smaller than usual skirt she was illegal from purchasing, and gone out riding in vehicles with young men to darlings' path.

Leaving the washroom, Aubree was hanging tight for her external the entryway, and she gave Isabel a splendid grin. "It's just plain obvious; I disclosed to you that you would look incredible."

Isabel saw her blue sweater and scaled-down skirt and the Samara sweater and small skirt Aubree was wearing. It felt so cool to be dressed equivalent to Aubree, yet she questioned her folks would feel a similar way.

Aubree took the basin containing Isabel's smudged garments. "I'll place these into douse, however, come into my space briefly or so first. I have a few things that may help you."

Isabel followed Aubree into her room, where Aubree got her boiling water bottle, a glass of water, and headache medicine. "I figured these might mitigate your spasms a piece."

"That is so pleasant of you, thanks once more," the appreciative Isabel said, sliding off her shoes and sitting shoeless on Aubree's bed, taking the ibuprofen and putting the heated water bottle on her stomach.

Aubree went down the stairs with the can containing Isabel's garments. She returned a couple of moments later, sitting with Isabel and conversing with her as the high temp water bottle managed its job and facilitated the difficult spasms in Isabel's uterus. The young lady lost from her humiliating experience. "You feeling somewhat better now?" Aubree inquired.

Isabel gestured and took the high temp water bottle off her midsection. "Indeed."

"What about we go to the first floor now?" Aubree proposed. "I have some schoolwork to do; I envision you have as well?"

"I would be wise to make a beginning on that exposition for English; I've been procrastinating throughout recent days," said Isabel.

The two young ladies went down the stairs into the parlor, and Isabel felt like she was in another country, not simply the house across the road at how schoolwork was finished here. Aubree, Brad, and Chip plunked down on seats working on different school tasks with the TV on showing a famous music and dance show. A great show that was never permitted to be on the TV in Isabel's home whenever considerably less when she and Peter needed to concentrate in complete and outright quiet.

What struck Isabel as she removed her eyes from the high contrast TV screen and started work on her English exposition was that in the Clayton house's casual air, Aubree, Brad, and Chip concentrated perseveringly; it didn't care for schoolwork was an errand for them. Ben Clayton found a spot at a table close by, finishing some administrative work for his electrical contracting business.

Isabel noticed Aubree, who had pre-warmed the broiler, went into the kitchen, and put four TV suppers inside to warm up. Brad and Chip kidded that, at any rate, they weren't going to get food contamination which was likely the situation if Aubree arranged supper herself. Aubree reacted with amiable prodding about how the young men's endeavors to make spaghetti had brought about a pot loaded with paste, and Ben thus had kidded that on the off chance that they couldn't get along together, he would make supper for the family and that the young men presumably didn't need that to occur. Brad and Chip had concurred with this slant, and Isabel ended up truly getting a charge out of going through her evening with the Clayton family. She wanted that the conditions of how this came about had been extraordinary. However, nothing could change that, and Isabel concluded that she should make the best of the circumstance.

In the rear of Isabel's brain notwithstanding was the information that this would conclude, and sure enough, Isabel looked out of the front room windows to see her folks' vehicle maneuvering into their carport. She peered down at her smaller than expected skirt, or to be accurate, Aubree's little skirt, and dread filled her face at disclosing to her folks why she was wearing Aubree's garments.

Aubree saw the appearance all over. "Would you like me to converse with your mom?"

Isabel gestured anxiously. "Indeed, please."

"It'll be OK," said Aubree as Isabel battled to her feet.

"Shouldn't something be said about my Dad?" Isabel asked, dread clear in her eyes.

"I'll deal with him," said Ben, he and the two young men following Aubree and Isabel as the two young ladies strolled across the road to where her folks and Peter were escaping the carport.

Reverend and Mrs. Samara held back, their mouths dropping open as they got a quick look at their adolescent girl attired in a sweater and scaled-down skirt with the young lady they disliked most. Peter was more intrigued by the moon, which was out very early this evening. If Isabel had been wearing a swimsuit, a jokester ensemble, or an old burlap sack, he would probably have not seen this all things considered.

When the thing they saw was not a twofold visualization, Reverend and Mrs. Samara stepped forward, looks of devout irateness on their countenances. Isabel felt the nerves in her stomach, and she took a gander at Aubree, who was quiet and gathered.

"Isabel, your mom and I need a clarification of what you are doing dressed that way," said the Reverend Samara, fixing Isabel with his strictest articulation.

"What befell the garments you wore to class earlier today, young woman?" Mrs. Samara needed to know.

"Reverend and Mrs. Samara, there's an entirely consistent clarification to this," said Aubree. "Yet, it is best for everybody if this stays between Mrs. Samara, me, and Isabel."

"Reverend, maybe you could accompany the young men and me, and you can disclose to us your mystery on how you keep your nursery so clear of weeds," said Ben.

"Well, quit worrying about that, Mr. Clayton," ranted Reverend Samara. "I need clarification with regards to why my little girl is wearing your little girl's garments, and I need to know now. Isabel should dress that way, nor would she be able to dress that way. Simply take a gander at her!"

Aubree drew her breath. "Isabel was bolted out of the house when she returned home from school and was having a few issues with her monthlies."

Quickly, Reverend Samara's outward appearance and attitude changed, the man looking apprehensive and bothered, his face going red. "Um, really, what kind of weeds are you having issues with, Mr. Clayton?" he stammered, hustling over to Ben, Brad, and Chip at a close to run.

"They're directly out the back here," said Ben, he and his child and nephew driving Reverend Samara out to the back garden, the reddening minister exceptionally happy to get away and not be conscious of the discussion concerning private female things going to occur between his significant other, young little girl and the young lady across the road.

"I realized it was your time, yet I didn't have any acquaintance with you were having countless such issues," said Mrs. Samara to Isabel. "So what occurred?"

Aubree clarified the present circumstance, and Mrs. Samara, while at first offended to see her girl wearing a small skirt, had the option to see a completely sensible clarification. "All things considered, I surmise in the conditions this is all OK."

"I'll return Isabel's garments tomorrow when they've been washed and dried, Mrs. Samara," said Aubree.

"Indeed, thank you, Aubree," said Mrs. Samara. "I'll return the garments you've leaned to Isabel simultaneously."

The men got back from out of the back garden, and the Clayton family returned into their home, the Samara family to their own home across the road, where Isabel put on something else. As the crampy youngster sat getting her work done in absolute quietness that evening, she couldn't resist the opportunity to wish that she was in the significantly more fun and loosened up the air of the Clayton house.

*

Mrs. Samara, while thankful that Aubree had helped her girl when she required it, actually didn't care for nor trust the small-scale evaded teen across the road. She was berserk to wash the sweater, shirt, small scale skirt, and underwear that Aubree had advanced to Isabel and return them to her; least having such pieces of clothing in the house ought to cause the fierceness of the Lord.

In the week that followed, Isabel's musings were increasingly more fixated on Aubree, given the amount she had helped her. Her intense excitement at whatever point Aubree addressed her or grinned at her, and again toward the end of the week, she felt that odd sensation of jealousy when Aubree went out with companions on a Saturday night. At the same time, Isabel sat at home concentrating then tuning in to Peter's talk for nearly an hour about Neptune.

On the Thursday after lunch, Isabel was strolling with Aubree to Geography. The bashful brunette attempting to try not to gaze at the delightful blonde, today attired in her blue sweater and small scale skirt, similar articles of clothing she had advanced to Isabel the earlier week.

The young ladies talked about planning when abruptly they halted at the sound of a youthful male voice with a prodding tone. "Hello Aubree, what's under your smaller than expected skirt?"

Aubree and Isabel went to see the unwanted presence of Henry Jarvis, long the harasser of this current year bunch with his gang of four similarly juvenile domineering jerks behind him.

Aubree respected Henry with scorn. "Nothing you'll at any point will see, Henry."

"I don't think about that," said Henry. "I hear that heaps of folks will perceive what's under your skirt, tons of folks."

"I suppose you're the failure who doesn't look at that point," said Aubree contemptuously. "Please Isabel, we should class. We may wind up as imbecilic as these numbskulls if we remain around here chatting with them."

"You both have issues standing, Aubree," giggled Henry. "She's a challenged person, and you invest the greater part of your energy on your back." Like a bunch of hyenas, Henry's companions participated in the giggling.

Seeing the vibe of hurt all over, Aubree went to Henry with an angry appearance all over. "Don't you at any point call her that, not ever."

Henry pointed at Isabel's leg support, which was completely obvious today as she was wearing pants and a sweater. "It's what she is."

"Let us be except if you need me to punch you in the face," said Aubree, endeavoring to lead Isabel away.

"Leaving so quick, Aubree?" taunted Henry. "We haven't seen up your skirt."

"Continue dreaming Henry, it is never going to occur," said Aubree.

"It will depend on the off chance that we do this," said Henry. He moved quickly, finding Aubree napping and getting her topography course reading and throwing it to one of his companions. "We'll see bounty if you need to play get with a skirt that short."

"That is truly adult folks," said Aubree. "We're 18-years of age, not 8-years of age."

"Please, don't you need it back?" Getting Aubree's book and tossing it high noticeable all around, Henry taunted, trusting she would hop up to get it with her skirt flying up simultaneously.

"What about you let her be, Henry?" Isabel proposed.

"Furthermore, what about you avoid it, polio, young lady?" Henry said. "This doesn't concern you."

"Try not to call her that!" hollered Aubree, her face becoming a striking shade of red.

"What, you don't care for it when I call her a disabled person, and you don't care for it when I call her polio young lady?" said Henry as again he got Aubree's reading material and tossed it to another companion. "There's no satisfying you, is there Aubree?"

One of Henry's companions tossed Aubree's book. However, the kid he threw it to misconceived his catch, and the book fell onto the floor, right external the open entryway of the janitor's wardrobe. He went to get it, yet Henry halted him. "We'll see bounty on the off chance that she needs to twist around to get her book."

"Once more, not going to happen, Henry, grow up," said Aubree as she went to recover her book. Henry could see that Aubree would not permit any brief look up her skirt by the noble way the beautiful blonde bowed down to recover her course reading and immediately settled on another strategy to have a good time.

Hurrying forward, he pushed Aubree into the janitor's wardrobe. "Hello!" shouted Aubree as she went rambling, and Henry hammered the entryway shut, catching Aubree inside.

Aubree's face was simply noticeable to Isabel briefly before Henry finished the entryway and killed the light, yet Isabel could see a look of abject dread in Aubree's eyes. When the entryway was shut, Aubree shouted like a banshee and started beating on the entryway. "Allow me to out, let me out, let me out!" she shrieked, her voice insane.

Henry and his companions snickered, thinking this was every one of the major events. "What's the matter Aubree, you're not terrified of the dull, are you?" Henry called.

"Allow me to out; if it's not too much trouble, let me out," shouted Aubree, presently crying and her voice giving indications of frenzy and hyperventilation.

Isabel was appalled. Aubree was alarmed, and these dolts thought it was each of the gigantic jokes. Isabel pushed ahead as quickly as possible to where Henry held the entryway shut, the frozeAubree beating on the threshold and wailing on the opposite side.

"Allow her to out!" shouted Isabel, attempting to compel Henry far removed so she could free Aubree, who was beating on the entryway in a craze. Yet, Henry was a lot greater, taller, and more grounded than her also healthy, and it was never going to be a challenge.

One push from Henry and Isabel's wobbly left leg before long gave way, the youngster going rambling and hitting her head on a seat on her way down.

"What's happening here?" called a youthful male voice.

Isabel, scouring her aching head, admired see Brad running towards Henry and his force of menaces as Aubree shouted and wailed inside the storage room. Brad's face was a cover of wrath.

"That is my sister in there!" hollered Brad. "Let her out at this point!"

"You going to make us for sure?" Henry tested.

"No doubt!" said Brad. Without wavering briefly, Brad conveyed a punch to Henry's face, sending him rambling. Two of Henry's companions went to battle Brad, yet the angry young fellow pushed them to the side with the power of outrage and opened up the janitor's storeroom's entryway.

Inside, Aubree was a wreck, shaking in dread, crying, and hyperventilating. Brad took his panicked twin by the hand and drove her out, Aubree's eyes going wherever like a scared deer. Isabel felt frightened. What might have caused a particularly rough response in Aubree? Isabel felt vulnerable as Aubree stood crying.

Brad went to Henry, who was all the while recuperating from the hard punch he had gotten. "You think this is interesting, Henry?" Brad requested.

"It's not my deficiency your sister can't take a joke, for what reasons is she is continuing like such a churlish brat?" jeered Henry.

His face dazzling red, Brad surged forward, his clenched hand raised when the sound of the Principal's voice repeated through the hall. "No more."

The young people went to see the tall, silver-haired figure of the school chief stepping towards them, and quiet fell. "What's happening here?" No answers. "No one has anything to say?" The Principal pointed at Henry and his companions. "What an unexpected Henry, seeing you and your companions at the focal point of any difficulty. Get up to my office and sit tight for me."

Henry and friends turned and shuffled towards the workplace, an excursion all had made commonly before.

The Principal went to Brad, who was shaking with anger and attempting to quiet his upset sister. "Brad, take Aubree up to the medical attendant's office and hang tight for me there."

Brad guided his shaking, crying sister away toward the medical caretaker's office, and the Principal went to Isabel. "IsabelSamara, it's an amazement to see you of all young ladies here. What occurred your face?" The Principal demonstrated the scraped area on Isabel's brow.

"I attempted to get them to allow Aubree to out of the storeroom," said Isabel.

"Isabel, accompany me to the attendant's office so she can investigate you, and afterward, I think we would be wise to have somewhat of a discussion," said the Principal.

Isabel followed the Principal to the medical caretaker's office and could see into the neighboring room, where Aubree sat on the bed wailing and still obviously panicked. So upset was Aubree that the medical attendant put a pail on the bed alongside her to safeguard the off chance that the young lady heaved.

Brad sat adjacent to his twin, attempting to get her to quiet down. Noticing the sibling and sister, Isabel could see that the two common some uncommon bond, yet what it was Isabel couldn't tell. Isabel's heart hustled as she attempted to comprehend what had caused such degraded fear in Aubree, who was ordinarily a particularly certain young lady, not anxious or restless by any means.

The Principal went into the room where Aubree and Brad sat. "Brad, take Aubree home, and you're both on debilitated leave for the following two days," said the Principal. "I will call your dad to talk about what occurred here today."

"So we're getting rebuffed its Henry and his companions who ought to be suspended from school," fought Brad.

"Brad Clayton, I recommend that you realize when is a fun opportunity to stay silent," said the Principal. "You are on wiped out leave for two days, so you both have the opportunity to quiet down; you are not suspended. On the off chance that your dad wishes to rebuff you for battling in school, it is his choice and his alone. The chip will gather any schoolwork for you and Aubree during the following two days. Presently, I propose you get your sister home and that she rests for the remainder of the evening."

Brad was baffled and irate yet could see that nothing he said or did would have any effect. "Indeed, sir," he said to the Principal before driving his sister out of the debilitated space to take her home. While she had now quit crying, Aubree was white as an apparition, and her legs precarious as she followed her sibling in total quietness.

The Principal and the attendant at that point directed their concentration toward Isabel in the next room. The medical caretaker analyzed the scraped area on Isabel's temple, and the Principal addressed her.

"Isabel, might you want to disclose to me how you came to be engaged with the unsettling influence in the passage this evening?"

"Henry and his companions secured Aubree in the storage room, and they wouldn't allow her to out; I attempted to get them to open the entryway."

The Principal shook his head, doubting. "So you got into a battle with five young men?"

"No, I didn't attempt to battle them," Isabel dissented. "I simply attempted to get them to open the entryway. I was just defending my companion."

"I'm amazed at you, Isabel," said the Principal. "A young lady with your constraints and the Reverend's little girl ought not to get herself associated with the tricks of Aubree and Brad Clayton and Henry and his companions. You ought to get an hour's detainment at any rate for this. Be that as it may, given your conduct is ordinarily magnificent, you'll just get thirty minutes."

Like Brad before her, Isabel could see that awful would come from discussing the matter further. Detainment for 30 minutes after school was another experience that she could have done without. Yet, she had the fulfillment of seeing Henry and his companions getting rebuffed by pruning a fence - with hand scissors.

Isabel missed her customary transport and had a severe sit tight for the following one. Getting off at her stop, she trusted her folks would not test her a lot on why she was late home. Isabel looked at the Clayton house. She had stressed constantly over Aubree the entire evening and needed to ensure she was OK. She could see that Ben Clayton's van was stopped in the carport and was enticed to proceed to thump on the entryway, yet chose to leave things for the occasion.

Going in her own home's front entryway, everything hushed up until Isabel heard her dad's voice. "Isabel, would you be able to come into the kitchen, please?"

Isabel strolled through into the kitchen to see her mom and father situated at the table, both brilliant wearing garments, however looking generally disappointed.

"Isabel, for what reason are you late home from school today?" Reverend Samara needed to know.

Isabel endeavored to sound easygoing. "Goodness, I missed the transport."

"You missed the transport?" Reverend Samara inquired.

"Indeed, I surmise I just forgot about the time, and I needed to sit tight for the following transport," said Isabel. "Sorry about that."

"Did you have a decent day at school today?" Reverend Samara inquired.

Isabel shrugged. " I presume."

"What befell your face?" enquired Reverend Samara. "You have a wound on your temple."

Again Isabel attempted to sound windy in her answer. "I hit my head on the entryway of my storage."

"Simply a customary Thursday at that point?" Reverend Samara said. "Not all that much or distinctive occurred?"

"No, simply one more day," Isabel said.

"All in all, you ordinarily get into battles and are given detainment? That is simply one more day at school for you?"

Isabel's mouth fell open. "How could you know?"

"Your Principal called me about it, Isabel," said Reverend Samara angrily. "By what other method do you think I think about it?"

"It wasn't my issue; I was simply defending Aubree," said Isabel.

Reverend Samara feigned exacerbation. "Aubree, obviously she would be engaged with this."

"Father, you weren't there; it wasn't Aubree's shortcoming. If you'd just hear me out ..."

"No, Isabel, I won't listen to you. Do you realize why I'm not tuning in to you? Since you don't hear me out. On the off chance that you'd have tuned in to me, you would have remained far away from Aubree Clayton, and none of this would have occurred."

Isabel shook with wrath. "I'm mature enough to choose who I need to be companions with. Aubree helped me when I required it a week ago, recollect?"

"As you bring that circumstance up, when you consider it, that was your shortcoming for failing to remember your home key. Please leave me alone exceptionally clear with you,

69

Isabel. At the point when you live in this house, you live by my principles. I revealed to you not to connect with Aubree and her family, you neglected to tune in, and you engage in battling at school, being set on detainment and afterward lying about it." Reverend Samara stopped, cleaning sweat from his bare head. "Also, I'm not the one you ought to be generally stressed over challenging. Recall that God can see all that you do, each idea you have, each transgression you submit."

Isabel glared back at her dad and conveyed an answer loaded up with mockery. "God, yes, obviously everything has something to do with God. It's all I've heard for what seems like forever."

Reverend Samara's demeanor turned out to be angrier. "Also, what is that expected to mean?"

" God truly looks out for me, doesn't he?" Isabel tested her dad. She demonstrated her leg support. "I got polio at a children's book of scriptures camp on the off chance that you recollect. Was God getting away when that occurred? Shouldn't something be said about kids who deteriorated than me? Where was God at that point? Is it true that he was looking out for them? What about kids who kicked the bucket from polio? Was God paying special mind to them and their folks who needed to live with losing their kids?"

"I realize that you're irate right now, Isabel, so I'll imagine you didn't say any of that," said Reverend Samara. "However, I will disclose to you a certain something. There's an 18-year-old young lady from Raleigh, North Carolina, grounded for about fourteen days and just permitted to take off from the house to go to class and go to chapel on Sunday. Do you know who that young lady is? I'll provide you some insight; it's you. Presently, your mom, sibling, and I will go to the congregation social this evening, and you will remain here to contemplate. Is that reasonable, Isabel?"

Isabel saw her dad's face as a combination of disobedience and impoliteness. "Missing a congregation social? I'm heartbroken."

"Where did you figure out how to be so impolite?" snapped Reverend Samara. "Aubree Clayton, her sibling and their companions, no uncertainty. Get your schoolwork, and begin." Reverend Samara turned and shouted to his child. "Peter, please, we're going to the congregation."

Isabel saw her mom, and her mom glanced back at her. "Your dad is correct, Isabel," Mrs. Samara said.

"Do you in every case simply concur with him, Mom?" Isabel inquired. "Don't you at any point have an independent mind?"

Mrs. Samara remained quiet, and Isabel feigned exacerbation and murmured noisily in criticism at her mom's absence of confidence.

"Isabel, you regard your mom and don't talk anymore," raged Reverend Samara. "I'm so disillusioned in you."

The Reverend and Mrs. Samara, alongside Peter, who regularly appeared to be unmindful of his other relatives' issues, advanced out the front way to the vehicle. Isabel, still angry, followed them out. "You think you know everything Dad, except you know short of what anybody. What incredible things have you at any point done in your life to make you think you reserve the privilege to pass judgment on individuals you scarcely know?"

Reverend Samara was seething yet also stunned at the conduct of his regularly peaceful and consistent girl. "You don't have the foggiest idea when to stop while you're ahead, do you, Isabel? You're presently grounded for a month. Is that unmistakable? Presently return inside."

Isabel remained in the front yard in peaceful disobedience as Reverend Samara switched out of the carport and drove towards the congregation. Isabel's anger towards her folks was over-shadowed by her anxiety for Aubree and the alarming occasions at school that evening. As the young person attempted to figure out the alarming circumstance, a male voice to her side broke into her considerations, surprising her to some degree.

"You alright there, Isabel?"

Isabel went to see the tall, attractive type of Ben Clayton to one side, the man giving her a grin. "Apologies, I didn't intend to frighten you," Ben grinned. "I would prefer not to get you furious; you as of now look bounty irate, all things considered."

"No, that is OK; I'm not irate at you, exactly at my Dad," said Isabel. "He doesn't get any person or thing."

"You shouldn't slight your dad; you should take a gander at things from his viewpoint. Your Dad acts how he does due to his past encounters throughout everyday life," said Ben. "It's the equivalent for us all. I act how I do give my background, and you'll act in a path on account of things that happened to you in your life."

"I was unable to mindless if I never see my dad again," said Isabel.

Once more, Ben cast the young lady a friendly and knowing grin. "I knew a child who sounded actually like you once. A kid who was a genuine hot-head and thought he knew better than every other person around him. When he was 16, he chose to lie about his age and flee from home to join the military and go to the conflict. His dad attempted to stop him, they had a gigantic contention, and the kid stomped out and said that he trusted he never saw his dad again. The kid got into the military utilizing manufactured records,

72

battled in the conflict, and when he got back three years after the fact, his sister was sitting tight for him and revealed to him that their dad had passed on a year prior. The kid laments the exact opposite thing he at any point said to his dad right up 'til the present time."

Isabel pondered this for a couple of moments. "You're discussing yourself, aren't you, Mr. Clayton?"

Ben snickered daintily. "That undeniable, right? Furthermore, kindly call me Ben."

"I only sort of speculated," said Isabel.

"I figured you would," said Ben. "At any rate, I needed to thank you for supporting Aubree today."

"I was unable to do a lot; I was no assistance at all true," Isabel mourned.

"No, you went to bat for her against five male harassers all greater and a lot more grounded than you," said Ben. "I'm speculating that you're quite befuddled about what occurred at school today?"

"You could say that," said Isabel. "How is Aubree? I'm so stressed over her."

"Brad took Aubree out for a drive to attempt to get her to quiet down a digit," said Ben. "Chip's out as well - at swimming club practice. That kid invests such a lot of energy in swimming training. I think he'd have been more joyful on the off chance that he was conceived a dolphin. Aubree was stressed over you seeing what you did, that you would be frightened. She inquired about whether I could converse with you; Aubree said she would be too disturbed even to consider discussing it herself. What about you go over to my home, and I can disclose things to you?"

With her annoyance levels lessening, the agreeable, respectful Isabel, who never tried to ignore her folks, returned all of a sudden. "Shouldn't take off from the house; I'm grounded."

"I will not tell your folks on the off chance that you don't," said Ben, to which Isabel gestured and followed the more seasoned man across the road. A tall man whose youngsters had the option bodied, Ben without intuition strolled excessively quick for Isabel, who battled to keep up before Ben acknowledged what was going on and strolled at a more slow speed. Ben opened the entryway and accompanied Isabel into the lounge room.

"Would you like a tea or an espresso?" Ben inquired.

"An espresso, please," Isabel said, sitting down on the lounge chair and tuning in as Ben heated the pot in the kitchen; at that point, got back with some tea and espresso, Ben putting the espresso mug on the table before Isabel.

"Much obliged to you," said Isabel, getting the cup and taking a taste.

"I got the propensity for drinking tea when I was in England," said Ben as he drank his tea. "If I drink espresso currently, I'm until late."

"Aubree and Brad referenced that you were in England when you were in the military," said Isabel.

Ben gestured. "Truth be told. My detachment was there a few times in the later phases of the conflict."

"They said you got the Medal of Honor," said Isabel. "You should feel so pleased."

Ben becomes flushed. "I wish they hadn't said anything regarding that."

Isabel's heart hustled. "Apologies, I didn't have the foggiest idea ... I don't need them to fall into difficulty ..."

Ben gave her a consoling grin. "It's alright, Isabel. They will not be in a difficult situation. I was granted the Medal of Honor, and my children are glad for that. It's justifiable they would be. I simply wish I was glad."

"You're not pleased with getting the Medal of Honor?"

"To be honest, Isabel, I feel sort of humiliated by it."

Isabel was stunned by the man's response. "Humiliated?"

"Indeed," said Ben. "The decoration dwells in my sock cabinet now. Each time I take a gander at it, I consider men who were more courageous than me and weren't perceived or never returned from the conflict. I consider my activities that prompted my enrichment, and I think if there was something different, I might have done to save more men in my company that day. However, in particular, I consider things I found in Germany."

"What kind of things?" Isabel inquired.

"It's better that you never know the full subtleties, else you would never be a cheerful lady," Ben guaranteed the young lady. "There were places awful places in Germany. Camps where they kept Allied POWs, Jews, Gypsies, and different gatherings the Nazis despised. The things I saw, heard, and smelled some things would remain in my psyche until the end of time."

"It should be troublesome," said Isabel.

"As I said before, encounters in life influence how you respond to things," clarified Ben. "I can live with my encounters in the conflict. It isn't in every case simple; even now, almost 20 years after the fact, I stir a few evenings after dreams. However, I can adapt to it—a few men I unexpectedly presented with think. For a few, their conflict encounters were similar to a terrible day at the workplace. Different men discovered their encounters excessively. Some have lost themselves in the jug, and some couldn't bear going on and are never again are with us."

"I believe no doubt about it," said Isabel. "You were my age - younger than me - serving in the conflict."

"I don't consider myself daring," said Ben. "I believe you're more daring than me."

Isabel was stunned. "Me? Valiant? I don't think so. For what reason am I fearless?"

"Since you went through something as a youngster that has consistently scared me. Something I question I might have adapted to had I confronted it myself."

Ben's look floated to one side leg and her support, and the youngster was stunned. "Polio?"

Ben gestured. "Indeed."

Isabel shook her head. "I'm not valiant. Heaps of children had polio in the mid-1950s."

"Polio was the one thing that consistently terrified me more than all else," said Ben. "As a child, I was constantly terrified I would get it, that my sister Jane would get it, or that our cousins or companions would get it. Fortunately, none of us did. What's more, when Brad and Aubree were conceived, I stressed over them constantly."

"However, they were OK," said Isabel.

"Indeed, yet not without an enormous alarm. One morning in summer 1952, when there was that truly downright terrible pandemic Aubree and Brad woke up with hardened necks and high temperatures. My blood went cold; it resembled the world had quit turning. They'd been playing with Chip and Katie the other day, so getting on the telephone to Jane and Donny was one of the most noticeably terrible calls I've at any point made. Fortunately, it turned out the children had influenza - truly downright awful - yet not polio. For those couple of hours, however ..." Ben's voice followed off, and he shook his head.

"I can see how you and your sister and brother by marriage were so stressed," said Isabel, again bewildered by the shortfall of Aubree and Brad's mom from this story. She was starting to contemplate whether the twins even had a mother. The family photos in the front room did not indicate a spouse or mother. Maybe as newborn children, Aubree and Brad were saved close to home one morning by a stork?

"It was the most startling involvement with my life, far more awful than anything in the conflict," said Ben. "Simply the possibility that my child or my little girl could wind up injured, in an iron lung, or more awful. I can't envision what it might have been wanting to encounter it without a doubt."

Dread filled Isabel's beautiful face at the troublesome recollections. "I was so terrified," she said in a little voice.

Ben gestured. "Having polio would have been an encounter to influence your life, how you see the world, how you respond to various things, various individuals, various circumstances. I envision certain things take you back there, to when it occurred?"

"The smell of medical clinic sanitizer," Isabel advertised. "Furthermore, the sound of children crying. It constantly happened in the ward when I was in a medical clinic. Once in a while, it would be the young lady in the bed close to me. In some cases, the kid across the path from us. Once in a while, it would be me crying, and I didn't have any acquaintance with it."

Ben gestured purposely. "Indeed, I can get that. It very well may be a normal day, and I'll be driving as it were or grinding away, and I'll see, hear or smell something. Out of nowhere, I'll be directed back in Europe during the conflict, either under substantial German fire or going into one of those awful places to see the most horrible of what people can do."

"At the point when Peter was 12, and I was 14, he broke his arm," said Isabel. "It was his flaw; he scaled a stepping stool to draw a nearer, take a gander at the moon, and tumbled off. In any case, sitting in the clinic lounge area with Mom and Dad while the specialist put Peter's arm in a cast, I could smell the sanitizer, I could hear a child crying, and I sensed that I was directed back in the polio ward. I felt unnerved and simply needed to leave as quick as possible."

"That affirms what I was saying about past encounters influencing individuals and how they will act in specific circumstances," said Ben. "Take your folks. I don't have any acquaintance with them well enough, yet from what I do realize, I can see that their confidence is vital to them, that it generally has been a critical piece of their lives and will decide how they respond to conditions."

"Indeed, they're both exceptionally strict," certified Isabel. "All things considered, with my Dad being a clergyman, there would be an issue if he weren't."

"You most likely can't help thinking about why I've been conversing with you pretty much the entirety of this instead of coming to the heart of the matter and clarifying about Aubree," said Ben. "Aubree and Brad have had things happen to them in the life that causes them to carry on unquestionably. Disclose to me, Isabel, have either Aubree or Brad referenced their mom to you?"

"No, not even once," said Isabel.

"I figured that would be the situation," said Ben. "Have you at any point asked why?"

"I thought perhaps your significant other had died, and Aubree and Brad were so tragic about it that they never talked about their mom."

"From numerous points of view, that would have been simpler to adapt to," said Ben. "To appropriately disclose the entirety of this to you, I need to return to before Aubree and Brad were conceived, and I showed up in England with my unit. You've found out about the thing England resembled during the conflict?"

Isabel gestured. "It was quite awful, right?"

"Indeed. Times were hard; they had quite recently experienced the Depression; presently, there was all the apportioning and deficiencies and the horrible bombings. One thing that we saw was how satisfied the young English ladies were to see the appearance of the American powers. Numerous sentiments were created, and it was the same for me when I met Rose."

"Rose is Aubree and Brad's mom?"

"Believe it or not," certified Ben. "Albeit not straight away. I met her, and immediately I thought I was enamored. I think she thought she was as well, yet we were youthful, and we thought we knew it all. We fraternized in England, and when I was away with my company, we generally kept in touch with one another. At any rate, we were together around Christmas 1944, preceding my detachment got back to Europe for the last mission to crush Germany. I ought to have been eased that the conflict in Europe was finished. However, I continued stressing over what might occur with Rose when I got back to America. I was apprehensive I could never see her again. When I was back in England, this was responded to in due order regarding me. Rose and I needed to get hitched, and she needed to return with me to America as my better half. You comprehend why that was, don't you?"

Given that Aubree and Brad were brought into the world in September 1945, the reasons regarding why Ben needed to wed Rose were self-evident, and Isabel just gestured in understanding as Ben proceeded with the story.

"A ton of American servicemen wedded young ladies from England and different nations like Australia and New Zealand and got back to America with them when the conflict was finished," said Ben. "War ladies, they were called. I can't represent the Australians and New Zealanders; however, many young ladies from England had a wrong perspective on the United States. They thought it was all Hollywood fabulousness and style, New York refinement, or the New England states' magnificence. A great deal of them discovered the most difficult way possible that things are similarly just about as hard and intense as in Britain."

"So your significant other was troubled when she came to America?" Isabel inquired.

"Despondent is putting it mildly," said Ben. "Rose was so disillusioned with America and detested it from the beginning. I offered lenient gestures given what she'd experienced in the conflict. Rose was from a helpless family in London's East End, where the bombarding was a portion of the most exceedingly awful. They were bombarded out in the main seven-day stretch of The Blitz, and the crisis convenience where they were remaining got obliterated as well. Rose thought that it was difficult to adapt to the bombings, bomb stun, I believe, is the thing that they called it. I was in a single air assault, and it was unnerving for me, and I was a warrior, prepared to manage things like that. I attempted to see things from her view, rationalized her, and attempted to assist her with acclimating to her new life. Jane made an honest effort to be companions and make Rose greeting in her new home. However, Rose was having none of it. At that point, Aubree and Brad were conceived, and I trusted things would change. They did, however, not how I trusted."

"Your significant other was upset when Aubree and Brad were conceived?"

"Actually, no, not in any manner," said Ben. "At the point when I previously saw my children after they were conceived, Aubree was sound sleeping, and she resembled a doll that a toymaker had made to act as an illustration of what an ideal infant ought to be. What's more, Brad was a particularly attractive child; I generally recall how he grinned and connected with me. Be that as it may, Rose hated them from first sight and scarcely needed to hold them."

"That is terrible." Isabel couldn't envision a mother hating her infants.

"I continued disclosing to myself that things would change, that Rose would develop to adore Aubree and Brad; however, she didn't. She did the absolute minimum to care for them as infants; however, she overlooked them. I was out working for extended periods, attempting to put food on the table, cover the bills, keep a rooftop over our heads, and feel awful about not investing more energy with the children, given their mom didn't need anything to do with them. There wasn't much I could do; if I didn't work, there was no cash, and we'd have been out in the city. Rose and I battled continually; she hated me for everything. I was a grown-up and settled on life decisions that prompted the present circumstance that I could adapt to. What's more, it takes two individuals to make a marriage work or a marriage come up short, so I was to blame as well. Yet, it was how she disdained Aubree and Brad that agitated me most. They were infants; none of this was their flaw. What's more, when you're in a terrible circumstance, you will, in general, go into refusal; you disclose to yourself that things will mysteriously improve when you realize where it counts that they won't ever will."

Isabel felt shocked that a lady could detest her significant other - a bold saint from the conflict - such a lot that she thus abhorred their children. No big surprise then that Brad and Aubree never talked about their mom. Also, Isabel could feel for Ben saying how he lived willfully ignorant during a terrible time in his life. For specific years after her sickness, Isabel would regularly disclose that she would get up one morning and track down her harmed left leg was mystically back to ordinary. She would disclose to herself that she was pleasant on the off chance that she carried out beneficial things for individuals and implored particularly hard to God that her leg would improve and she could walk regularly. It never did, and these dreams had a distant memory when she arrived at middle school.

Ben proceeded with his story. "I figured Rose might resemble an uncle of mine; he didn't appear to like our cousins without a doubt and invested as little energy as conceivable with them. That I might have lived with, yet when Aubree and Brad got more established and were strolling and going around the house, Rose thought that it was considerably harder to adapt to them. The children would consistently be energized when I returned home from work, and Rose would holler at me for making a fight with them, saying they had been getting out of hand throughout the day. At that point, things happened that began to make me considerably more stressed. One day Brad had a major wound on his arm, and when I got some information about it, she said that he'd fallen over going around the nursery. I didn't inquire her further; I mean, I can't keep those rowdy boys down, and I had many wounds and cuts when I was a child. At that point, about seven days after the fact, I returned home, and Aubree had been debilitated all down the front of her dress. Once more, I got some information about it, and she hollered that Aubree had just barely hurled before I arrived, that she had been occupied with Brad and hadn't had the opportunity to deal with Aubree, and for what reason didn't I do it. So I brought Aubree into the washroom to get her tidied up and figured out, and Aubree's regurgitation was dry. She has probably been strolling around like that throughout the day."

Ben completed the remainder of his tea and took a gander at Isabel. "I realize this is likely isn't the most joyful story you've at any point heard in your life Isabel, yet on the off chance that you will comprehend what happened this evening, you need to hear it."
"I comprehend," said Isabel.

"The alerts went off more grounded when Aubree and Brad started to talk more. They began talking, upsetting things that they were too youthful to even think about having concocted all alone. At some point, I saw Aubree hollering at her doll, saying, 'You inept, dumb, moronic youngster, for what reason wouldn't you be able to be dead?' Another day Brad was out in the nursery yelling at the neighbors' feline, which was perched wavering, saying that it was 'a greater bonehead than its sister' and that he 'despised it and wished it didn't exist.' The children were getting very forceful and would make statements like that to their cousins and different children as well, even though clearly, they had no clue about the thing they were saying. They would carry on in other unusual manners as well. Once I discovered them going through my apparatus chest playing with sharp things, and I reprimanded them for it. Aubree and Brad were terrified, even though I wasn't going to hit them, and scarcely even raised my voice. Sometimes, I fixed an entryway on a wardrobe, and Aubree meandered into the room and turned out to be exceptionally disturbed, crying and shouting at me to leave because the Devil may get me. She wasn't playing around. She was truly terrified."

"What did you do straightaway?" Isabel inquired.

"By that stage, I was persuaded that Rose was mishandling Aubree and Brad, yet I had no evidence. When I was around, Rose would act like - well, I wouldn't say an extraordinary mother; Rose was never an incredible or even a decent mother. I suppose you would say an uninterested mother - and that is no wrongdoing. I trusted in my sister, and Jane and I worked out an arrangement. One morning I claimed to leave for work, yet Jane and I snuck once again into the house without Rose or the children seeing us. Jane was there as an observer - else it was only Rose's statement against mine - and we had a journal with us to note down what occurred. It appeared to be odd - a grown-up sibling and sister taking cover behind the lounge chair - however, we needed to perceive what was happening. It wasn't some time before Aubree spilled her juice, and it drove Rose insane. She hauled Aubree across the floor by her hair to the storeroom, disclosing how moronic she was. Aubree was crying; Rose advised her to quiet down and snatched a length of the electrical link and hit Aubree with it. I needed to leap out at that point and stop her. However, Jane kept me down, saying we required more proof."

Isabel felt progressively sickened by the story, at how a mother could treat her children how Aubree and Brad's mom did.

Ben looked upset by the recollections. "At the point when Jane and I were kids, our folks exhibited to us that belts, the backs of hairbrushes, and wooden spoons had different uses on many occasions; however, I've never seen anyone hit their child how Rose belted Aubree. At that point, Brad begged his mom not to hurt Aubree, and Rose hit him with the electrical rope as well and inquired as to whether he needed to be secured in the storeroom with the Devil like his sister would have been. Brad was crying and eased off; at that point, Rose opened the wardrobe entryway and requested Aubree inside. Aubree cried constantly and asked not to be placed in there. However, Rose took Aubree's doll and revealed to Aubree that she would consume the doll in the fire before Aubree if she didn't get inside there. Aubree, at that point, ventured into the storage room entryway - she was totally scared - and Rose hit her once more, pushed her in there, and revealed to her that she trusted the Devil got her this time at that point, shut the entryway. Aubree was shouting and crying. We'd seen enough, Jane and I leaped out, and she took the children out to her vehicle. I disclosed to Rose that the marriage was finished, that I would petition for legal separation straight away, and that I would ensure she could never see the children again."

Isabel's enormous earthy-colored eyes were wide at the sheer ghastliness of what Aubree and Brad had experienced as kids on account of the individual who should adore and secure them most. How is it possible that any mother would misuse her kids the way Mrs. Clayton had done?

"I was concerned Rose may challenge the separation application or battle me for the authority of the children just to get at me, yet luckily she just evaporated off into the wide blue there, and we never saw or heard from her again," said Ben. "She didn't show up in court for the separation procedures. I don't have the foggiest idea of where she is currently - regardless of whether she remained in America or returned to England - or whether she is alive or dead. I couldn't care less, I never need to see her again, and neither does Brad or Aubree. It's one thing for her to detest me - a grown-up - however, to take it out on our children is something I can never excuse her for."

Isabel recalled a little while before, where Aubree had said something about her dad just committing one genuine error in his life, at that point getting unsettled and requesting that Isabel fail to remember what she had quite recently said. The bewildering discussion currently appeared well and well. "I can comprehend why Aubree was so frightened when she got driven into the wardrobe at school today."

"Indeed, Aubree is frightened by dull, bound spaces," said Ben. "Brad is claustrophobic as well, yet not to the degree of his sister. It appeared that Rose secured him in the storage room as well, but since he would be more consistent, it happened to him undeniably less. Aubree was in every case more difficult and would hold fast, and accordingly, Rose secured her in the storage room more."

"I recall that we had a topography trip at school to certain caverns a year ago," said Isabel. "I wasn't permitted to go; they said my leg wasn't up to the climbing, yet Aubree didn't go. She said that you had grounded her and wouldn't release her on the outing."

"Indeed, that was a pardon we worked out together. It's impossible Aubree could go in a cavern, and she would never have some work like a photographic artist that includes a dim room. Aubree was stressed. You would think she was insane after what happened today. Aubree isn't insane; it's simply that gratitude to how her mom dealt with her, she is seriously claustrophobic."

"I never thought Aubree was insane, yet I was so stressed over her. Brad as well, he was so furious after what befallen her."

"It resembles what I was saying before regarding past encounters influencing your life," said Ben. "If I hear a bizarre commotion in the evening, I'm wide alert and 18-years of age again and in the conflict. If you smell medical clinic sanitizer, you're back in the polio ward of the kids' medical clinic. Furthermore, when Aubree is set in a dull, limited space, she's unexpectedly an alarmed young lady again being secured in a storage room by her mom and advised that the Devil will get her. Since Brad had similar encounters and needed to perceive what occurred to his sister, he is exceptionally defensive of her and sees red assuming anyone harms Aubree." Ben stopped, trying to ease up the air kidded, "In any event, I realized that Aubree could never play the game Seven Minutes in Heaven at parties when she was more youthful."

Isabel grinned meagerly. "No, I don't figure she would. Is Aubree going to be OK?"

"Indeed, it will simply require her a couple of days. As I referenced before, Aubree requested that I address you as she was stressed over what you saw today and thinks it's difficult to talk about what occurred to her when she was a kid. Isabel, I believe you keep what I advised you to yourself and not talk about it to any other individual. Not to your folks, your sibling, your companions, or anybody from chapel or the area."

Isabel never planned to tell anybody anything of what Ben Clayton had advised her and gestured in certification. "I comprehend; I will not utter a word to anyone."

"I realize we can confide in you," said Ben. Seeing that Isabel looked troubled about her companion, Ben again grinned and said, "Aubree will be OK, I guarantee you. It will simply require a day or so for her to recuperate."

"Much obliged to you for disclosing things to me," said Isabel. She looked at the clock. "I surmise I would be wise to be returning home and make it appear as though I've in any event done some schoolwork."

Ben bade Isabel goodnight, and the young lady got back to her own home across the road. She thought that it was difficult to rest that evening, thrashing around and pondering the abhorrencesAubree and Brad had experienced on account of their mom. She trusted Aubree would be OK after the school's injury that day and again seethed at how individuals unreasonably decidedAubree and her family, not least Isabel's folks.

*

The Reverend Larry Samara was a man who was liable on the occasion of living trying to claim ignorance. In the kitchen on Friday morning, he saw Isabel finding a seat at the table, glancing coy in a light Samara dress, sewn white coat, and white level obeyed shoes, Isabel's long dim hair tied back in a braid with Samara lace. He expected that his agreeable and devoted little girl had returned and plunked down close to her.

Isabel respected him with an actual appearance on her lovely face, and Reverend Samara grinned at her. "I imagine that there's a young lady who needs to apologize and offer reparations for the mistakes of her methodologies."

Reverend Samara's words were conveyed in a similar belittling and deigning tone he regularly embraced with his little girl, like she was a getting rowdy youngster instead of the youthful grown-up she was. Isabel would have been willing to talk about things with her dad had he addressed her like a grown-up. Be that as it may, all the prevailing about doing was getting her considerably more off-side. Isabel frowned at her dad, stood up unexpectedly, and without a word, left the kitchen, giving him the silent treatment.

"You're not conversing with me at that point?" Reverend Samara asked the teen, who didn't react. "I realize that you'll come around to see things the correct way in the long run."

Isabel trusted that the transport would school with Peter, and her more youthful sibling annoyed her about things that were just important to him. As common, he was unaware that his more seasoned sister wasn't intrigued and that she was feeling terrible and not under any condition responsive. Yet, this was not an astonishment. He hadn't discovered that giving Isabel a lot of room like clockwork was a smart thought. The prior year had awoken Isabel at two AM to reveal that the planet Venus was so brilliant in the sky it showed up as more a circle than as a star.

Friday was a long, difficult day for Isabel. On the whole, the classes she imparted to Aubree, Isabel wound up taking a gander at the unfilled work area where Aubreeordinarily would have been sitting and wishing her companion was there. Pretty Aubree filled Isabel's creative mind throughout the day, and she trusted that the twins were doing approve.

The last ringer for the day rang, and Isabel returned home to a Friday night that was altogether different to ordinary. The main thing was very phenomenal. At 16 years old, Peter was going out to a sleepover, the first run-through in quite a while life he had dozed over at another child's home. This was a kid from the science club at school, and he was similarly as captivated by space as Peter was. Isabel trusted that Peter could make a certifiable companion this time, however, had her questions given her more youthful kin's history with making and keeping companions.

The Reverend and Mrs. Samara were likewise going out to supper with a family from their congregation, the Harris family, who were confronting a horrendous emergency. It appeared to be that their oldest child Tommy was especially taken with that new melodic gathering from Liverpool, England, which considered themselves the Beatles. Such an extensive amount a fan was Tommy that he had trimmed his hair to resemble the group of four of young fellows who contained the gathering, profoundly stressing his folks. Reverend Samara was certain that this gathering would rapidly disappear to haziness, however clearly, there was an issue in the meantime, and Reverend Samara was only the man to converse with teens, help them see the blunder of their methodologies, and set them back on the Lord's way. So Reverend and Mrs. Samara would eat with the Harris family, and a while later, Reverend Samara would have a meaningful conversation with Tommy and set him back in good shape.

Isabel, alone in the house, watched the comings and goings at the Clayton house across the street. First, Brad went out with his sweetheart Susie in the vehicle the three children shared, and afterward Luke showed up, and he and Chip went out together; Isabel contemplated attempting to meet two pleasant young ladies. Ben Clayton would get together with old companions from when he was in the military, and around evening time was one of those evenings, Ben going out not long after his child and nephew. However, of Aubree, there was no sign, and Isabel had not seen her throughout the day. She was clearly at home as the lights were on; however, Aubree herself didn't show up through the windows nor venture outside of the house.

Covering herself in her schoolwork, Isabel forgot about time as an hour passed by; then, her focus was broken as there came a thump on the front entryway. Getting up from the table, Isabel addressed the entryway. She was dazed to see Aubree remaining there, wearing a red smaller than normal skirt and coordinating with a sweater, a couple of white shoes on her feet, Aubree's delightful light hair hanging free over her shoulders.

"Hello Aubree!" shouted Isabel, her pleasure at seeing her companion self-evident. Isabel denounced herself inside at how she had responded; she seemed as though Billy did at whatever point Isabel showed up. "How are you feeling now?"

Aubree grinned. "I'm feeling greatly improved at this point. I wanted to would like to converse with you. Is it true that you are distant from everyone else right now?"

"Indeed, Mom and Dad and Peter are full scale. Come in."

Isabel and Aubree strolled to the couch and plunked down. Isabel saw the slightest look at white cotton undies texture up Aubree's smaller than normal skirt as the blonde young person folded her legs, Isabel criticizing herself intellectually for taking a gander at this.

"I requested that my Dad address you yesterday since I was stressed over you," said Aubree. "I needed to, yet I think that it's difficult to discuss how my mom dealt with Brad and me when we were young children. Seeing me in that state when I got pushed into the storeroom - you probably thought I was insane."

"Actually, no, not insane, but rather I was stressed over you and Brad," said Isabel.

"I realize you were; you're a truly old buddy," said Aubree. "You faced me against those blockheads."

"I was futile, they pushed me over, and I fell straight away," said Isabel. "You defended me more when they considered me a disabled person and polio young lady."

"That made me so frantic," said Aubree. "It shows how daring Henry and his companions are. How might they feel on the off chance that they'd had polio and someone prodded them about it?"

"The Principal made them cut the support with hand scissors," said Isabel. "I saw them doing it after school on Thursday."

Aubree grinned. "That is something at any rate. Furthermore, you weren't pointless. You're rarely futile, absolutely never say that regarding yourself."

"I feel futile now and again," Isabel deplored. "Like a bird with a wrecked wing."

Aubree gave Isabel a consoling grin. "Well, in case you're a bird with a wrecked wing, I should be a bird with a messed up cerebrum."

"I'm truly grieved about how your Mom dealt with you and your sibling when you were kids," said Isabel. "I was unable to trust it when your dad advised me."

Aubree gestured. "So now you realize why Brad and I never talk about our Mom."

"I'd generally felt that your Mom had passed on."

"She may well have since. However, I won't ever know. I never need to see her again, and neither brads. Every one of the ladies in London - or England as a rule - and Dad needs to succumb to her. However, Dad wasn't a lot more established than us at that point, and he didn't know what she would have been similar to, so it isn't his deficiency. What's more, when you consider the big picture, on the off chance that he hadn't met Mom, Brad and I wouldn't be here today."

"I surmise not; I never truly considered it that way," said Isabel.

"Discussing guardians, I heard you got grounded for a month," said Aubree. "I'm heartbroken about that; it's so uncalled for. Everything you did was an attempt to help me."

"You understand what my folks resemble," said Isabel. "My Dad and I aren't getting along excessively well right now."

"So would you say you are just permitted to take off from the house to go to class?"

Isabel gestured. "Indeed, school and church. Even though I wish I'd been grounded from the chapel as well. I can't tolerate churching. Father's messages are so exhausting. It's something very similar after quite a while after week."

Aubree snickered. "Perhaps it's better that you go to chapel? On the off chance that you don't go for about a month, Billy would be shattered."

Isabel become flushed and chuckled marginally. "No doubt, he most likely would be. He's liked me for quite a long time."

"I can't help thinking about what Billy is up to right now?" Aubree pondered, a naughty grin on her beautiful face. "Tallying during the time to chapel on Sunday? Composing love verse about a specific Reverend's girl named IsabelSamara maybe?"

"I don't think any sonnet Billy composed would be an example of writing," said Isabel. She demonstrated her Samara dress. "Once, he said that this dress fit me because my last name was Samara."

"Billy's not, in reality, wrong there," said Aubree. "You do look extremely lovely wearing Samara."

"I'm not pretty," said Isabel modestly.

"Indeed you are. A considerable amount of folks say how lovely you are."

"You're the beautiful one, Aubree," said the becoming flushed Isabel. "Doesn't your sweetheart disclose to you that you're pretty?"

"My beau?" Aubree inquired.

"Indeed, the person you go out with at the ends of the week."

"Gracious, he's not my beau," said Aubree. "We've been a few dates, yet nothing genuine. He's pleasant, yet I don't believe he's the individual for me."

Again Isabel noticed that Aubree utilized the word 'individual' instead of 'man,' 'kid,' or 'fellow' when talking about sentiment, yet excused it. "I've never been out on the town," Isabel said.

"That is awful," said Aubree. "I'm certain Billy might want to take you out on the town."

" I'm certain he would," said Isabel. "Be that as it may, I'd never need to go out on the town with Billy."

"It's interesting how love functions aren't it?" asked Aubree. "Billy has a squash the size of the Grand Canyon on you, yet you would prefer not to go out with him. Furthermore, you imagine that the individual you like won't ever know how you feel, and you stress over how they will feel if they discovered."

Isabel felt nerves coursing through her body, gathered in her stomach. Was Aubree simply talking logically, or when she utilized the word 'you,' was she tending to Isabel straightforwardly? Isabel took a gander at her little evaded companion, and Aubree had a slight look of entertainment all over, a look in her eyes that she knew something. Did Aubree know how Isabel felt about her?

"I - um - don't really like a person right now," Isabel stammered.

"I realize you don't really like a person right now, Isabel," Aubree guaranteed her.

"I have previously, however; I've liked young men previously. Heaps of young men. Not heaps of young men, simply normal pulverizes on an average number of young men." Isabel's face went red. She thought it was difficult to converse with Aubree without re-thinking herself under the most favorable circumstances; however, she just appeared to be fit for discussing jabber when anxious.

"I realize you have Isabel," said Aubree. "Most young ladies have liked a person in their life. It's simply that a few of us create squashes on young ladies as well."

"Not me," the anxious Isabel proclaimed. "Not ever."

"Truly?" Aubree inquired. "I surmise I failed to understand the situation at that point. It's a pity. However, I was truly complimented when I thought you liked me."
Isabel's genuine like it may blast out of her chest, so quick and hard was it beating. The young lady felt numb, thus apprehensive it resembled she was some way or another out of her own body, watching herself. She saw Aubree's face and could mention that regardless of what she said, Aubree knew the reality. Nervous perspiration coursing through her face, there was nothing left but to ask in a bit of voice, "How could you know?"

Aubree chuckled agreeably and drew nearer to Isabel, taking her companion's hand in her own to console her. "Isabel, on most occasions, you can tell when someone likes you. I could see the signs."

Isabel felt an irregularity creating in her throat, similar to she planned to cry, and she needed to fight hard not to break down into tears. "I'm so heartbroken, Aubree. I didn't intend to get a pulverize on you; I made a decent attempt not to ..."

"Isabel, it's alright; I'm not irritated with all."

"I feel horrendous about it. I shouldn't feel how I do."

Aubree pressed Isabel's hand tighter and investigated her huge, wide earthy-colored eyes. "What is there to feel horrendous about? Since when is it wrongdoing or a transgression to have heartfelt emotions about a companion?"

"What parted with me?"

"Gracious many things. How you took a gander at me, how you generally appeared to be so cheerful when I was there, however, so apprehensive about what to say to me simultaneously."

"Does any other individual know?" Isabel asked, shocked that others may have worked out her mysterious squash as effectively as the object of her expressions of warmth.

Once more, Aubree snickered her charming chuckle. "On the off chance that you acted a similar path around me a similar way Billy does around you, at that point, you'd have a lot to stress over. However, you're protected. Do you know why?"

Isabel shook her head, and Aubree expounded. "The possibility of the sweet, honest Reverend's little girl falling for a young lady who wears smaller than usual skirts, doesn't go to the chapel and sins a ton isn't reasonable, and accordingly, individuals will not see it. Also, you did a very great job of concealing how you felt, simply not exactly adequate to trick me."

"I figured you would be furious, vexed, or humiliated if you knew how I felt about you," said Isabel, especially soothed by Aubree's response.

"No, none of those things," Aubree guaranteed her companion. "However, there are things you don't see. You imagine that the lone young lady on the planet who likes young ladies just as young men, and you additionally feel that Billy is the lone individual who prefers you as such. You're off-base there on the two tallies. There's another young lady who likes young ladies just as young men and who likes you more than as a companion."

Aubree's hand moved to Isabel's knee, and she investigated Isabel's face. The beautiful brunette's eyes went wide with stun. "You?" she gasped.

"Me," said Aubree.

"No, you're trying to say that to cause me to feel much improved," said Isabel.

"I'm not, I swear," Aubree guaranteed her companion. "We're both what is called sexually open. I like folks; I like folks a ton. However, I like young ladies and one specific young lady - you - much more. Also, you like folks as well, yet you like me more."

"I could never have imagined that," said Isabel. "Never."

"Indeed, you now you do know. What is your opinion about that?"

Isabel was as yet staggered. "I don't have the foggiest idea, swell, I presume."

Aubree chuckled. "Well, I didn't think about that, yet I get it is swelling."

Isabel was adrift regarding what she ought to do straight away. "What would it be advisable for us to do about it?"

"I know precisely what we ought to do," said Aubree certainly. "We should begin dating, enlighten everybody concerning it, make out in the central avenue of town and circumvent school together clasping hands. Furthermore, from that point forward, we should go around giving out socialist distributions to every one of the children in school."

Isabel grinned daintily. "I get it. We need to hush up about it and not inform any other person regarding it."

"That is 100% right," insisted Aubree. "I wish it was extraordinary. I'd love it if we could go out together on dates to the drive-in or the film; that we could clasp hands together when we stroll down the road and that we could go to sweethearts' path and park, yet we can't. Perhaps one day, young ladies like us can date appropriately? Yet, for the time being, we need to keep things calm. It doesn't imply that we can't have a good time when we're distant from everyone else, however, similar to the present moment."

Isabel was sweating from nervous energy. However, it was the most remote region of the young person's body that was getting wettest. Isabel's vagina felt like it had taken on a unique kind of energy, the influxes of delight from her clitoris coursing through her whole body and her ladylike excitement making the seat of her undies get sodden. Isabel contemplated whether Aubree's vagina was carrying on a similar path as her pussy. On the off chance that she had the option to see through Aubree's miniskirt's texture and the cotton of the lovely blonde youngster's underwear, she would have gotten an agreed answer. Aubree could scarcely stand by so excited was her young pussy, her undies saddle getting wetter and wetter as time passes to such an extent it nearly felt like she had begun her period.

"You've never been kissed, not appropriately, have you?" Aubree asked her unpracticed companion.

Isabel reddened and laughed anxiously. "No."

"Well, this is the day all that changes," said Aubree. She moved her hands and accepted Isabel, attracting her companion nearer until their covered breasts were squeezed against one another. Isabel could feel Aubree's hand running here and there on her back, the lovely blonde's fingers waiting on occasion on Isabel's bra ties and fasten and sending shudders of joy up her spine. The anxious yet energized Isabel took cues from Aubree, running her hand all over Aubree's back; her sensations of pleasure multiplied when her fingers felt the ties and fasten of Aubree's bra through her sweater and shirt.

Aubree and Isabel gazed longingly into one another's lovely faces for a couple of moments before the more experienced Aubree took the main action. Bringing down her face into Isabel's, she kissed her gently on the lips. This basic activity caused the generally stirred Isabel's vulva to get considerably damper, and the delight again expanded when Aubree again kissed her on the lips, shallow and erotic. When the teens kissed for the third time, their lips remained together more, and their fourth kiss transformed into a sexy French kiss. Isabel, her heart hustling, felt Aubree work her tongue into her mouth as the young ladies bolted lips, their hands running everywhere on one another.

Driving her tongue into Aubree's mouth, Isabel lay back on the sofa Aubree on top of her, proceeding to make out. Isabel couldn't accept that she was doing this with a young lady; she had consistently envisioned kissing a kid along these lines. Furthermore, she preferred this young lady so much, and her folks didn't, and they were doing this in her folks' home just added to the experience's rush and energy. Isabel's pussy got wetter and wetter in her underwear, as did Aubree's pussy in her undies.

The two young ladies quit making and sat up on the sofa, Isabel and Aubree both sitting with their knees marginally separated so if an easygoing eyewitness turned out to be in the room, the person would have seen up to their dress and skirt individually and the white undies the two teens wore.

"So, how was your first kiss, Isabel?" Aubree inquired.

"Astounding," said Isabel, the teen battling for words in her Sapphic energy.

"No doubt," Aubree concurred. "Have you at any point considered what your first time would resemble?"

Isabel had since a long time ago idea that her first time would be on her wedding night if she were ever ready to discover a man - other than the blundering chunk Billy - who was able to wed her. "At the point when I get hitched," she said timidly.

"I figured such a lot," said Aubree, her grin making her considerably prettier before talking in a low and tempting voice. "Sex with folks is extraordinary, understand me, yet sex with young ladies is surprisingly better. Vaginas fixate young men, but since they don't see how young ladies brains and bodies work, they misunderstand things a large part of the time. But since young ladies comprehend different young ladies, it is far hotter, undeniably more lovely. There's likewise zero danger of falling pregnant, and for your situation, at any rate, you stay a virgin. It's past the point of no return for me. That boat has effectively cruised."

Isabel's mouth was open. "You've done it with folks - and with young ladies?"

"Try not to look so stunned," giggled Aubree. " I have. It's typical for people to need to engage in sexual relations. I'm here because two individuals had intercourse, you're here because two individuals had intercourse and each individual to have at any point lived -

aside from Adam, Eve, and Jesus - are here because two individuals had intercourse. So what about we go higher up to your room and incredibly have a good time."

Isabel didn't require any further provoking and let the route up to her room. On the steps, she felt Aubree's hand on her posterior, the excellent blonde inclination Isabel's undies lines through her dress, at one phase softly lifting the flexibility of Isabel's undies away from her left butt cheek. Albeit still apprehensive, Isabel put her hand to Aubree's base, and Aubree had finished with her felt versatile of Aubree's undies through her smaller than expected skirt.

As yet thinking that it's difficult to accept she was doing this, Isabel advanced into her room, followed by Aubree, Isabel feeling the delightful blonde young person's blue eyes looking at her base. The two young ladies sat on Isabel's bed and taken off their shoes, and the youngsters were presently shoeless.

Isabel stood up and started to detach her polio support. "This is the main thing that requirements to fall off," she said.

"If there's anything awkward for you that harms your leg, just let me know," said Aubree. Isabel cast her abhorred leg support aside. "Much obliged Aubree, I ought to be alright, yet I'll tell you." She took a gander at Aubree's fine high school figure as she sat on the bed, twisting and uncurling the toes of her naked feet. She could hardly imagine how she was going to see Aubree bare and that Aubree was going to see her in a condition of complete bareness as well. On the off chance that Isabel had the option to do rec center, the two young ladies would have seen each other's nubile, stripped adolescent bodies before now when they showered after rec center class. Sitting down close to Aubree, Isabel started to unfasten her coat just for Aubree to stop her.

"Allow me to do that, and afterward, you can do likewise with me," Aubree encouraged.

"Alright," said Isabel, feeling herself getting damper between her legs as Aubree unfastened and took off her coat. Standing up once more, setting one hand on the bed to keep her consistent without her support, Isabel looked as Aubree unfastened her dress; at that point, came to down and grabbed hold of the sewing of the skirt, lifting the article of clothing and leaving Isabel wearing just her white bra and her white underwear.

"My turn currently," said Aubree, standing, trusting that Isabel will uncover her.

Isabel, all around acquainted with discovering methods of keeping her equilibrium moved, so her hip was leaning against her bed and left two hands-frees. Her shuddering fingers parting with her nerves and enthusiasm, Isabel eliminated first Aubree's sweater and afterward her pullover, Isabel's large earthy colored eyes devouring seeing Aubree's young breasts growing out in the cups of her white bra. At that point, Isabelconstantly unfastenedAubree's little skirt, with Aubree venturing her naked feet out of it. Both Aubree and Isabel have attired something similar, shoeless and wearing a white bra and white underwear.

Isabel went to reach despite Aubree's good faith to eliminate her bra. However, Aubree halted her with a grin. "One moment there, it's consistently amusing to play around in your bra and undies first."

The two teens lay back on the bed together, and as they had done on the sofa ground floor started to make out, their hands meandering over one another's clothing clad bodies, most often finding their way to one another's firm, youthful breasts and their underwear. Following a couple of moments of deep, enthusiastic kissing, the two young ladies sat on the bed confronting one another, their legs crossed. The explicitly unpracticed Isabel took a gander at Aubree with the inquiry, 'What next?' clear in her eyes.

"You have the prettiest hair in school," said Aubree, running her hands through Isabel's earthy colored braids.

Once more, unassuming, Isabel reddened. "No, I don't." Isabel ran her hand through Aubree's plush light hair. "Your hair is a lot prettier than mine; you have the hair of a holy messenger."

"Indeed, I haven't seen a heavenly messenger face to face, so I don't have the foggiest idea," Aubree giggled as she wriggled the toes on her exposed feet. "Something else I haven't seen is the hair in another piece of your body, and that is presumably the one thing I need to see more than all else on the planet."

Aubree's fingers grabbed hold of the flexible belt of Isabel's undies. They held it out, peering down at Isabel's female hill canvassed in a woodland of dim earthy colored twists, Aubree's wet pussy getting increasingly more excited at seeing Isabel's public hill. Isabel felt a little reluctant about Aubree holding open her undies and taking a gander at her pubic hair. However, she energized simultaneously and quick to peer down Aubree's underwear at her pubic hair.

Isabel's anxious fingers grabbed hold of Aubree's underwear belt and held it open, the young lady seeing Aubree's pubic hill and the twists of light hair that filled in wealth there. With Isabel unfit to take exercise center class, she had never seen her schoolmates exposed, and in this way, she was astonished to see that Aubree's pubic hair was blonde. Given that Isabel had just seen one vagina in her life - her own - she believed that all young ladies had earthy colored pubic hair as she did herself.

"Your hair down there is blonde!" Isabel shouted, incapable of keeping her hunger under control.

"It is; my hair is regular blonde, not out of a container," said Aubree. "If you peered down a redhead's underwear, she would have red pubic hair. I take it you like what you see there?"

"I sure do," said Isabel, unfit to tear her look from Aubree's public hill.

Aubree gestured. "Better believe it, me as well. I mean, folks have pubic hair as well. However, there's simply something unique about a young lady's pubic hair." She eliminated her hands from Isabel's underwear, Isabel doing likewise with Aubree's undies, and again, the two youngsters took a gander at one another. "You know what else improves young ladies than folks?"

Isabel shook her head. "No, what?"

"Folks can't do this." Aubree came to despite Isabel's good faith and unclasped her bra, pulling the bra away from Isabel's body and leaving the teen sitting uncovered breasted, currently wearing just her underwear.

Isabel chuckled. "To be reasonable for folks, they don't wear bras."

"Indeed, yet folks are fixated on what bras contain, yet attempting to get to them is a major test for them. Not so for us young ladies."

Isabel, her heart dashing at the possibility of seeing Aubree's revealed breasts, interestingly came to despite Aubree's good faith, unclasping her bra and pulling it away as Aubree had finished with her brassiere. The two young ladies gazed at one another's stripped teen breasts, each getting increasingly more energized between their legs as they rubbed and touched the firm, youthful tissue. Aubree brought down her head into Isabel's chest, kissing and licking first Isabel's left and afterward her right breast, her tongue

104

waiting around Isabel's hard nipples, sending her body to more noteworthy statures of delight.

With Aubree driving and Isabel following her model, Isabel, at that point, started to lick and kiss Aubree's boobs how Aubree had done to her. She cherished inclination her tongue and lips against the delicate substance of Aubree's firm breasts, and particularly her companion's hard nipples. Aubree thought it was difficult to stand by on the sleeping cushion with being so stirred, the twofold cotton of her underwear saddle currently highly wet. She was in good company there, with the twofold cotton of Isabel's underwear saddle so wet that Isabel felt like she had a feminine setback.

The two young ladies traded another energetic Sapphic kiss on the lips, their hands everywhere on one another's breasts again before Aubree said, "Presently is the second I've been hanging tight for. I get into IsabelSamara's jeans, and IsabelSamara gets into my jeans."

Aubree slid her left hand into the front of Isabel's undies, her fingers investigating her pubic hair before sneaking further and tracking down the wet access to Isabel's tight, young vagina, Aubree's forefinger going directly to her clitoris, making Isabel wriggle in enchant.

"I don't know, Isabel, you're a miscreant," Aubree giggled. "The nearby Reverend's little girl is letting a corrupt Catholic young lady who never goes to chapel put her to give over her undies and up her vagina. What might your folks say on the off chance that they could see you at present?"

"They would detest it; I figure Dad may tumble down dead from a coronary episode," said Isabel.

"You understand what they would loathe considerably more? If you put your give over my undies and up my vagina simultaneously."

Isabel required no further greeting, and inside the space of seconds, her left hand was down the front board of Aubree's underwear, feeling the magnificent twists of pubic hair that developed everywhere on her hill and going further into Aubree's underpants until she tracked down her pussy. Not at all like Isabel's pussy, Aubree's vagina was a long way from virginal; however, feeling her companion's finger on her clitoris, Aubree felt like she was burning between her legs, so magnificent was Isabel's touch down there.

"We would be wise to give our correct hands something to do," said Aubree, before sliding this give over the rear of Isabel's underwear and feeling the firm, youthful substance of her posterior. Isabel did likewise, cherishing the vibe of Aubree's base inside the delicate cotton of her underwear.

Aubree's fingers went further into Isabel's base, sliding between her hindquarters as Isabel did likewise to her. Isabel, at that point, felt Aubree's correct pointer against the tight opening of her rear-end, and she reddened and chuckled apprehensively.

"What's wrong? Don't you like to be contacted there?" Aubree inquired.

It had unquestionably been an alternate encounter for the virginal young person, leaving Isabel feeling unsure from the start. Typically just two things came into close contact with Isabel's rear-end; tissue clearly when Isabel went to the restroom and washcloths when Isabel was scrubbing down or shower and washed her butt-centric region. Someone contacting her in the most private piece of her body was somewhat of stun from the start, yet now she was cherishing the inclination of Aubree's finger against the passageway to her insides.

"No, it feels extraordinary yet as long as you just touch me outwardly just back there," said Isabel.

"That is something similar for me; I love fingers outwardly, yet having fingers or whatever else embedded up my backside isn't something I need to occur," said Aubree. "It is an exit, not a passageway, all things considered."

Isabel's fingers moved further between Aubree's bum, feeling the tight opening to Aubree's butt, actually thinking that it's difficult to accept that her left forefinger was embedded into Aubree's vagina and her correct pointer against the passageway to the lovely blonde's rectum. She figured she might stir any moment. In any case, it was all genuine, just like Aubree's fingers inside her pussy and another finger down the rear of Isabel's undies, feeling the tight opening to her rectum.

The two young ladies, with some hesitance, removed their hands from one another's underwear and stooped on the bed, confronting one another. "You know how I disdain dull bound spaces?" Aubree asked, to which Isabel gestured. "There's on the exemption for that, as you've most likely speculated. Presently go down on all fours, and I'll show you."

Isabel got in line, her base covered by white undies push noticeable all around enthusiastically anticipating Aubree's touch. Aubree got behind her companion, Isabel feeling she may detonate from fervor as Aubree took Isabel's underwear belt in her grasp and pulled her undies down to her thighs, leaving her uncovered base uncovered, a sight Aubree found a long way from horrendous. In any case, before directing her concentration toward Isabel's base and vagina, Aubree brought down her face into Isabel's brought down underwear, her noses retaining the brilliant female scents on Isabel's sodden undies saddle.

"The Reverend's girl isn't intended to get her undies wet like this by deduction evil contemplations and to do wicked things," said Aubree teasingly.

"I know," snickered Isabel.

"So the thing are you going to do when your mom does the clothing?" Aubree inquired.

"I'm certainly electing to do the clothing this week," said Isabel.

"I believe that is entirely reasonable," Aubree concurred. "I don't have that issue, just like the lone young lady in my home, I do all the clothing."

"That doesn't appear to be reasonable; what do the young men do?" Isabel inquired.

Aubree snickered. "On the off chance that they did the clothing, I would be wearing some exceptionally distorted and weird shaded garments. Young men and clothes washers are not a decent mix, trust me." She removed her face from Isabel's undies and stood looking at Isabel's base, the beautiful brunette's vagina hardly obvious between her legs.

Isabel felt Aubree's delicate hands on her base, separating her bottom to completely uncover the most private pieces of her high school body. Aubree's blue eyes took in Isabel's full shrub of pubic hair, her pink, oval-formed, and balanced vagina, and Isabel's tight, star-fish molded butt. She could smell Isabel's ladylike excitement which prompted her energy as she brought down her face into Isabel's pussy and embedded her tongue into her vagina.

Influxes of energy went through Isabel's body as Aubree's tongue navigated her vulva, going along her pussy lips, now and again waiting on her clitoris and different occasions going to the delicate skin that isolated Isabel's vagina from her butt. Shudders ran up her spine, and her toes twisted as Aubree licked her pussy more profound and more profound. Aubree's vagina, while accepting no manual incitement at this stage, was getting increasingly more animated as the beautiful blonde tasted Isabel's pussy, cherishing each taste from Isabel's vagina. While Isabel might have joyfully remained in this situation for the entire night, she realized she needed to accomplish something else. This was done very similar things to Aubree as Aubree was doing to her now.

Aubree removed her face from Isabel's pussy and, looking most fulfilled, said, "It's your turn now."

Aubree moved, so she was down on the ground and push her underwear canvassed ass, noticeable all around. Isabel, her underwear still around her thighs, moved behind her and grabbed hold of Aubree's undies by the belt, pulling them down so like her own underpants they were around her thighs.

Breathing intensely, Isabel saw Aubree's uncovered exposed base and her female region, beginning with her blondie shrubbery of pubic hair, the thin pink lips of her vagina, and her tight butt. She could smell Aubree's stimulated pussy unmistakably as she sniffed the soggy seat of Aubree's brought down underwear how she had finished with her, cherishing all of Aubree's ladylike scents that entered her noses. Directing her concentration toward Aubree's base, Isabel brought down her face into Aubree's vagina and started to lick her private female zones. Aubree let out a screech of enjoyment as Isabel's tongue went to her clitoris, at that point to the lips of her vagina and the region of skin between her vulva and her rear-end.

Aubree's stimulated vagina was running like a cracked fixture as the energetic Isabel kept on going down on her pussy, Isabel adoring each smell and each taste from Aubree's twat, Isabel feeling a portion of the beautiful blonde teen's pubic hairs stimulating her nose.

109

Aubree would have been glad to remain like this until Isabel's tongue carried her to climax, however clearly, being the more experienced of the two had a far superior peak for the two arranged. Demonstrating for Isabel to stop, Aubree turned over and said, "If you loved that, you should perceive what I have made arrangements for us now."

Connecting, Aubree grabbed hold of Isabel's now brought down undies. She pulled the white cotton underwear down her legs until they contacted her naked feet, at that point, eliminated them inside and out. Isabel, as she had done throughout the evening, taken cues from Aubree and pulled the blondie's dropped white undies down her shapely legs and off over her naked feet, leaving the two nubile 18-year-old young ladies bare.

Isabel and Aubree each respected the other young lady's stripped body; their beautiful appearances, their uncovered breasts, their thin figures, their pubic hair, their vaginas, and their exposed bottoms. The youngsters embraced and for the following five minutes lay together on the bed, French-kissing while their hands investigated each other's exposed body, the two young ladies scouring their naked feet together to give additional incitement.

"Untruth level on your back, open your legs," Aubree coordinated. Isabel did only this, spreading her legs wide, putting her adolescent pussy on full showcase.

Aubree rode Isabel until her female region was over Isabel's head; at that point dropped her vagina down, her shaggy blonde young pussy going into Isabel's face. Aubree got herself agreeable, at that point inclined forward and put her face into Isabel's pussy, retaining the awesome scents from between Isabel's legs, Isabel similarly appreciating the smell of Aubree's vagina as she sat all over.

"Presently, we continue to go until we arrive at the climax," said Aubreebefore licking Isabel's vagina with incredible eagerness. Isabel was no less anxious to embed her tongue into Aubree's pussy, and adored the flavor of Aubree's vagina as she licked her clitoris.

The Sapphic scents from the two stirred youngsters' vaginas filled Isabel's room as the young ladies kept on licking each other's pussies. Their soft, muted female groans and the manners in which their fingers and toes grasped and unclenched were proof to any outsider who may have noticed the two young ladies in such a personal circumstance that both were making the most of their adoration making widely.

After nearly seven minutes of this magnificent experience, climax's main indications started to approach, sentiments that were extremely recognizable to Aubree, however not so for Isabel. Aubree could feel the discontinuous influxes of joy from Isabel's tongue on her pussy transforming into one incredible sensation, her vagina getting wetter and wetter. Similarly, for Isabel, a hard lick on her clitoris by Aubree's tongue put the teen on target for her climax, and there was no retreat now.

Aubree felt the muscles in her vagina fix, as did those in her rectum, the muscles of Isabel's vagina and her rectum fixing at the same time. The hard nipples of Isabel and Aubree's firm high school breasts shivered persistently, and the toes of their naked feet gripped. Aubree's shout of joy as she contacted her peak was suppressed by her face being somewhere inside Isabel's orgasmic pussy. The two teens' vaginas let out a surge of pussy juice into the other young lady's face, the Sapphic scents getting more grounded in the room. Both winded and with their appearances flushed radiant red after their climaxes, Aubree took herself off Isabel and lay adjacent to her, the two young ladies recuperating their breath and wet from sweat and their pussies.

"I bet you didn't anticipate being doing that this evening," said Aubree as she stroked Isabel's hair.

"No, that was inconceivable," concurred Isabel, still difficult to accept she had done such taboo, private and provocative things with the lovely young lady her folks objected to.

"It doesn't stop there," said Aubree. She hopped off the bed, her legs going wide, showing her vagina all the while. "We both need a shower. Do you figure we can remain this way?"

Isabel could feel how wet and tacky her vagina was. "No, I surmise not."

"Precisely, and I believe I should open this window to get some air into the room," said Aubree. "It smells a piece - um - how might I put this - ladylike - in here."

Isabel giggled as Aubree strolled over to the window on her exposed feet, Isabel appreciating her shapely base. Ensuring her naked breasts were covered by the curtains, Aubree opened the window a couple of inches. She turned around, Isabel getting a charge out of the front perspective on Aubree with her shapely breasts and triangle of blonde pubic hair similarly as much as the back perspective on her companion.

"Do you need your support to get to the washroom?" Aubree inquired.

Isabel sat up on the bed with her legs somewhat separated, showing her pubic hair and vagina, Aubree's eyes taking in every last trace of Isabel's groin. Isabel shook her head. "No, I can get around the house OK without my support insofar as I'm cautious and I utilize the rails."

Standing up, Isabel clutched her bed at that point strolled on her naked feet across her room floor, holding onto the rail then into the corridor, the young lady again utilizing the rail to get herself to the restroom. The bare Aubree followed, respecting how Isabel got around regardless of her incapacitated leg. She likewise extraordinarily respected Isabel, cherishing seeing her exposed companion's uncovered breasts, a triangle of thick dim earthy colored pubic hair, and her exposed base.

Going into the restroom, the two youngsters made straight for the shower, and Aubree turned on the water. As the warm drops fell onto the two young ladies' nubile youthful bodies, they embraced and started to apply cleanser to one another, foamy white air pockets covering their skin and their pubic hair, running down their legs to their exposed feet and the shower floor.

The two young ladies kissed profoundly and ran their hands over one another's wet bodies, their fingers finding their breasts, bottoms, and pubic hair before going further between their legs, Isabel almost losing her balance as Aubree embedded her finger into her vagina as Isabel in like manner fingered Aubree's vagina.

Moving out of the shower, the young ladies dried one another; at that point, the two stripped youngsters returned to Isabel's room to get dressed. The initial two pieces of clothing they went after were their underwear, yet the two young ladies stopped, seeing that the wetness on the seats had now started to dry, making putting them on an unappealing possibility.

"What about you acquire a couple of my underwear? You loaned me some last week when I required them," Isabel recommended, as she took two new combines of undies from her clothing cabinet, saving one for herself and holding out the second pair to Aubree.

"Much appreciated, Isabel," said Aubree, taking the undies from Isabel and venturing her exposed feet into them before pulling them up and changing them around her pussy and her base, at that point slipping her undies into her tote. "I'll wash and return them to you - without your folks getting some answers concerning it."

"Better believe it sure," said Isabel, as she pulled up her undies and ensured they were agreeable around her pussy and base. She put a grin all over, a grin that showed modesty, cleverness, and enchantment in equivalent measure. "Or, on the other hand, don't wash them; I wouldn't fret."

Aubree, who was securing up her bra, looked astonished. "You have a touch of a terrible side to you under, haven't you, Isabel?" she snickered.

Isabel cut up her bra. "Over the most recent few days, I've been given confinement, been grounded for a month, and now around evening time ..."

"We'll need to trust your folks and sibling to go out more regularly while you're grounded so we can have a great time together," said Aubree, who put on her smaller than expected skirt, shirt and sweater while Isabel put on her dress and coat. She looked at the morning timer on Isabel's bedside table. "They've been out sometime around evening time."

Isabel gestured as she put on her leg support. "Peter rested over at another kid's home around evening time, and Mom and Dad have gone out to eat with Mr. also, Mrs. Harris from our congregation. They're stressed over their child. He enjoys that new gathering from Liverpool - The Beatles - such a lot that he's starting to trim his hair like them. They needed Dad to converse with him about it and set him back on the correct way."

Aubree chuckled. "Do they realize that the Reverend's little girl is grounded?"

"I figure they may have excluded that piece," said Isabel.

The two young ladies put on their shoes and went to the first floor, stopping at the front entryway. "I think we'll be having much more mystery fun together later on," said Aubree.

"I suspect as much as well," Isabel concurred before she and Aubree traded a deep French kiss, and Aubree left, stopping to give Isabel a cordial, neighborly wave as she got back to her own home, a motion Isabel returned. Isabel had a glance around to check whether there were any neighbors around who may have seen Aubree take off from the house and may transfer this data to her folks, yet she saw no one, and they were by all accounts free. Not that any of the neighbors like her folks could at any point have longed for what she and Aubree had done this evening. They would expect that they had trespassed otherly, like tuning in to take care of business music, drinking liquor, or perhaps speaking shamelessly about young men.

*

It was pouring when Reverend and Mrs. Samara showed up home from their evening with the Harris family, and Isabel had headed to sleep. Reverend Samara was fulfilled that his discussion with Tommy Harris after supper with their family had gotten the job done. Sure the adolescent would accept regard of his wise counsel that trimming one's hair in the style of a group of four of youthful artists from Liverpool that everyone would have overlooked in a year was a poorly conceived notion that could just lead him down the way to additional enticement.

Reverend Samara trusted that the awful young people across the street, who right now were remaining in the yard talking and tuning in to a little portable radio, would likewise regard the expression of the Lord and maintain a strategic distance from wrongdoing. Yet, there appeared to be little any expectation of this as they were non-rehearsing Roman Catholics and consequently not a piece of his congregation. Furthermore, their dad was no place to be seen. The Reverend Samara wished he could fabricate a divider to get them far from his girl and child, similar to the divider raised in Berlin two years before keep the Western and Eastern Zones isolated.

The minister respected the youngsters across the road with an additional harsh glance through his glasses. There was the red-haired cousin Chip, the dim-haired child Brad alongside his team promoter sweetheart Susie, and far most noticeably awful of all the blonde little girl Aubree, dressed as consistently in a smaller than usual skirt. Reverend Samara's devout articulation became significantly sterner as Aubree crossed and uncrossed her legs. Even though it was dim and pouring, he had the option to see her white underwear immediately. Not wishing to perceive any more sin and impropriety from the high school young lady across the road, Reverend Samara followed his better half inside.

Higher up, Isabel was sleeping sound snoozing with her room entryway open, and Reverend Samara cast a look at his resting girl. Isabel had been irksome of late because of the terrible impacts across the road; however, at any rate, this evening, he hadn't get back home to her associating with them as they sat on their entryway patio.

Isabel's demeanor was quiet, honest as she rested, and Reverend Samara was certain that she was learning her exercise and this time would comply with both him and her mom, not submitting any more sin. Brushing his teeth before hitting the hay, Reverend Samara had no clue that his resting girl's fantasies required her back a few hours to her Sapphic experiences with Aubree in this very house and that Aubree's underwear that he had immediately seen were indeed his little girl's undies.

Explicit Erotic Sex Stories

Catalina the Dense Gold Digger

Seductive and Real Secret Sapphic Sex

*****

Sitting in the back of her folks' vehicle, 18-year-old Melissa Jenkins felt like she had visited her gynecologist and been given a chemical infusion that allowed her a year of PMS on the double, even though her genuine-time was not due for an additional fourteen days or something like that.

The pretty and dainty young lady with long earthy colored hair, a doll-like face with profound earthy colored eyes, and an ideal, normally tanned appearance because of an Italian foundation on her mom's side, had a beautiful, sensible day this fine spring Wednesday at the secondary school on Chicago's North Shore she went to as a Senior, and from which she would move on from in two months as a component of the Class of 1991.

Between her legs, Melissa could feel her undies riding up between the cheeks of her base, and the young person discretely came to down to change them through her pants. Nonetheless, uncooperative underwear, while disturbing enough, was not the fundamental driver of Melissa's irritation. One wellspring of bothering was in the back of the vehicle with her; the different anticipated her at their objective this evening.

Looking into the front of the vehicle, Melissa saw her folks Warren and Fran. Her dad drove peacefully, her mom sat in the front seat additionally peacefully, their outward appearances uneasy as they expected what anticipated them at their objective.

Other than Melissa, two of the four individuals in the back of the vehicle were her siblings, Seth and Josh. The construction of the Jenkins family was very bizarre. In November 1972, Fran had brought forth congenial twins Melissa and Seth, and for exactly 15 years, the Jenkins family was an ideal family unit – mother, father, child, and girl. In 1987, Fran Jenkins discovered she was late – late – and woke up feeling squeamish each day. On different occasions, she would get up in the center of the night to fix herself peanut butter, celery, grapefruit, and pastrami sandwiches. As anyone might expect, from the get-go in

1988, Fran, at age 41, brought forth Josh and Seth and Melissa had a child sibling 15 years their lesser. This age distinction caused shame on a few events, such as a day at the zoo when Melissa and her mom took Josh on an excursion, and a few groups expected Melissa to be a youngster mother and Fran the kid's grandma.

This evening, youthful Josh sat in his sponsor seat, inverse Melissa playing with a toy robot, the three-year-old euphorically unaware of the worries of his folks and his more established sister. Melissa looked towards her twin and considered that to be common. He was gazing at the object of his warm gestures with an affection debilitated, marvelous look in his eyes that were earthy colored like those of his twin sister.

The object of Seth's expressions of warmth was the primary wellspring of Melissa's disturbance this evening. Her name was Kelly Crane, and she was a thin and pretty 18-year-old redhead, her long red hair tied back in a braid with a blue strip that coordinated with the shade of her eyes. She had taken a crack at Seth and Melissa's secondary school toward the beginning of their lesser year, and Melissa could just revile the Illinois Education Department and their spending cutting measures. The adjoining secondary school Kelly had recently gone to had declining participation, so the choice was made to close the school and back range the understudies to the three neighboring secondary schools. On the main day of junior year, the recently shown up Kelly took a gander at Seth, Seth took a gander at Kelly, and that was it, all-consuming instant adoration.

In his more youthful years, Seth and his companions had consistently adored sci-fi. When Kelly showed up on the scene, Melissa snidely imagined that possibly she came from a cosmic system far, far away, as opposed to an adjoining North Shore suburb. Yet, Kelly was no sci-fi fan, indeed an incredible inverse. The solitary books, TV shows, and motion pictures Kelly was keen on were associated with one book, potentially the most popular book on the planet.

Kelly's dad was the Minister of a fundamentalist Christian church, and Kelly – the second oldest of six children - accepted each expression of the Bible was in a real sense valid. The young lady was persuaded that the Earth was just 6000 years of age and excused as nonexistent infuriating things like dinosaurs, trilobites, wooly mammoths, saber-tooth felines, and Neanderthal men that may have provided reason to feel ambiguous about her convictions, notwithstanding fossil proof to demonstrate their reality.

Kelly showed up at her new school with a more youthful sibling and sister, two cousins, and a group of companions from the shut secondary school. Every fundamentalist Christian and another Christian inner circle quickly made its essence felt in the school. Seth was so besotted by Kelly, chasing after her like a canine with its tongue hanging out, that he was quickly brought into this gathering away from his current friend network and was before long going to book of scriptures study and supplication gatherings, advancing restraint, helping his sweetheart in getting the mainstream tabletop game Dungeons and Dragons restricted at the school, and passing out strict handouts to different understudies as they showed up for school.

Kelly's main characteristic was that she thought everything throughout everyday life – great, terrible, or detached – was brought about by God's desire. This evening was no special case. "Didn't Our Lord furnish us with a particularly delightful spring day?" Kelly inquired.

"He sure did," Seth concurred.

Melissa smothered a moan and gazed out the vehicle window to mask her eye-roll. Chicago had an enjoyable spring day because of good climate conditions over Illinois and Lake Michigan, not because of a higher force's desire. Furthermore, love-debilitated Seth needed to concur with all that Kelly said. If Kelly said that orange was blue and lemon was purple, Seth would concur.

In any case, in any event, Kelly's assessment on the climate was minor contrasted with a portion of the feelings Melissa had heard the young lady express. Half a month sooner, Melissa and her closest companion, a lovely 18-year-old Jewish young lady named Gretchen Goldstein, were in the young ladies' room; both inclinations wore out as they had their periods and terrible feminine issues. As they were remaining at the sinks taking a few tablets to reduce this, in strolled Kelly, who was likewise at this stage in her month-to-month cycle. The lovely redhead said as she gulped her period torment tablets that it was God's will that decided when ladies got their periods and that any uneasiness they endured during this time was because He tested their confidence. Melissa and Gretchen would, in general, accept that this was brought about by the way that they and Kelly had all neglected to fall pregnant during their present feminine cycles, and they were shedding the linings that had framed on the dividers of their uteruses, yet clearly, Kelly knew more.

Once more, Melissa observed Kelly and Seth fortify their hand hold and gaze at one another with great eyes and wanted that she had a basin close helpful on the off chance that she hurled from all the saccharine. The youngster could likewise see by investigating the vehicle's front that her folks were not so excited by their child's sweetheart's decision and the tight controlling hold she had over Seth. In any case, however much Melissa detested the way that her twin sibling was under the spell of his better half, he was not by any means the only male in her family to turn out to be besotted by a beautiful young lady as of late. The other man was her fatherly granddad Stan. It was to his home, for his seventy-10th birthday celebration where they were going. Furthermore, hanging tight for them would be his sweetheart Catalina, the second female who was causing Melissa such aggravation on this usually lovely Chicago evening.

*

As a kid and more youthful teen, Melissa had adored visiting her grandparents on the two sides. Her maternal grandparents, somewhat more youthful than her fatherly grandparents, she and Seth consistently called 'Nonno and Nonna' because of their Italian foundation, were truly making the most of their retirement, both fit and dynamic, cherishing investing energy with their grown-up youngsters and grandkids.

Until quite a long while back, Seth and Melissa had consistently appreciated investing energy with their fatherly grandparents Stan and Mary. Be that as it may, from the get-go in 1989, Grandma Mary was determined to have the pancreatic disease and was gone inside about a month and a half. The demise of his better half of such countless years sent Stan's wellbeing into a descending winding, and inside the space of months, he had transformed from a reasonable, able. Free senior resident into a fragile, distracted, and doddering elderly person who could scarcely recollect his name a few days, and different days would accept he was before. Time and again, Stan received he was as yet a GI raging the sea shores of Normandy during D-Day in 1944, as opposed to a retired person in rural Chicago in 1989.

Similarly, like other older individuals with mature related medical issues, Stan got obstinate and hard to dissuade and opposed any endeavors by his grown-up children and girls to help him. Absolutely against moving to a mature consideration office or, in any event, going to live with family members, the older adult would fake it to specialists that he was completely alright and fine to live alone.

One thing Stan recollected was a similar mix of numbers he and his late spouse had consistently decided for the lottery that they had played each week for quite a long time, always failing to win more than fifty dollars. He always remembered to purchase a lottery ticket, albeit one day he did forget as he would prefer a home from the retail plaza, not exactly a mile from his home after purchasing a ticket and wound up in Joliet, running on empty in a significant crossing point. Luckily Stan did discover as he would prefer home alright after purchasing the Christmas 1989 ticket. What's more, the victor of 4,000,000 dollars was Stan Jenkins.

The Jenkins family were no less stressed over the older adult since he was a multi-tycoon; truth be told, they stressed him even more. The 4,000,000 dollar prize was kept into a low revenue investment account at the bank. However, Stan didn't alter his way of living and unflinchingly wouldn't tune in to the appeal of good-natured relatives. Despite having the cash to pay experts, Stan chose to re-paint the outside of his home himself, recovering from the carport dried out brushes and a wide range of shaded jars of paint – some water-based, others oil-based - containing leftovers that were many years old and making the outside of the abode appear as though it had been shrouded in spray painting by a visually challenged jokester. The solitary ones who had to go through cash were Warren, and his sibling, repairing their dad's wreck had made of his home.

Requests by Warren, his sibling, and two sisters to their dad to go through a portion of the cash to move to a helped living office for the old all fell upon hard-of-hearing ears. At that point, as though by enchantment, along came Catalina, and out of nowhere, Stan had no issue spending his riches.

Warren moved toward the road where his dad's home was found and took a gander at his significant other. "I don't have the foggiest idea what to be more stressed over, Fran," he said. "That thing will not be extraordinary, or that thing will be unique."

Fran gave her better half a cynical grin. "With your dad and Catalina, the sky is the limit."

"I believe it's superb that Jesus sent Catalina to your dad to stay with him in his more established years," remarked Kelly.

Once more, Melissa feigned exacerbation discretely. Kelly thought Catalina's appearance was because of higher intercession, not a mooching and boneheaded young lady seeing a frail older man with a 4,000,000 dollar bank surplus as a simple supper ticket and moving in like a hyena or vulture searching on the body of a dead wildebeest on the African fields.

"Indeed, the house is as yet standing, and Dad hasn't had a go at painting it once more," noticed Warren as the house came into focus, and the absence of some other vehicles showed that they were the first to show up.

"Yet, that is new," said Fran, pointing at what stood further up the carport, the jaws of Melissa and her folks falling open in stun at the boat that sat on a trailer. On the boat stood Stan Jenkins, the older man wearing an ocean chief's cap and gazing blankly out into the dimness.

"I have a truly downright terrible about this," said Warren, as he escaped the vehicle, stress appearing all over, and gazed toward his dad. Stan neglected to recognize his child's presence, little girl in-law, grandkids, and more established grandson's better half.

"Um, hey, Dad, upbeat birthday; what are you doing up there?" Warren asked his dad uncertainly. In any event, his dad had never communicated any longing to claim a boat when more youthful and capable. And keeping in mind that Catalina never had any issues persuading Stan to go through cash upon her, for example, her costly vehicle that was left in the carport, gems, and many, many garments, a boat truly didn't seem like such a thing she would need by the same token.

"I'm cruising my new boat," Stan reported gladly.

"I see that," said Warren. "Anyway, how long have you had your new boat?"

"We got it this Monday," came a youthful female voice, piercing and innocent; everybody was going to see Catalina leave the front entryway of the house and stroll towards the family. A sensibly tall and incredibly appealing young lady, 23-year-old Catalina had the good Midwestern look of long light hair, styled with an unmistakable periphery, enormous blue eyes, and a reasonable ideal composition. She wore a light blue tee-shirt that highlighted her enormous breasts and on her base a large portion of some dark stirrup pants that flaunted her shapely legs and bum, the stirrups tight around Catalina's bare feet. Melissa couldn't resist seeing when Catalina drew nearer that her tight stockings likewise showed the young lady's underwear lines and the space of her vagina at the front.

"Having a great time up there, darling?" Catalina called to Stan, the young lady giving the older person a wave.

"Goodness indeed, parcels," concurred Stan, proceeding to gaze out across the road. "I cruised it on Lake Michigan yesterday."

"Hey Warren and Fran," said Catalina in her sharp voice. "Howdy, kids!"

"Hi Catalina," said Warren, keeping an even tone. "I need to ask, what is the story with the boat?"

"Stan figured it would be a smart thought to get it," said Catalina. "Along these lines, here it is."

Different individuals from the Jenkins family firmly questioned this, yet Stan was so careless it is hard to learn the reality. As yet remaining on the boat, the old man gazed blankly into the night skies before exclaiming, "Michael Jordan sold us the boat."

"Michael Jordan? The b-ball player?" asked a doubting Warren.

"Believe it or not, he did," Catalina attested to Stan before going to Warren and Fran. "He didn't actually; the boat sales rep just looked like Michael Jordan."

"If it's not too much trouble, disclose to me that Stan didn't take the boat out on Lake Michigan?" asked Fran, thinking about the abhorrences this could cause.

"No, my stepfather Jim took the boat out, and me, my Mom, my closest companion Vanessa and Stan were travelers," said Catalina. "Jim loves cruising and fishing. The boat is a large portion of speculation."

"A large portion of a venture?" Warren, who worked in the account, realized Catalina was not knowledgeable in this field. Her lone handle of acquiring cash was filtering off a feeble, older man with a significant bank balance. So what was the brainless blonde airhead on about now, discussing 'half speculations?'

"That is to say, it's a large portion of our boat and a large portion of Jim's boat," said Catalina. "Indeed, it was Jim who said what a smart thought it is to purchase a boat, and he said he'd pay a large portion of the cash towards it when he gets his expense discount."

Warren, Fran, and Melissa all traded a look. It appeared well and good at this point. What wasn't clear was whether boneheaded Catalina had been conned herself or was in on the plan with her stepfather; however, getting to reality would be troublesome. Not because Catalina was an incredible liar, but since she was too moronic even to consider holding an appropriate discussion with.

Seth and Kelly didn't trade the look of Seth's folks and sister, as they were excessively bustling gazing into one another's eyes as they clasped hands. Three-year-old Josh had no comprehension of any of this and was more intrigued by his toy robot and the kids' book his mom had offered him to keep him involved.

"Why not all come inside?" Catalina said, driving the route towards the front entryway. Stan did not endeavor to get down from the boat, the older adult proceeding to gaze blankly into space.

"Um, Dad, why not accompany us?" Warren recommended, his dad either intentionally overlooking the idea or having no understanding of his child standing in that general area.

"Gracious, he's fine up there; he adores it, don't you, Stan?" asked Catalina. The older man gestured in understanding. "It's obvious, he's fine," the young lady declared.

"Indeed, yet shouldn't something be said about when he needs to get down from that point?" Fran inquired. She realized her effortlessly confounded dad-in-law was fragile, and getting down the stepping stool to the ground would be hard for a man in such chronic frailty.

Catalina shrugged detachedly. "He's never had any issues getting down. He'll descend when he's all set."

With some hesitance, Warren and Fran followed their entertainer inside, Warren directing Josh and Fran conveying a cake in a container, trailed by the youngsters.

"I trust you're eager since I've been cooking throughout the evening," said Catalina.

Once more, the Jenkins family took a gander at one another, considering what repulsions this could involve. Catalina showed not very many abilities throughout everyday life, and cooking was unquestionably not among them.

"Do you like Chinese food?" Catalina inquired.

"Um, yes," said Warren, his voice brimming with vulnerability. A tall blonde Midwestern young lady couldn't watch more strange getting ready Asian food.

"Great, you'll love my home-made sushi and sukiyaki at that point," Catalina stated.

The baffled Fran shouted out. "Catalina, you do understand that sushi and sukiyaki are from Japan and not China, don't you?"

Catalina gazed back at her with a befuddled, empty articulation in her blue eyes as her mind attempted to bits things together. "Aren't they something very similar?" the young lady in the end reacted.

"No, certainly not," said Fran. She smothered a murmur. A seemingly insignificant detail called the Second World War was unquestionable evidence that Japan and China were not indeed the very same.

Once more, the Jenkins family could see Catalina attempting to sort things out in her brain gradually. "However, they're both Asian," the young lady at last said.

"Indeed, they are both in Asia," said Fran, contemplating how long she could last before becoming irritated. At the point when more youthful, Fran's sibling had been an Italian Casanova-type, getting one young lady after another, a significant number of them not excessively honored with minds. What's more, as a school administration official, Fran had met many moronic individuals in her work – children, guardians, and even educators who had by one way or another got their showing recognitions – however, nothing to equal dopey Catalina. "However, they are various nations."

"Goodness," said Catalina. The blondie reconsidered. "Is that like Canadia and us?"

Melissa put her hand over her mouth to smother, chuckling at how Catalina had misspoken the country to their northern boundary. One thing was without a doubt, if Catalina visited 'Canadia,' she wouldn't have any desire to utilize that elocution to a gathering of loggers or ice hockey fans.

"Indeed," said Fran briskly, as Catalina's consideration – restricted, best case scenario – went to Josh.

"You simply get greater and taller each time I see you," said Catalina, twisting around to pat the little kid on his head. With Catalina has returned to the next relatives, Melissa couldn't try to see the oval state of Catalina's pussy through the tight texture of her stirrup pants.

"Your book looks genuinely fascinating," Catalina said, taking a gander at the kids' book Josh conveyed. "It looks genuine instructive as well."

Melissa looked at Kelly, seeing the slightest trace of objection playing about the young lady's mouth. Kelly trusted in pushing her strict convictions upon every individual who ended up intersecting her way. Her method of accomplishing this with her beau's a lot more youthful sibling was to purchase the young man a progression of the book of scriptures-based picture books as a Christmas present. Be that as it may, to Kelly's mistake – and Melissa's priggish fulfillment – Josh didn't warm to the excellent book story books and responded to them with a complete lack of concern.

Satisfied by Catalina's advantage, Josh opened his book to the main page, pointed at the letter An and said, "A," preceding going to the following page and saying "B," at that point going to the following page, "C, etc.

Catalina was exceptionally dazzled and went to Warren and Fran. "He can say the letters in order?"

"Indeed," said Fran. "We showed Melissa and Seth to peruse and check before they began kindergarten, and we are showing Josh as well."

Seth, who searched for any opportunity to bring Kelly into any discussion, added, "When Kelly was four, she knew the names of the relative multitude of books in the holy book, and what every one of them was about." Kelly dressed at the recognition of her sweetheart.

"Amazing, you should peruse genuine great," said Catalina. She turned around to Josh. "Things being what they are, would you say you are anticipating beginning kindergarten, Josh?"

"Indeed," said Josh.

"You realize, Josh, when I was a young lady, I was fortunate," said Catalina. "I truly preferred kindergarten, and afterward, one day, my Mom said I was such an exceptional young lady that I was picked to have one more year there, and I would have a great time and meet a ton of new companions. I was so satisfied."

Melissa turned and gazed at the divider, making a decent attempt not to snicker. That she had been left back a year in kindergarten appeared to be absolutely out of Catalina's cognizance. Yet, from Melissa's experience of Catalina since she showed up on the scene a year ago, it was anything but an astonishment.

"Would you like me to peruse your book to you?" Catalina asked Josh.

"Indeed, please," said Josh.

"OK, at that point, how about we mess around with your book," said Catalina, driving the kid to the lounge chair, where he sat close by her. Catalina opened the book and took a gander at Fran. "What's the book about?"

"It's about a pig who travels with all his other creature companions," said Fran.

"Right," said Catalina, gazing at the page where the letter 'A' was conspicuous across the top, with beautiful delineations of the pig and the creatures beginning with A. She gazed at the page and started to peruse resoundingly. "Sometime in the distant past – three – there – was a pig called Pat-rick. He was going on vay-cay-teen with his an-nee-mal beasts - companions. First, he went to co-lect the an-nee-mals who start-ted with A, Ad-dam the subterranean insect tel-open, Ally-child the – Allie-gay-pinnacle, and Melissa the ..."

Catalina went to Melissa. "Hello Melissa, there's a creature with your name here."

Melissa, who had perused the book to her sibling ordinarily with far more unique capability than Catalina, figured out how to stammer out, "Indeed, truth be told."

Catalina glanced back at the book, unmistakably confused. "What kind of creature is Melissa? A-Aardvark?"

131

"An aardvark," said Melissa, actually attempting to abstain from giggling.

"Gracious right," said Catalinabefore before turning the page. "Billy the honey bee is, Bob the buff-far-low ..."

Melissa could take Catalina's abominable perusing of a kids' book no more, and the giggling youngster made a rushed flight for the kitchen, astounded to see her granddad at the seat. By one way or another, Stan had returned inside through the indirect access and keeping in mind that Catalina was carelessly permitting a particularly delicate older adult to ascend and down from the boat all alone; clearly, nothing terrible had occurred.

What was of worry to Melissa was that her granddad utilized an electric container to fix himself some tea. Power and bubbling water were an awful mix where her granddad was concerned. He gazed toward his granddaughter as she entered the kitchen. "Hey, April!" he said.

"It's Melissa," said the young person, used to her granddad stirring up her name. "Is it true that you are alright there, Grandpa? Would I be able to assist you with that?"

"Fine says thanks to Alice," said the elderly person before investigating his cup with alarm. "I don't care for the teabags Catalina purchases."

"What's going on with the teabags?" Melissa inquired.

"They don't have an aftertaste like tea, and they absorb all the water," whined the elderly person.

"Allow me to see that," said the baffled young lady. Melissa strolled over to the seat and held back as she saw the tampon her granddad was hanging in the cup by its blue string, the white tube-shaped article swelled to a monstrous size from retaining the bubbling water.

"The teabags Catalina purchases are truly abnormal," remarked Stan.

Melissa grabbed hold of the cup and tossed the soaked tampon into the kitchen garbage. "What about I make you a pleasant cup of tea, Grandpa?" the young person proposed.

"Are you going to utilize Catalina's teabags?" Stan needed to know.

"No, Grandpa, I'll make you a legitimate cup of tea you'll truly like," Melissa guaranteed her granddad, getting a new cup and an appropriate teabag, setting the container to bubble once more.

"Much appreciated Emily," said Stan, again failing to remember his granddaughter's name.

From the lounge, the semi-proficient Catalina was proceeding to falter and stammer her way through the youngsters' book, with the lone two creatures she articulated accurately first time in 'C' and 'D' feline and canine.

Going to get some sugar for her granddad's tea, Melissa stopped and peered down at the two financial records in the name 'Catalina Rhodes' and figured how the young lady couldn't have had a less proper last name. The last individual on the planet to be offered a Rhode's Scholarship to England's renowned Oxford University would be Catalina.

On top of each financial record was a check with the cabinet Stan Jenkins to pay the full – and generous sums – of each. The youngster like printing and how the word 'thousand' was spelled 'thousand proposed Catalina had worked out the checks; however, the bug-like scribbling of a mark was that of her granddad, the weak man scarcely ready to hold a pen without shaking.

Melissa shook her head in disappointment. Again Catalina burned through cash on herself, and again her granddad took care of the bills with no thought of what he was marking. Catalina hadn't paid for classes for grown-ups to improve their perusing abilities; Melissa thought as she returned into the front room with her granddad, where the dazed blonde inquired as to why there was a sheep on the 'G' page, Fran clarifying that the creature was truth be told a goat. Catalina battled through the kids' book with difficult gradualness, stumped on the last page where there was an X, however no creature beginning with this letter to go with the yak and the zebra. Youthful Josh gave first Catalina, at that point his folks and afterward his more established sibling and sister a bizarre, confounded look, having never heard his #1 book read like that previously.

Ordinarily, this part of the Jenkins family were as yet the solitary ones there, Stan's other grown-up kids and their life partners and families consistently put off appearance to the last possible moment, abhorring investing energy with a frail older adult whose time on Earth was attracted to a nearby, and the characterless vulture appreciating what she could now and who might almost certainly appreciate much more when Stan's opportunity at long last arrived.

However many occasions as she had seen it previously, Melissa would never adjust to seeing her granddad sitting close by a lovely youthful blonde instead of her late grandma, and it generally felt odd. The remainder of the family appeared to be similarly tense as Stan guzzled at his tea, and space-cadet Catalina sat close to him gazing blankly into space. Melissa would never choose what was more regrettable with Catalina; when she expressed moronic things or when she was too idiotic even to consider considering anything to say, so she said nothing by any means.

At long last, Warren made some noise, not anticipating a coherent reaction from his dad. "So Dad, another birthday today. One year off until the enormous eight-zero."

Stan gazed vacantly at his child. "Whose birthday, right?"

Catalina laughed her energetic chuckle. "It's your birthday, senseless."

"Is it?" the befuddled Stan inquired. "Goodness. I went to Australia for my birthday today."

"You went to Australia?" asked the puzzled Warren.

"Indeed, I drove there," said Stan. "Furthermore, I saw a kangaroo, an emu, a koala, a crocodile, and a huge reptile."

"You headed to Australia today?" Warren affirmed, not interestingly considering what his dad was discussing.

"Sure did," said Stan. He completed his tea and took a gander at Melissa. "Much appreciated, Agnes; you improved a much more cup of tea than the tea from Catalina's white teabags."

"White teabags?" the confounded Catalina asked before Melissa quickly stepped in to stay away from humiliation.

"How could you drive to Australia, Grandpa?" Melissa inquired.

"I got in my vehicle and went there; it wasn't exceptionally far," said Stan.

"If it's not too much trouble, disclose to me he didn't drive his vehicle out and about — all alone?" the daunted Warren asked Catalina.

Catalina shrugged. "He demanded."

"Catalina, I believe it's better for everybody if you do all the driving," said Warren. While Catalina was an awful driver, her out on the streets was a better possibility than Stan driving.

"In any case, I can't drive his vehicle," Catalina dissented. "It has this bizarre stick thingy and a bolster."

Melissa again needed to cover her mouth to forestall, giggling resoundingly while Warren rectified Catalina. "You mean it has a manual transmission and a grip. Also, simply take him in your vehicle."

"Discussing vehicles and driving, this truly abnormal letter showed up from the DMV saying that Stan needed to step through his driving exam," said Catalina. "It probably been an error; Stan's had his permit since he was sixteen, so for what reason would he have to step through a driving examination?"

"Catalina, individuals of Dad's age, need to re-sit their driving tests," Warren clarified. "How did you manage the letter?"
"I tossed it in the junk — I expected it was a slip-up," said Catalina. "In any case, no damage is done; we'll simply say we never got it. I trust they don't make me step through my driving examination once more. Multiple times is sufficient." She took a gander at Melissa, Seth, and Kelly. "Didn't you simply abhor going for your driving tests on every one of those occasions?"

The three young people took a gander at one another. "We as a whole breathed easy," said Seth.

"Goodness, you should be genuine acceptable drivers," said Catalina, plainly dazzled. "My closest companion Vanessa got her to permit the first time, and I generally thought Vanessa resembled some driving virtuoso or something."

"My driving test was extremely hard," said Kelly. "The inspector picked this truly difficult situation along the edge of the street and advised me to invert park into it. I was so anxious my hands were sweat-soaked, yet then Jesus gave me the strength, and I got in there first time without any issues by any stretch of the imagination."

"I disdain switch leaving, so some of the time when Stan and I go out together, I let him dominate and leave my vehicle for me," said Catalina.

The hopeless Warren put his head in his grasp. Until quite a long while back, his dad could drive any vehicle capability, yet now the possibility of Stan equal leaving a vehicle was a bad dream.

Sitting alongside her better half, Fran was all the while contemplating about her dad-in-law's demand that he had been to Australia that day, given he had never been to the country and was resolved to do quick work of this. "So Dad, you were saying you went to Australia today. Where did you see each one of those Australian creatures?"

"They were remaining by the roadside in a line," said Stan. "What's more, there was a major sign with Australia on it as well."

Fran thought briefly and acknowledged what probably occurred. Around 20 miles away, an Australian-themed natural life park kept kangaroos, wallabies, emus, koalas, dingoes, crocodiles, Australian snakes, reptiles, and frogs, cockatoos, and Tasmanian Devils. Various Australian creatures' sculptures were at the front passageway, alongside a huge sign that read 'Welcome to Australia.' Her dad-in-law probably determined past the natural life to stop and become befuddled, which was a concern given it was an exceptionally bustling street.

"The Australiana Wildlife Park, obviously," said Fran, her significant other and teen children acknowledging what had happened as well.

"I didn't realize that Australians drive on a similar roadside as we do now," said Stan.

"They do?" the critical Warren inquired.

Stan gestured. "Believe it or not. I thought they drove on the left-hand roadside as they do in England, so when I got to Australia, I thought it would be wise to change to one side as well. Be that as it may, incidentally, they drive on the right-hand side as well." The older adult took a gander at his child. "The Australians aren't too agreeable; truth be told, they're truly unpleasant. They were yelling and swearing at me, blaring their horns and glimmering their headlights, and some of them shook their clenched hands at me as well."

Warren didn't have the foggiest idea what to say, the man just covering his face in his grasp despondently. Catalina, unaware of course, said, "I'd truly prefer to go to Australia. I'd love to go to Melbourne so I can see the Sydney Harbor Bridge and Opera House."

Melissa saw her folks scowl considerably more, and again the teen needed to smother chuckling. Catalina probably had many educational weaknesses when at school; however, her geology educator most presumably had ended it all instead of the face showing a young lady who believed that the Sydney Harbor Bridge and Opera House were situated in the Australian city Melbourne as opposed to in Sydney. Melissa's assignment of monitoring her chuckling was made much more troublesome when Catalina said, "And the young Australian ladies look so beautiful in their frilly dresses." Melissa contemplated whether Catalina thought Brisbane was found near Vienna, given she clearly couldn't distinguish between Australia and Austria.

"So Catalina, how did you and Mr. Jenkins initially meet?" Kelly inquired.

"It's a genuinely fascinating story," said Catalina. "I was accomplishing humanitarian effort for a Senior Citizen's Center where Stan goes, and we got to talking, and we truly enjoyed one another, and that was it. Possibly this is because we're both Aries."

Or, on the other hand, possibly because Stan had 4,000,000 dollars in his financial balance, the negative Melissa thought as she took a gander at the beautiful shoeless blonde. Furthermore, Catalina was not accomplishing charitable efforts at the Senior Citizen's middle out of her heart's integrity; she had been requested to do as such by an adjudicator because of her powerlessness to stop legitimately her inability to pay the numerous resultant fines. Melissa couldn't be certain whether Catalina was lying by oversight, realizing that she was requested to accomplish local area administration work by a court would look awful, or whether the moronic young lady earnestly thought she was accomplishing humanitarian effort as opposed to local area administration forced by an adjudicator.

Melissa looked at Kelly, seeing the young lady's objecting yet firmly controlled articulation as Catalina referenced the zodiac. Kelly thought anything was against God's desire and as awful as fiddling with the mysterious to calls dark powers with an Ouija board. In any case, as common, she kept up her affableness with Catalina. Melissa knew why that was. Kelly had been customized since early on by her strict family to influence anyone who crossed her way to the fundamentalist Christian lessons she followed. Almost certainly, Kelly saw stupid Catalina as an obvious objective for teaching. Yet, what Kelly hadn't understood was that Catalina was very moronic to be conditioned.

"You had a birthday as of late excessively at that point?" Kelly inquired.

Catalina gestured. "No doubt, on April first." Again, she looked bewildered. "One thing I would never work out when I went to class was the way I was brought into the world in April. However, I was consistently the most seasoned child in the whole of my classes. I got some information about it once, and Vanessa advised me to work it out for myself. I surmise Vanessa didn't have the foggiest idea why by the same token."

Again, Melissa needed to monitor her chuckling. With the most appropriate birthday conceivable, Catalina couldn't work out that she because the most established in the class was that she was held back a year in kindergarten.

Kelly, missing any humor in Catalina's birthday and the clearest part of her character, said, "All things considered, April is by all accounts a well-known month for birthday events. My grandma is turning 75 on Sunday, and we're having lunch to celebrate. Seth, Melissa, Josh, and Mr. furthermore, Mrs. Jenkins are generally coming. Why not and Stan go along as well?"

"Why says thanks to Kelly, Stan and I couldn't want anything more than to come, wouldn't we, darling?" Catalina said.

Stan gazed blankly back at his sweetheart. "Whose birthday is it on Sunday? Is it my birthday?"

Melissa thought Catalina would be in for a major shock when she ventured into the Crane home and met Kelly's family. Furthermore, the Crane family would be in for a similarly large astonishment when Catalina went into their home and looked as strange as an Eskimo in the Sahara Desert.

The front doorbell rang, flagging the appearance of more family members. Warren went to answer the entryway, and Stan looked befuddled as he heard the voices of his other child, girl-in-law, and Seth, Melissa, and Josh's cousins as they entered. "For what reason are largely these individuals here?" the elderly person inquired. "Did Mary welcome them? Have you seen Mary around? Where right? I haven't seen her the entire day."

*

So particularly far as Melissa knew, Catalina's work history was all in the accommodation business as a sandwich shop chaperon, a worker in a roasted chicken café, a server in a burger joint, and gratitude to Catalina's propensity for not intuition before she talked, as a mixed drink server in a strip club. Notwithstanding, getting ready food was not something Catalina was put on this Earth to do, confirmed by the horror that she had arranged for Stan's birthday supper.

Melissa figured she might have a pardon of escaping eating the Japanese food Catalina had arranged because of a serious hypersensitivity to fish and fish. A couple of drops of shellfish sauce was all it required to dispatch Melissa to three days of having her head in a basin and running for the restroom with one loose bowel assault after another.

Catalina, as it ended up, despised fish, so nothing from the ocean was in the Japanese food, she arranged. She had bubbled rice such a lot of it was more similar to an English rice pudding sweet and subbed spinach for ocean growth. The fish segment was a fill-in for chicken — a basin of seared chicken from a neighborhood remove. Catalina realized that the Japanese ate crude fish in their sushi, yet additionally expected that the meat in sukiyaki was left uncooked, so this dish had enormous chunks of crude meat joined with generally cut celery containing the leaves, chime peppers that had been sliced to incorporate every one of the seeds and carrots including the skins. A Catalina side serving of mixed greens was destroyed with her bare hands (that she neglected to wash heretofore) icy mass of lettuce and toss it into a bowl.

Sauces were critical to planning credible Japanese food, so Catalina had bought prepared and satay sauce containers, leaving the secretive teriyaki sauce on the grocery store rack. One real Japanese fixing that Catalina bought was wasabi mustard, yet the young lady thought this resembled American mustard one put on a sausage. The outcome was true to form when she gulped down an entire piece before anybody could stop her.

Catalina's resultant sniffling and hacking fit frightened Stan, the older adult letting out his dentures from stun. Youthful Josh had gazed in interest at his granddad's battle to re-fit his false teeth, declaring to his folks that he needed to have teeth very much like his Grandpa and attempting to check whether his teeth could be removed from his mouth.
Kelly and Seth saying Grace together didn't help the off-kilter air of the evening. Nor did Stan demand that his sibling Homer and sister Agatha had been to see him that day. Stan's kin demonstrated a genuine illustration of terrible things occurring in threes. Homer had kicked the bucket from coronary illness and Agatha from a stroke, both under a quarter of a year after Mary passed on of malignancy. Melissa was exceptionally happy when the night at last found some conclusion.

Presently, lying in bed wearing a blue tee-shirt over a couple of white cotton swimsuit-style undies, Melissa was wide conscious contemplating her sibling's tenacious and controlling strict sweetheart and her granddad's gold-digger sweetheart. However, irritation was one distinct feeling as the pictures of red-haired Kelly and blonde Catalina swam into her inner consciousness; another feeling filled the teen's mind – one of sexual excitement. Coming to under her shirt, Melissa pulled her undies down to her thighs, uncovering her triangle of dark pubic hair that filled in bounty over her ladylike hill, and

142

drove her fingers into the tight, warm, sodden inside of her pink vagina. Melissa's lovely face showed the delight of masturbation, and under the covers, the youngster's bare toes grasped the sheet. Under her tee-shirt, Melissa's areolas shivered and were hard against the texture.

DespiteMelissa's excellence, with her olive appearance, luxurious dim hair, and huge earthy colored eyes from her Italian legacy on her mom's side making her quite possibly the most shocking young ladies at her school, she didn't have a sweetheart, nor did she need one, not currently and not ever. Many folks at her secondary school had asked the lovely teen out on dates. However, she had cordially denied each time, saying that dating folks she went to class with resembled two work partners dating and not a smart thought. She would like to focus on getting passing marks for a school where she wanted to concentrate on a bookkeeper's vocation. Notwithstanding, she had thumped back date demands by folks out of school as well.

Melissa just had no interest in young men, yet it was an altogether different matter with young ladies. While she attempted to smother her Sapphic longings and could never talk about them to anybody, a beautiful young lady caused Melissa's clitoris and vagina to react, and the young lady's undies seat would wind up quite sodden. Also, however much Melissa attempted to deny it to herself, she was a lesbian. An extremely lovely, exceptionally female lesbian who maintained her mystery bolted somewhere inside. However, a lesbian, as much as some butch dyke trims her hair in a group trim, wore overalls and battle boots, and lived transparently with another lady.

Melissa enjoyed school because she was in the young ladies' soccer group, so this implied double seven days; she had the opportunity to see her schoolmates getting undressed, changing, and showering both from her group and from normal exercise center class. At the point when Melissa saw her companions, for example, Gretchen bare or in their bras and underwear, it turned her on, yet she generally felt regretful about looking them that

143

way. Nonetheless, as she loathed Kelly, she could take part in anonymous voyeurism with her and not feel regretful, and it was a similar story with the similarly irritating Catalina.

Previously, Melissa had discretely situated herself to see up Kelly's skirt when her sibling's better half went higher up or looked at Kelly's hot adolescent ass when the lovely redhead twisted around in tight pants or shorts. Over and over at the Crane house, Melissa had taken her risk to recover a couple of Kelly's well-used undies from her clothing hamper, breathing in the delicate stale-smelling ladylike smell Kelly's vagina left immediately cotton undies saddle, causing her undies to get clammy simultaneously.

One thing Melissa had considered in the past was if the Crane family were strict to such an extent that they didn't self-teach Kelly and different children. There were two explanations behind this. Right off the bat, their posterity could help with spreading their religion to schoolmates, and also, the children were all acceptable at sports; Kelly herself a capable soccer player. While Kelly was as aggravating as could be expected as an individual from the young ladies' soccer crew, saying that God had a significant job in the group's fortunes, Melissa was furtively happy to have her in the group. This managed the cost of Melissa a lot of opportunities to observe Kelly getting uncovered and her stripped under the shower, water falling down her light complexion and her adolescent tits and down her thin figure to her enticing exposed base and the twists of her red pubic hair, before streaming down her legs to Kelly's exposed feet.

Melissa had never seen Catalina bare. However, she would take part in similar voyeurism strategies with her granddad's gold digger sweetheart whenever the opportunity emerged. Like with Kelly, she had up-avoided Catalina a lot of times, making the most of her perspective on inept Catalina's underwear as she went higher up wearing an exceptionally short skirt. Likewise, she took the risk to recover Catalina's swimsuit style underwear from the hamper on a few events and appreciated the smell of Catalina's vagina on the cotton. Melissa had not gotten the opportunity to do this around evening time, however as the youngster squirmed under the covers stroking off, her inner consciousness thought about Catalina's tight stirrup pants that showed the lovely blonde's underwear lines, her ideal butt, and the state of her vulva.

Getting wetter and wetter as her finger surrounded her clitoris, Melissa considered a sensual dream she had half a month prior of showering close to Kelly in the young ladies' change room when in strolled Catalina, the more established young lady stripping and joining the bare youngsters under the warm water. So much did Melissa appreciate the dream that it made her have an uncommon female wet dream, the youngster's vagina delivering a tsunami of sticky wet pussy juice as she arrived at the climax in her rest?

This ought to have made Melissa drench her cotton undies. Yet, for once, Melissa was happy to have her period when this occurred, as the discharging youngster's cushion consumed her ladylike energy just as her menses and protected her underwear. In any case, the orgasmic Melissa had awoken in the night to an immersed sterile napkin that she expected to change. Taking her parcel of cushions, Melissa had strolled shoeless to the restroom and spruced herself up between her legs before appending a new sterile cushion to the seat of her underwear. Shockingly, as Melissa flushed the restroom, washed her hands, and left the restroom, she found Seth, her sibling, having awoken in the night to pee, and the twins traded an abnormal hi as Seth saw the female cleanliness items his sister was conveying, Seth gazing at the roof, Melissa at the floor.

The memory of smelling a couple of Catalina's white cotton undies that she had been energized while wearing was sufficient for Melissa to arrive at the climax. The young person heaved and smothered a groan as the muscles in her vagina and rectum contracted, and her wet, tight pussy delivered a surge of pussy juice, which splashed her fingers and ran down the region that isolated her vulva from her tight back-ends.

Recuperating her breath, Melissa contacted to get a few tissues and utilized them to retain the clamminess of her post-orgasmic vagina. Expecting to pee, the young lady swung her legs up and strolled on her exposed feet down the foyer to the washroom, turning on the light and shutting the entryway behind her. Putting down the restroom seat, Melissa lifted her tee-shirt, slid her white underwear down to her lower legs, and sat the firm cheeks of her uncovered base down on the restroom seat. The sound of the young person peeing filled the washroom as Melissa's pee stream went into the restroom bowl, and when this lessened, she loosened up certain sheets of tissue to wipe her pussy. Discarding the wet tissue and the pussy-scented tissues into the bowl, Melissa stood up off the restroom and flushed it before pulling up her underwear and washing her hands; returning to bed, the young person nodded off, contemplating how great it is to see her sibling's better half-stripped in the shower after soccer this coming Friday.

*

At secondary school on Thursday morning, pretty brunette Gretchen Goldstein rapidly lamented getting some information about how her granddad's birthday supper went. Following twenty minutes of continuous whining from her closest companion about how she needed to endure her sibling's controlling Christian sweetheart and her granddad's moronic gold digger of a sweetheart, Gretchen was happy her more seasoned sibling was dating an ordinary young lady and that the two arrangements of grandparents were intellectually and genuinely equipped.

Melissa and Gretchen, wearing sweaters and short skirts, their dark hair tied back in pig tails, strolled through the hall after analytics, making for the young ladies' washroom before they went to the cafeteria for lunch. "Did I reveal to you Catalina and her stepfather conned Grandpa into purchasing a boat?" Melissa inquired.

Gretchen moaned and changed her hair. "Indeed, Melissa, a few times."

"Grandmother's been dead just two years, and she comes in and begins going through his cash like it's her own," Melissa proceeded. "Also, in addition to the fact that I have to go to Kelly's home on Sunday, she welcomed Catalina and Grandpa as well."

Gretchen trusted that something would end up diverting Melissa as they moved toward the young ladies' room, and keeping in mind that she got her desire, it was not by and large in the manner she needed. Turning the corner was, in all honesty, Kelly, wearing a green sweater and green plaid skirt and appended to Kelly's hand like a canine on the chain was Seth.

"Hello there, Melissa, greetings Gretchen," Kelly called, waving to the two young ladies with her free hand.

"No doubt, hello there, Melissa and Gretchen," called Seth to his sister and her dearest companion.

"Hello," Melissa and Gretchen said accordingly.

"I'm happy I got you," said Kelly. "Melissa, Seth, and I and every one of our companions are going to my home after school. How might you want to come as well?"
Melissa shook her head. "Sorry, Kelly, I'd love to come yet, Gretchen, and I need to consider financial matters, you know how it is." Melissa expected to do some financial aspects study, yet not really to keep her inside for the whole evening after school. Melissa realized that Kelly held up any expectation of teaching her into her circle of strict fixated companions, given how effectively she had brought Seth into her web. Yet, there was no chance Melissa would be going to the Crane house for a book of scriptures study meeting after school.

Gretchen didn't realize whether to feel alleviated or offended by her absence of a welcome when standing in that general area. Gretchen realized that Kelly saw Melissa – like a large portion of her family, a non-rehearsing Roman Catholic – as a reasonable objective to be brought into her Christian gathering alongside her twin sibling. As Gretchen was Jewish, Kelly considered her to be a non-practical recommendation, and accordingly, the scorn. Be that as it may, besides getting assaulted by a multitude of Africanized honey bees, there were not many things Gretchen needed less to occur than go to Kelly Crane's home to spend time with her strict oddity companions and family members.

"We'll see you later Kelly, we're simply going to the young ladies' room before lunch," said Gretchen.

"All things considered, I was as well," said Kelly. She unraveled her hand from that of her beau. "Simply stand by here, Seth."

Gretchen and Melissa traded a discrete eye-fold and went with Kelly into the young ladies' washroom; a long room containing twenty restrooms slows down with a sinks inverse column. Different young ladies involved, a few slow down further along, and Kelly, Melissa, and Gretchen went into three vacant slows down towards the middle. The youngsters shut and bolted the entryways behind them, the green 'Empty' locks changing to a red 'Drew in' on each. Inside their particular slows down, Kelly, Melissa, and Gretchen all checked for a tissue before lifting their skirts, sliding their underwear down to their lower legs, and sitting in the restrooms.

There was a considerable measure of room under the restroom entryways and slowed down parts, so it would have been workable for anybody passing by to see the feet and brought down two-piece style cotton underwear of the three young ladies – Kelly's white with pink blossoms, Melissa's white and Gretchen's light blue. The sound of the three teens peeing was discernible before their pee streams subsided, and every young lady

148

loosened up a length of tissue to wipe her wet pussy, Gretchen, and Melissa's dark earthy-colored pubic hair appearing differently about Kelly's red pubic hair.

Kelly, Melissa, and Gretchen stayed sitting in the restrooms for the following five minutes or so to purge their entrails, every young lady loosening up and utilizing tissue as she required it. The entire time, Kelly didn't quit talking, principally about how the beneficial things that had happened so far that day were because of Jesus. In her slow down, Gretchen murmured and peered down at her feet and brought undies as Kelly proceeded down to chatter endlessly.

In the middle of slow down among Gretchen and Kelly, Melissa was similarly bothered by Kelly's relentless talking. Yet, in the youngster's brain, she continued considering how she was between two alluring young ladies, and the two of them like her had their undies around their lower legs and felt her clitoris shivering.

Loosening up certain sheets of tissue from the move, Melissa coincidentally intentionally dropped the toilet paper onto the floor and inclined forward on the restroom to recover it, looking to one side at Gretchen's brought down blue undies, seeing the twofold cotton underwear saddle that would go through a large portion of the day in contact with Gretchen's youngster pussy.

Feeling remorseful as consistently when she took a gander at her closest companion in a sexual manner, Melissa went to one side, and her earthy-colored eyes devoured seeing Kelly's youngster underwear, so lovely with the pink flower design on the white cotton. On Kelly's underwear saddle, Melissa could make out a slight pussy stain and contemplated whether Kelly had been turned on some way or if it was essentially the aftereffect of her vagina self-purging. Melissa's pussy got clammy as she thought about the smelly female aroma that would be apparent on Kelly's undies, totally different from the botanical fragrance that the blossoms that enhanced the youngster's underwear would radiate, in actuality. Sitting back up with the length of bathroom tissue in her grasp, Melissa felt the paper adhering to her vagina as she cleaned herself, and the lovely young person wriggled on the restroom seat as the tissue stimulated her private ladylike zones.

Melissa and Gretchen completed at a similar second, the young ladies standing up as one, putting down the restroom tops and flushing the restrooms, before pulling up their underwear and changing them around their pussies bottoms, at that point smoothing down their skirts.

"Hello, hang tight for me!" Kelly called as Gretchen and Melissa opened their slows down. Inside her restroom, slow down; Kelly loosened up a length of tissue to get done with cleaning herself before standing up and flushing the restroom after putting down the top. Kelly pulled up and changed her undies around her pussy, and the firm cheeks of her base as Melissa and Gretchen had done, at that point smoothed down her skirt.

Leaving the slowdown and joining Melissa and Gretchen at the sinks, Kelly proceeded to talk and talk as the young people washed and dried their hands before leaving the washroom, where Seth stood standing by quietly as Kelly has directed him to.

"Did you miss me?" Kelly asked, promptly taking a tight hold of Seth's hand.

"Sure did," said Seth, as Kelly drove him away towards the cafeteria, Melissa and Gretchen following behind.

Melissa thought it was best that Seth had done what he was told, to keep away from a rehash of what had occurred at the shopping center half a month sooner. Kelly had gone to the women's room and advised Seth to sit tight outside for her, yet Kelly – probably having a few issues with her stomach-related framework - had taken ages to get back from the restroom. Seth had gotten drilled and meandered into the hardware store neighboring the bathrooms, where he was watching a rap music video on one of the TVs. So much was Seth getting a charge out of the music video that he neglected to see the beautiful redhead enter the hardware store and remain behind him, active hips with an absolute look of dissatisfaction all over? At the point when Seth did at long last acknowledge Kelly had returned, he was educated beyond all doubt that he had been recently urged that he was restricted from tuning in to any rap, hip-jump, or heavy metal music and that his better half didn't value his offense. Seth, at that point, wound up waiting on the post-trial process for the remainder of the week for his horrendous sin.

Strolling close to Melissa, Gretchen additionally noticed Seth and Kelly. Gretchen had a sweetheart out of school, yet they had a typical, loose, and equivalent relationship. Gretchen couldn't envision what life would resemble if their relationship resembled the couple before her, one controlling the other. At the opposite finish of the scale was Melissa and Gretchen's now and then idea that her companion was possibly excessively honest about school by ceaselessly thumping back demands for a date.

In the school cafeteria, Melissa and Gretchen were the first to show up of their gathering of companions and sat with their plates at their table. Kelly and Seth found a spot at an alternate table with their Christian companions and, as frequently as she had seen it previously, couldn't stop herself wincing as the gathering supplicated before eating.

Two rappers passed by with their plate and glanced in dismay at the scene. "Man, did you see that?" one of them inquired.

"Those children imploring at school? Better believe it, I saw it," the subsequent rapper affirmed.

The top rapper shook his head. "I thought perhaps I was getting a fever or something and envisioned it."

"No, you didn't, yet the man, I wish you had," his companion guaranteed him as they went to their table where different rappers were sitting tight for them.

Melissa knew Kelly and her loved ones supplicated before eating any food – even bites. Yet, since Seth had begun supplicating before dinners at home and in any event, when Kelly was nowhere to be found, bits of gossip had spread to Melissa's great shame that the Jenkins family were likewise peculiarly strict.

Gretchen feigned exacerbation. "Hmm, I can hardly wait until soccer practice with Kelly tomorrow around lunchtime."

"Me by the same token." Melissa's reaction sounded as wry as Gretchen's, yet while Melissa, to be sure, discovered burning through the majority of Friday evening with Kelly bothering, there was for her a result. Kelly would change out of her customary garments and into her soccer uniform, and a short time later would strip down to the bare and shower. Also, this was something Melissa anticipated each Friday.

*

Melissa burned through all of Friday expecting soccer, and time appeared to move gradually through the entirety of her morning classes. Be that as it may, adequately sure, it at long last showed up, and Melissa attempted to monitor her eagerness as she advanced toward the exercise center with Gretchen and different young ladies in the soccer group, Kelly notwithstanding.

Before long, the change-room was loaded up with pretty and fit 18-year-old young ladies taking off their customary garments to change into their soccer garbs. Melissa removed her shoes, sweater, skirt, and tee-shirt and stood shoeless in the pink bra and pink undies she was wearing. Her lovely earthy-colored eyes took in the nubile female types of her partners. Melissa felt her clitoris shiver and her vagina dampen between her legs as she noticed different young ladies disrobe and are happy she was a young lady. If she were a kid, her energy would be very clear at this point.

As Melissa eliminated her bra, the firm fragile living creature and dark skin of her high school tits noticeable, she looked to one side at Gretchen's above and beyond C-cup breasts, as her closest companion remained close to her shoeless and wearing lilac shaded undies. Simply before her, Kelly was additionally shoeless and in her white bra and undies; before the beautiful redhead eliminated her brassiere, the light complexion of her breasts with pink areolas now obvious. At that point, as one, Melissa, Gretchen, and Kelly pulled down their undies and stood bare, Gretchen and Melissa's dull pubic hair appearing differently from Kelly's red pubic hair. Melissa's eyes flittered around the change-room, taking in the earthy colored, blonde, and red shrubs of her partners, their uncovered breasts, and exposed bottoms.

Melissa couldn't avoid Kelly's discrete look. With her legs marginally separated and her adorable bare ass noticeable all around, Melissa got a decent perspective on Kelly's thin pink oval-molded vagina and the tight pink starfish-formed opening of Kelly's back-end. Melissa felt her clitoris shiver at the great sight. She considered how she had seen a greater amount of Seth's sweetheart than her sibling had most likely seen and how he would need to stand by until he and Kelly wedded to perceive any of Kelly's appealing resources that her bra and underwear covered.

The young ladies all put on their games briefs and sports bras, at that point their soccer regalia – light blue shirts and shorts with dim blue decorations – and their preparation shoes. The Chicago climate was still decent and unexpectedly warm for April, and the young ladies all burned some serious calories during their extreme instructional course.

Melissa's games briefs were sweat-soaked enough from the extreme exercise. Yet, a portion of the moistness from between her legs was from noticing the nubile young groups of her colleagues and expecting the showers subsequently.

Getting back to the young ladies' change rooms to shower after training, Melissa, as she generally did, felt like she had passed on and gone to Heaven. Her subtle youthful body was only one of numerous bare, shoeless 18-year-old young ladies who remained under the shower heads, the water falling down their bodies as they washed away the sweat with cleanser, the vast majority of the young ladies having uncovered breasts and pubic hair splashed with cleanser and water.

Aside from Melisa was Gretchen, who was applying cleanser to her uncovered base when the bar sneaked out of her hands and onto the shower floor and Gretchen's exposed feet. Promptly, Gretchen bowed down to get it, and Melissa again felt similar sensations of hunger and blame as she saw between Gretchen's legs and her dim pink vagina and the more obscure pink of her tight butt.

On Melissa's opposite side was Kelly, stripped like the wide range of various young ladies and her red hedge filled drenched with cleanser and water. She said to Melissa, "I can hardly wait for Sunday, can you? It will be great, your granddad and Catalina tagging along."

"No, I'm truly anticipating it as well." Melissa's dull articulation that parted with none of her actual feelings would have made her a decent expert part in Las Vegas or Atlantic City.

"I figure your Grandpa will have a ball," Kelly proceeded. "I think he is quite possibly the most honored individuals I have met."

"Truly?" Melissa inquired. She was unable to consider anybody less honored than her granddad. He had lost his better half of numerous years to malignant growth, was in chronic weakness truly, couldn't recall his name most days, and given that he had filled in as an architect with asbestos for a long time, was living on a foundation of uncertainty time. It was improbable Kelly was alluding to her granddad's bonanza lottery win – cash didn't appear to be too imperative to her, dissimilar to the draining Catalina.

Kelly gestured in confirmation. "Indeed, God has chosen to give your Grandfather one more year to appreciate on this superb world He made, and surprisingly however your Grandmother has gone to be a holy messenger with Jesus, He sent Catalina to your Grandfather so he wouldn't be desolate."

With that, Kelly ventured her nubile adolescent body free from the shower and gathered her towel, getting dry as she strolled on her exposed feet back to the primary change room region.

"Is she genuine?" asked Gretchen. Kelly never neglected to stun her, yet her last remarks were past uncouth in any event for her. Also, how should she not think, even in any event briefly, that a young lady as appealing as Catalina may be pulled into the older man's significant bank balance more than the man himself?

"She is," moaned Melissa, as she and Gretchen moreover ventured out of the showers and gathered their towels, the two teens drying their vaginas.

"In this way, on Sunday, I'm going out with my sweetheart to the lake," said Gretchen, a naughty grin on her lovely face. "What are you doing on Sunday?"

"Ok, shut up," said Melissa, pushing her closest companion warmly on the shoulder.

The Saturday saw Melissa working her low maintenance work as a server at a shopping center restaurant. She had a fascinating encounter holding up upon an Asian-American family with two school-age kids, a child and a little girl. The child was not exceptionally discrete, looking at Melissa's hot adolescent ass each time she strolled by. However, the youngster was undeniably more discrete in looking at the young fellow's sister, envisioning what the youthful Asian excellence would resemble naked. At one phase, the Asian young lady got up to visit the women's room, Melissa getting a quick look at her lovely white underwear as her skirt immediately rode up.

A couple of moments after this, Melissa saw two recognizable figures pass by the restaurant. One was the weak figure of her granddad, Stan strolling with a stick with excruciating gradualness, projecting confounded articulations at his uproarious and swarmed environmental factors. To his side was the tall, blonde figure of Catalina, the young lady wearing a dark tee-shirt and some denim shorts so close and short that she should have quite recently gone out wearing undies. In any case, going with them was a third individual whom Melissa had never seen.

The third individual was a young lady about Catalina's age, as tall and as lovely as her yet with long red hair tied back in a pig tail. The redhead wore a white tee-shirt, sleeveless denim coat, and short denim smaller than a normal skirt. Melissa pondered who the redhead was, potentially Catalina's dearest companion Vanessa whom she had much of the time talked about yet who Melissa had never met. Neither Catalina nor Stan saw Melissa, something the teen was appreciative of.

The two young ladies guided Stan's advances; Melissa ventured to where they could go through a greater amount of his cash. A few groups saw the rare sight of an older man with two pretty young ladies, every one of whom was adequately youthful to be his granddaughter, many giggling, others offering intriguing or trashing remarks. Melissa became occupied tending to tables through the remainder of her day of work, so gave her granddad, his gold-digger sweetheart, and the obscure redhead little thoroughly examined next couple of hours.

Gretchen functioned as a clerk at a general store in a similar shopping center. When their works day completed in the early evening, the two closest companions advanced home together, talking about what might happen when dopey Catalina met different individuals from Kelly's family and Kelly's family met dopey Catalina. It would be intriguing at any rate, Gretchen mentioning a full report of what occurred.

Seth was up most punctual of the Jenkins family on Sunday morning, shuddering with fervor at going to chapel for the early morning message with Kelly and her family. As Melissa got up to go for a Sunday morning run, she saw her sibling run for the Crane family vehicle loaded up with zeal, similar to going out to an amusement leave for the day instead of a Fundamentalist Christian church.

Melissa shook her head as she set off running on one more fine and bright spring morning. Fran and Warren got their bikes out of the carport and went out for a ride, Josh in a seat on the back of his mom's bike.

Seth had gotten back to Kelly's home after chapel to help her family set up for their grandma's birthday lunch, so it was simply Fran, Warren, Melissa, and Josh for breakfast. Similarly, as the family was completing and tidied up the table, the phone rang, and Fran went to respond to it.

"Hi?" she asked, her face falling at the voice on the opposite end. "Goodness, howdy Catalina, how are you?"

Warren's face soured at the notice of his dad's sweetheart, and he was happy he wasn't the person who had picked up the telephone.

"Catalina, you sound surprised. Is everything alright?" Fran questioned. She smothered a murmur at Catalina's reaction. "Kelly gave you the location to her folks' home, didn't she?" Again Fran tuned in to what Catalina said and feigned exacerbation. "You can't work out how to arrive? Have you had a go at glancing in the road catalog?" Fran shook her head. "No, Catalina, you don't need to point the road index toward the path you are going ..." her voice followed off. Thinking about an answer, the exasperated Fran said, "Catalina, why not roll here? At that point, you and Stan can follow us over yonder? OK, we'll see you later."

The disappointed Fran put down the beneficiary, shaking her head. "Is something interesting you, Melissa?" she asked her little girl to some degree cuttingly, as Melissa couldn't contain her delight at her mom's phone discussion.

It wasn't well before Catalina showed up in her vehicle, Stan in the front seat. The young lady crashed into their carport excessively quickly and shrieked to a stop simply before the carport. Peering out the window, Melissa watched Catalina escape the driver's side. She was unable to have been dressed less suitably for lunch with moderate Christians, wearing a white short-sleeved shirt that showed a lot of her all-around satisfactory cleavage, a short blue extravagant scaled down skirt, and white shoes, Melissa seeing the white texture of Catalina's underwear as she left the vehicle.

Stan stumbled out of the traveler's side on insecure legs before strolling around to the driver's side and getting into the seat. He shut the entryway behind him, and for a couple of seconds, fear rose in Melissa's stomach as she suspected her granddad was going to drive.

Luckily he did nothing of the sort, yet in Stan's matured mind, he was driving. He claimed to guide the vehicle while noisily making vehicle commotions, "Brush– brush – brush," the elderly person shouted. Melissa felt her cheeks flushing super hot as a portion of different understudies from her school were passing by and watched the older man proceeds to profess to drive. "Brush, brush – blare, signal, blare!" the elderly person called out while promising to turn a corner.

The children giggled and tattled as they strolled up the street, actually watching Stan; however, two of the young men were more intrigued by the female type of Catalina as the tall blonde strolled towards the front entryway unmistakably uninterested by Stan sitting in the vehicle professing to drive.

Melissa was substantially more concerned. No big surprise everyone believed that their family was insane. If individuals weren't expecting that Melissa was Josh's high school mother instead of his a lot more seasoned sister, there was Seth and his imploring and tough talk and being driven like a canine on a rope by his Jesus crack sweetheart, neighbors naturally imagining that Melissa and her folks were likewise oddly strict like their most established child. At that point, there was her granddad, right now causing him to notice himself by claiming to drive a vehicle in full perspective in the public road, however, who previously pulled in a lot of consideration by having a moronic blonde sweetheart more youthful than his most established grandkids. It was fortunate that none of the neighbors realized that Melissa's sexual direction inclined towards individuals who, like her, had two X chromosomes, as opposed to the individuals who had one X and one Y chromosome. A lesbian girl would be what tops off an already good thing.

"Hi Catalina," said Warren, likewise with incredible hesitance, he permitted the young blonde into his home.

"Why howdy Warren," said Catalina in her sharp Midwestern pronunciation.

"Is Dad OK in the vehicle like that?" Warren asked, seeing his dad making many clamors, claiming to drive Catalina's vehicle in the carport.

"He's fine; he's simply having some good times; he does it constantly," said Catalina. She saw Fran show up behind her significant other. "Hello Fran," Catalina waved.

"Indeed, hi Catalina," said Fran. She took a gander at where her dad-in-law was drawing the consideration of the quiet rural road. "You removed the keys from the start, didn't you?" The prospect of Stan beginning and heading out in the vehicle was a scary one, to be sure.

"They're here; I'm not senseless," said Catalina. The beautiful blonde glanced through her untidy handbag, Warren turning away his eyes when a period cushion was one of the things the young lady removed; however, one thing that neglected to show up was the keys to Catalina's vehicle. "Hold up for a second; perhaps I left the keys in the start," Catalina surrendered.

"I'll get them," said Warren curtly. He stepped towards the vehicle, his dad neglecting to enlist his quality, and came to through the window, eliminating the keys without a moment to spare to keep Stan from turning them in the start, and returned inside.

In the lounge room, Catalina glanced around, and her blue eyes picked saw a video from the neighborhood rental store – a homicide secret set in the realm of corporate money and high society in New York - that was sitting close to the VCR. "This is a decent film; I saw it a week ago on TV," she said.

"Indeed, Fran and I were wanting to watch it this evening," said Warren. "We appreciate watching secret films."

"It was somewhat confounded now and again," said Catalina. "I could hardly imagine how the child in-law ended up being the killer; he appeared to be a truly decent person."

Warren and Fran murmured profoundly and feigned exacerbation as one. "Well, expresses gratitude toward Catalina; that is one thing I didn't have the foggiest idea," said Fran.

"God helps us; I didn't ruin the closure for you?" Catalina inquired. She winced. "Sorry." She plunked down on the love seat, Melissa again seeing up the blondie's skirt and her white undies as she crossed her long, shapely legs. "So would Josh like me to peruse him another story?"

"I believe he's useful for the occasion; he's playing in his room," said Warren.

"I would be wise to get something to keep him involved when we go to the Crane house," said Fran.

"I'll accompany you," Melissa chipped in, going with her mom higher up. The young person was wearing a dress that came over her knees, and if anybody had been remaining under the steps as she climbed them, they would have seen that she was wearing apricot-hued undies.

"So what toys might you want to take with you today?" Fran asked her child as she went into his room.

Josh was perched on the floor playing with the toy dinosaurs Melissa had bought for him for Christmas – a tyrannosaurus, a stegosaurus, a triceratops, a brontosaurus, a plesiosaurus, a duck-charged dinosaur, and a pterodactyl – and he had no faltering in saying, "The dinosaurs, please Mom."

"He sure loves the toy dinosaurs he got for Christmas, Melissa," said Fran.

"He does, doesn't he?" said Melissa. The youngster couldn't have been more joyful with her more youthful sibling's decision of toys for now. Kelly and her strict family discovered dinosaurs disturbing, and Josh playing with toy dinosaurs would add to their anxiety. Melissa wanted that there was a toy trilobite she could purchase for Josh to agitate Kelly and the remainder of her family significantly more, yet questioned that there would be a business opportunity for trilobite toys.

"Maybe Josh may grow up to be a scientist?" Fran proposed.

"He's brilliant enough," said Melissa. "Insofar as Catalina doesn't peruse to him any longer."

Fran giggled. "That is valid; I stress it very well may be getting." She put the dinosaurs into a plastic holder to ship them. "I wish that there was a TV show about dinosaurs that Josh could watch."

"You mean like a narrative?" Melissa inquired.

"No, I mean like fun, instructive children show with a cordial dinosaur as the principal character," said Fran. "It would keep Josh involved, that is, without a doubt. I figure different children might want it as well, and guardians or more seasoned children and teens who are infant sitting could never become weary of it."

The two ladies accompanied Josh first floor, and everybody prepared to leave.

"Thus, I'll follow you," said Catalina, remaining back and holding on to follow the Jenkins family, unmindful of the way that her vehicle hindered the carport, so she would need to retreat first.

"Um, Catalina, you'll need to turn around out first so I can get the vehicle out," said Warren.

"Yet, I don't have the foggiest idea about the way," Catalina dissented. "I can't drive out first."

"Indeed Catalina, however with your vehicle there, I can't get my vehicle out of the carport," said Warren, with trouble holding his understanding, an assignment made even more troublesome with his dad proceeding to sit steering the ship of Catalina's vehicle making vehicle clamors. "Invert out into the road, stand by a moment or something like that, at that point follow me when I back out, alright?"

Catalina remained there looking exceptionally befuddled, thinking continuously about how it would function before her face lit up. "Alright, I have it now."

After another brief pause – Stan was getting a charge out of claiming to drive Catalina's vehicle and just hesitantly surrendered his situation steering the ship – they were on their way, Catalina following Warren as he headed to the Crane house.

*

With her short free skirt and uncovering shirt, Catalina did to be a sure post of a spot at the Crane house with their traditionalist fundamentalist Christian loved ones. Kelly, holding tight to Seth's hand and not allowing her sweetheart to far away from her, glanced pretty in her Sunday best green dress, yet the article of clothing seemed like it was from

1961 instead of the current year 1991. Melissa got the slightest look of dissatisfaction on Kelly's lovely face at Josh playing with the toy dinosaurs. She felt fulfillment at Kelly's distress of seeing things that introduced such a test to her confidence.

Because of the fine warm climate, the Reverend and Mrs. Crane chose to have the lunch outside, something Melissa was appreciative of. The Crane house was dreadful. Not on account of the unusual occupants, who implored before each supper, including when one of them took an apple, orange, or banana from the organic product bowl as a tidbit. Not in light of the more youthful Crane youngsters who intensely watched strict projects for youngsters on the TV and once in a while talked a sentence without utilizing the word 'God' or 'Jesus.' It was a direct result of how the house was embellished. Strict artworks canvassed the dividers in basically every room, and Melissa consistently felt the eyes of Jesus and other scriptural figures chasing after her.

The restrooms were about the solitary spot liberated from strict artistic creations. However, they had outlined sacred writings to adorn them. Kelly delighted in perusing scriptural entries at whatever point she was perched on the restroom with her skirt around her midriff and her undies around her lower legs. However, Melissa was not a significant enthusiast of perusing parcels from the holy book in the restroom.

While Stan was thoroughly out of it and had no cognizance of where he was or why he was here, Catalina figured out how to track down some shared view with Kelly and a portion of her different family members.

"Did you find as you would prefer here, alright?" Kelly inquired.

"Gracious yes," said Catalina. "I didn't know what direction to guide the guide toward arriving, yet then I had a splendid thought and followed Stan's folks here. I would not like to get lost or be late. I disdain to be late. It resembles when they change the timekeepers forward or back for sunlight saving, I can easily forget what direction, and now and again, I've been two hours ahead of schedule or two hours late. Sunshine saving time is so confounding. I disdain sunshine saving."

"I don't care for it either," said Kelly. "The Lord chooses what time the sun rises and sets every day, and by changing this around, all we are doing is contradicting His will."

Different individuals from the Crane family affirmed their arrangement before Seth said, "I concur with Kelly. For what reason do we as men need to change the time when it is chosen for us?"

"Gracious, shut up Seth, if Kelly thought it was a smart thought to bounce in a fountain of liquid magma, would you concur with her at that point?" the exhausted and pessimistic Melissa murmured, the teen checking her watch and seeing that time had advanced with anguishing gradualness.

Feeling the call of nature, Melissa went inside the house. The ground floor restroom the visitors were utilizing was situated close to the indirect access, and a humiliating scene promptly faced the young lady.

Her befuddled granddad, having no clue about why he was at this unusual house, had gone to search for his better half inside the house, passing by the restroom as one of the young ladies from the Crane family flushed the restroom and arose in the wake of washing her hands.

Seeing no hint of Mary inside, Stan had advanced back outside once more, and again passing the washroom, noticed that the restroom reservoir was delayed to top off. Accepting that the restroom was broken somehow or another, Stan concluded he would investigate himself and fix the issue. Until quite a while back, Stan had been an extremely equipped home jack of all trades; however, now he was not, and keeping in mind that the restroom wasn't broken, previously, it was when Stan began to dismantle the storage.

"I'm so grieved about this," Warren was saying 'sorry' to his hosts, as he and the Reverend Crane attempted to fix the flushing component, while Mrs. Crane remained outside the restroom with the extremely befuddled Stan.

"Melissa nectar, on the off chance that you need the restroom, you'd best utilize the one higher up," said Mrs. Crane as she noticed Melissa.

"Indeed, thank you, Mrs. Crane," said Melissa. She mounted the steps to the second floor, where everything was tranquil, but instead of making straight for the restroom, the youngster made a diversion to somewhere else – Kelly's room.

In contrast to most adolescent young ladies, Kelly didn't have banners of pop stars or attractive entertainers finishing her room; however, huge pictures of Jesus, Melissa again feeling the eyes pursuing her around the room. Her heart rippling with anxious energy, Melissa made for Kelly's bureau and opened the subsequent one – the one wherein Kelly kept her clothing.

To one side were the bras that held Kelly's firm high school tits under tight restraints, and to the privilege was her cotton underwear that covered Kelly's red pubic hair, firm bum, and pretty pink vagina. In the cabinet's focal point were the two articles that had the opportunity to go into Kelly's undies and vagina – a bundle of sterile cushions and a container of tampons.

While taking a gander at Kelly's spotless teenager undies in her clothing cabinet was very acceptable, something better was in the room – the clothing hamper in which Kelly positioned her pre-owned garments. Shutting the cabinet, Melissa advanced toward the hamper. She lifted the top and promptly noticed a couple of Kelly's underwear laid conveniently on top – white with purple leg and abdomen versatile and violets.

Venturing into the hamper, Melissa, with shaking fingers, removed Kelly's dirty undies. Inside her undies, Melissa's vagina got wetter and wetter as her eyes took in the velvety pussy stain that Kelly's vagina had left as soon as possible cotton of the seat. Raising Kelly's underwear to her nose, Melissa consumed the delicate, smelly, ladylike smell of Kelly's virginal vagina, wishing she could encounter the smell between Kelly's legs for genuine when licking her pussy. This obviously would never occur, however, in her mind; her creative mind had no restrictions.

Smelling Kelly's pussy once more, Melissa again contemplated why she just did this with the two young ladies in her day-to-day existence she hated most when strides on the steps broke her out of her fantasy world. Setting Kelly's undies back in the hamper in a similar flawless position their proprietor had, Melissa trusted that the new introduction was not Kelly as it is difficult to clarify why she had been in her room. Nonetheless, not Kelly and Melissa moaned to see that Catalina's individual who mounted the steps.

With the waiting smell of Kelly's grab still in her noses, Melissa watched Catalina go into the washroom and close and lock the entryway behind her. Melissa recalled that she expected to go to the restroom herself. "Damn," Melissa mumbled faintly as she went to stand by outside the restroom entryway, a representation of Jesus straightforwardly inverse the washroom gazing at her, its eyes appearing to say, "That is the thing that you get for taking a gander at the underwear of quite possibly the most committed individuals from my herd."

The sound of Catalina peeing into the restroom was perceptible in the tranquil lobby. When her pee stream decreased, other sounds from inside the restroom demonstrated that the beautiful blonde was currently discharging her guts. Melissa surrender to a considerable delay when amazingly, the shrill voice of Catalina, a hint of frenzy in her voice, came from the restroom. "Goodness dangs it, hi, would anyone say anyone is there? I need assistance in here, please!"

"Hey Catalina, it's Melissa. Is everything OK in there?" Melissa inquired.

"Melissa, thank heavens you're here. There's no tissue, and I'm abandoned in the restroom. Generous assistance me!"

"Alright, Catalina hold on, I'll discover some tissue for you," said Melissa.

"Much obliged to you!" Catalina got back to.

Melissa strolled to the divider storeroom inverse the restroom, opened the entryway, and recovered a move of bathroom tissue from the parcel. "I have a few; I'll simply need to open the entryway and pass it to you." The washroom entryway was bolted, yet the feeble inward lock was handily opened, just barely cut. The youngster strolled into the restroom holding the tissue roll and quickly held back.

Catalina was perched on the restroom directly before her, her short skirt up around her midsection and her white swimsuit style undies down around her lower legs. One thing Catalina hadn't thought to do was to close her legs, and her knees were widely separated, showing her twists of light pubic hair and her vagina.

Melissa had needed to see Catalina's pussy for a very long time. Yet, she hadn't expected that today would be the day and not in the conditions of Catalina abandoned on the restroom with no paper. Catalina's pink pussy had thin lips and was distinctive to how Melissa had envisioned it. Her pussy reacted to the sight. However, she knew that she could not continue to gaze at Catalina's groin, much as she needed to. Getting bothered,

Melissa took a gander at the ground and at Catalina's brought down undies, seeing a rich pussy stain on the cotton saddle.

Catalina could see Melissa's inconvenience, and the young lady's light complexion become flushed as she contacted her own – and off base – decision about what this was. "Apologies, I'm somewhat foul today," she was sorry, with a nervous, humiliated laugh, still careless in regards to the real her legs were widely separated.

Melissa hadn't seen any smell whatsoever, being excessively occupied by Catalina's pussy and undies. "That is OK," she figured out how to stammer. She held out the move of tissue. "I um – got you some bathroom tissue."

"Much obliged, Melissa, you saved my life," said Catalina, taking the tissue roll and starting to change the unfilled move for the full one.

"I'll simply leave you to have some protection," said Melissa. Retreating from the washroom, she shut and bolted the entryway behind her, hanging tight outside for her turn, her inner consciousness loaded up with the pictures of Catalina's brought down undies, her blonde pubic hair, and her vulva. The sound of Catalina discontinuously loosening up bathroom tissue from the move holder was perceptible for the following five minutes before Catalina flushed the restroom, washed her hands, and arose, changing her underwear through her short skirt.

"The restroom's all yours, Melissa," said Catalina.

"Much obliged, Catalina," said Melissa, going into the restroom and shutting and bolting the entryway behind herself. At the point when she completed, flushed the restroom, washed her hands, and arose out of the restroom a couple of moments later, as Catalina changing her underwear through her skirt, Melissa was astonished to see that Catalina had stayed higher up and was gazing at one of the numerous strict canvases in the passage.

"Much appreciated again for protecting me," said Catalina. "Would you be able to trust I was adequately senseless to plunk down on the restroom without checking for paper?"

Melissa could well trust it; however, to be respectful, they said, "I get it could happen to anybody."

"It's happened to me a great deal," Catalina yielded. "Indeed, both my Mom and my companion Vanessa said that on the off chance that I at any point stalled out on the restroom with no bathroom tissue once more, they would simply leave me staying there to become familiar with an exercise. Brain you, today was Stan's flaw. He's a flawless man, yet he can be genuine senseless at times. This could never have occurred if he hadn't messed around with the restroom first floor."

"Indeed, I saw that as well," said Melissa. "Father and Kelly's dad was attempting to fix it."

"I'm happy they just had a book of scriptures things with enormous words in the washroom, not artworks like that one," said Catalina, pointing at one of the strict artistic creations of Jesus which gazed back at them with unblinking eyes.

Melissa chuckled, happy that the Jesus painting was not in the restroom gazing at her while she was in the restroom with her dress hitched up and her undies pulled down around her lower legs. "Indeed, it would be peculiar in the washroom like that."

"It helps me to remember my stepbrother Joey," said Catalina.

"Your stepbrother appears as though Jesus?" Melissa inquired.

"No, however, he had these large eyes that used to gaze at me," said Catalina. "It was more terrible when he was in the restroom with me."

"Your progression sibling used to go into the washroom with you?" the stunned Melissa inquired.

Catalina gestured. "Indeed, I thought it was somewhat bizarre from the start. I would have to go to the restroom or have a shower, and he would go in there too to brush his teeth or shave. My Mom was a single parent, and I was an alone youngster, and she wedded Jim when I was eighteen, so I'd never grown up with siblings or sisters. Joey said siblings consistently went into the restroom with their sisters, and Joey ought to have known, he was a year more established and more brilliant than me."

"He disclosed to you that?" Melissa asked, significantly really distrusting.

"Indeed. I suppose you and Seth are more accustomed to it when you're in the restroom together?"

Melissa was lost for words, shocked by the possibility of her utilizing the restroom or showering when Seth was in the washroom shaving or brushing his teeth. She was certain that this situation, whenever introduced to her twin, would bring about him fleeing so quick that an hour later, he would be in Texas. "Um, Catalina, Seth, and I never go to the restroom together."

"You don't?" Catalina looked confounded.

"Actually, no, not ever," said Melissa solidly. "Catalina, didn't you feel awkward with him in there with you?"

"I didn't care for it without question," conceded Catalina. "He used to gaze at me when I was perched on the restroom having a crap, and he wouldn't turn away every time I got bathroom tissue and utilized it to wipe my base. It was multiple times more regrettable when I had loose bowels or my period."

"My God," said Melissa, rubbing her forehead in despair.

"Joey was continually saying Chicago had water deficiencies, so we needed to shower or have a shower together," Catalina proceeded. "Once more, I didn't care for it, particularly when it was my time. However, Joey said that the public authority had requested all families to shower or have showers together to ration water, and we'd get a huge fine in the event. That we didn't."

Melissa shook her head. "Catalina, if you didn't care for it and needed security, for what reason didn't you bolt the restroom entryway or converse with your Mom about it?"

"I bolted the entryway, yet Joey would simply open it," said Catalina. "Joey said that all guardians realized it was typical for their children to go into the restroom together yet never talked about it, and I thought on the off chance that I disclosed to Mom it would snitch."

"Catalina, that truly is such a thing you ought to have gone to your Mom about," said the shocked Melissa.

"I contemplated getting some information about it. However, Vanessa just has sisters, so I didn't figure she would comprehend. In any case, I enjoyed my more established stepbrother Richie much more," said Catalina. "He was in every case genuine pleasant to

172

me, never followed me to the restroom, and once he attempted to help me become a model, you know."

"A model?" Melissa didn't care for how this discussion was going, and her feelings of trepidation were affirmed when Catalina kept on talking.

"Indeed, he was continually saying how beautiful I was and how I ought to be a model, and one day he came over totally energized and said that his photographic artist companion from a demonstrating organization was visiting the area, and he was able to shoot a full displaying portfolio that was typically 2,000 dollars free of charge."

"How did you respond?" Melissa inquired.

"It sounded genuine great, I went with Richie to this stockroom, and I met the picture taker," said Catalina. "He said I was genuine pretty and would make a genuine decent model. Richie and this other person who was an attorney went behind a shade, and the photographic artist made every one of these efforts of me. I was somewhat anxious when he said that he expected to take pictures of me in my bra and my underwear and bare; however, the photographic artist said that all models needed to have these photos required to show their inward excellence to customers, so I did it."

Melissa recoiled. "What occurred straightaway?"

"The attorney — even though he didn't resemble a legal counselor, he appeared to be somewhat youthful; he made me sign this agreement with every one of these huge words to say I'd never enlighten anybody regarding it," said Catalina. She looked stressed. "You will not tell anybody, will you?"

"No, swear on my mother's grave. So did you get any demonstrating offers?" asked the dubious Melissa.

"Tragically no," said Catalina, not to Melissa's great amazement.

Catalina and Melissa advanced ground floor, Melissa currently encountering an alternate inclination towards Catalina, one of compassion at how the genuine and unintelligent young lady had been exploited by her deadheads of stepbrothers and their companions, the phony photographic artist and fake attorney to fulfill their debilitated sexual corruptions. Melissa had never met both of Catalina's progression siblings yet swore on the off chance that she did, she would kick these degenerates in the balls on the off chance that they got excessively near her. The psychological pictures of Catalina and her progression sibling in the restroom together and her 'displaying shoot,' joined with the genuine pictures of Catalina's groin while she was in the restroom, remained in her mind and guaranteed that Melissa was certainly not the energy everyone needs, not that it was a lot of fun in any case.

When the lunch ended up mid-evening, Catalina again needed to follow the Jenkins family back to their home to get her heading. Stan's demand at some tea implied that they remained an additional, prior hour getting back.

The strain of expenditure the majority of Sunday with their child's super controlling strict monstrosity sweetheart and her comparative family, the decrepit patriarch of the Jenkins family and his moronic gold-digger sweetheart was sufficient to guarantee that Warren and Fran opened a jug of wine at supper, and enjoyed a glass or two too much.

Time was slipping away into the evening when Fran saw a remedy bottle on a table. She got it and murmured as she read the mark resoundingly, "Stan Jenkins, for the help of angina." She went to her better half. "Warren, your dad will require his drug."

Warren went to his twin child and little girl. "Do you feel like a drive to your granddad's home?"

"OK, Dad," said Seth. He drove out to his granddad's home, Melissa in the front seat. Maneuvering into the carport and stopping, Seth and Melissa approached the front entryway, and Melissa rang the ringer, the sibling and sister hearing the tolls.

Anticipating that the tall blonde figure of Catalina should reply to the door, Melissa and Seth were stunned when rather the entryway was opened by a tall and gorgeous redhead. The young lady's long braids hung down free behind her, and her thin body with enormous breasts was attired in a blue football shirt, her shapely legs and feet exposed. Seth had not seen her previously, yet straight away, Melissa perceived the young lady as the one from the shopping center on Saturday who had been with Catalina and Stan.

The young lady took a gander at the teens, her pretentious outward appearance unpleasant, just like her discourteous hello. "Indeed, would I be able to help both of you?" The young lady's pronunciation was particularly Midwestern. However, her tone was far more complex than Catalina's juvenile voice.

"I'm Melissa, and this is Seth, and we're Stan's grandkids ..."

"Gracious indeed, I've seen your photos; I remember you presently," said the young lady contemptuously.

Catalina's voice was perceptible before she could say any more and affirmed Melissa's speculation that this baffling redhead was Catalina's companion she had talked about previously. "Vanessa, would somebody say somebody is at the front entryway?"

Vanessa feigned exacerbation, which was a strange unadulterated green. "No, Catalina, I rang the doorbell, opened the front entryway, and now I'm conversing with myself."

Catalina showed up in from another entryway, her long, light hair-free. Like Vanessa, she wore a larger than usual tee-shirt – Catalina's pink shirt appearing differently about Vanessa's blue shirt - and her legs and feet were uncovered, Catalina's sufficient youthful breasts rounding out the front of her nightwear.

"Goodness greetings Seth, howdy Melissa, what are you both doing here?" Catalina asked as she joined Vanessa at the front entryway.

"Grandpa failed to remember his heart prescription," said Melissa, holding up the little white container. "We were simply bringing it back if he needs it."

"Why, thank you," said Catalina. She opened the front entryway and took the jug, yet pondered the mark. "I don't think this is Stan's drug; it's for someone called Angie."

"Angina!" Seth, Melissa, and Vanessa adjusted the blonde all the while, every one of them showing restlessness in their voices.

"Who's Angina?" Catalina needed to know.

"Catalina, angina is an ailment, a heart condition," Melissa clarified. "Grandpa has it."

"Gracious," said Catalina. "I didn't realize that."

"Where is Grandpa?" Seth inquired.

"He's hit the hay," said Catalina. "He had his supper, watched the news, and was worn out, so he went higher up and nodded off. Anyway, you haven't met Vanessa previously?"

"Consider it Catalina; this is the first occasion when I've been anyplace simultaneously as them," Vanessa called attention to.

"Well, Melissa and Seth, Vanessa is my dearest companion perpetually," said Catalina.

"Dearest companion perpetually?" asked Vanessa disparagingly. "That sounds stupid; no one except for you will at any point say that, Catalina." She went to the teens. " Catalina is my dearest companion. Here and there, I can't help thinking about why, however, she is."

"Vanessa is remaining over for a couple of days," said Catalina.

"I don't have a lot of decision," said Vanessa to Seth and Melissa. "My flatmate Lisa, her beau Paul is on leave from the Navy for a week, and when Lisa and Paul are fraternizing, I can't get any rest whatsoever."

"Lisa and Paul have loads of uproarious sex together, and it keeps Vanessa conscious throughout the evening," Catalina exclaimed.

"Indeed, thank you, Catalina; I think they previously worked that out for themselves," said Vanessa. "No doubt, I figured Lisa and Paul could utilize some time alone together, so I approached stay with Catalina for a couple of days."

Vanessa, at that point, yawned and took a gander at the clock. "Is that the time? I suppose both of you would do well to return home; you have school toward the beginning of the day." With that, Vanessa unexpectedly and inconsiderately shut the entryway shut on the young people, yet it was not quick enough to keep Melissa from seeing Catalina gazing at

Vanessa. Given Catalina's absence of insight, the young lady regularly would stare with an empty articulation. However, the look she was giving Vanessa was a significantly odd one, her eyes wide and fantastic.

Seth and Melissa got into the vehicle, and as Seth began the start, he went to his sister and said, "Did you see that Kelly and Vanessa have precisely the same shading hair and skin?"

Melissa carried her eyes out the vehicle window. Her sibling utilized any pardon to bring Kelly into any discussion. Yet, as far as possible home, and after heading to sleep, all Melissa could consider was Vanessa's appearance on the scene. Unfit to rest, the teen got up and gotten the book she should peruse for English, and awkward under the covers, she lay on top of the bed on her stomach wearing a larger than usual tee-shirt over white underwear, swinging her bare feet back and forward as she attempted to peruse, yet just finished a passage or something like that.

Consuming the young lady's brain was Vanessa. The new introduction onto the scene no uncertainty was a bitch, given how inconsiderate and wry she had been not exclusively to Melissa and Seth however Catalina, even thoughMelissa imagined investing such a lot of energy with Catalina, and her stupid inquiries would drive anyone up the wall.

It was difficult to miss that Vanessa was the predominant, more clever, powerful, and streetwise pair than Catalina. Vanessa was presumably simply one more vulture that moved in to take care of like her inept companion. Given her overbearing character, it could just prompt more difficulty and a different channel of her granddad's cash. Melissa's brain continued thinking about the odd dynamic of Catalina and Vanessa. However, the young lady surrendered that given the restricted measure of time, she had needed to notice them because of Vanessa needing to dispose of her and Seth as fast as could be expected, that she could be envisioning things.

*

Melissa was not by any means the only high school young lady contemplating a secret that evening. A suburb or so away, Kelly had put on her pink nightwear and stooped shoelessly close to her bed to say her supplications. Taking the underwear she had been wearing that day, Kelly went to place them into her hamper yet held back as she saw the white undies with violets she had set in the hamper that morning were not in the correct position. Kelly consistently positioned all her garments, including her undies, into the hamper flawlessly, not scrunched up like this underwear were.

Venturing into the hamper, Kelly fixed her white underwear with the purple violets and set the white undies she had changed out of to head to sleep perfectly on top of them. Swinging her exposed feet under the covers and killing the light, the beautiful red-haired young person considered on the off chance that she had truly been so untidy as to throw her well-used undies into the hamper that way simply.

*

Monday brought one more fine radiant Chicago day that was unexpectedly warm for April. Melissa dressed for a secondary school in a lightweight light blue sweater, a short naval force blue creased skirt, and a white tee-shirt. Melissa wore white tennis shoes and white lower leg socks on her feet, and her hair was tied back flawlessly in a pigtail with a blue scrunchie.

Large numbers of the seniors had the last period free in the early evening, and Melissa was among them. Gretchen was driving her more youthful cousin to a dental arrangement while Seth and Kelly were getting ready for an evening of clasping hands while gazing into one another's eyes, so Melissa advanced home to an unfilled house, her folks at work and Josh at childcare.

While strolling to the house, Melissa saw that the plant beds that developed near the carport were getting dry because of the surprisingly warm spring climate of late. She recovered her Walkman from inside alongside a watering can, and keeping in mind that tuning in to music, set to work watering the plants.

Melissa, in her music, was so retained as she watered the remainder of the plants nearest to the carport that she neglected to hear the commotion of a vehicle move toward their carport at extraordinary speed while in some unacceptable stuff. It was just when the young person cast a casual look towards the street as she strolled before the carport entryway that she saw the auto went directly toward her at speed. Her beautiful earthy-colored eyes loaded up with ghastliness, her heart dashing and the stun sending floods of adrenaline through her body, Melissa flung herself aside, her dull blue creased skirt flying up flaunting her white swimsuit style underwear with blossoms of different various styles and shadings as she went rambling.

Melissa prepared herself for the sound of the vehicle colliding with the carport entryway at speed, however rather, the brakes screeched as it shrieked to an end simply an inch from the entryway and sat over-firing up. In nervous sweat and her heart beating in her chest, Melissa got to her feet, breathing vigorously. On temperamental legs, her mind began to clear; Melissa had no trouble perceiving her granddad's vehicle or her granddad in the driver's seat. Smoothing down her skirt and eliminating her earphones, Melissa was thankful that she had been to the restroom not long before leaving school. Else, she would have endured a most humiliating destiny. She additionally pondered about how long her close shave from being squashed to the death against the carport had removed her life and thought that by around 2020, Seth and Josh would allude to her as their late sister or would tell individuals they met that they once had a sister called Melissa, yet she had passed on youthful.

Neglectful of how he had almost executed one of his granddaughters, Stan killed the vehicle's start and stumbled out of the entryway. He took a gander at Melissa and gave her an amicable wave. "Hey, Fran."

"Melissa," the young lady reminded her granddad.

Stan's face took on a confounded demeanor. "No, you're Fran, my child Warren's better half, the beautiful Italian young lady. Melissa's your girl; she's a young child. It was her and her sibling's fourth birthday celebration a few days ago. Mary made her another dress, and we as a whole took the two children to that new Sears Tower working for the afternoon."

Straight away, Melissa realized her granddad was on one of his outings back to the past. The day he portrayed did for sure match her restricted recollections of her and Seth's fourth birthday celebration; however, this was over 14 years prior. Given that Melissa appeared as though her mom was more youthful, no uncertainty added to the older adult's disarray. "Thus, what are you doing here?" she inquired.

"Have you seen Mary?" Stan inquired. "She went to the store toward the beginning of today. However, she hasn't returned yet, and I'm beginning to get stressed. I figured she might have halted by here. I went to see our companions Fred and Doris to check whether Mary was there. However, they probably moved without advising me because Japanese family was living there now."

Not interestingly, Melissa felt a sense of foreboding deep in her soul at the trouble of her granddad glancing around to no end for her late grandma. Also, the companions Fred and Doris that Stan had talked about had kicked the bucket a couple of months after Mary had. Gulping hard to forestall tears welling in her eyes and running down her face, Melissa's misery went to outrage.

Her dad had particularly revealed to Catalina not to allow her granddad to drive, and only five days after the fact, he had turned up driving his vehicle, totally bewildered. He had almost dispatched Melissa to an early grave or life in a wheelchair, and the young lady hated to think what ruin her granddad had made on the streets here. She half anticipated that a police car should move toward the carport, yet luckily one didn't. The solitary thing Melissa was appreciative of was that in any event, her granddad had turned up here and not at a dangerous skyscraper lodging project like Cabrini Green or one of the ghetto neighborhoods in South Chicago. Not exclusively was Catalina moronic, yet she was untrustworthy as well.

"So Fran, Mary hasn't been by here by any stretch of the imagination?" Stan needed to know.

Melissa was never certain whether it was smarter to cooperate with her granddad when he was this way or address him, yet settled on the previous choice given how confounded he was. "You realize, Dad, I figure Mom may have effectively gotten back and been pondering where you are," said Melissa. "For what reason don't I drive you home at this point?"

"Much obliged Fran; however, I'll be alright to drive," said Stan.

"Indeed, yet you drive such a lot of that I figured you might get a kick out of the chance to be driven for a change," Melissa proposed.

"Alright, says thanks to Fran," said Stan, giving Melissa the keys and getting into the traveler's side, his granddaughter into the driver's seat. Melissa was not excessively acquainted with driving a vehicle with a stick-move. However, she figured out how to drive the manual vehicle more ably than her granddad, not that this was an extraordinary accomplishment.

"Shouldn't something be said about your children?" Stan inquired. "They're not at home alone, right?"

"Goodness, Seth, and Melissa are having a play date with their companion, Gretchen," said Melissa nonchalantly.

"That is acceptable," said Stan. "Before it slips my mind, two young ladies are remaining at our home right now, one a blonde and the other a redhead. Mary more likely than not welcomed them to remain; I believe they're her sister's girls. Time passes quickly; they've grown up to such an extent."

Melissa's disturbance at the unreliable Catalina developed as her granddad's home became visible. Presumably, Catalina and her companion Vanessa had been out going through much a greater amount of Stan's cash and left the older man with admittance to his keys and vehicle. The youngster trusted they were back, as she was in a state of mind to go up against the two young ladies, and there was no chance she was going easy. Melissa pulled her granddad's vehicle to a stop in the carport, left the car, and hammered the entryway shut.

Stan escaped the traveler's side and took a gander at the yard, which was perfect and had been cut inside the most recent week. Notwithstanding, Stan didn't view it as such. "Take a gander at how congested the grass is!" he shouted. "I would do well to deal with it, I have work tomorrow, and I will not have time."

"It's fine," Melissa guaranteed her granddad, yet the elderly person was not going to tune in to his granddaughter and made for the carport and recovered an old manual push-style lawnmower that he had bought during the 1940s.

It had no edges and was corroded and ought to have been discarded years prior, yet Stan had no understanding of this. He pushed the cutter onto the grass and started to push it to and fro, meanwhile making lawnmower commotions, "Brush, brush, brush, brush, brush!"

A woman across the road looked across at the uproar and shook her head at seeing the older man across the street acting insane as common and returned inside. Leaving her granddad to his uproarious imagine grass cutting, Melissa strolled to the front entryway. She was going to ring the chime yet saw the entrance had been left unlatched. Melissa shook her head. Ordinary Catalina, anybody might have strolled in. Without ringing the chime or thumping, Melissa chose to stroll in to make her statement to Catalina about going out opened.

It wasn't long until Catalina came into Melissa's view when she rose out of the lounge room, the tall blonde shoeless and wearing a dark tee-shirt and super short dark small scale skirt. Catalina was in her very own universe and didn't see the more youthful young lady by any means.

"Hi Catalina," Melissa called out.
Not anticipating that anyone should be there terrified Catalina, the young lady shouting in stun and pivoting to see the dainty figure of Melissa remaining there, the youngster remaining with her arms crossed.

"Melissa, what are you doing there? You terrified me," said Catalina, tapping her chest.

"Great, since I got the fear of my life not exactly 30 minutes prior," said Melissa.

Catalina, as a regular, was puzzled. "So you came here and frightened me? You know, it's not extremely considerate to give yourself access to another person's home without thumping or ringing the chime, Melissa."

"But it isn't your home, is it Catalina? It's my grandpa's home. What's more, I wouldn't have had the option to get inside if you had bolted the entryway like you ought to have done. You're fortunate it was me; it might have been anybody. However, in particular, I wouldn't be here at all on the off chance that you would assume some liability for once in your life."

Catalina stood astounded by the furious young person. She could just handle each thing in turn gradually, and Melissa had tossed a considerable amount of data at her that she was unable to measure effectively. In the house's calm, the weak sound of someone propelling the tissue move inside the ground floor washroom was perceptible. The restroom flushed, and the taps ran, and Vanessa arose wearing a white tee-shirt and changing her corrosive wash denim pants, her feet exposed like Catalina's feet.

"Catalina, what's happening around here?" came her disturbed voice. "Wouldn't I be able to try and sit in the restroom and take a crap in harmony and calm ..."

Vanessa's voice followed off as she saw the angry Melissa remaining there. "What's Melissa doing here?"

"I'm here because I almost got murdered when my granddad drove his vehicle into our carport and almost squashed me against the carport," spat Melissa. "I wet myself."

"Ew!" shouted Catalina. "Melissa, would you say you aren't somewhat old to in any case be peeing yourself?"

Before Melissa could say anything, Vanessa said fretfully, "Catalina, she didn't wet herself. She said 'for all intents and purposes,' if she'd wet herself, she would have said 'in a real sense,' wouldn't she?"

Catalina thought for a couple of moments. "Don't know," she advertised.

Vanessa gazed Melissa upward and down. "You seem as though you're having a terrible day. What's the matter child, you got your period or something?"

Melissa's thin body fumed with rage. "No, I don't." She went to Catalina. "I'm irate because you let Grandpa out and about in his vehicle. You were advised a few evenings ago not to allow him to drive. Didn't you remove his keys?"

"Better believe it," said Catalina.

"So, how did you manage them?"

"I put them in Stan's bedside cabinet."

Melissa raged. "Furthermore, you didn't believe that he may get them out and use them?"

Catalina shrugged. "Thus, he returned like he generally did, and there was no damage done."

"Aside from me almost getting run over? Also, it's fortunate that it was me there; it might have been my younger sibling. Furthermore, at some point, if he continues driving, he will cause an intense mishap, and someone will get executed."

"Well, you've truly got your underwear in a pack," said Vanessa, her chuckle like she thought this a major joke driving Melissa insane considerably more. "That searing European temper of yours is coming through."

Catalina shouted out. "Vanessa, Melissa isn't European. Her Mom's family is Italian."

Melissa gritted her teeth, and Vanessa put her hand on her brow, shaking her head. It was Vanessa who shouted out first. "It seems like you have a genuine issue, Melissa, so why not simply come out and say anything you desire to say?"

The more youthful young lady saw no reason for keeping down. "Catalina, what are you doing here with my Grandpa? He's an old and debilitated man. At the point when he showed up at my folks' home, he was searching for Grandma, and she's been gone more than two years now. Presently, he's externally claiming to trim the grass. Furthermore, Grandpa will not be with us, especially more."

Once more, Catalina's beautiful face showed disarray. "Where's he going?"

"I mean he will pass on!" spat Melissa. "Catalina, don't you have any feeling of disgrace? Would you be here if Grandpa had ten dollars to his name? All the stuff you get him to purchase ..."

Melissa raged into the parlor, the two more seasoned young ladies following. "Like the enormous TV here." She pointed at the huge, costly TV.

"Is there any valid reason why we shouldn't have decent things?" Catalina inquired. "Stan likes the new TV."

"Grandpa doesn't comprehend TV any longer," said Melissa. Her lovely earthy colored eyes spied something on the table – a traffic encroachment gave to a Miss Vanessa Doyle, a check for the sake of Stan Jenkins connected to it. Melissa got the two records. "What's more, I wouldn't call this something decent."

Melissa saw her granddad out the front windows, still in his very own universe claiming to trim the grass. She turned around to Catalina. "Catalina, you're an alluring young lady. If you need cash without finding a new line of work like typical individuals, why not discover some elitist and be his prize sweetheart, all things being equal? What might you share practically speaking with my granddad? Do you know when he was conceived?"

"Last Wednesday?" proposed Catalina. "You came here, recollect?"

"Indeed, to praise his birthday, not that there was a lot to celebrate," said Melissa. "No, he was brought into the world on the 10th of April 1912. Do you know what else happened that day? The Titanic set sail on its launch."

Catalina thought for a couple of moments. "In any case, the Titanic wasn't genuine."

Melissa was utilized to Catalina's moronic assertions, yet this was another one in any event for her. "Indeed, it was."

"No, it was in a film I saw once. Films aren't genuine; they're just pretending."

"It was a film about the Titanic. There's been a considerable amount of films made about the Titanic, and they may even make much more motion pictures about it. In any case, the

Titanic was an open boat, and it sank on April 15, 1912 – 79 years before the day. Grandpa was a multi-day-old child when it occurred."

Melissa could see that Catalina didn't trust her, and Melissa took Vanessa's gander for help. However, Vanessa appeared to be too interested to even think about interposing. "Try not to take a gander at me; this is all information to me," she said egotistically.

"I'm befuddled, so was Stan on the Titanic?" asked Catalina.

"Not," snapped Melissa restlessly, wanting to be on the real Titanic so frigid water would stop this discussion. "Catalina, do you realize who was President when Grandpa was conceived?"

Catalina considered the big picture. "Abraham Lincoln?"

"No, William Taft," said Melissa, getting significantly more disturbed by the presence of the grinning Vanessa.

"I've never known about him," said Catalina.

"So I assembled," said Melissa. "Furthermore, when Grandpa was conceived, George V was the King of England."

Catalina chuckled. "You're not tricking me. I realize that England has a Queen, not a King."

"They have a Queen currently, yet back in 1912, they had a King," seethed Melissa.

Catalina again looked distracted, thinking about her next question progressively before saying, "I've confounded again, so for what reason would you say you are discussing the Titanic and this genuine old King and President I've won't ever know about?"

"I was utilizing them as guides to show how old Grandpa is and how you could share nothing for all intents and purpose, yet that didn't work," said Melissa. "Allow me to put it another way when Grandpa was conceived, the Chicago Cubs' World Series dry spell was just four years of age."

"Haven't the Cubs won the World Series since ..." Catalina attempted to work out which year was four years before 1912, yet couldn't do as such.

"Since 1908," Melissa said.

"Truly, I thought they won it a couple of years prior?" asked Catalina.

"No, they haven't won it for a very long time."

"At the point when will they next win it?" Catalina needed to know.

"In 2016," said Melissa snidely, picking that future year at arbitrary.

"Truly?"

"How could I know?" Melissa snapped, her terrible humor not improved by Vanessa's priggish sniggering.

"You get how life resembles for me presently, don't you?" Vanessa asked Melissa. "Now and then, it resembles I have my pet dodo bird."

"Aren't dodo birds wiped out?" Catalina inquired.

"Not every one of them," said Vanessa.

Catalina, as normal, missed the mockery. "Gracious, that is acceptable. I'd love to see a dodo flying around."

"I'm composing a book, you know," said Vanessa to Melissa. "It's a book pretty much every one of the imbecilic things Catalina says and does. Up until this point, it's more extended than War and Peace."

"Is War and Peace like a reference book or something?" Catalina inquired.

Melissa could see the discussion had well, run off the tracks, and quickly come to her meaningful conclusion to Catalina and Vanessa. "Wouldn't you be able to see that you being here doesn't help Grandpa by any stretch of the imagination? He doesn't have the foggiest idea who is dead and who is alive most days. He thought I was my mom before. He should be in a protected where individuals deal with him appropriately. The exact opposite thing he needs is to live with you, Catalina."

"Amazing, don't gloss over it, Melissa," said Vanessa.

"I'm glossing over it," said Melissa. "Both of you vultures need to proceed to discover another person to use as your feast ticket. Simply let my Grandpa be, alright."

"I probably won't have been in the keen classes in school, yet I know a certain something, and that will be that there is not anything you can do about it," said Catalina.

"Indeed, yet I can disclose to you how wiped out and messed up I think this is, Catalina," said Melissa. "Helpless Grandpa thinks Grandma is as yet alive, and afterward you get into bed with him for um, relations ..." She shivered. "I don't prefer to consider everything." A magazine grabbed Melissa's attention lying on the table – a magazine that one matured under 18 couldn't buy. She opened the magazine to the pictorial of an alluring youthful African-American model expressly exhibiting that individuals of color have dazzling pink vaginas and held it up for the two more seasoned young ladies to see. "What's more, you purchase porn for him to peruse? Do you know how this rottenness deals with his mind?"

"You understand what I see?" Vanessa inquired.

"No, what do you see, Vanessa?" Melissa snapped back.

"I see a minimal fraudulent lesbian who is upon her ego trip when she doesn't have the foggiest idea about the real factors," said Vanessa. "You say the magazine is rottenness, yet if you glanced through that, your undies would be doused through in under a moment."

Melissa held back, her skin burning hot. "What?" she stammered. "That is absurd; I'm not a – well, one of those ladies."

"You can deny it all you like," said Vanessa. "However, the proof says something else."

"What proof?" asked Melissa.

"That you generally look into my skirt and smell my underwear whenever you get an opportunity," said Catalina. "Furthermore, it's not simply me; I realize you do it to your sibling's sweetheart Kelly as well."

"That is strange, Catalina," said Melissa. "I don't need to tune in to these untruths."

"I've seen you doing it," said Catalina. "At the point when you came over for Easter, you slipped away, and I saw you getting my undies out of the hamper and smelling the seat. What's more, yesterday, when I went higher up to go to the washroom, I saw your appearance in a mirror when you were in Kelly's room. I realize that you got a couple of Kelly's underwear – the white undies with violets on them – out of her clothing hamper and were smelling them."

"How could you know Kelly's undies were white with violets on them?" Melissa inquired.

"Furthermore, how would you understand what your sibling's better half's underwear resembled?" asked Vanessa.

Melissa held back, realizing that she had talked herself into a corner. She realized she could outsmart Catalina – this wasn't troublesome as a sheep or a turkey could outmaneuver Catalina – yet the more streetwise Vanessa had come through and conveyed checkmate. "I didn't, Catalina said they were ..." Melissa stammered before Vanessa put her finger over Melissa's lips to stop her talking.

"I think you would do well to come higher up with us so you can perceive how things truly work around here," said Vanessa.

Her heart hustling, Melissa followed Vanessa and Catalina higher up, and surprisingly, however apprehensive and bewildered, the more youthful young lady couldn't resist the opportunity to take a gander at the appealing bottoms of the two more established young ladies, Vanessa's through her corrosive wash pants and Catalina's through her dark little skirt.

"This is your Grandpa's room," said Catalina, showing Melissa into the room, which was as yet enriched equivalent to when Mary was alive. At that point, the three young ladies went into an adjoining room, which was all the more silly in the plan. "Furthermore, this is my room."

"You don't lay down with – um – my Grandpa at that point?" stammered Melissa.

Catalina shook her head. "No. I rest in my room. Your granddad is an exceptionally sweet man, and I'll kiss him goodnight or give him an embrace; however, that is it."

"You don't ..." asked Melissa.

"No, one since he's such a ton more established than me, two since he's not alright to be keen on such a thing, and three ..." Catalina's voice followed off, and she laughed apprehensively.

"What's three?" Melissa inquired.

"Since regardless of whether your Grandpa was so fit and attractive like he was in that huge conflict back in like the 1940s – was it the First or Second World War – I can easily forget – I wouldn't have any desire to um, do it with him."

"You wouldn't?" asked Melissa.

"Good gracious," said Catalina. "There's just a single individual in your family who I need to do it with."

"Also, who may that be?" Melissa inquired.

Catalina laughed. "You obviously, senseless."

Melissa's head was turning like she was on a thrill ride. "Me! Thus, you're a – um – one of, no, you can't be ..."

"A lesbian, you can say it," said Vanessa. "Catalina's a lesbian, I'm a lesbian, and you're a lesbian. I think three lesbians together can say the word lesbian. That magazine first floor – it's not your granddad's – it's our own."

Melissa recalled the earlier evening and the odd unique she had seen among Catalina and Vanessa the last night presently appeared well and good. "So you're more than companions?"

Vanessa gestured. "Gracious better believe it. The previous evening, I wasn't too upbeat when you and Seth turned up so late because Catalina and I were going to - all things considered, you know."

"We were going to hit the hay to have intercourse," said Catalina in her piercing voice.

"Much obliged to you, Catalina, I think she got it," said Vanessa. "In any case, each opportunity I come here, I take a gander at your photographs, similar to you one at Christmas, and I get so wet in my underwear."

"Vanessa implies her vagina gets all wet and tacky because you turn her on, not because she pees her jeans," Catalina chipped in.

"Once more, thank you, Catalina," said Vanessa snidely. "I think she got that and didn't accept I circumvent pissing my jeans the entire day."

"So how long have you been ..." Melissa started.

"Screwing one another?" Vanessa completed the sentence for her. The beautiful redhead chuckled. "Two or three years. We met at that honorable man's club where Catalina worked as a mixed drink server."

"Vanessa works there; she's a sensual artist," said Catalina.

"I'm a fascinating artist," moaned Vanessa. "How often do I need to advise you?" She turned around to Melissa. "Even though Catalina is directly in one sense, it is likely more sexual than outlandish."

"Pause, you're a lesbian; however you dance at a strip club – for men?" the confounded Melissa inquired.

"Better believe it, truth be told," said Vanessa. "It may appear to be bizarre, yet I love prodding the dumb folks and deviants who go to the club, realizing that there's nothing left but to look except for never contact, making them believe that I need to screw them when the prospect of screwing them causes me to feel debilitated. Yet, the best thing is I met Catalina. I'll always remember the day I was on the stage and saw this one misunderstanding orders, neglecting to serve a few tables, spilling drinks, stumbling over, and not having the option to check out fundamental change."

"Hello, I wasn't unreasonably awful," Catalina dissented.

"Indeed, you were," Vanessa stated. "In any case, hello, I wasn't griping since you're acceptable at different things, similar to this."

Vanessa brought down her beautiful face into Catalina's lovely face, and Melissa observed wide-peered toward as the redhead and the blondie traded a deep, enthusiastic French kiss, their lips interlocking as their hands wandered everywhere on one another. Between her legs, Melissa's clitoris shivered in hunger, and she felt her undies saddle hose as her vagina got wet.

The two more established young ladies opened their lips and went to Melissa. "Thus, you need any more verification?" Vanessa inquired.

"No," Melissa shook her head.

"You understand what we like considerably more than engaging in sexual relations with one another?" Vanessa inquired.

"No." Once more, Melissa shook her head.

"Having intercourse with another young lady who turns us on as you do," said Catalina. "You generally get me so hot. I realize you like to look into my skirt and smell my underwear. Also, I generally do likewise with you. On Sunday, you were wearing apricot-shaded undies. What's more, when Stan and I came over half a month prior, you'd been wearing the undies that humiliate you most, the huge beige-shaded full concise underwear. They smelled pretty wonderful, however."

Melissa becomes flushed. "It was clothing day; I was coming up short on clothing ..."

"Regardless of what kind of undies you were wearing, Melissa, the one thing I realize I would need to do is to get into them," said Vanessa. "At the point when Catalina previously said she thought Stan's granddaughter was a lesbian, from the outset, I was dubious. As you probably are aware, Catalina isn't the sharpest tool in the shed, and you must be mindful to ensure that she has it right."

"Hello, it's not ideal to say that I'm imbecilic like that," Catalina dissented. "I'm here."

"Catalina, would you be able to try and spell the word 'moronic'?" Vanessa asked her companion.

"Obviously," said Catalina. "D-U-M – imbecilic!"

Vanessa shook her head. "Catalina, would you say you are certain your mom didn't take Thalidomide when she was pregnant with you?"

Catalina considered everything for a couple of seconds. "No, I don't think so. Mother said she had nicotine desires when she was pregnant with me, so she smoked two bundles of cigarettes daily rather than her standard one parcel. Do you feel that is the reason I had truly downright terrible when I was a young lady?"

"That clarifies a ton, and not simply your asthma. I'm simply happy your Mom was just pregnant once; delivering a few Catalina's would be a lot for the world to deal with," said Vanessa. "In any case, were right? Indeed, Catalina said you were a lesbian, and I was pessimistic from the start; however, when she said more, I realized that she had it right for once. And afterward, I saw your photograph, and I realized that I needed to get into bed with you and Catalina and the two of us to screw your adorable little ass off."

Melissa felt Vanessa's hand on the trim of her short creased skirt going up to brush the cotton of her undies, and soon this was joined by Catalina's hand.

"So what about it, Melissa?" Vanessa tested. "You need to would what you like to do most throughout everyday life and get into bed with Catalina and me, and we rock your reality and make you flood like a stream, or you need to spend the remainder of your life wishing you had?"

Inside her bra, Melissa's areolas shivered and were rock hard; inside her underwear, her clitoris was sending floods of delight through her container and getting her actual moist, and inside her body, her heart was hustling, and her adrenaline is siphoning. On anxious legs, the youngster strolled to the bed and sat on the edge, opening her legs to permit the young ladies to see up her skirt and her fancy white underwear.

Vanessa grinned. "Shrewd young lady."

Catalina and Vanessa proceeded to sit on each side of Melissa, and Catalina came up and eliminated Melissa's scrunchie and unfastened her braid. Hence, her lovely dull hair was free and outlined her beautiful face. The young person's huge earthy-colored eyes took a gander at the two more established young ladies, nerves apparent. "I've never done this," said Melissa in a bit of voice.

"Try not to stress; we'll show you," said Catalina.
Melissa's shaking hands went to eliminate her sweater, yet Vanessa halted her. "Allow us to do that for you," she said as she stroked Melissa's face with delicate fingertips.

Vanessa went to one side foot and Catalina to her correct foot and loosened her perfect white shoes, leaving her in her white cotton lower leg socks, before taking off one sock each out, leaving Melissa shoeless the two more established young ladies.

"You have such lovely, petite feet," Vanessa noticed, her hands stroking and touching Melissa's left foot, Catalina her correct foot. Melissa wriggled on the bed, the sensitive young person's toes twisting and uncurling at the two more seasoned young ladies' superb delicate bit.

Vanessa and Catalina moved their hands from Melissa's exposed feet. Vanessa eliminated the teen's sweater and Catalina her tee-shirt, leaving Melissa wearing just her bra on her top half. Eliminating Melissa's short naval force blue creased skirt was a collective endeavor, Melissa taking her base off the bed and Vanessa and Catalina loosening and eliminating the skirt. Presently Melissa's nubile youthful body was clad just in a white bra and white undies with pretty blossoms on at that point.

"Your underwear is so lovely, Melissa, with each one of those blossoms," spouted Catalina, her hands everywhere on the delicate cotton of Melissa's undies, her touch making the more youthful young lady wriggle as her clitoris reacted.

"They sure are," Vanessa concurred, joining Catalina in caressing Melissa's underwear. The lovely redhead followed an example around a pink rose on the front board. "However, I bet your underwear covers the best bloom of all," she added interestingly, Melissa feeling Vanessa pull marginally on her pubic hair through her undies.

Vanessa and Catalina ran their hands up Melissa's flawless olive skin to her breasts and the two more established young ladies burned through no time in stroking Melissa's brilliant teen tits through the texture of her bra.

"Almost certainly you're not kidding," noticed Vanessa, as her finger prodded the hard areola of Melissa's right breast through her bra.

"It's that undeniable, is it?" asked Melissa with a chuckle.

"Gracious better believe it, she's turned on okay," screeched Catalina as she stroked Melissa's left breast.

"OK, presently it's your chance to strip us down to our bras and our undies," said Vanessa, she and Catalina eliminating their hands from Melissa's firm, youthful boobs and standing shoeless before her.

Melissa got to her feet and her hands, shaking with hunger, fully expecting stripping two appealing young ladies, went first to Vanessa's white tee-shirt, Melissa getting wetter and wetter as the clothing article was eliminated and Vanessa's enormous boobs clad in a white bra came into focus.

Presently the ball was in Catalina's court. Melissa eliminated the lovely blonde's dark tee-shirt, leaving her wearing a pastel pink bra on her top, a large portion of Catalina's enormous tits filling the cups.

Melissa's hands moved to Vanessa's tight corrosive wash pants, loosening the denim article of clothing around the redhead's thin midsection and pulling the pants down, Vanessa's white cotton swimsuit style underwear with the blue abdomen and leg versatile materializing, the young lady venturing her bare feet out of the pants when they contacted her lower legs. Melissa's mouth watered as she could see the state of Vanessa's female hill and the space of her vagina at the front of her undies.

Again moving to Catalina, Melissa loosened her dark small-scale skirt and permitted it to slide down the blonde's shapely legs, Catalina venturing her exposed feet out of it when it arrived at the floor. Seeing the space of Catalina's vagina in the pastel pink cotton two-piece style undies she was wearing, the texture coordinating with that of Catalina's bra precisely made the teen get significantly more energized between her legs.

The three young ladies lay back on the bed, shoeless and in their clothing, the modest brunette Melissa in the taller blonde and redhead. Once more, Melissa felt Catalina and Vanessa's hands everywhere on her nubile youthful body. This time, she reacted by stroking Catalina and Vanessa's breasts through their bras, feeling how hard the two ladies' areolas were. Their hands moved to one another's undies, stroking each other's pubic zones through the cotton texture, Melissa adoring the vibe of feeling the space of Catalina and Vanessa's vaginas as much as when Catalina and Vanessa's fingers went to her groin and stroked the layout of her pussy through her underwear.

"You at any point kissed a young lady previously?" Vanessa asked Melissa as the three young ladies stooped on the bed.

Melissa shook her head. "No," she said modestly.

Minus any additional provoking, Vanessa brought down her face into Melissa's face and planted a kiss all the rage. It was shallow from the start, yet soon Vanessa worked her tongue further into Melissa's mouth and the two young ladies French-kissed, the toes on their exposed feet twisting and uncurling at the sensation, their vaginas getting wetter and more energized. Vanessa put her arms around the teen, stroking Melissa all over her back, tinkering with the catch of her bra, and foundling the cheeks of her base through her underwear.

Melissa reacted by doing likewise, adoring the delicate sensation of Vanessa's light complexion, the non-abrasiveness of her undies, and the state of the more established young lady's firm base.

Catalina's beautiful face showed charm at seeing the two different young ladies making out. "That is so hot!" the shoeless blonde screeched. She sat on the bed close to them with her legs wide separated, the state of her vagina apparent in the twofold cotton saddle.

Slipping one of her fingers under her undies saddle, Catalina started to stroke off her pussy, the young lady groaning and wriggling with her exposed toes holding and unclenching.

Vanessa and Melissa completed French-kissing and opened their lips. "You've kissed another young lady now," Vanessa reported victoriously.

" I sure did," said Melissa, actually feeling dazed.

Catalina removed her finger from her underwear and pussy. "Furthermore, you will kiss another," she reported.

The tall blonde and the dainty brunette embraced and kissed. Like Vanessa had done, Catalina kissed Melissa on the lips from the start before the two young ladies started to French-kiss all the more profoundly, their hands wandering everywhere on one another. Her tongue interlaced with Catalina's, Melissa felt the more seasoned young lady's hand everywhere on her underwear-covered base, and Melissa immediately moved her hands to Catalina's base, feeling the blonde's bum through her undies.

"Those aren't your solitary lips that we will kiss today," Vanessa guaranteed the teen, Melissa feeling her vagina shiver in expectation as she and Catalina opened their mouths. Melissa came to behind herself to unclasp her bra, yet Vanessa halted her. "One moment, we'll do that for you."

"We need to accomplish something different first," said Catalina, chuckling in expectation.

"What's that?" Melissa asked, her heart vacillating in energy.

"You like underwear," said Vanessa. "Think about what we do as well. You look so adorable in those elegant little undies of yours, and we need to appreciate them however much we can. Here's a sample of what we need to do to you."

Her huge earthy-colored eyes wide, Melissa looked as Vanessa and Catalina got into a similar position. The two Sapphic darlings would have gotten into on the off chance that they would have intercourse in the 69-position, Catalina lying on the base, Vanessa on the top. Catalina opened her legs wide, and Vanessa put her head into Catalina's undies-covered groin, and a similar time bringing down her undies-covered pussy into Catalina's face.

Melissa looked as the two young ladies smelled each other's underwear, at that point kissed and licked at the cotton, Catalina and Vanessa getting a charge out of giving the more youthful young lady this exhibition. Following a moment or so, they escaped this position, and Vanessa said to Melissa, "It's your turn now."

Catalina and Vanessa guided Melissa down, so she was lying level on her back and tested her sanity separated. She could see Catalina's blue eyes and Vanessa's green eyes gazing at her undies, and it made the youngster hot in her pussy, this lone expanding as Vanessa brought down her face into her groin, breathing in the smell of Melissa's vagina through her underwear.

"You smell so wonderful down there," Vanessa remarked as her noses retained Melissa's ladylike smell.

Catalina put her face into Melissa's pussy, smelling the youngster between her legs, cherishing the smelly, private, female fragrance of pussy on the more youthful young lady's underwear. "She smells pleasant," Catalina concurred. "She possesses an aroma like pussy."

"What else do you believe she will resemble between her legs?" Vanessa brought up her imbecilic companion.

Melissa wriggled in charm as Catalina kissed the seat of her underwear, the lovely blonde's tongue navigating the delicate flower cotton that covered her vagina. At that point, Vanessa set her head back between the youngster's legs and, like Catalina had done, licked her vulva through her beautiful little undies.

Vanessa removed her head from Melissa's groin and the magnificent appealing ladylike scents the young lady's vagina was making with some hesitance. Melissa went to sit up. However, Vanessa halted her. "We know how you love the smell of undies, so we have a genuine treat for you.

Vanessa remained on her exposed feet and situated herself, so she was riding Melissa over her head; at that point brought down her undies covered base down into Melissa's lovely face, so the texture of her white undies was in direct contact with the young person's face. Melissa moaned in please as Vanessa's female smell filled her noses.

"Try not to be timid, kiss me, lick me through my undies," encouraged Vanessa.

Melissa required no inciting and kissed and licked Vanessa's vagina through her undies as the more seasoned young lady had finished with her, the redhead squirming with delight as Melissa's tongue pushed the cotton up into her pussy.

Vanessa hopped off Melissa with Catalina having her spot, and as Vanessa had done before, she brought down her base covered by pink underwear into Melissa's face. The smell of Vanessa's gentility was supplanted by a similar smell from Catalina's vagina.

Melissa kissed and licked the beautiful blonde's pussy through her undies as Catalina sat simply over her face with extraordinary eagerness.

When Catalina stood up, Vanessa arraigned for Melissa to sit up, and the young lady did as such, the three young ladies presently sitting all around. "Presently, it's off with your bra," said Vanessa, she and Catalina coming to behind Melissa and unclasping the young lady's bra before pulling off the piece of clothing to uncover the firm, youthful breasts that the underwear had encased, the two more established young ladies salivating in expectation at Melissa's tits.

"Presently, you and Catalina take my bra off," said Vanessa. Melissa and Catalina took one side every one of the catches of Vanessa's bra. They unfastened it, the redhead's huge and enticing breasts coming into focus as the brassiere fell away and the young ladies eliminated it inside and out.

"My turn currently," screeched Catalina, Melissa, and Vanessa unfastening and eliminating Catalina's pink bra. Melissa adored seeing Catalina's enormous, firm boobs, so enticing, so welcoming.

Presently all uncovered breasted yet at the same time wearing their underwear, the three young ladies touched and stroked each other's boobs, rubbing the firm tissue, prodding their hard areolas with sexy fingers.

"You know how you can tell we're all lesbians?" Vanessa inquired.

"No, how?" Catalina inquired.

"Short fingernails," said Vanessa, showing that she, Catalina, and Melissa kept their nails managed back.

"Please, not all young ladies with short fingernails are lesbians," snickered Melissa. "I keep mine short since it's more helpful, and I play soccer at school."

"Valid, not all ladies with short fingernails are lesbians," said Vanessa. "What's more, your explanations behind keeping your nails short are functional. However, subliminally, you do it since you realize that long nails and vaginas don't blend. Also, in particular, you need another young lady's fingers up your pussy, don't you?"

With that, Vanessa set her to give over the front of Melissa's underwear, her fingers brushing through the abundance of dim twists that covered her pubic hill and into the damp, dim regions between Melissa's legs. Navigating the lips of Melissa's high school twat, Vanessa pushed her fingers all the more profoundly into her wet vagina, Melissa wriggling at the touch to her clitoris.

"Goodness, you are so close up there!" shouted Vanessa. "Hello Catalina, come and feel this – I've never felt a tight pussy."

Catalina joined Vanessa in placing her hand into Melissa's underwear, and like Vanessa was struck how close Melissa's vagina was. "Goodness, she truly is tight!" Catalina screeched.

"Thus wet as well, it seems like you're on your period down there, Melissa," said Vanessa.

"No doubt, it does sort of," said Melissa timidly.

"I'm possibly utilizing cushions now when I have my period," Catalina remarked totally at arbitrary, leaving Vanessa and Melissa to trade a perplexed look.

"Also, for those of us in the world Earth?" Vanessa provoked her companion.

"Throughout recent months, my tampons have quite recently continued disappearing," said Catalina. "I'm certain I purchase more, however when it's that time, I can't discover any."

"Are you certain you have been getting them?" Vanessa inquired. "You're not efficient."

"Uh-huh, I have been getting them," Catalina kept up, "yet someone has been taking them. Perhaps there's an apparition in this house?"

"Indeed, because apparitions need female cleanliness items to deal with their periods Catalina, it happens constantly," said Vanessa snidely.

Melissa, actually appreciating having two alluring young ladies with their hands in her private female zone, believed it best to say nothing regarding how she realized her decrepit granddad was confusing the tampons with teabags and pointlessly endeavoring to fix himself cups of tea with them. Considering her granddad, Melissa became worried that he may return inside, however from outside, the sound of him making lawnmower commotions was as yet discernible, so they were protected in any event for the time being.

Vanessa and Catalina removed their hands from Melissa's undies, the young person's excitement expanding as the two more seasoned young ladies put their fingers in their mouths, drawing off Melissa's sticky pussy juice.

"Goodness, she tastes great!" screeched Catalina.

" I can hardly wait to lick that at its source," concurred Vanessa. She took a gander at Catalina and Melissa, a coy appearance on her lovely face. "Right, presently, it's the ideal opportunity for my underwear to fall off."

Catalina took one side of her better half's undies, Melissa the other, and gradually they pulled them down, Melissa gazing at the brilliant sight of Vanessa's perfect triangle of red pubic hair, like the pubic hair of Kelly. Catalina and Melissa slide Vanessa's underwear down her long legs and bare feet before slipping them off.

Sitting on the bed, her legs separated indecently, flaunting her grab – a pretty and dim pink vagina that had an ideal oval shape; Vanessa said, "OK Catalina, your turn now." With that, Vanessa and Melissa pulled Catalina's pink undies down her shapely legs to her beautiful uncovered feet. They left her exposed, her blonde pubic hair looking enticing to the next two young ladies.

Anticipating that Vanessa and Catalina should pull down her undies, Melissa took her back off the bed. However, Vanessa halted her. "I have a superior thought, get down on the ground."

Uncertain of what planned to happen yet energized in any case, Melissa got down on the ground, and Vanessa gave her a light slap on her undies-covered base. "Push that adorable little ass of yours uncertain," the more seasoned young lady coordinated, to which Melissa got in line.

The youngster shuddered as Catalina and Vanessa grabbed hold of her colorful white underwear and pulled them down to her thighs. The two more established young ladies pulling down her undies was the most sensual thing she had at any point felt, and as they gazed at her uncovered base, Melissa could feel herself getting wetter and wetter.

Vanessa and Catalina stroked and rubbed Melissa's exposed base's cheeks before they started kissing and licking her on her butt cheeks. Melissa couldn't abstain from snickering and wriggling as the two more established young ladies' tongues navigated her plumber's butt, licking her and messing with her delicately, here and there moving their heads lower to smell the seat of Melissa's brought down undies.

"You like that, don't you?" Vanessa inquired.

"No doubt," said Melissa.

"All things considered, you'll like this significantly more," Vanessa guaranteed. She spread the cheeks of Melissa's base more extensive still, so her ideal pink oval-formed vagina and the tight, starfish-state of her back-end were in full view.

Again, Melissa felt Catalina and Vanessa's fingers on her vulva, driving profound into the tight, soggy bounds of her pussy.

"So close, so close," Vanessa noticed again. "All in all, I take it the lone things that have gone up there are fingers and tampons?"

"Something to that effect," said Melissa.

"Furthermore, I bet it's considerably tighter up here," said Vanessa. Melissa felt Vanessa's pointer move from her vagina to the delicate skin that isolated her vulva from her back-end until it was straightforwardly on her butt-centric opening. Melissa felt Vanessa's finger surrounding her back-end for a couple of seconds; at that point, the youngster wheezed as Vanessa squeezed her finger profound into her rectum.

Melissa gasped, never having had anything embedded into her insides previously. Vanessa felt Melissa's butt-centric sphincter tight around her finger and how hot and tight the young lady was in her rectum. "No doubt, that is unquestionably just been utilized as an exit, never a passageway."

Melissa snickered apprehensively, as yet attempting to get adjusted to having something inside her rectum, while simultaneously Catalina was fingering her vagina. With the two openings so near one another, a suggestive inclination was so new to her.

"What's the matter Melissa, don't you like things up your butt head?" Vanessa asked challengingly.

Melissa was currently getting more used to the inclination. "I wasn't excessively certain from the start," she said timidly. "It seemed somewhat like when I go to the restroom; however, now I'm utilized to it, I like it."

Catalina's grab was dribbling at seeing her companion's finger embedded into the more youthful young lady's butt-centric opening. "You must allow me to attempt that!" she screeched.

Vanessa hauled her finger out of Melissa's insides, and Catalina had her spot. Her fingers very much greased up from Melissa's pussy, Catalina burned through no time in embeddings her forefinger up Melissa's back-end. Like Vanessa, Catalina could feel how hot and tight the inside of the young person's rectum before her. With some hesitance, she removed her finger from Melissa's back entry at the bearing of Vanessa.

"It feels so great with things embedded in your vagina and back-end simultaneously," Melissa noticed, the young lady still incapable of accepting that she was stripped down on the ground on a bed with her underwear around her thighs, doing provocative things with her granddad's idiotic gold digger sweetheart and her streetwise companion.

"It does," Vanessa concurred. "Hello, you need to see something scorching?"

"Alright," said Melissa energetically.

Vanessa leaped to her feet, Melissa appreciating her exposed base as she opened a cabinet and recovered a pink sex toy. At the front was a huge phallic molded penis, at the back a more modest limb.

"This is truly hot if you like something up your pussy and your butt simultaneously," said Vanessa. "I got it for Catalina; a couple of months prior, she was genuine horny and needed sex so terrible, yet it was that week when I was unable to play ..."

"Vanessa had her period," Catalina cut in.

"Once more, thank you, Catalina; I think Melissa worked that out all alone," said Vanessa. "In any case, I offered it to Catalina, and Catalina being Catalina; she was unable to work it out by any means. She had the restricted dick at the front, the large dick at the back and was asking why it didn't go up to her pussy appropriately."

"I didn't have the foggiest idea how it functioned," Catalina dissented.

"Sound judgment Catalina, a little something many refer to as the presence of mind," said Vanessa. "In any event, you didn't attempt to stick the enormous dick up your butt; I would not like to drive you to setback and clarify how you harmed yourself. So, Melissa, you need to check it out?"

"I figure I do," grinned Melissa, preparing herself as Vanessa bowed alongside her and embedded the enormous piece of the sex toy into her vagina, sliding the smaller limb into her butt. Melissa gasped as the plastic filled her pussy and rectum and felt her clitoris shivering as Vanessa jerked off her with the sex toy, controlling it back and forward.
"It's likewise acceptable if you need to encounter what sex with a man feels like, without enduring a man mounting and stuffing you," said Vanessa. She pulled out the sex toy

from Melissa's vagina and butt and put it aside. She grinned enchantingly at the more youthful young lady. "Brain, you, with us young ladies tongues work comparably well."

Melissa was getting somewhat of a sore back bowing on the bed with her can noticeable all around for such a long time. However, this was immediately forgotten as Vanessa got down low and embedded her tongue profound into Melissa's vagina. Vanessa's tongue crossed Melissa's teen twat, diving deep inside to lick up her pussy juice, at times waiting on the young lady's clitoris, different occasions returning and forward on her vaginal lips.

Catalina rolled in from over the top and brought down her face into Melissa's exposed base; Melissa before long inclined the firm strokes of Catalina's tongue on her back-end and different occasions on the delicate skin that isolated her vulva from her back-end. At that point, the young ladies changed position, Catalina going down on Melissa's vagina and Vanessa on her butt, Melissa's naked feet holding and unclenching at the awesome vibe of accepting oral to both her pussy and her back end simultaneously.

"Goodness look, we've neglected to take your lovely little underwear totally off," said Vanessa, as she and Catalina eliminated their heads from Melissa's private ladylike region. The teen again felt the hands of the more established young ladies on her underwear as they were slid down her legs and off over her exposed feet. Presently, she like Catalina, and Vanessa was bare.

"Presently, we have considerably more fun," Vanessa guaranteed. The three bare, nubile young ladies lay back on the bed, Melissa between the two more established young ladies, and they embraced firmly and exotically, their hands wandering everywhere on one another's exposed bodies; Melissa looked aside and saw a great appearance in the mirror, that of the firm, peach-formed cheeks of Catalina's uncovered base. Her pussy feeling like it may detonate from the magnificent sight as Vanessa's fingers prodded the cheeks of Melissa's uncovered base, multiplying the joy for the young lady.

The smell of three excited pussies filled the room with an appealing, welcoming Sapphic aroma as the three young ladies squirmed on the bed together. Melissa felt like she may stir from the most sensual dream of her life at any second and thought it was difficult to accept this was going on without a doubt. One second had her head between Vanessa's legs eating out her pussy, while Catalina went down on Melissa's butt before exchanging and licking Vanessa's back-end. The following Catalina was playing with Melissa's dull pubic hair. At the same time, Melissa thus ran her fingers through Vanessa's red pubes, and Vanessa's fingers were going through the blondie twists that filled in bounty over Catalina's female hill. At that point, they exchanged around, Catalina's fingers going into the red pubic hair on Vanessa's hill, Vanessa's fingers in Melissa's grab playing with her pubes, and Melissa's fingers investigating the great blonde pubic hair around Catalina's pussy.

Now and then, the young ladies' exercises were more steady, yet regardless erotic. For a couple of moments, they lay on their backs, their hands playing with one another's breasts while their wonderful exposed feet prodded and interweaved, following back and forward along their bottoms and around their lower legs, their beautiful toes flexing and un-flexing in joy. At that point, the young ladies gathered their undies and smelled every one of them thus, engrossing the female scents the proprietor had made on the cotton. Melissa smelled Catalina's undies, while Vanessa smelled Melissa's underwear, and Catalina smelled Vanessa's undies. At that point, exchanging around, Catalina's nose breathed in the smell of high school pussy on Melissa's elegant white underwear. At the same time, Melissa delighted in the pussy scented white and blue undies of Vanessa, and Vanessa's noses were blessed to receive the enticing smell of twat Catalina had left on her undies.

So much did Melissa appreciate these random Sapphic sex acts with the more seasoned young ladies that it was difficult for her to consider one she enjoyed the most? Be that as

214

it may, one stuck out. Vanessa and Catalina got on all fours as Melissa had done before, pushing their bare bottoms not yet decided.

Seeing two firm asses, amazing pink vaginas, and tight butt-centric openings were paradises to Melissa, and she burned through no time embeddings her tongue into Vanessa's twat, while fingering Catalina's vagina, the blondie squirming and screeching, her pussy juice immersing Melissa's fingers.

Vanessa groaned as Melissa licked her vagina harder and licked the cheeks of her base before moving her tongue to the territory between Vanessa's vulva and butt before Melissa went down on the tight opening to the redhead's back-end licking her long and hard, feeling Vanessa wriggle. The smell of excitement of her container getting more grounded.

On her right hand, Melissa could feel her forefinger was very much greased up with Catalina's pussy juice, so she moved her finger gradually along Catalina's twat to her can. She orbited Catalina's back-end with her finger before pushing it up into her guts, Melissa feeling how hot and tight Catalina was in her back section as the dividers of her rectum shut around Melissa's finger.

"Wow, Vanessa, look what she's doing!" Catalina shouted, her companion projecting an investigate her correct shoulder and preferring what she saw.

"She's a brisk student, isn't she?" Vanessa remarked.

Melissa kept on going down on Vanessa's pussy and butt face while fingering Catalina in her vagina and back-end for one more moment or thereabouts before she changed her position. This time, the youngster went down on Catalina's delicious twat, adoring the blonde's pussy wetness in her mouth while fingering Vanessa's vulva.

The young lady ventured things up, and like with Catalina, got her finger overall quite wet in the tacky pink inside of Vanessa's vagina, before following her forefinger in reverse from her vulva to her butt, feeling that like Catalina Vanessa was hot and tight in the limits of her guts, her rectum appearing to swallow Melissa's finger. Her different fingers she used to invigorate Vanessa's twat, seeing the redhead's naked feet responding to the incitement, her toes holding and unclenching.

Licking Catalina's vagina with energy, Melissa started to lick Catalina between her butt cheeks, on the zone between Catalina's vulva and back-end. Lastly, her back-end itself, Melissa pushing her tongue down hard on the opening to Catalina's guts, the blondie's screeches of enjoyment showing the amount she loved this.

The three young ladies were all inclined to climax. Vanessa – clearly smarter than Catalina and more experienced than Melissa – took control to ensure that the experience was awesome for everybody.

"I'm cumming soon; I can feel it," said Vanessa. She plunked down on the bed and spread her legs wide; she grabs uncovered, her legs so far separated that her back-end could be seen under her vagina. "Alternate to eat me out; at that point when I cum, you both lick me. From that point onward, it's Catalina's chance to get eaten out, and Melissa, no doubt about it."

Catalina was the first to bring down her face into Vanessa's red muff and her wet pussy, licking her companion's vagina hard and gulping the wetness the stimulated young lady's vagina delivered in abundance. At that point, Melissa proceeded the female smell of excitement solid as she embedded her tongue into Vanessa's vagina, surrounding her clitoris, Vanessa pounding her pussy in Melissa's face, the red pubic hair stimulating the youngster's nose. Catalina took over again that Vanessa's back angled, and the muscles in her pussy and rectum fixed, her clitoris feeling on fire. Vanessa accompanied a surge of

216

pussy juice in Catalina's face with a noisy screech as her climax went through her body, the redhead panting for breath.

Catalina licked up a portion of her companion's pussy juice, at that point, removed her face from Vanessa's groin so Melissa could likewise experience Vanessa's post-orgasmic vagina. Melissa did precisely that, licking the tart taste of twat from between Vanessa's legs as the young lady recuperated her relaxing.

"That was amazing!" said Vanessa as she stood up and gave Catalina an energetic slap on her exposed base. "Your turn now, Catalina."

"Whoopee!" shouted Catalina, having Vanessa's spot on the bed and spreading her legs wide so different young ladies would have simple admittance to her pussy. The pink vaginal opening with thin lips, blonde pubic hair obvious at the main, a tight star-fished molded butt under was not a greeting different young ladies were going to thump back.

Vanessa put her face into Catalina's vagina, kissing it first at that point, licking her clitoris, Catalina's wetness getting on Vanessa's mouth. As Catalina had done, Melissa at that point moved in for her turn, licking Catalina's pussy with long hard strokes, making the blondie squirm on the bed and her toes to hold and unclench. Drinking Catalina's pussy juice, Melissa eliminated her head to allow Vanessa to lick at her companion's crate once more before Melissa proceeded again. Melissa could judge by how Catalina was constantly squirming that her climax was close, and when she screeched, and her body went unbending, the second showed up.

Like Vanessa before her, Catalina felt the muscles in her vagina and rectum fix, and her climax spread through her body. The lovely blonde screeched and accompanied a tremendous tacky surge directly in Melissa's face, the youngster drinking the pussy juice cherishing each drop, at that point eliminated her head from between Catalina's legs so

Vanessa could likewise eat out Catalina's post-orgasmic vagina. Catalina, her face red, battled to draw breath, panting for breath before recuperating herself and getting to her feet.

"Presently for you," Vanessa said, Melissa feeling the more seasoned young ladies' hands on her breasts, pubic hair, and exposed base as she plunked down on the bed where Vanessa and Catalina had been before her. Albeit the young ladies had done such countless attractive things up until this point, the unpracticed Melissa felt anxious about what was still to come.

Her heart vacillating, Melissa spread her legs wide separated as Vanessa and Catalina had done, the young lady uncovering her lavish twists of earthy colored pubic hair, her oval-formed vagina, and her tight back-end. Vanessa was anxious to be the first to put her head between Melissa's legs and cover her face into Melissa's youngster pussy, the stripped redhead licking the brunette's vagina with eagerness making Melissa's clitoris send rushes of joy through her dainty body, Catalina gazing at her companion eating out Melissa's virginal vagina with a look of enjoyment on her beautiful face.

"Your turn now," Vanessa said, as she hauled her face out of Melissa's vulva after altogether licking it from the more youthful young lady's clitoral hood to the passageway to her back-end.

"Can hardly wait!" shouted Catalina, jumping recklessly into Melissa's muff and licking her vagina hard and first, the erotic impression of the blondie's tongue, the teen's pussy like a spilling tap. Melissa's toes flexed, and un-flexed and her hips pivoted at the magnificent sensations of Catalina licking her pussy, at one phase making out with Melissa's lower lips as she kissed her vulva.

Again it was Vanessa's chance to go down on Melissa, yet she was such a near climax now that there was no retreat. The shivering sensations from her clitoris transformed into one colossal influx of joy before spreading through her vagina and butt, the muscles contracting and causing the young lady to feel like her uterus and rectum were going to detonate. Melissa had climaxes before while stroking off. However, she had never engaged in sexual relations with anybody – male or female previously – so this was a lot more pleasurable than any climax she had encountered before.

Her lovely face was wet with sweat and showing the power; all things considered, Melissa's as of now immersed vagina delivered a flood of pussy juice into Vanessa's mouth and face. Melissa proceeded to climax as Catalina put her head into her vagina, keep to lick the teen's pussy as she was cumming, and was compensated by the second part of tacky pussy sogginess that went into Catalina's face, the excellent blonde lapping it up with enchant before she and her darling Vanessa traded a deep French kiss, the flavor of Melissa's vagina clear in their mouths.

"Indeed, if you had any questions, you were a lesbian; I imagine that they've gone currently," said Vanessa, the three stripped young ladies lying on the bed stroking and touching their nubile youthful bodies, recuperating their breath, their silly scents clear in the room.

"So Melissa, did you like it?" Catalina asked Melissa as she scoured her exposed foot against one of the teen's naked feet.

"That was the best insight of my life," said Melissa, actually thinking that it's difficult to accept that this had occurred.

Vanessa scoured barefoot all over Melissa's leg. "All things considered, you'll need to visit more, will not you? Furthermore, it's not finished at this point. There's still shower time."

219

Gathering their garments, the three young ladies strolled stripped to the washroom up the lobby, their uncovered breasts and differentiating red, blonde, and brunette hedges looking extraordinary from the front, and their shapely exposed bottoms and legs incredible from the back.

As Vanessa shut the restroom entryway, Melissa as consistently after a climax, wanted to pee. "I um – need to go to the restroom," she said to Vanessa and Catalina.

Vanessa pointed at the restroom. "Take yourself out, Melissa."

Melissa started to become flushed. Even though she and Gretchen had peed before one another previously, utilizing the restroom before different young ladies caused her to feel reluctant. Vanessa saw Melissa's anxious articulation and chuckled. "What's wrong? You're not timid about peeing before us after everything you did in there; would you say you are?" Vanessa thought briefly and said, "You do have to pee, isn't that right? On the off chance that you need to go for a poo, the restroom's all yours, Melissa, trust me."

Catalina snickered. "No doubt, we sure would prefer not to be in here in case you will have a crap." She waved her fingers right in front of her and afterward held it.

"No, I just need to pee," said Melissa, actually reddening.

"All around, please, don't be timid; we will not look or chuckle or anything," said Vanessa.

As yet becoming flushed, Melissa advanced toward the restroom and sat her base down on the seat. It felt odd to be perched on the restroom totally exposed; typically, when she utilized the restroom, she was dressed yet had her underwear and other attire like pants, shorts, pantyhose, or nightgown pulled down. However, it wasn't half pretty much as abnormal as utilizing the restroom with two different young ladies in the washroom with her.

The call of nature was more grounded than Melissa's timidity, notwithstanding, and as she sat in the restroom, Melissa started to pee, the yellow fluid tinkling into the restroom bowl, the perfect water becoming a brilliant shade of yellow from the surge of pee from her urethra. At the point when her pee stream at last subsided and her bladder was vacant, Melissa loosened up some tissue and dried her wet pussy, at that point flushed the restroom.

"That was a monstrous measure of pee for a little young lady," Vanessa remarked to Melissa as she washed her hands. "What's more, think about what, presently I need to go as well."

Like Melissa before her, Vanessa At the point when completed, Vanessa cleaned her vagina, stood up, and flushed. At that point went to wash her hands.

"Presently, I need to go also," said Catalina. The beautiful stripped blonde plunked down on the restroom and started to pee. As the sound of Catalina peeing filled the washroom as the yellow fluid went into the restroom bowl, she said to Melissa, "We're somewhat even at this point. You've effectively seen me in the restroom; presently, I've seen you on the restroom."

Vanessa held back. "What was that?" she inquired. "Might someone want to fill me in?"

Catalina completed the process of peeing, got toilet paper, and cleaned her wet pussy. "On Sunday, Melissa sort of needed to protect me at Kelly's home ..."

Vanessa murmured and feigned exacerbation. "Did you plunk down on the restroom without checking for bathroom tissue once more?"

Catalina looked timid as she stood up and flushed the restroom. "I may have."

"Catalina, even you ought to have the option to work out that when you need to take a poop, you check for bathroom tissue before you sit on the restroom." Vanessa went to Melissa. "Melissa, on the off chance that she does it once more, leave her abandoned on the restroom to get familiar with an exercise. It's the thing I will do from here on out."

"It wasn't my shortcoming," Catalina dissented. "I was a piece cracked by all the Jesus compositions in the house, so it slipped my mind."

Vanessa came to under the shower to turn it on, and the three young ladies ventured under the warm water, washing away the sweat and the remaining pussy juice between their legs. Sharing a sensibly little shower break made it very confined. However, Melissa sure wasn't gripping as she, Catalina, and Vanessa washed each other's bare bodies. Cleanser and water ran down their bodies, their firm breasts and posterior shrouded in white foam and bubbles and doused their pubic hair before more water emerged from the showerhead and washed the cleanser down their legs to their naked feet and down the channel. This was such a great deal more sizzling than the showers with her soccer group after Melissa's school.

When Vanessa killed the shower, and the three wet young ladies got out and took towels to dry themselves, Vanessa asked, "Melissa, is their one kindness you can get done for us?"

Melissa put the towel between her legs to dry her vagina and said, "Sure, what right?"

"Your sibling's sweetheart Kelly, any possibility you could bring her here to have a foursome?" Vanessa inquired.

"I would cherish that; she is thus, so hot!" shouted Catalina. "What's more, her undies smell so wonderful."

Melissa giggled. "You realize Kelly is a fundamentalist Christian, isn't that so? I don't believe that will occur. She advances restraint – a ton."

Vanessa grinned a cunning grin. "Try not to be so certain. You wouldn't know it. However, I experienced childhood in a severe Catholic family. I went to parochial school and Mass and Sunday school each Sunday. My auntie was even a religious recluse. I used to accept that having intercourse before you were hitched – to a man – was one of the most exceedingly terrible sins you could resolve to challenge God. What's more, peer how I ended up. A lesbian who fills in as a colorful artist at a strip club flaunting my tits, ass, and pussy to sick people and failures."

"I don't believe that will occur with Kelly," said Melissa.

"Perhaps, perhaps not yet, it's ideal for dreaming," said Vanessa.

"You are so fortunate having Kelly in your soccer group and having the chance to see her stripped in the showers after games," said Catalina.

"You're not off-base there," concurred Vanessa.
"Possibly we could go to their secondary school and shower with them after the game?" Catalina recommended.

"Better believe it and get captured for it," Vanessa brought up.

Catalina contemplated this and said, "What might be said about your companion Gretchen, the lovely Jewish young lady? Would she be keen on a foursome?"

Melissa snickered. "I don't think so. Gretchen has a genuine sweetheart."

"Fortunate Gretchen's sweetheart," said Vanessa.

Presently dry, the young ladies started to dress, pulling up and changing their undies around their vaginas, at that point covering their breasts with their bras. The young ladies put on their garments, and as Melissa tied back her hair in a pigtail, her blue sweater, creased blue skirt, and white shoes and lower leg socks gave her a reasonably tidy appearance, totally at chances with what she had been up to not exactly 30 minutes sooner. Just if one somehow happened to lift the teen's skirt and check the twofold cotton seat of her white botanical underwear, would one have any hint that she had even engaged in any sexual musings?

Stan had completed his 'grass cutting' outside the house and looked puzzled as the three young ladies moved toward him. "I went through longer than an hour taking care of this lawn, and it looks the same," he griped. "I'll need to go to Harry's Hardware and get some new edges."

"What's Harry's Hardware?" Vanessa inquired.

"It's a tool shop run by Grandpa's companion Harry," said Melissa. She turned down the volume. "It shut down around ten years prior, and Harry himself passed on around five years prior."

Catalina looked confounded. "For what reason would Stan need to go to a tool shop that shut down?"

Vanessa and Melissa feigned exacerbation, and Melissa said, "I'll likely need to go currently to get the transport."

"Try not to stress; we'll drive you," said Catalina.

Vanessa's face showed entertainment at the appearance of dread in the more youthful young lady's eyes at getting in a vehicle driven by boneheaded Catalina, and she giggled. "Try not to stress; I'll drive."

Melissa lose. "OK, at that point, much obliged."

"Tag along, Stan, we're going for a drive," said Catalina.

"Catalina, did you lock the house?" Vanessa inquired.

"Um – ah – possibly - simply a second," said Catalina, running for the front entryway.

Vanessa shook her head. "One day, you'll fail to remember your head, Catalina."

"So, where are we going?" Stan asked as Vanessa upheld her vehicle out of the carport, Catalina in the front seat, Melissa and her granddad in the back.

"Gracious simply on a little drive," said Vanessa.

"Be cautious," Stan prompted her. "I took my vehicle out before, and there were every one of these awful drivers going the incorrect far up the road, and afterward this senseless young lady stepped before my vehicle." He took a gander at Melissa. "You know, dear, the young lady who got before my vehicle looked a great deal like you."

Melissa said nothing, and Stan, depleted from his meeting of imagining grass cutting, nodded off when the vehicle arrived at the corner. The older man possibly stirred when Vanessa maneuvered into the Jenkins family house's carport, and he took a gander at the home with disarray. "I think I was here recently." He, at that point, reconsidered. "No, stand by, I wasn't. I should get confounded."

"Much obliged for the lift," Melissa said to Vanessa as she escaped the vehicle. "I'll see you both later."

"Make it as soon as possible," said Vanessa interestingly; as she switched out, she and Catalina waving to Melissa, and Melissa waving back as the vehicle drove away up the road, Stan effectively solid sleeping in the back of the vehicle.

Returning inside, where she was as yet the just one home, Melissa considered the stunning turn a common Monday had taken. She didn't care for how Catalina, Vanessa, and Catalina's family were utilizing her granddad like an ATM; however, for once, Catalina had been right in saying that there was no way around it. From this point forward, Melissa figured that she would visit her granddad frequently and make the best – the absolute best - out of an awful circumstance. Inside her undies, Melissa's vagina reacted to the prospect of her next visit to her granddad's home and investing energy with dumb Catalina and her Sapphic streetwise companion Vanessa.

END

Explicit Erotic Sex Stories

HER CARELESSNESS

Finley faces a challenge with SELENA (Lesbian)

Pamela Vance

Prologue: (Past, California)

Brandon Edevane heard the way to his examination open. "You're early," he mumbled, not gazing upward from his work.

"I'm quite on schedule," Gregory Wright remedied, "On the off chance that you had a check-in here, you wouldn't need to keep guessing..."

Brandon waved his hand pretentiously, "They're diverting. I don't think well with one in the room."

Gregory sunk into the solitary another seat in the inadequate room, "You know, a great many people would be astonished to see that your examination looks like a seventeenth-century study hall. Clear dividers, one table, one seat... this chair..."

Brandon thought down at his 'work area', a long table with different paper and books piles flawlessly positioned. He slid along the seat starting with one end, then onto the next in a rehearsed float, and halted, "This works for me. If it ain't broke..."

"No, you distraught virtuoso, I wasn't discussing the utility of your ludicrously straightforward boards of wood," Gregory laughed at his dearest companion, "I was saying that individuals most likely expect you take care of your job in something likened to the size and magnificence of the Library of Congress."

Gregory murmured at Brandon's empty look before clarifying, "... since you and your family's gotten more cash-flow than practically any other person on earth..."

The numb look transformed into a more awkward one.

"... Apologies, bud, I call them as I see 'em..." Gregory shrugged.

The fortunes and impact of the Edevane family combination were broad and profound. Brandon, for whom the 'virtuoso' name was not a long way from reality, further added to the family's abundance with his enormous arrangement of licenses and licenses. Gregory was Brandon's sole school flatmate; both had gotten along promptly, and a deep-rooted companionship was fashioned. Gregory proceeded to cut a well-deserved way to progress as the seat and senior litigator at Halprin Uxley and Beckett, one of the biggest and most esteemed law offices on the planet. The two men remained steadfastly engaged with one another's lives and in closeness as they each wedded and had kids. They had little girls a similar age - fortuitously conceived minutes separated - who grew up more like sisters than companions.

The two families lived inside a five-block span of one another on the Lower East Side of California, each shunning the more extravagant homes of the City's Upper East Side. In truth, the Edevanes lived in an all-around delegated - however, mysterious-looking - four-story carriage house on Eldridge Street, so it was as yet a pearl of a property. The Wrights lived in a three-room condo close by on Broome Street.

Life turned along easily until Gregory abruptly got himself a single man and a single parent. His little girl Marlo was going to turn thirteen when their reality turned over. Gregory quit his place of employment, removed Marlo from school, and both of them went on a one-year vacation to venture to the far corners of the planet, halting in as numerous urban areas and waypoints as they could. The holiday filled some needs: It gave the two of them some distance to deal with Marian Wright's deficiency and gave them the important time and experience of being a two-person family versus a three-person family.

At the point when father and girl got back to the States, two things turned out to be clear: First, the Edevanes accepted them both as a feature of their family; second, Gregory had no revenue in getting back to the existence of a sought after corporate legal counselor. Brandon Edevane burned through no time in poaching his closest companion's honest insight and scholarly pull. Brandon had quite a while in the past surrendered the running of the aggregate to his significant other Juniper, herself a prepared veteran of Wall Street; further, he understood he came up short on the fortitude to control and convey adapt his developing archive of advancements. Gregory was the ideal General Counsel the Edevane Group had been hanging tight for.

Liberated from corporate administration obligations, Brandon cheerfully went through his days in his Spartan examination, thinking up groundbreaking thoughts. As a rule, Gregory and Juniper needed to persuade Brandon out of his scholarly casing. His inclination for staying under the radar frequently hurt him in the realm of substance over-burden: his quiet was thought to be vainglorious, his absence of effort an indication of haughtiness. A new BNL article was the ideal contextual investigation.

"You know," Gregory proceeded, "On the off chance that you'd simply consider somewhat more PR, individuals may see you for the profoundly humanitarian geek that you are, rather than the malicious big shot accumulating cash in your house."

Brandon moaned, "That is not a story that PR would settle. Did you see the Business News Ledger article today about my absence from charity? Well, that is saying something - the BNL, the most favorable to business, supportive of entrepreneur paper - composing a gnawing evaluate about my charitable giving."

"They put in a decent picture, however," Gregory noted with a sound dab of mockery.

Brandon grunted, "They superimposed a crown that says "Ruler Edevane" on it. Like I'm some Marie Antoinette same. They can think what they need - however, we most likely ought to do much more."

"I know the proofreader at the BNL; I can converse with him. In private. They don't have the foggiest idea what they don't have a clue, Brandon. You're an obvious objective: You disdain exposure, all your generosity is carefully mysterious, and you never put any misinformation to rest... you just come to me and say, 'we need to accomplish more.'"

"There's in every case more to do," Brandon demanded, "... furthermore, try not to converse with the manager of the BNL..."

"Stunner," Gregory shrugged, "I guarantee I will not. No, no, no, don't return to your work. We need to go through some school stuff for the children. If it's not too much trouble, sign these things first... you've been perched on these for quite a long time."

Gregory gestured prudently at Brandon's look of shock, "That's right, it's here, elderly person, your oldest is set for school. Also, no grumbling from you - in any event, Finley's simply going to be an hour's drive away. Marlo takes off to Los Angeles one week from now. I may very well ask Halprin to take me back and let me work out of their LA office."

"You will not have to ask. You can get me as their greatest record," Brandon's rationale regularly stepped over others' endeavor at humor. He marked the pile of school structures for Finley: medical services intermediary, HIPAA waiver, and some different ones with his significant other's unique effect on them.

Gregory giggled, "I was simply joking. I'm not returning to following my life like clockwork. Furthermore, I'll utilize your fly to see Marlo. She's been sulking around; I believe it's just hitting her now that she will be on the opposite side of the country to most of us."

"Finley will miss her; I was asking why the two of them have stayed together the recent days," Brandon moved off the seat, "Please, we should go to lunch; what time, right?"

Gregory checked the time, "Noon. We're just ten minutes late."

Brandon whitened, "Juniper will murder me. Please, we should go."

The two men advanced out of the examination, through the library, and down the stairs to the lounge area. Brandon's eyebrows weaved with disappointment when he saw a roughly made crown sitting on his place setting at the lounge area table. The crown was annoyingly like the one in the BNL article.

"Too early?" snickered Finley, "Marlo made me one, as well!" She came to under her seat and put an absurdly luxurious plastic crown on her head. Marlo figured out how to express "Princess Finley" in indelible marker, subbing one of the imitation gems for an "o."

Brandon whirled the crown around his forefinger, fairly assuaged by his little girl's pleasantness, "They had a point, you know, we need to accomplish more, improve."

"They don't know all that you as of now do," Finley answered, "It was certainly not a reasonable article."

Brandon shook his head, "It's not tied in with being reasonable. Since you can never sit in a house this way and get instruction like the one you're going to get and talk with any believability about reasonableness."

The table fell quiet.

"Not to heap on the blame, wow," Juniper tutted. She gave her significant other a harsh look, "Sweetheart, perhaps next time go after the methodology of a hundred one-minute chunks of insight versus 100-ton guilt trip in sixty seconds? If it's not too much trouble, wrap up, everybody, the food's getting cold."

"Try not to stress Brandon," Marlo spoke up, "I'm glad to call her 'Princess Finley' from this point forward to keep her legitimate!"

Finley's more youthful sister Sophie stifled on her water, "Marlo for the success!" she spat.

Finley stuck her tongue out at Sophie and gave Marlo a firm elbow in the ribs. She shifted the crown on her head, "Indeed, Marlo, this unmistakably implies I'm wearing the jeans in this relationship!"

Marlo reddened; Finley's utilization of the word 'relationship' was easygoing and wry. However, it evoked an emotional response somewhere down in Marlo's heart, awakening her mysterious expectation and longing. Marlo recuperated rapidly; however, "emergency room, I'm wearing the jeans right now, Finley. You're wearing a dress..."

Everybody giggled.

"Whatever, Marlo, you understand what I implied," Finley began eating, "Hello mother, did I get any mail from Avington?"

"Not today, but rather you got something yesterday," Juniper said calmly. She held up two huge school direction envelopes with the Avington logo on them.

Finley's eyes streaked, "You kept those from me? Give them here!"

"Eh, eh, eh!" Juniper rebuked, "Finish lunch first, please."

The prospective first-year recruit immediately ingested lunch as Finley tore open the envelope, "Where is it?" She murmured as she looked over the pile of papers and flyers, "Aha! Flat mate tasks!"
Finley ran her eye rapidly down the task, "Not the most noticeably terrible! I'll be living with Mona Winchester from Brooklyn. She went to Windcroft High School... was the Valedictorian... B-ball group... The seat of Windcroft's LGBT-Allies group..."

Just Juniper saw Marlo's eyes take on a marginally worried look.

Finley inhaled out a moan of help, "Sounds like a typical average secondary school over-achiever. Shouldn't something be said about you, Marlo?"

Marlo blew a raspberry, "Got my direction parcel in my email inbox earlier today. I need to get off-grounds lodging. It's alright - they cautioned us that this was a chance. Father and I, as of now, investigated some stuff."

It worked out that everybody had an assessment of where Marlo should live, which didn't help Marlo's developing fear about living in another city without anyone else. She'd decided to go to school in LA to move away. Presently, as her trip toward the West Coast lingered, the distance felt like over the top excess. Marlo had come out toward the start of her senior year... to precisely zero exhibition from her dad and the Edevanes. She hadn't come out with every bit of relevant information. However, her developing appreciation for

Finley felt verboten from multiple points of view. California's tattle editorialists had been immediately stimulated by the information on Marlo's sexual direction, and that was at that point past what Marlo needed the Edevanes (by relationship) to need to bear. The world may be pushing ahead regarding the acknowledgment of the LGBT people group. However, there were deep pockets of traditionalism not worth inciting (the Edevanes truly couldn't have minded less, yet they weren't aware of Marlo's ponderings on this specific subject). Above all, Finley appeared to be bound for a specific Camelot-type future, with venerating paparazzi following afterward. Marlo didn't perceive any motivation to disturb that direction, not least because Finley's present beau was proof enough of where her sentiments would take her.

Sometime after that, Marlo laid on her bed, thinking about her issue. Her indecision about school was exacerbated by the information that Finley planned to have a gay flatmate. Marlo felt promptly desirous of Mona, even though there was no motivation to be. Marlo needed to be far away and nearby at the same time. "This is so moronic!" She said for all to hear.

"What's dumb?" Marlo's father ventured into her room, grasping her wireless, "You left this first floor, and it's been humming perpetually."

"Much appreciated," Marlo opened her hands to flag her father to throw the telephone, which he did. She immediately checked her messages, "Gracious, Finley's been messaging me. No big deal."

"Mmmm. You OK?" Gregory realized his girl was in a disposition, "I thought you planned to spend time with Finley throughout the week?"

"Nah," Marlo mumbled, "Likely better to begin sorting out LA logistics..."

"... which you're doing by lying in bed and gazing at the ceiling...?" Gregory chose to press, only a tad, "I've been told by my little girl that I'm a very decent listener..."

That got a slight grin out of Marlo, "I'm fine, father... there's a great deal to consider, that's it in a nutshell."

"All good," Gregory gestured, "I will accomplish a little work. Trattoria Nuova for supper?"

"Sounds great!" Marlo gestured as her father left the room. She got her telephone and looked through the messages from Finley.

{FE} Hey - for what reason did you leave unexpectedly early?

{FE} Did I annoy you or something?

{FE} Seriously. Is it safe to say that you are there?

{FE} What got into you today? Could you pls react?

Marlo chose to utilize a conventionally possible answer, {MW} Summer's closure too early. I was feeling blah.

{FE} Same. Is it accurate to say that you are returning over around evening time?

Marlo smiled; a naughty sense was dominating. {MW} Does Princess Finley require the organization of this modest worker?

{FE} You're never going to let that bite the dust, right?

{MW} No, your Greatness, I unquestionably won't. Marlo was grinning more extensively presently, getting a charge out of the energy of her prodding.

{FE} You = ghastly.

{MW} Something vexes you, my lord?

Before Marlo could type her next word, her telephone rang. It was Finley.

"Indeed, your highness?" Marlo laughed.

"Marlo, stop it." Finley sounded more delighted than anything.

"I can't help myself. This is an excessive lot of fun."

"Until somebody gets a grip of our writings and misunderstands the idea..."

"Fine. I'll keep it offline..." Marlo was very much aware of the newspaper's extraordinary interest

"Much appreciated," Finley moaned.

"My pleasure, Princess..." Marlo began snickering, "Apologies! It's excessively enticing!"

"Butt head." Finley was snickering too.

"Liable as charged." Marlo extended.

"Is it accurate to say that you are returning over for sure?"

"I'm going to supper with Dad. And afterward, I think we need to hunker down and sort out where I'm going to live."

"Come over more often, Wright. I'm certainly troubled about you being 3,000 miles away when school begins."

"You can't have everything, Finley..." Marlo said this daintily; however, her heart was beating.

There was a beat of quiet before Finley moaned, "I will miss you; that's it in a nutshell."

"Me as well."

"Stop by tomorrow?" Finley said, "Please?" She was unable to have speculated the impact her words had on Marlo.

"OK," Marlo concurred. She would never deny Finley.

"Guarantee?"

"Guarantee." Marlo finished the call and murmured. This is so inept.

"Life's not reasonable," she helped herself to remember Brandon's words, "Simply manage it, Marlo."

Chapter 1: - A Pleasant Dinner (The More Recent Past - Five Years Ago, California)

Finley's telephone quavered for what felt like the 100th time that day. In contrast to the wide range of various calls, however, this one made Finley grin. She got right away.

"Marlo!" Finley's telephone screen exchanged into video call mode, and the picture of her closest companion appeared out of 1,000,000 pixels of shading and light.

"How's the Big Apple?" Marlo was some place outside. It was splendid.

"Fine. An excessive number of gatherings. Father's beginning to feel weary of investors and specialists." As usual, the simple truth of conversing with Marlo was sufficient to cause Finley to rest easy thinking about her day.

Marlo smiled, "They don't help themselves... Yet, no doubt about it!"

"It's tiresome, without a doubt. In any case, I'm not whining - we're perched on a triumphant lottery ticket. A little torment with the brokers is great!"

Finley was downplaying the truth of what was happening. Numerous years prior, her dad had dabbled with another build for semi-conductors. As of late, Brandon tidied off the patent for it and began to create possible applications for sun-based boards. Some way or another, the Silicon Valley types got wind of the exploration, and the wild offers for the licensed innovation came flooding in. Admittance to Edevane's innovation would rake in tons of cash for many individuals.

Marlo glared, "They'd auction you piece by piece if they could. Be cautious."

Finley's heart warmed with Marlo's anxiety, "Father and I play great cop-awful cop well. No one's contacting our IP until we say as much in any case. Quit worrying about them. How's your gathering going?"

Marlo shrugged, "a few groups the previous evening that I hadn't found in years, which was pleasant. Some rando came up asking me for a signature toward the beginning of today."

Finley snickered, "Which one was it this time? Did they think you were Tilda Swinton or David Bowie?"

This was a formal event for Marlo, and mixed-up personality instances increased dramatically when Marlo returned to LA.

"Tilda. I just marked it. I was at that point late, and you realize how individuals get all rude when I say I'm not who they think I am..."

"Indeed, I'm certain you made Tilda's fan glad today."

Marlo raked her free hand through her short light hair, "No doubt, I presume. What are you up to around evening time? You said you might go to your get-together supper... yet, if I know you, you've effectively thought of 1,000,000 reasons not to go... am I right?"

Since Marlo and Finley graduated that same year, it was inescapable that their get-together years would agree on a normal five-year rhythm. Finley joined the Edevane Group not long after graduating, yet Marlo proceeded with her investigations in Los Angeles, proceeding to procure a Ph.D. in Chemical Engineering. Marlo might have had her selection of labs wherein to work. Yet, she decided to fill in as an expert, advantageously, frequently for the Edevane Group's innovation business in San Francisco.

No one thought that it was important to remark, as Marlo was right around an individual from the family.

"I'm correct, aren't I?" Marlo squirmed her eyebrows. She realized she was correct. Finley's gathering greeting sat under a heap of papers around her work area, consigned to gather dust. Following a day of gatherings, Finley was not in any manner roused to be social.

"I was thoroughly going to go!" Finley dissented, "Yet I altered my perspective when our last gathering of the day hauled into its third hour... I've had sufficient gathering and hello for some time. I will remain in. Try not to see me like that. You realize you'd say yes to lager and pizza with me if you were here..."

"Valid," Marlo gestured, "Yet I'm not there, so go be social as opposed to covering up at home."

Finley put on an overstated frown, "Don't wanna."

Marlo couldn't avoid prodding her companion, "Everyday life is difficult, your Greatness, suck it up and bargain!"

"You're unimaginable; you realize that?" Finley grinned back at her companion tenderly, "Enough with the princess horse crap. What's more, what plans do you have? Some hot lady standing by to hop into bed with you? Goodness. My. God. You're reddening! You thoroughly do!" Finley shook her head, "You do, don't you, Marlo?"
However long Finley has known her companion, Marlo's constantly had a simple appeal about her. Indeed, even before Marlo came out, young ladies would play with her. They were attracted to her, such that Finley needed to wonder about. As Marlo grew up and

sunk into her sex personality, there was an unending stock of ladies who needed the attractive butch to inspire them deeply.

"Hello, there's nothing amiss with having a good time!" Marlo squirmed her eyebrows.

"Somewhat fun? Dr. Marlo Wright, I know you and your adventures! Should change your name to Don Juanita..."

Marlo smiled, "Envious? You should attempt it at some point!"

"Attempt what? Being one of your casual sexual encounters?" Finley giggled. This was a long-running joke among them. Throughout the long term, such countless individuals have conjectured about their kinship - and whether it was something else they chose en route to participate. For Marlo, it was the ideal feign: she could play with Finley under the misrepresentation of kidding around. For Finley, she could make the most of Marlo's advances without standing up to her interest when it went to her affections for Marlo. Marlo was never a long way from Finley's contemplations at whatever second. However, Finley never permitted herself to think too profoundly about the explanation; there were too many 'what uncertainties' and instabilities holding up traffic.

Thus Finley became tied up with the running joke without reservation, "You know I'm not that sort of young lady!"

Before Marlo could reply, Finley's call holding up pinged, "Gracious! That is Mona calling me. We've been playing telephone label throughout the day. Have a great time around evening time. Call me tomorrow!"

Marlo saluted nonchalantly as her picture vanished, and Finley accepted the approaching call.

"No, Mona, don't cause me to do it." Finley was half grinning as she said this. Since they were allocated as flatmates the first year, Mona Winchester and Finley have kept a profound and enduring kinship. Mona's playful nature was the main motivation why Finley didn't go through her four years in school stayed outdoors in the library.

"Finley, you don't have the foggiest idea why I'm calling!" Mona was completely set up to tidy off her 'come to have a great time' powerful thinking.

Finley began to pace a well-used way around her room; her telephone squeezed against her ear. She realized Mona was calling to persuade her out to their Class supper, "No, Mona, I truly have no interest in finding 200 of my previous schoolmates... I needn't bother with individuals getting into my business."

"Your business as in the way that you're a beneficiary? Or then again your business as in the way that you all hold the way into the greatest mechanical jump of the following 25 years?"

"Every last bit of it. They needed me to feature the renewables class tomorrow. Fortunately, I fly to London tomorrow evening, which made it conceivably genuine to decay without culpable anybody. I figure I should remain in bed until my flight leaves."

"Please! You can slither into bed when you get to London. Truly!"

"I have no more energy left to manage individuals... or then again drive out to campus..."

"I have you covered. Finley, it'll be ten or twelve individuals at my condo. It'll be private and a ten-minute ride from your place. A small-scale gathering off-grounds," Mona clarified, "We're excessively old for parties in any case. This is the first occasion when we've all been in a similar city simultaneously in years! "

"I've been in gatherings the entire day; I don't believe I'm up for another arrangement of new faces."

"You know the majority of them - there's just perhaps one individual you haven't met; a companion of Liz's from the west coast. I guarantee you it'll be superior to sitting in at home going over pitch books with your father."

Mona was directly around a certain something; Finley was finished with work, "I would prefer not to talk any business. What's more, no notice of my family."

"Check and check. Everybody coming around evening time thinks about your family and is long past mindful. SELENA - Liz's companion - wouldn't give a rodent's rear end regardless of whether you disclosed to her you were the Queen of Mars."

"I bet everything of Mars doesn't need to manage the paparazzi!"

"That is because the Queen of Mars doesn't possess the biggest secretly held organization on the planet that is perched on a lot of licenses worth billions of dollars..."

"Ugh," Finley scowled.

Mona rushed to answer, "Gracious, please, Finley. Nobody who's coming this evening often thinks about any of that. Also, if they do, I'll tear them another one, what about that? Presently get your can here."

Finley laughed, "OK. I suppose I'm in."

After two hours, Finley felt suddenly appreciative of Mona: The evening ended up being very charming, pleasant, even. Mona had designed the specific good gathering of previous school companions, each of whom treated Finley's family foundation as an oddity instead of a personality. She'd failed to remember what it very well may resemble to invest energy with genuine companions. Maybe Mona realized it'd been something Finley had profoundly missed yet couldn't expressive. It caused her to feel - if just for one evening - liberated from every one of the obligations and commitments she'd been hauling near. Finley wandered into the kitchen, where she discovered Mona giving the cooks a minute ago guidelines. Spontaneously, she gave Mona a huge loving squeeze from behind.

"Ooof!" Mona turned and shifted her head maternally at Finley, "What was that for?"

"To thank you for hauling me here this evening. It's acceptable to be in this world for a tad. Furthermore, far superior to any of the get-together occasions nearby around evening time."

"I'm so happy!" Mona embraced her back, "Liz is practically about finished with sleep time with the children and supper's prepared. Thank god for cooks... Who would you like to sit with?"

"Shock me," Finley grinned.

Mona slanted her head somewhat, "Challenge acknowledged, please through to the lounge area."

Finley followed Mona towards the long rectangular table. "Sit with Ivar," Mona demonstrated to an unfilled seat, "he chose to stop the scholarly community a month ago, so he will have parcels to say about that... furthermore, he's a decent drinking mate. I'll go along with you momentarily."

"Ivar!" Finley recalled the tall, bespectacled Swede from some time ago when. The two companions embraced and fired, making up for lost time right away.

Mona grinned cheerfully and guided the remainder of the gathering toward their seats. Mona searched for her significant other with three places unfilled, whom she at last found in the corridor, freeing two containers of wine from SELENA.

"Please, both of you, we're going to begin. SELENA, you sort of cut it somewhat close! We weren't going to keep an eye out for you to get your butt in gear." Mona gave SELENA a well-disposed gesture of congratulations.

SELENA shrugged in conciliatory sentiment, "Sorry - I was helping my father out with something." The three advanced into the lounge area. Liz sat down in the center of the table, leaving SELENA the top of the table's top or the unfilled seat inverse to Finley. She picked the last mentioned. Mona sat down at the top of the table, with Finley to her left side and SELENA to her right side.

Finley was somewhere down in discussion with Ivar and didn't completely enroll in SELENA's appearance. When one of the servers hindered to offer Ivar his decision of wine, Finley turned and looked at SELENA interestingly. Mona, ever the quintessential host, saw her opening, "Finley, this is Rowan Kan, Liz's companion who's meeting from San Fran... otherwise called SELENA. SELENA, this is Finley Edevane, one of my closest companions from school."

SELENA inclined across the table and shook Finley's hand, especially valuing the presentation. Meals with Mona and Liz were continually fascinating undertakings, and being situated inverse, an excellent lady was a promising beginning. The face and the name were natural, yet before SELENA could say whatever else, she saw two jugs of wine floating behind her, proffered by a server. With SELENA diverted, Finley went to Mona and mouthed, "Amazing."

Mona lifted an eyebrow intentionally. SELENA consistently knocked some people's socks off. Straight or gay or some place in the middle, ladies wound up attracted to SELENA. Tall, with short earthy colored hair, she had delightful brown eyes and an attractive face that was enticingly male/female. This wasn't the first run through Mona's seen a lady's compulsory fascination in SELENA's easy sex claim. While Mona wasn't astonished by her companion's response, she was shocked by how unguarded Finley was about it. In school, Finley had once admitted to being gently pulled into ladies and to be somewhat interested in Sapphic love, yet she never appeared to have followed up on it. It created the impression that the interest had waited.

Finley herself was amazed. She was unable to quit taking a gander at SELENA. There was an attractive quality about the lady before her; there was something in particular about SELENA's characteristics, something about how SELENA consumed space that was inquisitively charming. Whatever that something was, it was excessively significant and undefinable for Finley to sort it out at that point. Accordingly, she ended up getting a handle on any trace of shared characteristics among her and SELENA to make a big difference in the discussion. SELENA, who was very much polished in the specialty of enticing chitchat, was glad to oblige.

Mona felt like she was the seat umpire of a fervently challenged tennis match as her two visitors inconspicuously, however, definitely transformed unremarkable points into a stewing consume of shared tease. Liz, a few seats away, detected a famous unsettling influence in power and shot her better half a wary gaze. Mona shrugged and took a taste of wine; this wasn't something she could (or needed to) get control over; the train was at that point leaving the station.

At the point when the entire course finished, Mona chose to mix the pot. Only a tad. Overlooking Liz's wide-peered toward look of stun, Mona stood up and pronounced, "Please, Finley, trade with me, I'm feeling like the unnecessary extra person wheel here... also, it'll allow me to converse with Ivar... Ivar, what about we split the chocolate cake?"

Finley didn't protest and moved her wine and water glasses as Mona exchanged seats with her.

From her seat at the table, Liz watched the pastry course served and devoured. She knew SELENA, and she knew where this would end if she didn't step in. She was less acquainted with Finley, however as indicated by Mona, Finley had in every case painstakingly dealt with her heartfelt undertakings with an eye towards security and not chumming the waters for the sensationalist newspapers. However, from where she was sitting, Liz saw decreasing limitation and expanding tease (which Mona appeared to egg on, annoyingly.)

"Hello, SELENA!" Liz called as the servers tidied up the table, "Come here, I need to converse with you for a brisk sec."

SELENA gestured and went to Finley, "Hold that idea. I'll be directed back."

SELENA's nonappearance appeared to snap Finley back to the real world. What the heck was that, and what occurred in my mind? She got up and gone to the washroom.

Liz saw Finley leaving and went to SELENA, murmuring, "Terrible Rowan! That is a positive, 100% certain, no exemptions ever, clear and brilliant line NO!"

"Who? Finley?" SELENA asked guiltlessly.

Liz folded her arms, "SELENA! Try not to even... Don't - Go - There. Guarantee me."

"We're simply having a good time, Liz. Unwind." SELENA's cocksure smile was irritating.

Liz maneuvered SELENA into the kitchen, assessed individuals in there, altered her perspective, and maneuvered SELENA into the investigation. She shut the entryway for great measure.

"Finley is the future CEO of The Edevane Group!" Liz spat out. Seeing SELENA's casual face, she talked gradually and unmistakably, "The Edevane Group. Possesses about a large portion of the world. She's beneficiary to the whole thing. Do you get it now? She can't be screwing around with you!"

SELENA shrugged, "What difference does it make? Regardless of whether she was the President of the Universe, whom she fucks around with is up to her."

Liz moaned in dissatisfaction, "Definitely, yet you destroyed her with your voodoo. She doesn't at any point fuck around. Like, EVER. That is the reason you need to ease the hellfire off, SELENA. This isn't another of your welcome farewell successes where you tempt a wonderful lady and leave."

"I've scarcely made proper acquaintance!" SELENA said guiltlessly.

"You're so goddamn enraging, SELENA! You're now pondering taking her bed. Also, what might be said about Alice? Is it true that you should be seeing her this end of the week?"

SELENA shrugged, "She headed out to Paris. Yvette welcomed her to some gathering there, and we haven't been in touch since."

Liz shook her head, "We're going off point. See, SELENA, would you be able to if it's not too much trouble, ease off? You realize I never meddle in your business. However, this is unique, alright? Also, SHE'S STRAIGHT!"

"I don't believe she's that straight..." SELENA squirmed her eyebrows, "And possibly you folks are correct... perhaps I do have a perfect partner, and it's Finley! Perhaps she's the one genuine romance all of you think I've been sitting tight for!"

SELENA's mocking tone was combined with a suspicious slant of her head. SELENA's friend network had been (fruitlessly) attempting to match her off with a sweetheart who'd last in excess several months. SELENA remained relentlessly resistant to sentiment. One-off flings, then again, were particularly invited.

"No, she isn't," Liz said mockingly, "You wouldn't perceive a perfect partner if she came and kicked you in the ass!"

"That is because I don't need one. That is to say, don't misunderstand me; I'm excited that you and Mona are into the until the end of time thing; however, that is never fascinating to me. 'Perfect partner' a.k.a. sentiment a.k.a. passionate snares. It's excessively confounded."

"Muddled? Do you need to evade 'convoluted'? At that point, ease the hellfire off, Finley! This has newspaper outrage composed on top of it. It's not great. For both of you."

SELENA pushed her hands in her pockets and was tranquil as Liz's words soaked in. A little flash got back to her eyes as she reclined against the work area, "What about this? I'll ease off. In any case, if she welcomes me over, I'm not going to say no."

Liz considered the big picture briefly, "OK. All good. Be that as it may, she won't welcome you. You know why? Since you will disappear before you voodoo that idea into her cerebrum. You will imagine some anecdote about gathering companions for drinks and get the damnation out of here."

"You're showing me out? You don't confide in me to ease off? Liz, on the off chance that I said I'll ease off, I will."

Liz opened the investigation entryway, "It isn't so much that I don't confide in you. I don't confide in your entire hot vibe thing."

"It's straightforward: Two individuals becoming friends. Furthermore, I don't have a provocative vibe thing."

"Indeed, you do. It's freaking deadly. Presently go wash up and offer me this one kindness. If it's not too much trouble."

"Fine," SELENA streaked her smile once more, "I can't accept you're showing me out."

"Indeed. Sorry. I love you definitely, yet you need to leave now."

"I will bid farewell, alright? That is permitted, right?"

Liz gestured her head hesitantly. SELENA stepped past her, overlooking her glare of objection.

Finley was conversing with Mona in the parlor when SELENA returned. The two ladies scowled when they saw that SELENA wasn't remaining.

"You're leaving?" Mona inquired.

SELENA inclined down and gave Mona an embrace, "Definitely, I'm meeting somebody for drinks. Finley, it was truly ideal to meet you! Safe ventures tomorrow."

Finley gestured, not exactly sure what to say. SELENA's disposition had changed. It was by all accounts all business now. Finley gestured once more, "Great to meet you, as well."

SELENA gave Liz a fast side-embrace farewell, and, like that, she was no more.

Mona took a gander at Finley, "You appear to be frustrated."

Finley ran her fingers through her hair, "I was interested. SELENA is captivating. I loved becoming more acquainted with her."

"You're in good company. Numerous ladies discover SELENA fascinating." Mona laughed.

"She's very... something." Finley needed to choose to utilize the word 'something,' even though it didn't get what she felt. Possibly kidding around with Marlo around casual sexual encounters started the interest hidden the entirety of this. Perhaps it was the way that Marlo was untouchable in some way or another, and SELENA wasn't...

"Why? As a result of the beautiful butch lesbian thing? I thoroughly understand it - I wedded Liz..."

Finley hushed up for a beat, "It's not simply that. There's something that's... I don't have the foggiest idea... it resembles I have an association with SELENA... however, it's so out of nowhere. It doesn't bode well; I mean, I just met her!"

"How fascinated are you?" Mona slanted her head, "This is a little out of your typical safe place, Ms. Edevane!"

Finley reddened. She contemplated where she was at that point... furthermore, where she would have been in 24 hours. She contemplated how, all her grown-up life, she'd been wary and purposeful about individuals she'd dated. Why? Perhaps it was the wine, or possibly it was the organization. However, Finley felt firmly spurred to split away from the point of reference.

Smothering a startling flood of tears, Finley looked at Mona dead without flinching, "On the off chance that I don't venture out of the safe place now, I may never get to. Also, that is frightening."

Mona let out a lazy breath, "Fi..."

Finley held up a hand, "No, it's OK. Look. I'm presumably going to be beneficiary clear for the following years and years. My father's fit and trim. Which implies a couple more many years of being the Perfect Daughter. Also, then..." Finley slowly inhaled, "I'll be sixty... also, old... furthermore, wedded to some person... with a glimmering neon sign that says 'caught in a plated confine' pointing directly at me."

"He may be a pleasant fellow and the man of your dreams...?"

Finley grinned straight, "Not likely. Less and fewer men in those sorts of dreams, Mona..."

The two companions bolted eyes for a beat.

"Gracious," Mona felt such compassion toward her companion, "I had no clue... That is to say; I sort of did... but..."

Finley lifted her eyebrows and shrugged, "I was inept not to attempt to sort this out prior."

"Perhaps you weren't prepared. Also, does it truly matter in any case? You will be the supervisor woman of everybody. Wed a lady, if you need. I'd prefer to see somebody attempt and blacklist you, folks!" Mona stopped and afterward squeezed her hands together, "Yet not SELENA, Finley. Please, for the love of all that is acceptable and blessed, not SELENA."

Finley chuckled, "Goodness, I could advise that she's not one to remain with one individual for long. She's excessively alright with the being a tease."

Mona chuckled, as well. "Disregard 'for long.' SELENA's a 'one and done' type. We thought she was at last prepared to settle down when she met Alice, yet we were dead off-base."

Finley hushed up briefly. Mona got a wine bottle and topped off their glasses. A little fluid boldness is likely useful here...

"Thanks..." Finley held her breath briefly before allowing it to out, "One and done... one and done..."

Mona took a gander at her companion and positioned an eyebrow, "Where are you going with this?"

"I think," Finley said as she took a major swallow of wine, "that I'd like you to tell SELENA I need to meet her this evening."

Mona didn't dare to move. Finley becomes flushed once more. Mona was one of Finley's most confided-in companions whose watchfulness was just about as dependable as the sun rising each day. Mona was the storehouse of Finley's school smashes, unexpected failures to comprehend the issues at hand... furthermore, other capers not befitting The Edevane Group's scion. It appeared to be that there would be one all the more such occasion around evening time.

"Indeed," Finley said, all the more certainly now, "If it's not too much trouble, let SELENA realize I'll meet her at my lodging... the Brackenridge. If it's not too much trouble, let her realize that I'm anxious to proceed with our discussion."
"You're not kidding." Mona was stunned. "You truly are not kidding!"

"Indeed," Finley smoothed down her dress, "If she's so disposed, and I think she is, I'd like SELENA to drop by this evening."

Mona whistled. "Alright. Is it true that you are certain? Since, supposing that I hand-off your message, she will appear."

Finley gestured as she stood up, "I will spruce up and head out. I'll message you once I get to the inn. Mona, much obliged. I would not joke about this."

In a little while, Liz discovered Mona composing into her telephone.

"Finley just sent me her lodging information for tonight..."

"Inn data? What are you doing?" Liz glanced on with sickening dread as she saw the beneficiary of Mona's content.

{Mona} SELENA, Finley requested that I let you realize that she's remaining at The Brackenridge this evening. Room 1208. She needed me to disclose to you that she's anxious to proceed with her discussion with you.

"Try not to HIT SEND!" Liz yelled, "What the heck, honey!!???"

Mona's finger floated over the "send" button, "This is all Finley, Liz. It's what she needs. Furthermore, don't see me like that! You're the person who welcomed SELENA!"

"Jesus," Liz murmured.

"I was too clear about SELENA's history. I guarantee. She needs this. Fair!"

"We're going to set off the beginnings of a gigantic outrage," Liz murmured as she ran her eyes over the content Mona just composed.

"Possibly not," Mona countered, "SELENA resembles a fricking vault." With a little screech, Mona hit "send."

"However, there're similar to 1,000,000 cameras and staff..."

"Finley realizes how to deal with all that. It's her inn for the wellbeing of god. She needs this. I think she knows she's out of her defensive air pocket for one evening and one night as it were. She needs this."

SELENA grinned when she got the content. There was as yet an opportunity Finley would ease off from allowing anything to occur. However, it merited seeing where the evening took them. SELENA enjoyed turning the roulette wheel in the circumstances like this; she loved the air of shock, the unforeseen.

Finley didn't need to stand by well before hearing a soft yet sure thump on her entryway. I just settled on a goods decision. Good lord. I just settled on a goods decision, and she's here.

Finley opened the entryway. SELENA smiled and lifted a hand in hello.

Oh my goodness, she looks astonishing. "Hey! I couldn't say whether you'd come."

SELENA quirked an eyebrow.

Finley reddened when she understood the risqué statement she'd expressed, "Um, why not come... er... come in... come in here..." Holy crap, I just did it once more.

SELENA grinned and strolled into the room, "Pleasant burrows."

"Much obliged. One of the advantages of claiming a lodging network. An advantageous hideaway directly in the center of the city."

SELENA gestured in comprehension.

"So," Finley chose the couch in the room and tapped it for SELENA to join her, "What were we discussing? You know, before you vanished on me." What the hellfire am I doing? Making casual banter? Really??!!

SELENA obliged, apparently glad to participate in the ludicrously hackneyed, and plunked down close to Finley, "Your birthday celebration a month ago where you handled some improper inquiries from your folks out on the town you brought..."

"Ok, yes. My folks were first disturbed that I didn't have a date, and afterward, when I brought a date, they thought that it was important to contest his essence." No compelling reason to expound that I deliberately picked somebody whom I knew would kindle a response... Finley grinned at the memory, feeling the little triumph of public insubordination. She'd quite a while in the past surrendered finding a perfect partner - being next in line for a prominent privately-owned company made it close to unimaginable. It didn't assist with being contrasted continually with her more youthful sister, who was joyfully hitched with two young men for sure. Benji can accept the responsibility the second he moves on from school; I can resign and pass on indefinite quality.

SELENA looked doubtful, "Indeed, because being in your thirties implies who you date is still a reasonable game for parental denial."

"Forties, SELENA. I turned forty a month ago."

"Liar!" SELENA was amazed. It understands, course: Finley and Mona were school counterparts. The two of them looked youthful for their age. SELENA frequently failed to remember the Mona was more established than her by ten years.

"Truth! Droopy boobs and decreasing sex drive are all coming right up!" Finley was shocked by the words that emerged from her mouth. Where did that come from?

"To begin with, I profoundly question the droopy boobs part..." SELENA's eyes cleared certainly across Finley's chest.

Finley nearly let out a little whine. SELENA watched Finley's lips part marginally in response to her intentional visual touch. Awesome.

"Second, no better time than right now to take one's sex drive for a spin..." SELENA's mouth twisted unquestionably into an arrogant smile.

Finley set both her hands level on her lap and said, with some doubt, to test SELENA's purpose, "Here? On the couch, SELENA?"

SELENA needed to recalibrate; she would not like to move excessively fast, even though Finley was putting out the desired signs. She inclined forward and read Finley briefly before shrugging with an innocent appeal. SELENA got another great sign in shutting the distance between them: Finley's eyes shined briefly and never jumped.

"I'm available on the off chance that you are... what's more, the couch is nevertheless one of the numerous options..." SELENA started unobtrusively. She set her pointer on the highest point of Finley's center finger and delicately stroked it.

SELENA's touch hypnotized Finley's eyes and skin. The more seasoned lady shifted her head, "You sound colossally certain... might I advise you that I figure a lot of things would have to occur previously... um... anything could happen...?"

SELENA nearly didn't sleep for a while that Finley sent her direction, yet there was no mixing up the course the night was going. There was a ton to appreciate about the current circumstance: The verbal dressing, the thriving science, and the association's immediacy.

SELENA took a ton of fire most days for exploring every available opportunity. However, she saw no motivation to think about settling down when nights like this existed.

SELENA squeezed her case, "Ah! Lucidity of direction. I like a lady with an arrangement. Which one of those 'number of things' would it be advisable for us to handle first?"

Finley snickered apprehensively, "I don't have a clue!

SELENA grasped Finley's hand and kissed it, "There are numerous choices: seriously kissing... undressing... talking... or then again every one of the three simultaneously... or then again we could talk. Your call."

Finley was having what must be depicted as a psychological emergency. SELENA was not too far off, totally open to anything Finley desired. In however the several hours unfurled, it would be at Finley's caution... or on the other hand, carelessness.

"I don't have a clue what to do," she admitted, "I disclosed to Mona I needed to disassociate from my typical air pocket of a day-to-day existence, I don't..." Finley felt pointlessly bumbling.

"We can simply talk," SELENA offered truly. She would not like to push.

"I would prefer not to talk," Finley shook her head.

SELENA's heartbeat hopped, "That is fine, as well."

Finley chuckled apprehensively.

"Come here," SELENA inclined forward.

Finley agreed, and SELENA gently brushed their lips against one another. Finley cherished it. She hurried nearer, her whole body humming.

They kissed for quite a long time... hours... an unfathomable length of time. SELENA's hands had been tangled in Finley's hair this time. However, they began to wander lower. SELENA got a handle on Finley's midriff and pulled her nearer, procuring her a groan that reverberated profound from inside Finley.

SELENA's hands meandered further and squeezed Finley's bosoms interestingly.

"Good lord!" inhaled Finley. This was an alternate sort of foreplay through and through. As far as she can tell, foreplay was careless - and for the most part agreeable - introduction to the sex act. This was a different encounter: SELENA appeared to be in no rush by any stretch of the imagination; she was unintentionally and mindfully animated. Finley was sure that on the off chance that she'd been a person, she'd have been accomplished for quite a while past.

"Bed. Bed!" Finley yelled as SELENA's thumbs made a pass across her nipples. The texture of her dress demonstrated no safeguard against SELENA's touch.

SELENA stood and offered her hand to Finley.

Finley didn't know she would have been ready to remain with any nobility; SELENA had obliterated all similarity to actual coordination. When she figured out how to get to her feet, she became intensely mindful of the zone between her legs and the impacts of SELENA's ministrations. < i> Jesus. How is she doing to me? I'm not some confused virgin who's never had intercourse! However, my goodness, I'm so wet...

Some way or another, Finley wound up lying on the room's huge jumbo bed. SELENA had - mysteriously, it appeared - eliminated the covers... also, similarly as mystically, eliminated her dress. Finley, a rehearsed hand nearby self-regulated joy, struggled to change SELENA's overwhelming and certain rhythm. Finley flickered and attempted to zero in on all that SELENA was doing to her. Her eyes at long last worked once more, just to see SELENA's mouth dropping upon her bra-encased bosoms.

"Gracious!" Finley shouted as she felt SELENA's testing tongue work its way across every nipple.

SELENA adored causing a lady to submit to joy. Finley was an excellent and exciting accomplice. SELENA delicately eliminated Finley's bra, and the second her bosoms were uncovered, she covered them with consideration. Finley couldn't shape words any longer; her body was beating with need. SELENA eliminated the last piece of clothing and devoured Finley's sex. A profound, throaty groan ejected from Finley's mouth. It seemed like SELENA's fingers and tongue were all over the place, inside, outside, on her bosoms, grasping her thighs... Finley had never come this hard. She didn't have any acquaintance with it was conceivable.

However, SELENA's impulses revealed to her that Finley wasn't anyplace close to done, which fit SELENA fine and dandy. Her capable tongue manufactured new ways and better approaches to satisfy Finley, who felt continued many a rush of orgasmic euphoria. Finley got herself again astounded. She had never come this hard, this often previously. My goodness...

SELENA watched Finley descend off her peak. She crept up and loosened up close to Finley. SELENA cherished this second: a lady taking in post-coital rapture was straightforward flawlessness. It was flawlessness improved all the because she knew there would be no epilog to this evening. There would be no sweetheart's spat or relationship intricacy to deface the memory of this second.

The two ladies recuperated in peaceful quiet. Finley, at long last, opened her eyes and saw SELENA seeing her, "How could you do that?"

SELENA grinned, "I figure you did its vast majority."

"You're still completely dressed," Finley went after SELENA's shirt, "That doesn't appear right..."

SELENA shook her head, "No, it's about you around evening time." Why ruin something worth being thankful for? Leave now, and everybody rests cheerfully.

Finley shifted her head, "That doesn't appear to be ok," she said once more.

SELENA inclined down and kissed her on the button, "You have itinerary items tomorrow, and I have a morning meal meeting in a couple of hours. It's late."

Finley took a gander at the clock and was stunned to see that it was very nearly two AM. SELENA sat up and got her shirt into her jeans.

Without the deduction, Finley mumbled, "One and done..."

"Sorry?" SELENA went to confront Finley.

"Mona. She said you proceeded onward rapidly. 'One and done,' she said. That is to say, this turns out great for me... however, you truly don't wait, isn't that right?"

SELENA shrugged, "I like leaving on a high note."

"Imagine a scenario in which there are higher notes that you pass up because you don't stay."

"Things get confounded on the off chance that you stay," SELENA clarified, "I favor things not getting muddled."

Finley gestured, "All good." She sat up and wrapped a bed sheet around herself.

"I had a great time around evening time," SELENA smiled, "and prepare to have your mind blown.

"What?"

SELENA strolled over to the entryway and turned around with mischief in her eyes, "You certainly don't have floppy boobs, and you unquestionably don't have a reducing sex drive. I can bear witness to those two realities, without a doubt."

Finley turned beet red and examined unadulterated frenzy all over.

SELENA stepped back to the bed and plunked down until she was taking a gander at Finley, "Hello. Hello. Finley. I was joking. I will not utter a word to anybody. I guarantee."

Finley's gut nature was to confide in SELENA, "Alright," she gestured, "OK."

"Truly," SELENA grasped Finley's hand and crushed, "I will not inform a spirit concerning any of this. Not even Liz and Mona."

"Not even your future spouse?" Finley prodded.

"Amusing. There'll certainly be no future spouse," SELENA expressed solidly, "It's all acceptable."

"Never say never, SELENA," Finley sang out, "Spousal advantage. It's a genuine article."

"You need genuine? Three things in life will consistently be valid: demise, charges, and me not truly getting hitched," SELENA headed towards the entryway, "Straightforwardness, not entanglements, 100% ensured."

Finley floundered in reverse into the pads once SELENA had gone. "Good lord," she said for all to hear. She replayed the night in her mind over and over. It felt increasingly more dreamlike the more she considered everything. And afterward... out of the blue... I keep thinking about whether this is what it would feel like if Marlo and I had intercourse...

Goodness. Goodness!

"Blessed. Crap." Those were the only words Finley could reasonably create. Marlo... sex with Marlo... gee... sex with Marlo... Finley felt a tasty shuddering that has nothing to do with SELENA.

"My goodness," Finley murmured once more. Since quite a while ago, secret truth was unstoppable at this point. SELENA's ministrations were orgasmically explaining. Finley needed more... yet, not from the beautiful butch lesbian that as of late left her lodging... she needed it from the one who'd been sitting in the plated confine with her from the start.

On auto-pilot, Finley went after her telephone and messaged Marlo, {Finley} What are you doing?" She contemplated whether Marlo was at that point in bed with another person. Finley pressed her eyes shut. The envy curved and twisted around itself with earnestness. This was the reason she had never let the playing with Marlo get past the easygoing jokes. In any case, it was past the point of no return presently; she'd at last conceded reality: She needed Marlo... all to herself.

She gazed at her telephone, willing Marlo to surrender her tryst and react. At the point when her telephone remained tenaciously quiet, she crept under the covers and turned off the light. Resting appeared to be the solitary conceivable approach to prevent her mind from collapsing with its most recent disclosure.

As she was going to float off to rest, however, her telephone rang. Finley snapped the light on and addressed the call. It was Marlo, and it appeared as though she was in a gathering going all out.

"Where the hellfire are you?" Finley murmured, folding the sheets over herself.

Finley's exposure didn't get away from Marlo's notification. However, she claimed not to mind, "Cassie Beaumont's home. For what reason would you say you are up so late?"

Finley's eyebrows shot up, "The Cassie Beaumont from that hero establishment? She welcomed you to her home?"

"Sure," Marlo made an effort not to allow her eyes to wander over Finley's sheet-encased structure, "She was at one of those get-together talks, and she welcomed me over."

Finley's heart gripped, realizing beyond any doubt what Marlo had come up for the evening, "OK. Have a good time. I'll see you when you get back."

"Stand by!" Marlo scowled, "It resembles just about three AM for you, correct? It is safe to say that you are alright, Finley?"

"Indeed! I needed to say goodbye."

"Are you certain?" Marlo gazed at her companion, who gestured, "OK - I'll see you back in California."

Finley watched Marlo's picture vanish and slid the telephone onto her bedside table. She wished her emotions away. Marlo's never going to quit exploring every available opportunity. Individuals don't change... She didn't see I was exposed!

"Presently, it will be convoluted." Finley pressed her eyes shut, "I disdain it when things get confounded."

That evening, Finley promised - if SELENA could keep it straightforward, she could too.

Chapter 2: An Unexpected Piece of News (Present Day, San Francisco)

Finley stirred to the delicate ringing of a morning meal plate determined to the table in the abutting room. Not interestingly, Finley praised herself in deciding to take up home at the Brackenridge in San Francisco. Living in an inn addressed a huge number of accommodations, of which breakfast room administration was one.

"Hello, ma'am," Paula said unobtrusively. Paula has been the assigned orderly for Finley since she moved into the penthouse suite a year prior after Brandon Edevane passed on startlingly in his rest. The family was all the while faltering from his misfortune, and the house on Eldridge Street has been standing void since his passing. None of the family needed to move in; his quality was still excessively firmly felt; however, none could stomach selling it by the same token. As the recently printed CEO, Finley made the most extraordinary stride of getting the nation over toward the West Coast; she advocated it by referring to the developing base of business the Edevane Group had with Silicon Valley.

"'Morning," Finley answered drowsily. She cushioned off to the restroom and returned before long, "How's the early daytime unfurling?"

"Great, ma'am," Paula had productively spread out two settings of breakfast, "Dr. Wright is holding up outside."

"She demands the formality..." Finley blew a raspberry at her room entryway, "... what's more, that is my opinion about it!!"

Paula laughed, "Will I request that she come in?"

Finley's eyes streaked fiendishly as she said in a voice that conveyed, "No, I figure we should make her pause."

"I heard that!" came a stifled voice from past the entryway.

Paula's eyes ping-ponged between Edevane Group's CEO and the lodging entryway. Aside from Finley's mom, Marlo Wright was the lone individual with free admittance to the CEO. It didn't take long for Paula to comprehend why the talk factory demanded sustaining the possibility that Finley and Marlo had a closeted illicit relationship. Both of them had an association, that is without a doubt, yet it was puzzling why neither appeared to need to take it past companionship.

Finley had kept her promise from five years prior. Admirers made their advances. However, she generally rebuked them. Finley's disclosure about her sentiments about Marlo remained securely stowed away from seeing: it was less convoluted that way... not least because Marlo confirmed no aim of busy except for bedding however many ladies as she could. Finley chose to sustain her fellowship with Marlo; there were no ambiguities there: They were each other's must confide in a partner and progressively share the obligations of Edevane's issues. Once more, nobody thought it was important to remark; it appeared to be normal and inescapable.

There was, nonetheless, one thing that had changed since Finley took over CEO obligations a year prior: Marlo started demanding formalizing their cooperations every step of the way, looking for meetings with Finley when none was vital, taking remarkable lengths to show concession to Finley out in the open. She did it for the most part to bother Finley. It generally worked.

This specific morning, Finley decided not to react to Marlo's protestation. She took a seat at the table and started to have her morning meal, indefatigably overlooking the other spot setting Paula had spread out.

Finley took her first taste of espresso, claiming to not notification as the entryway swung open and a tall lady with a stun of bleach light hair ventured into the room. Paula pulled out the seat, and Marlo slid her tall edge into it.

"Will there be whatever else?" Paula asked the two ladies.

"No, thank you, Paula," Finley grinned at her.

"Excellent, ma'am," Paula set a heap of papers on the table and took off of the room. She grinned to herself as she shut the entryway, catching Marlo's calm, "You're such a butt head!" to Finley.

Finley blew one more raspberry at her companion, "Just you merited, darling."

Marlo feigned exacerbation, "There're conventions, you know?"

"Stop it. I'm not some ruined rich princess that gets off on bowing and scratching."

"No, no," Marlo's eyes shimmered fiendishly, "You're not Princess Finley, that is without a doubt... it's Queen Finley now... All hail the Queen!"

Marlo bowed richly, just to be met with a contemptuous snap of Finley's napkin across her shoulder.

"Cut that out, Marlo," Finley said in a firmer voice, "I can advise you without reservation that you can push your made-up conventions straight up your butt." Finley tossed a touch of toast at Marlo for accentuation.

Marlo recoiled as it hit her in the face, "Individuals will believe I'm taking freedoms... that I'm expecting excessively."

Finley sat up straighter and angled an eyebrow, "And what freedoms would that be, Marlo? That we're having some shameful issue?" Finley waved her hand hatefully, "Individuals imagine that as of now! Why give them the fulfillment of us changing our conduct?"

Marlo's mind mixed briefly. Getting sweltering and weighty with Finley was actually what she didn't require newly seared into her mind that morning.

This was an odd result of two individuals being long-lasting companions: Finley and Marlo were so acquainted that they'd quit attempting to sort each other out. In some other situation, Marlo would have gotten on the trace of bitterness behind Finley's eyes... be that as it may, she was excessively bustling attempting to conceal her affections for her companion. Jesus. Take a few to get back some composure, Marlo. She tasted espresso and conveyed an all-around rehearsed lie, "I was discussing irreconcilable circumstances and conventions. What's more, I understand what the newspaper tattle says. They're misguided, and I'm not taking care of that characterless pool of trash."

"Indeed, indeed, Marlo. I'm not your sort, and you're not into me that way. That line doesn't appear to reverberate with the gossip plant, however!" Finley prodded.

"They can't make up their brains about whether I'm accomplishing something improper with you or that I'm undermining you...!"

Finley snickered, "Genuinely? I surmise they have a point - possibly you should take a stab at dating one individual for over about fourteen days! That will give them something to expound on!"

"I'm not giving them that much control over my affection life. There's a lot of fish in the ocean, Finley; why not keep it intriguing?" Marlo squirmed her eyebrows lustfully.

This was a different line that Finley had heard regularly, and given the line of excellent ladies Marlo dated, there was never any sign why Finley would accept something else. What's more, subsequently, one more day passed in which two ladies were infatuated with one another; however, neither could see past their muddling of reality. The tattle writers endured, however, speculating that Finley had no interest in finding an accomplice because Marlo was the one keeping her bed comfortable around evening time.

"This is the reason individuals keep making up anecdotes about us!" Finley said great-naturedly, "To keep things fascinating!"

Marlo shrugged, "Indeed, however, now they're making crap up about the CEO of the Edevane Group; that is not cool."

Finley feigned exacerbation, "Look, in case you're stressed over individuals' over-dynamic minds with regards to you and me... I'll welcome Lawrence Halliday for the birthday celebration craziness one week from now he's been more than lovely. That will get the job done."

Marlo put down her flatware and took a gander at Finley, "Halliday?! He's keen on you?!!"

Finley tossed her head back and giggled, tickled by Marlo's response, "A great many people discover me very satisfactory, Marlo! Try not to act like you're stunned! Halliday's has been giving extremely close consideration - he even welcomed me to his child's wedding. I declined. I don't figure his ex would have valued it."

Marlo let out a derisive breathe out, "He's utilizing you."

"Calm down! Don't you realize I realize that? It'd be credulous to suspect something. Yet, we've discussed this, Marlo. Halliday can live like royalty me all he needs. I'm not intrigued. Be that as it may, no mischief in utilizing him to mix the pot of individuals' practically fanatical interest in who I engage in sexual relations with."

Marlo peered down, attempting to figure out how to discuss some different options from Finley's sexual coexistence. Marlo's charisma had different thoughts, however: Marlo was attempting to compel her eyes to remain bolted on her plate as Finley inclined forward to go after the salt. Finley's robe - as Marlo realized it would - fell open somewhat. Finley's noteworthy bosoms - perfect spheres of smooth caramel tissue - asked to be respected, even though Marlo made an honest effort to turn away. At last, as usual, she permitted herself a quick look, and what she saw animated her center and stirred up her longing for

Finley, scrambling her minds once more. Fortunately, the arcing clear of her lecherous look finished on the heap of papers on the table.

Marlo grinned, grateful to have tracked down an original method to change the subject, "I practically neglected - this came out today!" She pulled out the Business News Ledger, whose feature of the day declared that Finley had been named BNL's Person of the Year.

Finley glared hesitantly, "I get it's true! Did they take our alters?"

Marlo gestured, "They took out the 'guardian angel of the world' piece, yes. Please Fi, the main monetary paper on the planet believes you're great. Appreciate it a bit!"

Finley spread out the paper before her, "There's something excessively advantageous lauding the 'do-gooder very rich person.' There're a lot of individuals... people, who are more meriting the honor."

"No doubt about it," Marlo pointed at the article, recollecting the meeting when it had happened, "You pushed for some hard decisions when you got the proposals to purchase out your sun-based energy fire up. It's been draining millions every year. You denied the individuals who gave you a simple out to save your main concern. That takes strength."

Finley checked the article, "Marlo, you realize I was unable to do any of this without you, right?" She hung over and gave Marlo a modest kiss on her cheek.

This was something Finley had done multiple times, if not more, but rather the kiss waited on Marlo's skin, and the blonde's pulse sped up. Finley had consistently been a friendly individual; it never became obvious her to be in any case with Marlo, who was so natural to her, so courageous and indispensable. Marlo profoundly needed these minutes yet additionally dreaded what they would uncover. She had prepared herself to radiate a separation she didn't feel inside.

Marlo waved her hand pretentiously, "I'm the guinea pig. You're the genuine article."

Marlo and her group had been vital to Edevane's off-network energy technique, which tried to reclassify how power could be gathered. The most encouraging arrangement - another approach to building sun-powered boards - was near the real world. However, the sharks had been circumnavigating well before that. Finley held them all under control, like to accept the misfortunes as the specialists were solemnly contemplated, tried, and re-tried. Presently, ten years after the principal meeting with the sun-powered group, Finley was prepared to distinguish expected vital accomplices to talk about the ways forward. The BNL hailed Finley's patient methodology as the encapsulation of focusing on information over benefit, an advantage over acquire.

"Father purchased in as well! Furthermore, I will go to my grave shielding the choice to stand by," completed Finley. She took a gander at the clock, "Discussing which, you have your call with Gilchrist Labs coming up. They owe us an advancement report - reveal to them I'll go to California and inhale down their necks on the off chance that I need to!"

Marlo cleaned her mouth with a napkin and pushed back from the table, "What do you signify 'on the off chance that you need to'? You love California! What's more, the gathering's coming up - slaughter two birds with one outing!"

Finley shrugged, "Meh."

"I thought you made some great memories five years prior?" Marlo shifted her head inquiringly.

"You made some great memories at your get-together. I went to one supper. What's more, it was at my companion Mona's home. I surmise it'd be more exact to say I made some great memories spending time with my companions at Mona's home." Finley never explained what unfolded at that supper, nor did she at any point trace of the affair that followed.

"... so could you ask for anything better? You're five years more established at this point. Huge challenge! Doesn't mean a happy time can't be had, your majesty..." Marlo smiled.

Finley disregarded the burrow, "Indeed, indeed, because you figured out how to entice some closeted Hollywood diva at your last get-together doesn't mean age will not find you by the same token. Presently accomplish some genuine work and sort out if the Gilchrist public can create what they guaranteed! What's more, quit looking so egotistical!"

Marlo stuck her tongue out at Finley as she left the room. She jabbed her head back in immediately, "Gracious, and your mom needs you to affirm the wine list for the following week's supper, birthday young lady."

Finley murmured and frowned at the roof, "It's your birthday as well, Marlo. You pick the wine list."

"God helps us; she will not!" Juniper's voice became stronger as she drew closer.

"Marlo Wright, you set me up!" Finley heaved. Marlo smiled.

"Hello, Marlo, dear," Finley's mom proffered her cheek for a kiss.

"Hello, Juniper," Marlo obliged and, after tossing a 'gotcha,' take a gander at Finley, stepped off down the foyer.

"She saw you are coming, and she set me up," Finley griped.

"Indeed, she did," Juniper moved the envelopes she was conveying and gave her girl an opposing look, "You're as yet in your shower robe!"

"Whatever," Finley poured her mom some espresso, "Marlo's seen me in less." I could appear in her room exposed, and she wouldn't give it a second thought...
Juniper gave Finley a long, hard look before shaking her head with a moan. She left the suite, profoundly curious about the couple in the paper and considering what might have frightened her little girl like that.

When the entryway clicked shut, Finley got the paper and looked at the article about Rowan and Lauren ravenously.

Lauren Calder and Rowan "SELENA" Kan have hitched May seventeenth in a private function in California. The couple met a year ago while working at Winchester Brown, a worldwide venture bank...

There was more to the article. However, Finley couldn't resist gazing at the photo. Her mom was correct; they looked exceptionally content. In the photograph, SELENA's face was overflowing with affection and pride. It caused her to show up blissfully seraphic.

Finley felt completely deserted... what's more, deceived. She had a feeling that she'd made a settlement with herself to keep things straightforward. She had discovered the mental fortitude in her feelings to adhere to isolation since she realized that someplace out on the planet, SELENA was doing likewise. Yet, SELENA wasn't. SELENA had - some way or another - switched her assurance of staying unattached.

"SELENA..." Finley said discreetly, "What changed?"

Chapter 3: A Birthday Bash (A Week Later, San Francisco)

The inn staff was out in full power as Finley's birthday's final arrangements got in progress.

"This is the craziest misuse of everyone's time," Finley was pissed, "A gathering is the exact opposite thing I need."

"Remain quiet about it," her mom reproved, "Everyone's buckling down, kindly don't circumvent causing individuals to feel like they accomplished something incorrectly. Since they didn't."

"FINE." Finley stomped out of her mom's room and stepped furiously back to her suite.

Juniper murmured and went over the seating diagram once again. The family had taken up a whole floor of the Brackenridge for the week, paving the way to the enormous birthday festivities, and the vast majority of them had been grateful that Finley's suite was on an alternate floor. The future birthday young lady felt terrible essentially the entire week, which was exacerbated by Marlo's nonattendance. Marlo required a three-road trip to a gathering in Portland yet was expected back any moment.

Juniper turned upward hopefully when the way to the drawing-room opened, yet Gregory, not Marlo, stepped in.

"Everything's a solid first floor," he said brilliantly, "I just looked in on the A/V practices, and it's solid."

"Much obliged, Gregory. Is Marlo back yet?"

"Actually, no, not for another half hour, most likely." Gregory checked the time.

"Would you be able to send her straight in when she returns kindly?" Juniper grinned, "Nothing to stress over; I simply need a word with her."

"Obviously," Gregory gestured, "Goodness and the head gourmet expert are holding up outside. Would it be a good idea for me to have her come in?"

Juniper gestured, "Indeed, indeed, yes... much appreciated, Gregory."

Darla, the head gourmet specialist, came through and dove straight into the menu. Juniper gestured now and then; there was no compelling reason to do much else as Darla appeared to have thoroughly considered every one of the points and bunch dietary limitations.

A certain thump on the entryway declared Marlo's return. Juniper yelled for her to enter and highlighted the seat close to her. Darla accumulated her pile of papers and took off.

"Cheerful birthday Marlo," the more established lady inclined toward Marlo's side briefly.

"Much obliged, Juniper," Marlo reclined lovingly against the matron, "More established, yet not more shrewd!"

Juniper waved her hand contemptuously, "How was the flight?"

"Pretty smooth flight. The gathering was predictable... I have some excellent news that Finley will be glad to hear. Father said you needed to see me?"

Juniper moaned, "More like I needed to caution you: Her illustrious height has been experiencing a significant deficiency of relationship-building abilities this previous week. She's been a pill. Proceed with caution, uplifting news or not."

"Is it accurate to say that she is going nuts about getting more established?"

"No," Juniper ventured into an organizer and chose the Weddings Announcements page from seven days prior, "It was this. I incline it was this."

"Halliday's child's wedding?" Marlo sneered, "She doesn't care for the person!"

Juniper pointed at the article underneath, "No, this article. Do you know both of these ladies?"

Marlo ran her eyes rapidly preposterous, "Probably not. Never found out about them. Fi cracked around two ladies getting hitched?"

"She gazed at this article for some time and afterward sort of daydreamed. She's been a buzzkill from that point forward."

Marlo turned upward entertainingly, "How would you know the term 'buzzkill'?"

Juniper winked, "It assists with having grandchildren. Benji and Evan disclosed to me I was 'a significant buzzkill' a week ago when they asked for more frozen yogurt, and I said no! I thought that it was great!"

Marlo threw, "Alright. I'll see why Finley's by and large such a torment in the, guess what. May I have that article?"

Marlo turned the paper around and read through the article. There appeared to be next to no to clarify why it would cause Finley any trouble.

Stand by a second.

Marlo read out loud, "'The couple met a year ago while working at Winchester Brown. Winchester Brown. That is her companion Mona's firm. Her companion Mona, who facilitated the gathering supper five years prior... the supper where she returned saying she had a truly happy time, however, wouldn't reveal to me anything else...'"

Marlo gazed toward Juniper, who wasn't following Marlo's line of reasoning.

"What is it, Marlo?"

Marlo's cerebrum tumbled forward wildly as she got a handle on this line of request, "However, why get vexed about this declaration?"

Juniper pointed at the photograph, "She said she knows this lady... um... 'SELENA,' as per the article."

Marlo gazed at the photograph. Be that as it may, for what reason would she get all disturbed about these folks getting hitched? Except if she didn't need them getting hitched? In any case, is there any good reason why she wouldn't? She wouldn't participate if she... gracious!

"Blessed effing poop." Marlo felt like she'd been punched in the gut.

Juniper took one glance at Marlo's face, and a brilliant instinct fit properly, "You think Finley was associated with one of them!!??"

Marlo pointed at SELENA, "Her. Rowan... uh, SELENA..." Marlo needed to clear the smile off SELENA's face.

Juniper was stunned for a couple of moments, yet then she began gesturing, "Alright... On the off chance that Finley met SELENA at Mona's supper, and if something occurred... Indeed, that would clarify a ton."

It's unrealistic. Fi discloses to me everything. She would have advised me if she'd laid down with a lady! Marlo drooped once again into the seat. "Possibly nothing occurred between them; perhaps this Rowan lady only provoked her curiosity."

"I trust something occurred!" Juniper heaved, "At that point, at any rate, I'd realize she has a premium in taking a sweetheart!"

Marlo's eyes streaked, "You're not annoyed that she may have laid down with a lady?"

"I may be old. However, I'm not so sort of old. I've never been messed with you laying down with ladies... For what reason would I be messed with Finley laying down with a lady?"

Marlo jumped. The words 'Finley laying down with a lady' cut through her heart, and she neglected to imagine she couldn't have cared less.

Juniper contemplated Marlo's face intently, "What right?"

Marlo scowled, realizing that she'd said excessively. She kept her mouth shut.

"Is it accurate to say that you are annoyed because Finley left well enough alone from you? Or then again, are you troubled because she laid down with a lady and it wasn't you?" Juniper caused a stir. However, her eyes were delicate; she knew the appropriate response as of now. It's no time like the present. This all came out of the shadows!

Marlo froze. Around 1,000,000 feelings undulated through her blue eyes. She felt Juniper's hand on her lower arm, tapping her delicately.

"Marlo, goodness nectar, how long?"

"Since the dawn of time," Marlo attempted to battle the tears gushing in her eyes.

"At that point, go advise her, Marlo! What are you hanging tight for?" Juniper was at that point celebrating inside.

Marlo opened her mouth; however, no words came out.

Juniper tapped Marlo's hand, "Marlo. Quit slowing down."

"She doesn't need me. She needs her." Marlo pointed at the photograph of SELENA and Lauren.

"She's not accessible any longer. Stop. Slowing down."

All Marlo could feel was the sting of dismissal. Finley didn't need her, hadn't been straightforward with her, and had been feeling awful all week given a lady Marlo hadn't known existed before today.

"I'm going for a run."

"Marlo..."

"I can't converse with her at present, Juniper," Marlo strolled tragically out the entryway, "I wouldn't realize what to say."

Juniper assembled her contemplations briefly, processing all that that'd simply occurred. She shook her head, "So much for the younger age being less hung up on stuff this way."

Finley, then, was gazing lazily out the window, feeling more alone than any other time. SELENA, the stubborn 'one and done' enticer of ladies, had some way or another become hopelessly enamored and eagerly promised to remain consistent with one individual for the remainder of her life. It was puzzling. In a long time since meeting SELENA, Finley had clung to the way of thinking of "no convoluted ensnarements" - it was an advantageous method to keep undesirable consideration under control, and (all the more significantly) a method of persuading herself that considering anything with Marlo would be excessively confounded. Dislike Marlo would be distantly intrigued in any case... Finley counseled herself for the umpteenth time that day.

A glimmer of shading grabbed her attention. A sprinter, going across the road underneath, jogged alongside a natural loping walk. That must be Marlo. She didn't try to stop by after her excursion. We haven't said 'cheerful birthday' to one another. I truly will bite the dust alone and unkempt. A flood of self-centeredness washed over Finley. The second Marlo got to the opposite side of the road, Finley felt much more terrible. Marlo halted and accepted another lady, who'd been sitting tight for her. They talked for some time and set off together. The other lady was - infuriatingly - staying aware of Marlo's shuddering speed. At the point when the pair diverted and vanished from sight, Finley turned her eyes towards the roof and murmured.

That is presumably Marlo's date for this evening's supper. I must meet Marlo's date and grin like I believe it's the best thing ever that Marlo's found one more sweetheart to lure.

Finley abandoned the window and followed into the washroom. She turned the shower on and remained under the planes of warm water, which converged with the tears spilling down her face. "This is strange," she murmured, "Take a few to get back some composure, Finley!"

She took as much time as is needed getting dry and pulling on a wraparound before sluggishly looking through her email. Her inbox had kept on detonating with birthday well-wishes, and for once, she was glad to go through them. Should move the cards to say thanks...

Similarly, as she was going to go cross-peered toward with weariness, Finley snatched her telephone and called Mona.

"Fi!! Upbeat birthday, young lady!" Mona got very quickly, "I'm sorry we can't be there. Every one of the three children has their finish of school shows today and tomorrow, and we were unable to make the outing."

"I'd prefer to go to the shows with you, trust me!" Finley said harshly.

Mona made a thoughtful snort, "Neurosis? Please out to my place in Long Island - we're praising the start of summer this end of the week! An entire bundle of us old women is getting together for a gathering - we're dumping get-together occasions and digging in. Come!"

Finley turned when she heard a thump on the entryway. It was Paula, getting the outfit Finley was because of wear for the gathering.

"I may take you up on that. I was calling since I need some help." Finley waved her in and, seeing that Paula had hung up the dress, turned around towards the window. Marlo ventured into the room similarly as Paula was leaving.

"Name it," Mona answered on the opposite stopping point.

Finley slowly inhaled and said, "I need you to place me in contact with SELENA. It's significant."

Marlo couldn't accept that what she just heard. She'd cleared her head during her run and had made plans to, in any event, offer a friendly ear to Finley, however now she wasn't so certain. She shut the entryway uproariously enough and caused it to seem like she just strolled in. Finley gave her a little wave.

"Are you OK?" Mona inquired.

"I simply need to converse with her."

"Alright. She's back in California now... Finley, she... uh... she got hitched recently..." Mona's voice followed off.

"I know."

"Alright. I'll send you her contact information. She will be at my place at the end of the week. Is it accurate to say that you are certain you're alright?"

"Better believe it. Much appreciated, Mona," Finley said into the telephone, "I'll converse with you soon."

Finley hung up and gave Marlo a self-reproachful shrug, "Sorry to keep you pausing."

"I didn't intend to interrupt..." Marlo needed to get some information about SELENA yet kept it down.

"No, no... I was simply wrapping up." Finley said simultaneously. Marlo looked sufficient to eat, all flexible and gleaming post-run.

Marlo shrugged, "Uh, I needed to drop by and wish you an upbeat birthday. Uh, happy birthday, Fi..."

"Much obliged, upbeat birthday to you, as well. Did you simply go for a run?" Finley contemplated whether Marlo would refer that she'd carried a lady as a date to the gathering that evening.

Marlo gestured, "Definitely - ran out the wrinkles from the trip back."

"How was your outing?" Finley despised how commonplace this discussion was. Things with Marlo never used to feel repetition. Still no notice of the date...

"Not a big deal. Yet, I do I have some incredibly uplifting news," Marlo grinned interestingly since getting back,

Finley limited her eyes, "Gilchrist Labs?!!"

Marlo gestured, "Our bet paid off. All that time, individuals said we were squandering? It turns out it was not a loss by any means. We are presumably going to significantly increase - or even fourfold - the photovoltaic abilities of boards today. Dr. Hammond sent me the evidence yesterday. The Gilchrist group practically detonated with energy. They need to fly around here to meet with you one week from now."

Finley flickered. The news was staggering. To begin with, that their persistent effort was going to pay off; second, that Gilchrist Labs may join to be their greatest accomplice. Together, there was the possibility to jump third-era sun-based cells with steady, high-effectiveness arrangements that would characterize photovoltaics for quite a long time to come.

"Everything's going to change..." Finley considered.

Marlo gestured, "On the off chance that we thought individuals have been creeping up our rear ends... it will be dramatically more awful at this point."

"I'm Person of the Year - I ought to have the option to sort out an approach to not have ass-crawlers screw this up for us..." Finley watched out of the window, "Yet how about we stew in the uplifting news for the present. My cerebrum harms a lot today. We can plan and plan later."

"Birthday blues?" Marlo strolled into the washroom and sprinkled some virus water all over. She slicked her hair back and covered her face in a towel as she tumbled down on the couch.

Finley ran her eyes everywhere on her companion's body. It resembled assessing a major feline ... lean and strong... delightful and incredible. Without expecting to, Finley let out a major murmur.

Marlo looked into it, similarly as Finley turned away once more. Marlo tossed the towel behind her and strolled over to her companion, "What's happening?" Marlo gave Finley a cordial push.

I need to kiss you. However, I can't go because some airhead is hanging tight for you in your room! Finley needed to shout. All things being equal, she shrugged, "Mother's in pre-party mode and is making me insane. My sister's in pre-party mode and making me insane. You were gone throughout the week. None of my companions can go to the gathering since they all have children, and it's the latest seven-day stretch of school."

"You're envious because you need kids?" Marlo half-kidded.

"No! I'm simply saying... here we are once more—large gathering. I'm the visitor of honor. Be that as it may, every other person has activities. I'm the wearer of the dress and the shaper of the cake. It's genuinely discouraging, I advise you."

"Well," Marlo said discreetly, a grin pulling at the side of her mouth, "I have this little violin that I can play for you... tragically, it's so minuscule it's in a real sense difficult to track down."

"Annoy," Finley said, giving Marlo a little push. She realized Marlo was correct. She additionally realized she expected to move away for some time. Possibly I should go to Mona's at the end of the week. Indeed... that sounds amazing right about at this point.

"I talk truth to control," Marlo gave Finley a little push back, "Everybody's treading lightly because you've been so pissy. I realize you can hold it together until after the gathering, and you can go take off all alone for some time."

Finley gazed at her companion, "Amazing; it resembles you were guessing what I might be thinking or something. I was contemplating going to California for a tad."

Marlo's heart grasped with envy. She's going to California to see that lady. Marlo transformed and tossed her towel into the couch somewhat more powerfully than she intended to, "obviously. Why not?"

"What?" Finley couldn't see Marlo's face, yet there was no mixing up the chomp of mockery in Marlo's remark.

Marlo shook her head, "Nothin'. Um, look, I will go clean up and stuff. I'll see you at supper."

"Marlo!"

"WHAT?!" Marlo said far and away too strongly. Marlo realized she would start a ruckus, yet the picture of SELENA and Finley in bed together was taunting her agonizingly. It filled the persistent hurt and outrage that was detonating inside her.

Finley was shocked. "What do you signify 'what'? I said I planned to go to California, and you act like I'm submitting a cardinal sin or something. What's going on with you?"

Finley's tone was sharp and deigning, and it just served to stir up Marlo's rising protectiveness.

"NOTHING!" Marlo snapped back, "Nothing's the issue with me. You're the one taking off to California as a method for dealing with stress for your emotional meltdown!"

"You were the person who proposed I go out traveling someplace! Furthermore, where are you getting this emotional meltdown poo? Where's this abrupt aggression coming from?"

It was all going sideways, yet Marlo was lost in a twister summoned by the green-peered toward the beast. Her eyes streaked irately, "Antagonism? You're one to talk! Haven't you been woofing at everybody here throughout the week, your Excellency?"

Finley had never seen Marlo like this: her normally attractive, etched highlights were cold and loaded with disdain.

Marlo's dismissed heart was completely releasing long periods of stifled dissatisfaction, "Definitely. Everybody believes you're an egotistical bitch. No doubt you streaming off to California to fulfill some emotional meltdown is annoying me, alright?"

"No! NOT OKAY!" Finley raised her voice protectively, "And I'm NOT having an emotional meltdown. What's new with you?"

"Whatever," Marlo spat out, "Similar to you, give it a second thought."

Before Finley could react, Marlo turned and left.

"Marlo!"

Marlo continued strolling.

Finley yelled to Marlo's back, "Try not to go to my supper around evening time, Marlo!"

Marlo shrugged; however, they didn't think back, "FINE BY ME!"

Juniper was descending the corridor as Marlo stepped past, destroys streaming her face.

"Marlo... what occurred?"

Marlo pushed herself towards the lifts, "She just dismissed me from the list of people to attend for this evening."

"I'll return you on the rundown!" Juniper said serenely.

Marlo halted and turned, "Much appreciated, Juniper, yet I can think about 1,000,000 things I'd much preferably do over go to Finley's birthday supper. Sorry."

Juniper watched Marlo leave. She murmured and made a beeline for her girl's room.

"You made Marlo cry," she started as Finley's entryway respected Juniper's card key.

Finley was on the telephone yet feigned exacerbation significantly accordingly.

Juniper's eyebrows jumped upwards as she heard the following words emerging from Finley's mouth.

"Indeed, would you be able to have Eddie prepare the fly for tomorrow first thing? I'll fly out first thing. The objective is MacArthur Airport on Long Island, California... No, lone me... Fine. I'll take Tanya."
Finley put the telephone down and saw her mom, "No, I didn't make Marlo cry. She got stirred up without anyone else... Pause, she was crying?"

Juniper gestured, "Yes. She said you dismissed her from the list of people to attend."

Finley's eyes were limited, "She was an asshole...!"

"Is that why you're going to California?"

Finley took a full breath, "No. Marlo can pitch as large a fit as she needs. I couldn't care less. I will see Mona. My companion from school. I need some space, and she offered me to remain at her home on Long Island."

"There're a lot of different spots you can remain in - why Long Island? It's a long approach."

"Space. I need a great deal of it." Finley scowled at her mom, "Don't begin, mother. I'm going."

"Why? To go attempt to revive a relationship with the lady in the wedding declarations a week ago?" Juniper looked at her little girl without flinching.

Finley's breath got. What the heck? Does she think about SELENA?

Mother and girl were quiet for a couple of seconds.

Finley felt quickly protective, "It's not your opinion. What's more, it's not your issue to worry about, at any rate."

"I'm your mom," Juniper heaved, "And my girl is my business, so watch your tone."

"Simply kindly don't address me about being attentive. No one realizes SELENA and I went through the night together, alright? So don't go there."

"Give me a little credit, Finley," Juniper frowned at her girl, "I don't mind who you lay down with. I do mind in case you will attempt to separate a marriage. Since, in such a case that you are, I would be stunned and baffled. I thought you'd be superior to that."

Ultimately, Finley moaned and said unobtrusively, "No. Not to separate a marriage. I need to get why."

Juniper positioned her head, "Why what? Why she wedded another person and not you?"

Finley giggled after thoroughly considering the presumption behind her mom's inquiry, "God help us! SELENA and I weren't fascinated."

Juniper folded her arms incredulously.

"Truly!" Finley demanded, "Way off the mark. Yet, I thought we both had a similar demeanor to connections. It'd been consoling to realize that she and I had that equivalent arrangement. I need to understand what altered her perspective."

"Hm," Juniper strolled over to the love seat and plunked down, "For... what? Why? Whatever altered her perspective, that is her business, right?"

Finley plunked down close to her mom, "Indeed, yet she was completely clear that she'd never get hitched. It assisted me with adhering to my choice to not engage with anybody. However, presently it seems like I'm missing something..."

Juniper grasped Finley's hand, "Nectar, I don't think you need to travel to California to sort out the thing you're absent."

Finley gazed at her mom, "Gracious, what, you have every one of the appropriate responses?"

"No," Juniper shifted her head carefully, "Yet I don't think conversing with SELENA about her relationship will help you."

"Indeed, I believe you're off-base," Finley said with a shrug, "I'm going to California. Mona's children finish school this week, and she's tossing a huge summer festivity at her home on Long Island. SELENA will be there; it won't be serious. We're simply going to talk. "

"You appear, and it will be serious," Juniper caused a stir, "You showing up anyplace is serious."

Finley let out a long, full breath, "I understand what I'm doing, alright?

Juniper lifted a doubtful eyebrow, "You just advised your dearest companion not to go to your birthday celebration... I scarcely believe you're in the correct temper to understand what you're doing."

"I have no clue about why she provoked me, Ma; kindly don't see me like that."

"You should go get her and sort this out at this moment. You've never battled this way. Try not to allow it to rot."

Finley shook her head, "She has a hot date. I'm not going to proceed to stroll in on that." Finley frowned, the psychological picture of Marlo in another person's hug streaked agonizingly in her brain. "I will get dressed. I'll see you at supper, mother."

Juniper moaned and left the room. If she doesn't converse with Marlo, I will.

Yet, Juniper was past the point of no return. When she strolled towards Marlo's room, Marlo and another lady were taken off.

"Are you leaving?" Juniper inquired.

Marlo gestured, "Since my evening opened up out of the blue, I will exploit an uncommon night off from Edevane obligations - Meghan needs to leave in the first part of the day so that we will hang out."

Juniper turned and grinned at Meghan. Marlo recoiled, "Apologies. Where are my habits? Meghan, this is Juniper. Juniper, this is Meghan Randall, an old buddy of mine from graduate school."

"Ok! I recall Marlo discussing you," Juniper always remembered a name, "You all dated for some time, isn't that so? You should come to California for part of the late spring one year if I recall effectively."

Meghan was dazzled, "Yes! Goodness. I can't trust you recollect that. I got a ruptured appendix, so I was unable to travel. Goodness. That was years prior! That was my sophomore year, correct? When you were TA-ing?"

Marlo shrugged, "Sounds spot on."

"I'm so happy you folks are getting together; how pleasant that you've stayed in contact!" Juniper grinned heartily, "Any possibility I can persuade you to remain for supper?"

Marlo cut in, "No, I think best not to go over that. Meghan's moving out to California, and we need to make up for a lost time before she goes. We'll likely remain at my place around this evening."

Juniper gestured with abdication. This won't be settled around evening time. "All things considered, okay, both of you. Have a happy time around evening time."

Marlo and Meghan strolled to the inn entrance peacefully. The valet had Marlo's vehicle prepared, and both of them got in.

Marlo moaned uproariously lastly said, "I'm sorry Finley disinvited us from the supper."

"No compelling reason to apologize! Not my show, so there are zero objections from me!" Meghan was true; she was only glad to invest some energy with Marlo.

Marlo zipped expertly through downtown San Francisco roads, visiting the finish to get some supper from her #1 restaurant. Not long after, they pulled up to a high rise in Lower Haight.

Meghan meandered through the front room with the food as Marlo went into the kitchen to get a few beverages. One divider was loaded with Marlo's photos with her father, Brandon and Juniper, and with Finley and her sister Sophie. The connection among them was clear.

"I'm speculating you not going to the birthday supper this evening is serious," Meghan offered when Marlo returned.

Marlo shrugged, "I don't mind, sincerely."

"I'm likewise speculating that is not altogether obvious," Meghan said with a slight grin.

Marlo jeered and plunked down on the couch, "Fine. It's nearer to reality to say that Finley doesn't mind. Same contrast, however."

"When was this one taken?" Meghan tucked her legs under her as she highlighted a photograph outline on the table close to the couch.

"Just before Finley took over as CEO of the Edevane bunch," Marlo drooped into the couch, "She was preparing for an affair or something."

Meghan gazed at the photo. Finley was situated at a vanity, confronting the mirror yet taking a gander at Marlo's appearance. Marlo was remaining behind Finley, grinning at her. Indeed, even an imbecile would have the option to perceive the affection transmitting from Finley's look.

"She cherishes you without a doubt," Meghan said, pointing at Finley.

Marlo grinned sharply, "No doubt, I know."

"Goodness," Meghan misjudged, "You don't feel the equivalent way...?"

"Hm? No, I love her. She's my closest companion," Marlo murmured. Also, I just provoked her since I got desirous. I'm a butthead.

"No, no," Meghan tapped the photograph, "She adores you. Take a gander at the way she's taking a gander at you."

Marlo needed to take a gander at the photograph, yet she was unable to get the picture of Finley and SELENA off of her mind, so she reclined against the couch and shut her eyes, "You're perusing an excessive lot into that."

"I oppose this idea. Did she see you like this when we dated?" Meghan put the photograph outline down.

Marlo sneered, "Whatever. Likely not. I don't have a clue. Why?"

"Since!" Meghan shook her head, "I believe something's at last appearing well and good. See, I don't lament the time we spent together... also, I think we truly incline toward being companions... Be that as it may... um, you and I didn't turn out for various reasons, and I'm just presently understanding the main motivation was presumably Finley."

Marlo opened her eyes and gazed at Meghan, "Huh?"

Meghan snatched the photograph outline and put it before Marlo, "Quit messing with yourself, Marlo. She adores you."

Marlo took a gander at the photograph, "She doesn't adore me like that."

Meghan looked suspicious.

Marlo murmured, "She took part in an extramarital entanglement, quite a while back. With some lady. Recently, she made arrangements to see that lady once more. She doesn't adore me like that."

"That is the reason you were disinvited from the supper this evening? You defied her about this other lady?"

"No," Marlo put the photograph outline face down close to her, "She doesn't realize I know. I provoked her. It's a wreck." Marlo covered her face in her grasp, "It's a complete wreck."

"Hm," Meghan scratched her head, "Quelle outrage... Jumbles can be tidied up, you know?"

Marlo extended, "Perhaps."

"Furthermore, from what I see, it isn't so chaotic," Meghan considered, "You love her?"

Marlo gestured silently. Juniper knows, so who cares if every other person realizes that I'm the washout with the messed up heart?

"Like, you love her a ton a great deal?"

Marlo gestured once more. Failure, washout, washout, washout...

"I bet she cherishes you back. Comparably much."
"Why is she going to California to see a lady she had a toss with?" Marlo's voice shook.

Meghan hushed up briefly, "Most likely because she thinks you escaped with me around evening time... You put me on the list of people to attend, recall?"

"She's never thought about my dates," Marlo noted, "I believe you're adding a lot to it."

"Anybody taking a gander at this photograph would perceive what I see," Meghan demanded, "You're too obstinate even to consider letting it be known. No big surprise you can't submit. On the off chance that Finley's the affection for your life, no other lady could at any point have the right stuff!"

"Food's getting cold," Marlo snorted; she would not like to discuss it any longer.

Before Meghan could say anything accordingly, an ensemble of pops slice through the peaceful evening: Birthday firecrackers were detonating excitedly over San Francisco Bay. Marlo thought about how Finley was doing. Meghan's words aggravated her vibe. Perhaps this time, I've been driving Finley away... furthermore, this evening, I messed up and aggravated it...

Meghan didn't return to the subject and accepting it as a success when she'd get Marlo looking at the photo once in a while.

Chapter 4: A Helpful Intermission (Long Island, California)

Finley flickered her eyes open. Somebody was tenderly shaking her alert.

"Ma'am," it was Tanya Cross, her head of safety, "We're here."

"Much thanks to you, Tanya; I value you making this occur with almost no notification."

Tanya grinned, "obviously! I'm generally up for an excursion to California! Prepared?"

Finley gestured as everything was stacked into a holding-up vehicle. She sent a speedy content to Mona to say that she'd showed up.

They wove through the streets of the modest community of Brookes Cove before twisting through a long carport to Mona's home. Finley scarcely got an opportunity to extend before Mona flung the front entryway open.

"Nectar!!" Mona gave Finley a major embrace, "Welcome! How was the trip over?"

"Long, however unremarkable," Finley embraced Mona directly back, "This is Tanya; she holds me back from doing anything insane and holds my mom back from enjoying crazy jumpy dreams of me getting captured."

"Welcome!" Mona grinned energetically. She pointed at the right side of the house, "You folks should be crapped. We will place you in this piece of the house; it's parceled off a little, two rooms higher up and a little cave first floor. Ideal for when my folks or the parents in law come to remain. Liz is a fricking virtuoso - she had this assembled recently."

Finley grinned, "Much obliged for hanging tight for us."

"No compelling reason to express gratitude toward me! You're invited any time!" Mona answered, "You're the last to show up, a great many people arrived toward the beginning of today, and the neighbors will carry as the weekend progressed. Go get comfortable, and we can make up for lost time toward the beginning of the day."

Finley followed everybody into the house. At the point when she'd spruced up, she went down to the kitchen; she was too jetlagged to hit the hay.

"I'm making tea" Mona opened a bureau, "Do you need a few?"

"Sure," Finley slid into a seat at the kitchen table.

"I thought you'd need to crash..." Mona put the pot on.

Finley extended, "I'm on West Coast time... also, my cerebrum is on hyper-drive, so I wouldn't have had the option to rest at any rate."

"Would you like to discuss it?" Mona brought more than two cups of tea to the feasting table.

"Very little to say - I can't get it to bode well in my mind."

Mona blew on her tea, "Sort out what? Is SELENA getting hitched? What are you going to say to her tomorrow?"

Finley shrugged and measured her hands around her mug, "I inquisitive - profoundly inquisitive - to understand what adjusted her perspective. That photograph of her and Lauren, they look so upbeat. Furthermore, she was unyielding that it wasn't what she needed."

"You can't help who you go gaga for, Finley. SELENA fell hard for Lauren. We didn't trust it from the start, yet she did. Why's this essential to you?"

"I took a page from SELENA's book. I understood I shared her inclination for effortlessness. Connections - particularly in my specific circumstance - are convoluted.

She thought something very similar. I sensed that I found a partner in SELENA. In any case, it turns out she was the wedding kind, as well!"

Mona gazed upward curiously, "Connections for you are confounded because why? You fundamentally run the world?"

"Since individuals have assumptions and I may not need what they anticipate that I should want..."

"Be that as it may... who cares?" Mona raised an eyebrow, "It's your call. What do you need?"

Marlo. Finley murmured, "Something I can't have. Sort of makes it disputable; what others anticipate."

"Yet, who cares," Mona rehashed, "What's holding you up? To get what you need?"

"Marlo," Finley said discreetly.

"Marlo?"

Finley gestured. The mystery was difficult to discuss.

"Gracious, nectar," Mona realized Marlo very well - she was Finley's dearest companion. During school, Marlo had visited routinely. Gracious, I see... Mona gestured, abruptly believing that she comprehended the issue.

"Marlo struggles with you experiencing passionate feelings, right?" Mona speculated, "I mean, it bodes well, I presume."

Finley looked into her companion, puzzled, "What? Your meaning could be a little more obvious."

Mona shifted her head, "You said Marlo was the one holding up traffic of you having an affection life. Also, I think it bodes well. Be that as it may, - "

"Stand by," Finley interfered, "Apologies... hold tight, would you be able to clarify what you mean?"

Mona reclined and paused for a minute before she reacted, "When you said Marlo was the one holding up traffic. I contemplated each one of those occasions she visited you and every one of those occasions we as a whole hung out together, and it was clear - at any rate to me - that she was fascinated with you. That is the reason I said it sounded good to me that she'd be the one who'd have the hardest time with you being seeing someone... you know if she's as yet enamored with you."

Finley's mouth opened and shut. She multiple times and gazed down at her tea, astounded with stun. What? It can't be true...?

"I thought you knew, Finley," Mona was astonished... and surprisingly more befuddled currently, "I'm heartbroken. I thought you knew."

Finley was numb. Nothing was interfacing.

Mona sat ahead and put her hand on Finley's, "Gracious darling, I thought you knew. The first occasion when she and I met, do you recall? She went along with us for Spring Break - you'd persuaded your folks to allow you to accompanied us to visit my father's family in Barbados?"

Finley gestured, "Indeed, they concurred simply because Marlo planned to tag along."

"Do you recall that battle you had with Marlo when she initially showed up?" Mona lifted her eyebrows.

Finley glared and recalled her green beans year. Her eyes limited, "Yes! She said she was pissed because my folks made her dump arrangements with her better half or something."

"That was her story," Mona folded her arms, "She quit being pissy once I disclosed to her I wasn't attempting to date you."

Finley gazed at Mona in dismay. Mona gave a knowing look, "Swear on my mother's grave, that occurred. She got insane desirous after she heard my mom discussing how well you and I got along."

Finley's mouth dropped open, "It can't be valid. She dates... such countless different ladies! That is to say, she's revealed to me I'm not her sort a bigger number of times than I can tally. She's never shown any interest in me. She doesn't take a gander at me that way!" Finley's voice is poor toward the end.

"... what's more, you... need her to?" Mona was rapidly rethinking her theory; out of nowhere, it appeared to be agonizingly self-evident. "Goodness, Finley, perhaps you and Marlo simply need to discuss this!"

Finley thought it's difficult to zero in on anyone feeling; handfuls were flying at her immediately: energy, question, bewilderment, shock, misery, weakness, trust...

After a couple of seconds of quietness, Finley asked discreetly, "Did SELENA at any point mention to you what happened that evening? After supper at your place?"

Mona shook her head, "No."

"Recollect that I informed you there was something concerning SELENA that I couldn't exactly place?" Finley forgot about a deviant strand of hair on her face, "I didn't sort it out until SELENA left. That is to say, SELENA was wonderful..."

Finley becomes flushed at the memory. Mona laughed, "She used to get a great deal of good, uh, reviews..."

Directly at that point, a lady's delicate and critical groan floated into the kitchen.

Mona grinned more extensively, "... furthermore, Lauren unquestionably would concur!"

"That is coming from their room?" Finley becomes flushed once more.

"Something very similar as last night..." Mona laughed, "Perhaps it sounds recognizable to you?"

Finley held her hands up, "What happened that evening stays cheerfully before, yet my point was more about my acknowledgment that being with SELENA was my cerebrum's ungainly method of perceiving my affections for Marlo. I grew up with Marlo, and I generally felt safe and comfortable with her. It'd never happened to me that I'd been enamored with her this time. I figured becoming hopelessly enamored would be this thunderclap thing. Yet, it simply is that route with Marlo. I love her. Also, I feel moronic saying this since it's so clear at this point... be that as it may, it wasn't previously. However, Marlo wasn't a lot of help; she's shown no interest in me..."

Finley halted to slow down and rest. I love her! Furthermore, quite possibly... she adores me back!

Mona wrapped up her tea as she let Finley measure her contemplations. Ultimately, she asked, tenderly, "Why converse with SELENA? It appears to me that this is something you and Marlo need to sort out..." Mona got up and placed her mug in the dishwasher.

Finley shrugged, "from the start, I was frantic - I thought I had this close companion in SELENA in that we'd keep life basic... and afterward, she goes off and gets hitched! I needed to get her to mention to me what changed. Presently, I think I need to converse with Lauren..."
"Huh?"

Finley chuckled delicately at Mona's devoid look, "All things considered, if Marlo and I have been in shared refusal about how we feel about one another, I need a few hints from Lauren on how she won the core of the celebrated 'one and done' SELENA Kan."

"Straight young lady enchantment," Mona kidded.

"I don't mind what it was; I need however much assistance as could be expected if I will get my closest companion to view at me as a mate."

"Pfft," Mona sneered, "I bet Marlo's been difficult to nail down because she's attempting to divert herself from holding a light for you." Mona stopped briefly as a glimmer of mischief shined in her eye, "Even though I'm interested to perceive what Lauren must say for herself - SELENA fell so hard for her it's astonishing she didn't get a blackout!"

"Makes me need to meet Lauren considerably more," Finley snickered, "Do you figure it very well may be odd, though...? I understand I address a piece of SELENA's set of experiences that Lauren probably won't care for... even though I asked SELENA, and SELENA said it was cool..."

"Lauren knows who she has in her bed," Mona answered, "If SELENA says it's cool, she implies it's cool for the two of them. You'll comprehend when you see them together. Consider this; I truly needed to see it to trust it. However, even Liz is persuaded now, and she's known SELENA the longest and was the greatest doubter when SELENA and Lauren previously got together."

"Where's Liz?"

Mona attempted to smother yawn, "Milo's been awakening at two a.m. consistently this previous week for reasons unknown, and Liz took its brunt. She slammed around nine this evening. Which was close to the time SELENA and Lauren began their nighttime activities..."

The squeaks and calm clamors emerging from the opposite side of the house had not ebbed by any means. Finley snickered discreetly in compassion.

"I know," Mona yawned, "When you hear one bedspring working diligently... it's truly difficult to ignore..."

Finley noticed her companion's yawn and stood up, "Go put a few earplugs in! I've kept you up past the point of no return. Go to bed..."

Mona laughed and embraced Finley tight.

Finley grinned, "I need to say, they have endurance!"

Mona grunted, "Don't be astonished if I come running into your piece of the house if it fires up once more. Liz dozes like the dead and will be no assistance to me at all."

"Make sure to caution Tanya first - else you'll get tackled..."

Mona grinned and gestured, "Alright. All good. Is it accurate to say that you will be alright? This Marlo stuff's a great deal to measure."

"It's to a lesser degree a dumpster fire than previously... best I go gaze into space for some time."

"You sure?" Mona extended, "I'm glad to hear you out-think."

"Be cautious what you wish for... however, I believe I'm okay..."

Mona gave Finley's shoulder a crush, "Much obliged for confiding in me with this. I realize it hasn't been simple."

Finley murmured, "Feels simpler since I understand what my choices are. Much appreciated, Mona. I'll see you toward the beginning of the day."

The two ladies took off to their particular rooms. It was an anxious night for Finley, which was not aided by her mom's surge of writings begging her to call. When Tanya thumped on her entryway in the first part of the day to registration, the two of them looked destroyed.

"Great morning, ma'am," Tanya made a sound as if to speak, "You requested that I wake you at eight."

Finley moaned, "Goodness, East Coast jetlag's unpleasant by any stretch of the imagination."

"At the point when I said 'I'm generally up for an excursion to California,' I lied," kidded Tanya.

Finley laughed, "You should return to rest. Nothing will happen to me around here. This is Liz's old neighborhood; she can likely bring on the whole the fortifications we need if something insane occurred."

"Apologies, ma'am, no can do," Tanya grinned, "You're left with me."

Finley surrendered, "Fine. Have you eaten? I'm famished."

"I snatched some morning meal as of now. Your companions' children are truly adorable, incidentally."

"They're up to as of now?" Finley swung her legs off the bed, "I guess I should make myself presentable..."

Tanya grinned and said, "I'll sit tight for your first floor."

Finley rearranged into the washroom and cleaned up. The point when she advanced into the kitchen was at that point tumultuous and content with movement. Mona and Liz and their three kids were all younger than ten, Liz's sibling Stuart and his family, and somebody who presented herself as a neighbor. Tanya had tracked down a quiet spot directly off the kitchen. There was no indication of SELENA or Lauren.

"Say howdy to Auntie Finley!" Mona yelled to nobody specifically.

An offbeat volley of 'welcomes' followed as Finley made a straight shot to the espresso creator. Liz gave her a side-embrace as she flipped a mechanical production system of silver dollar flapjacks on the frying pan. Mona was close to her, slashing up some natural product.

"Sacred flapjacks, Batman, the number of are you making?" Finley was pre-espresso, yet she didn't require caffeine to realize Liz was making enough to take care of a military.

"There are six kids who are around a little ways from collapsing into an appetite fugue. The best arrangement is to stuff food into them... most of us elderly individuals can touch on the rest of the day wears on."

"What's more, trust me," Mona contributed, "none of us elderly individuals need to be up this early. It's a nurturing risk no one completely cautions you about heretofore."

As though on signal, one of the youngsters ran head-first into the edge of the counter. Stuart gathered up his shouting offspring and immediately pronounced an 'all reasonable.' The kid being referred to quit crying the second Liz's heap of flapjacks advanced toward the morning meal table.

Not long after every kid got their distribution of breakfast, a steady calm emerged in the kitchen.

Finley, who had chosen to remain in near closeness to the espresso producer, tasted her espresso and said, "Wow, Liz, you were unable to have planned that better."

Mona gave her better half a quick kiss on the cheek, "It's one of her uncompensated abilities."

"There is a wide range of kinds of pay, nectar," Liz grinned.

Mona didn't think twice, "I'll need to recollect that for some other time."

Finley snickered. She was going to say something when she heard her name. She turned towards the opening that associated the kitchen to the parlor and saw SELENA stepping in.

"SELENA!" Finley felt truly glad to see her recent supper buddy.

There was no cumbersomeness by any means; SELENA gave Finley a warm embrace, to which Finley cheerfully responded.

"Upbeat late birthday, coincidentally! Any dubious dates during the current year's celebration?" SELENA prodded.

Finley chuckled, dazzled with SELENA's memory, and shook her head, "No, I cut the cake completely all alone... albeit now my mom's ready to fight about me being lastingly single. Can't take care of business, I presume... furthermore, you! You owe me a clarification, Ms. Passing expenses and always failing to get hitched!" Finley folded her arms in mock outrage.

"I said that, didn't I?" SELENA laughed as she snatched two water bottles from a bureau, "I'm glad to argue my case after my run, I guarantee."

"Good day!" Mona interfered, "Where do you believe you're going, SELENA? You guaranteed Liz you planned to play escort today for the children's camps."

"I'll be back on schedule for that. Ellie and I will go for a fast run," SELENA clarified as she strolled over to the sink and began to top off the containers

As Mona and SELENA began talking about that morning's coordinations, Finley saw how, contrasted with five years prior, SELENA's vibe had changed. Discernibly. Previously, there was a practically crude, carnal sexuality that radiated from the taller lady. Liz considered it SELENA's 'voodoo,' and it was fitting - SELENA certainly had a path about her that was promptly alluring. In any case, to Finley, SELENA's once unbridled suggestion - that had been mortally indiscriminating in its effect - presently felt gloriously held. Maybe SELENA had completely acknowledged her superpower, and it was presently readily available to exhaust or retain as she wished.

Finley felt a hint of jealousy for Lauren. Since Lauren - of the relative multitude of ladies in SELENA's day-to-day existence - was the person who got ALL of SELENA: The superhuman SELENA, just as the adjusted inner self SELENA. I need to be that individual for Marlo... Finley wished quietly.

The hint of jealousy transformed into altogether envy simple minutes after the fact. SELENA had been conversing with Mona yet halted mid-sentence when Lauren strolled in. Mona wasn't misrepresenting; books could be expounded on how SELENA took a gander at her significant other. Finley saw SELENA's casual stance unexpectedly take on more mindful energy as Lauren's gravitational power pulled her in. On the off chance that solitary I had that sort of impact on Marlo!

313

"Great morning, everybody! Prepared, angel?" Lauren streaked SELENA a grin. Lauren was simple enough on the eyes as of now, yet that grin disclosed to Finley all she had to know. Mona watched Finley's response and quirked an eyebrow in an 'I advised you so' kind of way.

SELENA gestured, "Uh-huh. I was simply affirming times for the children's camps today. Gracious, Ellie, this is Finley. Finley, this is Lauren." She gave Lauren a water bottle.

"Much obliged," Lauren took the container and turned towards Finley, "Finley, ideal to meet you!" Lauren broadened a hand, which Finley readily shook; once more, with no hint of weightiness.

"We ought to get moving - I would prefer not to get damnation from Liz for being late," SELENA shifted her head towards the entryway.

Mona waved farewell to the couple and steered over to Finley, who was inclining toward the counter.

"Goodness," Finley murmured into her espresso cup as she tasted, "That is the genuine article."

Mona gestured, "I know; I continue to reveal to Liz that she doesn't see me like that any longer... typically gets the job done... gets her all disturbed up... which I like... a lot..." Mona's eyebrows did a tricky little wriggle.

"Hello, don't go adding insult to my injury... I don't have my poo figured out yet!"

Mona rang her mug against Finley's, "Leave it to me, darling; I'll ensure you will have some quality time with Ms. Lauren Calder for some ace tips..."

"I don't have a clue what to ask her," Finley said semi-dejectedly.

Mona positioned her head, claiming to be in profound idea, "Gee... What about, 'How did a straight lady tempt a responsibility phobic lesbian into married happiness?' That'll get the job done."

"Quite difficult," pondered Finley, "Even though I may wind up doing precisely that."

"That is my young lady," Mona laughed.

Consistent with her promise, as the different visitors and neighbors floated all through the house through the morning, Mona figured out how to design it to such an extent that Lauren discovered Finley sitting discreetly without help from anyone else on the deck a little before lunch.

"Psyche if I go along with you? SELENA just drove off with a vehicle brimming with children..."

Finley admired track down the blondie signaling to the parlor seat close to hers, "Not under any condition! I wanted to get some an ideal opportunity to converse with you!"

Lauren caused a stir, "Really?"

This wasn't simply the first run-through Lauren's discovered up close and personal with one of SELENA's exes. Indeed, many had been welcome to their wedding. Lauren deduced they'd all appeared at by and by affirming that SELENA had, truth be told, settled to venture out into monogamy. Finley didn't appear to be any changed: delightful, enchanting, and profoundly interested about SELENA's difference in heart about connections. SELENA had - as usual - been straightforward with Lauren about what occurred with Finley. It wasn't Lauren's #1 thing to catch wind of SELENA's precious darlings; however, fortunately, SELENA's past never felt threatening to her. Lauren was the person who got the proposition - and that was confirmation enough that SELENA had proceeded onward from that part of her life.

"I have an issue, and I figure you may be the ideal individual to help," Finley let out a short breath of assurance.

Lauren let out a quick chuckle, "Gracious great! I thought you'd planned to test me on how I got SELENA to stroll down the path with me!"

"Truly, it's associated," Finley waved her hand timidly, "I have somebody in my life who's similar to SELENA was before she met you. I'd prefer to attempt to convince this individual to consider settling down..."

Lauren moved a little in the seat, "Settling down with... you?"

Finley gestured, "That is my expectation."

Lauren was captivated however felt totally out of her profundity. She was sitting in the organization of quite possibly the most compelling business heads of the world. However, which was sufficiently amazing to be asked by Finley for relationship counsel appeared to be ludicrous. "Wouldn't you be able to purchase an island and propose in some extreme can't be-rejected sort of way?" She proclaimed.

Lauren quickly shrouded her mouth in stun, "Apologies. That was inappropriate. It just came out."

Finley snickered, "No, no, you're fine. Mona's been giving me poop for quite a long time. I can have issues as well, you know?"

"All good," Lauren said with some alleviation, "So... inform me regarding this individual you need to settle down with..."

"We grew up together. However, it wasn't long ago that I understood how I truly felt about her. I think about when you've adored somebody for that long; it's feasible to accept away how that adoration could change. Also, Marlo - that is her name - Marlo can be portrayed as difficult to nail down, best-case scenario, so regardless of whether I could toss cash at issue, I don't know she'd pursue a relationship with me." Unless Mona's privilege and we've been aimlessly disregarding each other's sentiments idiotically for every one of these years...

Lauren didn't have the foggiest idea what to say; there were such a large number of things going through her mind simultaneously... A multi-extremely rich person lesbian expert of the universe is staying here conversing with me??!! I should offer guidance regarding how to manage tragic love??!! I ought to have offered to drive the children to camp whenever I got an opportunity!

"She may pursue an indulgence, however?" Lauren asked, "Perhaps start there?"

"I'm old, Lauren," Finley said with amiableness, "I'm old, and I would prefer not to mess around. I understand what I need and who I need. When I understood it, I realized I didn't need an excursion... or on the other hand, a test."

"It resembled that for me, really, with SELENA," Lauren gestured, "Very quickly at the time that I met her."

317

"How could you all sort it out at that point? How could you get to 'I do'?"

"I don't think it was anyone thing specifically," Lauren grinned, "Sincerely. It sort of occurred."

"This isn't useful... however," Finley motioned for Lauren to continue to talk, "I need more info..."

"I succumbed to her consistently, yet SELENA demands she didn't get on it by any means. Albeit, at last, she got on..."

Finley sat up straighter, "How could she get on? This is the kind of intel I need!"

Lauren considered everything briefly and afterward said, "When somebody asked SELENA this as of late, she said that I kept her speculating. As indicated by SELENA, I wasn't out and out being a tease, yet she was unable to tell if I was unobtrusively a tease... she couldn't exactly sort me out."

"That is it? Being very dark?" Finley sounded wary, "And would you say you were intentionally playing with her?"

"I wasn't murky by the plan. I was attempting to figure out how I needed to be the point at which I was around SELENA. She could not sort out on the off chance that I was a tease since I didn't have the foggiest idea what I was doing! I was so stricken I was making an effort not to humiliate myself when I was in a similar room as her," Lauren clarified, "When I sorted it out, however, I wasn't timid about spreading the word about it. I was the person who took the principal action! Stand by, Finley, is there a chance Marlo feels something for you, as well?"

Finley shrugged, "Mona suspects such a lot. However, I haven't seen any sign she does. Even though Mona advantageously neglected to reveal this significant snippet of data to me until the previous evening... I haven't had the opportunity to test it out regarding associations with Marlo."

"Mona's senses are generally correct; she got on me playing with SELENA before SELENA did!" Lauren giggled, "I'd say that it was high time you left a few breadcrumbs for Marlo to follow. Try not to exaggerate your hand."

"How would I do that?"

"Streak her some skin when she least anticipates it... toss her a commendation that has some insinuation to it... let her find you are seeing her; however, don't make it self-evident," Lauren proposed, "Don't misunderstand me, I'm not saying you need to play mind games - I don't care for that stuff. What I mean is I conflicted with every one of the things she anticipated. It wasn't cared for; I had an arrangement. I attempted to figure out approaches to invest energy with SELENA, and when I did, we got along truly well! That is to say, I put some exertion into standing out enough to be noticed... yet, for the most part, the science was there, you know?"

Finley gestured along mindfully; an arrangement was beginning to shape.

At the end of the week, everybody tested out with thoughts. Liz attempted to persuade Finley to alternate route the entire thing, "Why not fly home now and bounce her bones? Complete it over and. You shouldn't need to overthink this."

"Gracious, I'm not," Finley said breezily, "Even though I would like to cause her to languish somewhat over not making advances on me sooner. Mona, in case you're correct and she's held every one of these affections for me, I'll be straightforward; I'm a little insulted that I wasn't more overpowering!"

Mona shook her head, "Indeed, you're going to retaliate for your honor... Poor Marlo, she won't understand what hit her."

Chapter 5: A Meeting of the Minds (San Francisco)

Finley flew home that Sunday night, adrenaline flooding through her in shocks as she expected the following few days. Mona bade her goodbye and wished her karma on "activity breadcrumbs."Finley was more thankful to her school companion than she might have at any point expressed.

Finley allocated herself seven days to carry out her arrangement - for the most part, to affirm Mona's hypothesis - since Finley realized what to pay special mind to.

The primary chance went ahead Monday when the Gilchrist group showed up to conclude their association with the Edevane Group. Finley had deliberately designed it to such an extent that she wouldn't see Marlo until the Gilchrist gathering. For the event, Finley picked a smoothly customized suit that was all business, matched with a pullover that had a plunging neck area. Finley's initial salvo was to give her cleavage a featuring job. If this doesn't stand out enough to be noticed, I'll have a harder fight ahead...

Marlo fully planned to get to the Monday early evening time meeting on schedule. However, she continued becoming mixed up in the idea. She'd been kicking herself the whole time Finley was gone. She realized she shouldn't have started a quarrel, and she'd anticipated saying 'sorry' the second Finley returned. In any case, there'd been no chance to do as such. Finley went directly to the lodging after landing (it was late) and decided to eat alone. Marlo went through the early daytime, attempting to sort out some way to spill her guts to Finley. However, the ghost of Finley's weekend in California lingered over her, projecting a long shadow of uncertainty and frailty over Marlo's considerations. She's most likely completely pissed at me. Ideally, the prep work I did with Gilchrist throughout the end of the week gets me some pats on the head... That was when Marlo saw her telephone and understood the gathering was going to begin.

"Crap!" Marlo snatched her stuff and hopped into the vehicle, reviling each red light tossed in her direction. The pendulum check in the inn doorway was finishing its rings when Marlo stepped into Brackenridge's business community.

"Where've you been?" Gregory Wright waved her in. Marlo murmured a calm 'sorry' and followed her father into the meeting room.

The about six Gilchrist colleagues were beginning to sit down along one side of the monstrous table. Finley was conversing with John Gilchrist and had her back turned towards Marlo, yet she detected that her dearest companion had shown up. She chilled out and effortlessly directed John towards the table.
"OK, John, how about we begin," Finley said to John, signaling towards the table. She took a gander at the Gilchrist group and shifted her head, "Please, folks, would you say you are truly going to all sit on one side and join forces against me?"

The Gilchrist group snickered, and some fired, taking up seats on the table's opposite side.

Marlo ventured forward and put her records close to Finley's seat. Finley turned and grinned, "Ah, Marlo to the salvage. I'm not going to be in isolation! Gregory, I'm happy you figured out how to discover her!"

Marlo's eyes met Finley's briefly before fluttering downwards for the smallest tick of time. Finley felt a rush rocket through her body. Finley's eyes shined wickedly as Marlo thought back up once more. Marlo realized she'd been gotten.

"Welcome back," Marlo faltered out. Did she find me gazing at her? Perhaps not?

"Much appreciated," Finley grinned, "I couldn't say whether you'd show today... however, I'm happy that you did!"

Blame washed over Marlo, "I'm heartbroken - "

Finley waved hand contemptuously, "We can discuss it later."

The CEO went to the gathered gathering, "I've explored the Partnership Agreement and the prep records you sent over - thank you for chipping away at it. Here are our imprint-ups. We can go over them at this moment. Gregory has a pile of remarks too, so we should begin."

Finley began sliding heaps of paper around, and as she turned towards Marlo, she hung over (barely) to slide the last heap of records her companion's way, "Here you go, Marlo, would you be able to separate those into three and pass it along?"

Marlo ended up gazing once more. Finley's shirt had ripped open for a negligible portion of a second, and Marlo's eager eyes got a brief look at the lacey bra under. Again, Marlo gazed upward and realized she'd been found gazing. Goddamit Marlo!

Finley's cherished it. She kept a poker face, however, and it left Marlo humiliated that the aloof exterior she'd built so cautiously throughout the long term had bombed her twice with hardly a pause in between.

Kindly, the gathering immediately requested everybody's complete consideration, not least when Gregory moved into high octane legal counselor mode to work through the legitimate terms among Edevane and Gilchrist. Finley didn't display her existing resources very as boldly from that point onward to Marlo's alleviation - albeit the tall blonde knew those blazes of tissue (whenever proceeded) would address a risky area for her. Marlo considered what had happened throughout Finley's visit to California and kicked herself by and by for having let envy over-run her feelings. Marlo additionally didn't exactly pay attention to her gut feelings, which revealed that Finley was, as a rule, purposefully provocative. In some other situation, Marlo would have seen an open door... yet, maybe her sonar had been stuck, and her mind wasn't preparing the signs appropriately.

Marlo was resolved to pull her companion to the side to dispel any confusion air. However, Finley didn't give her a possibility. As the gathering finished, Finley went to John Gilchrist and said, "Will we?"

John gestured and accumulated his archives, which he gave off to a helper.

"John and I will take care of some potential issues over supper. I guaranteed him Darla's famous Ahi fish dish. Much obliged to you for your work this previous week. The work is simply starting, and I'm eager to be cooperating going ahead."

The Gilchrist group alternated, shaking Finley's hand and expressing gratitude toward her for the chance. Marlo stood vulnerably by; she felt pointless and overlooked.

"Marlo," Finley at long last turned towards her, "We can look up some other time, yes?"

Marlo gestured, "Uh, sure. Do you-"

Finley picked that second to take her suit coat off. The sleeveless pullover uncovered itself altogether its magnificence, flaunting its proprietor's delightful arms... what's more, neck... furthermore, chest...

"Do I... what?" Finley asked straight, her face deceiving nothing.

"Goodness... uh... um, do you need me to take your stuff back to your office?" Marlo felt like the nitwit assistant that no one needed to converse with.

"Gracious, sure! Much appreciated Marlo," Finley gave Marlo the enormous heap of records and afterward went to John, "My mom may go along with us, coincidentally. I thought we'd eat out on the west porch. It's too pleasant ever to be inside, wouldn't you say?"

"As you wish," John Gilchrist slanted his head somewhat as both of them strolled towards the library entryways. Finley turned around towards Marlo, "Marlo, much obliged for everything." And at that point, with the smallest trace of a wink, she was no more.

Marlo felt moronic, holding the pile of papers... with no place to go. Her father had effectively withdrawn to his room, presumably to handoff the dealings' result with his group. Every other person appeared to eat designs as of now, and the room had gotten out.

Marlo set the records back on the oak table and slid into a seat, not quite certain what was happening with Finley. Marlo was thankful that Finley hadn't frosted her out totally, yet Finley had never been the sort to do that. What made it more befuddling was the inclination that Finley was practically trying Marlo to gaze, yet then she'd left so rapidly after the gathering. What a wreck...

Finley felt a little terrible about putting out contradicting messages; however, one thing was clear: she likely wouldn't require the entire week to bring in Marlo. Her companion's endeavor at unobtrusive lecherous looks felt astounding. She was, in reality, somewhat soothed to have a work supper drive a wedge between what occurred at the gathering with what her base cravings were asking her to accomplish (something as per hopping on Marlo and ripping each other's garments off). Her excellent target was for her and Marlo to deal with their affections for one another (to give herself wholeheartedly to Marlo decently fast before long).

"John!" Juniper shouted, "Beautiful to see you once more. Great gathering, I trust?"

John landed two warm kisses on every one of Juniper's cheeks, "I think it worked out preferable for Edevane over for us, yet I wouldn't have expected whatever else with your girl in charge."

Finley becomes flushed, "Gracious, quiet, John, you've been excessively liberal. We should sit."

"Marlo's not coming to supper?" Juniper inquired.

"Uh, actually no, not around evening time," Finley expressed just.

"There's another you don't play with," John said with friendliness, "Nearly pushed my group to the edge she worked them so hard a week ago. Also, still, they believe she's the best thing ever."

Juniper gestured, "She's a manager, that Marlo." Mother and girl traded a sharp look.

John tasted the water, "Don't I know it! I made Marlo a proposal to join Gilchrist, you know? In reality, I made her three offers - each with a bigger and bigger check. She didn't nibble."

Finley's heart begun pounding, "John Gilchrist, would you say you were attempting to take Marlo from me?"

Gilchrist set up his hand, "You can't blame a person for attempting. As I said, she never gave me a possibility. Said a completely 'no' without fail."

"You shouldn't be amazed; you'd need something more than cash to pry Marlo away from Finley," Juniper said intentionally.

Finley whipped her head towards her mom.

"Right!" John gestured, "I thought little of her devotion to you. Excuse me, Finley."

Finley shook her head genially as the server showed up to take their orders, "No damage, no foul."

"Great!" John grinned, "Women first!" He signaled towards them with the menu.

Them three immediately requested, and John pardoned himself, "If it's not too much trouble, excuse me, I recently recollected that I vowed to call my child this evening - he had a chess competition today."

The second mother and little girl were separated from everyone else; Juniper hungover, "Kindly reveal to me you have figured out the California frenzy. You would not accept my calls the entire week. I thought you were dead."

Finley feigned exacerbation, "Mother, stop with the acting. I answered your writings. You realized I was fine what's more, yes. I've got myself straightened out. I'm clear about that. That is not the issue."

"Really?!" Juniper reclined, "What's the issue?"

Finley shut her eyes and settled on a snappy choice. Her mom would be a considerable partner in assisting with 'activity breadcrumbs.' No torment, no addition. "The issue is Marlo. She probably won't feel a similar way."

"Are you saying what I believe you're saying?" Juniper couldn't conceal the joy in her voice.

Finley felt like a young person, seeing the excited look in her mom's eyes. She murmured with abdication, "Yes... what's more, kindly don't fold, mother. John will return any second."

Juniper fixed her back, "I don't fold. Since you've sorted out your affections for Marlo, I don't get what the issue is."

Finley did whatever it takes not to be irritated, "Uh, the issue is the way that she doesn't make connections? She may go into hypersensitivity stun if I propose the subject... furthermore, that is not even the most serious issue. The most concerning issue is her absolute lack of engagement in me."

"No. Wrong. It is anything but an issue," Juniper's words were staggering over themselves. She was so anxious to get them out, "She revealed to me she's been enamored with you since, goodness, a long time back. Could it be any more obvious? Don't worry about it."

Finley was paralyzed, "WHAT? You've known this, and you didn't advise me?"

Juniper squinted her eyes, "I urged Marlo to converse with you, yet that wound up being a finished fiasco. And afterward, you left and wouldn't return my calls."

"Alright, OK! Heavenly sh- - " Finley couldn't ward the grin off her face, "Presently what?"

"Eat rapidly. Rapidly. At that point, get Marlo. Disclose to John you're worn out from jetlag or something."

Similarly, as fast as the elation spread, reality began soaking in. Finley shut her eyes; she required everything to stop for one minute. "Mother, this won't turn out well with the PR people."
Juniper's eyes turned steely, "At that point, we have some unacceptable PR people."

"We will lose a huge load of business in pieces of the world that don't approve of stuff this way."

Juniper said nothing, yet there was little uncertainty about how she felt.

"Also losing business across an expansive area of the US. Furthermore, the press will go crazy."

"I bet we acquire allies, then we lose. Furthermore, the sensationalist newspapers have been circumnavigating around this for quite a long time, so this won't be new."

"We haven't endorsed with Gilchrist yet - he probably won't care for any of this..." Finley began to freeze. There was an explanation I chose to keep things straightforward! The expanding influences of this will be crazy...

"Finley." Juniper knew precisely the thing was going through her girl's psyche. She realized that all the disadvantage situations and every one of the negative results were thundering through Finley's mind dangerously fast.

"Mother, this isn't acceptable. This won't be acceptable."

"Nectar, don't conflate your dread of being involved with whatever else. Try not to let the 'what uncertainties' be your pardon for not sorting this out with Marlo. I'll converse with John. And afterward, we can sort everything out as we go. Since the world has deep pockets of disdain doesn't mean you should abandon Marlo easily."

Finley's brain was a haze of considerations. John Gilchrist got back to the table, and they three figured out how to have a completely pleasant supper. Finley was appreciative of her mom's awesome supper facilitating abilities. John Gilchrist was oblivious to the passionate strife Finley was grappling with.

A little more than an hour later, Finley courteously declined dessert and pretended exhaustion. She vowed to invest more energy with John throughout the following while the essential organization got in progress. Juniper everything except pushed Finley out of the café, and Finley ran back to her suite. She was scared in around ten distinct ways.

Finley dialed the one individual she realized who could talk her off the edge.

"I trust you're calling me to report having had some awe-inspiring sex with Marlo," came Mona's energetic voice.

"I'm going crazy, Mona," Finley answered.

"Gracious, nectar, what occurred?"

"Nothing. That is to say, it's unquestionably, presumably, without a doubt that we're truly into one another, and we've been imbeciles. In any case, I'm going crazy about the way that getting along with Marlo may be super awful information for my family and the farm that my family's developed in the course of recent many years."

"You are the biggest secretly held organization on the planet. There're no investors to battle with. You can lose the entirety of the arrangements in your pipeline and still be alright."

Finley took a full breath, "And now I will be that gay CEO. Regardless of what else I do, I will be the lesbian CEO. That will be my tribute."

"Try not to thump it until you've attempted it," Mona said discreetly.

Finley jumped, "I didn't intend to say it was something terrible - I simply imply that it will be the automatic, something dimensional that individuals will consider me."

"That might be valid for a few years, however Finley, that is not the feature any longer when individuals expound on me as CEO of Win-B. Sooner or later, the curiosity will wear off. I guarantee," Mona's tone was straightforward, "And truly, I figure individuals would invite this news. We've had too many butts face CEOs and sexual stalker CEOs overwhelming our features. You and Marlo openly pronouncing your affection for each other may break online media... positively."

Finley laughed, "You generally realize how to pull me back from the cliff... Much obliged."

"I'll generally be here for you. In any case, I'm booting you off this call since you need to figure out how to get into Marlo's jeans ASAP!"

Finley giggled, "OK... in any case; if this thing transforms into damnation on wheels, you must assistance I get the pieces - and no charging me those insane Win-B expenses!"

"Arrangement. Go tell your closest companion you're frantically enamored with her."

Finley hung up, a major smile all over. Perhaps this won't transform into a crap show.

Another full breath later, Finley dialed Marlo's number as adrenaline pounded through her.

"Finley?" Marlo was skulking around in her father's lodging.

"Marlo." Finley's voice shuddered with hunger, "I need to see you. Would you be able to meet me in my suite in 30 minutes?"

"You're finished with supper as of now? I thought..."

"No, I dodged out right on time. Not to stress, Gilchrist is still ready... or on the other hand, he ought to be... my mom's still with him."

Marlo tossed apprehensively, "Fingers crossed!"

"Have a little confidence in me, Dr. Wright; I understand what I'm doing." Finley put a little guarded edge to her tone.

"Gracious! I realize that Finley, I surmise I didn't anticipate that you should call, you know, after..." Marlo mishandled her words.

Finley grinned, getting a charge out of the way that she was proceeding to wrong-foot her companion, "I said we'd look up some other time, isn't that right? I haven't found a solution to my unique inquiry, coincidentally."

"Huh?" Marlo attempted to rewind the last moment of discussion. Gregory Wright gazed toward his girl's confounded face and raised an eyebrow. Marlo attempted to zero in on the thing Finley was asking, "What question?"

Finley let out a breath, "I said I need to see you. Would you be able to go to my room in, say, about 30 minutes?"

"OK. Why?"

Finley replied with her most imperious voice, "You provoked me and left without conversing with me about it. What's more, I'm your chief. Do I have to explain?"

Marlo's mouth hung open. Goodness crap. She's pissed at me. She's so pissed at me she took advantage. Which she's never done. Poop. I'm toast. She consumed fricking toast. "Uh, no, obviously not. I'll be there in 30 minutes."

Marlo hung up the telephone and murmured.

Her father gazed upward momentarily from the arrangement archives on his lap, "What was that about?"

"Finley's finished with the Gilchrist super early. Appears to be somewhat odd, right?" Marlo tapped the telephone against the side of her head.

Gregory Wright turned a page casually, "More limited gatherings are better gatherings; what's odd about that?"

"She needs to see me. Shortly... in her room..."

"Great."

"She's been hot and cold with me throughout the day."

"At that point, go fix it," Marlo's dad answered. He took a gander at his little girl over the highest point of his glasses, "And for hell's sake, kindly disclose to her how you feel. Juniper and I are prepared to disclose to her ourselves on the off chance that you don't come out with it soon."

"Wha-?" Marlo's eyes enlarged, "No. No, no, no, no, no. That is not on the table. No. I've irritated her enough for what it's worth. This will crack her out, similar to I've been some unpleasant stalker fan and... NO. I'm not going there."

Gregory took his perusing glasses off, "You're belittling her. Quit being a weakling. Disclose to her the genuine motivation behind why you blew a gasket on her last week. It'll be better. For the both of you. In any event, it'll be out in the open."

Marlo gazed at her dad a few beats, "I can't, father."

"She's your most seasoned and dearest companion," Gregory said as he set his glasses back on, "She merits reality. Else, you're a sorry companion, right?"

Marlo stood frozen in place, her dad's words soaked in - quick and profound. Gregory turned around to his paper; he'd said what he'd needed to say for some time. The rest was up to Marlo.

"I better go - I shouldn't keep her pausing," Marlo mumbled.

Gregory smiled, "Didn't she say she needed you to arrive in thirty?"

"Gracious... right." Marlo sank into a club seat inverse her father. The check-in room taunted her as it consistently... gradually... ticked and tocked as the seconds progressed.

Marlo didn't have the foggiest idea of what's in store. Finley had left so suddenly... furthermore, presently had called her so surprisingly. After the longest standby of her life, Marlo stepped through the lodging passageways and unobtrusively thumped on Finley's entryway.

There was no answer.

Marlo thumped once more. Nothing. She attempted the entryway and thought that it was opened. She opened the entrance and ventured into the room.

Finley rose out of the restroom, "Marlo. Much obliged for coming. All around coordinated, as well; I just completed my shower." Finley belted her robe.

Marlo remained by the entryway, uncertain of Finley's expectations, "I'm sorry it's been off-kilter since we battled "

Finley held up her hand, "Hold that idea. Could you kindly bolt the entryway?"

"Huh?" Marlo's mind was tumbling near; there was a look all over that was new. Marlo didn't dare name it.

"The entryway behind you. Kindly lock it."

Marlo's heart sped up. She came to behind her and turned the lock with an authoritative snap.

"I would not joke about this. I'm sorry we battled," Marlo began once more, "I'm sorry I expressed every one of those things. I was provoking you, and it wasn't reasonable."

"It was..." Finley inclined toward the arm of the couch, "... amazing, most definitely. I was unable to sort out what got you so frantic about me moving to California. That is to say, for what reason was it a serious deal?"

Come clean with her! A voice shouted inside Marlo's head.

Finley shifted her head and proceeded, "... Particularly since you had that delightful brunette going around with you that day... it didn't make any sense."

"She... uh, she didn't remain. She left."

Finley lifted her eyebrows, "Really? She didn't fall completely devoted to you, Dr. Wright?"

Marlo shrugged, "I... uh... she and I are simply companions. Nothing is going on between us past that."

Finley's heart jumped, celebrating at the data. She was unable to oppose a little burrow, "That is unordinary."

Marlo shrugged once more, "There was another person I needed."

"Ok. That is the Marlo I know," Finley scolded, "and who, ask, did you need?"

Marlo took a full breath and dove in, "Uh... it was somebody I provoked... furthermore, uh, that somebody took off to California for a piece."
There it was.

The two ladies gazed at one another. Every one of them looking at the other with a force that made words superfluous.

Finley's eyes gleamed with joyful tears.

Marlo raced to clarify, "I got desirous. I... I caught your discussion with Mona. About Rowan. What's more, you made arrangements to see her. I lashed out. I was unable to bear the possibility that you picked her-"

"Stop." Finley's voice was sharp. She cleared a finger under each eye and fixed her back, "Stop. I would prefer not to discuss our battle."

"Why-?" Marlo was confused. She thought she'd get a type of response from her admission. Yet, all things being equal, Finley was acting like she hadn't heard it by any stretch of the imagination. Additionally, there was something else about Finley's manner of speaking, about how Finley was taking a gander at her. It was the high-octane form of Finley that Marlo had fantasized about for quite a long time: One section majestic, two sections voracious, all parts hot. Nothing was seeming well and good. Marlo shook her head in disarray, "I don't comprehend."

"Your Queen is telling you to stop." Finley expressed once more. She interspersed it with a hidden wink.

Wow, that is the hottest thing I've at any point experienced. "Indeed, er, OK," Marlo murmured.

Finley strolled straight up to Marlo, "Don't... move... a muscle. Would you be able to do that for me?"

"Indeed," Marlo scarcely moved her lips. Marlo's blue eyes bolted onto Finley's earthy colored ones for a beat before Finley connected and put her hands on Marlo's chest and begun to unfasten Marlo's shirt gradually. Marlo wanted to recoil with excitement with each brush of Finley's fingers against her body.

"Stay still, Marlo," Finley murmured as she cleared her hands under Marlo's shirt and lifted the shirt and off Marlo's body, "I believe it's about time that this happened..."

Finley inhaled out with relish. She'd seen Marlo's middle many, often previously. In any case, presently, this is all mine. With somewhat shaking hands, Finley went after Marlo's belt. Her knuckles brushed against Marlo's lower mid-region, and Marlo needed to focus not to respond. Marlo felt Finley bring down her jeans and her clothing. Marlo watched Finley's eyes meandering ravenously all over her body.

Finley raised her eyes and saw Marlo taking a gander at her. Here goes nothing, Finley thought.

For Marlo, the next fifteen seconds occurred in extra lethargic movement. She saw Finley's hands fixing the belt of her robe, and afterward, supernaturally, the robe floated downwards. Marlo was too paralyzed to even think about doing anything but to gaze in marvel at the lovely lady before her.

Finley wavered. For what reason would she say she is simply remaining there? Goodness god, she doesn't care for what she sees... Finley had been fantasizing about falling into Marlo's arms and allowing their drives to dominate. Be that as it may, presently they were both remaining there, taking a gander at one another.

Marlo adored being the object of Finley's look. The blondie was acquainted with being respected - her build and sexual orientation introduction was striking, no doubt - except for it felt distinctive with Finley: Marlo felt seen - as an individual to be wanted, without a doubt, yet also as all the other things Finley realized that she would generally be.

Detecting Finley's passing aversion, Marlo quirked an eyebrow, "May I move now?"

Numbnuts! She didn't move since I revealed to her not to! Finley's face was an image of bothered cumbersomeness.

Marlo thought it was cute.

Counterfeit it till you make it..."Yes," Finley made a sound as if to speak, "yet just to take off your shoes and socks."

Marlo ventured out of the pool of apparel around her feet, dismissed from her shoes, and pulled off her socks. "Presently what?" She asked as her mouth brandished an abnormal smile.

"Well," Finley gave her head a slight shake, "I figure I may very well gander at you some more..."

"What's more, will perusing transform into something different, ma'am?" Marlo felt something incredible uncoiling inside her. Her senses were at last pinging on the correct recurrence once more, and they were shouting with, please.

"Gee, I trust so," Finley put her hands on Marlo's collarbone and hauled her fingers across Marlo's shoulders and down her arms.

Four common words, yet emerging from Finley's mouth, those four words were the hottest come-ons Marlo'd at any point heard. Marlo was by and by delivered puzzled. Finley's purposeful touch on her substance was practically difficult to measure: Elegant hands following electric lines of joy on her middle, drawing out each mind-boggling subtlety of Marlo's strong geography. The tall butch was perplexed for another explanation: She was acclimated with being in charge, establishing the tone, and being the one causing another person to feel better. Presently, she was submitting to Finley's purposeful investigation of her body. Marlo was astonished by the amount she was getting a charge out of it and how inconceivably stimulating it was.

Finley gestured towards the room. "Time to rests, Marlo..."

Marlo complied and watched with hungry expectation as Finley rode her across her stomach. There was a warmth transmitting from Finley that Marlo discovered overpowering.

"Amazing." Marlo began to go after Finley. However, Finley shook her head.

Marlo was kicking the bucket to contact Finley. However, she complied. Something was exciting and provocative about submitting to Finley. Marlo's sweethearts had consistently acknowledged Marlo's inclination to lead, which made Finley's initial salvo a striking takeoff from Marlo's typical experiences. But then... Marlo yielded. Since she'd been asked to... furthermore, more critically, she needed to.

Finley brought her lips down to Marlo's, and the two of them groaned with need. It was a first kiss that shut out the remainder of the world. In the long run, Marlo wanted to run her hands up Finley's body.

"Not yet, Marlo," gasped Finley. She kissed away along Marlo's neck and started laying a long twisting path of kisses down Marlo's body. Marlo was shaking with joy; she thought that it's hard not to move. It would have been incomprehensible for Marlo to think about the amount she'd love being kissed this way. Finley was rapidly losing herself in a mist of sensations. Marlo's skin was warm, smooth, and beat with sexual energy; Finley had been anxious - given her relative naiveté - however, since her mouth was connecting with Marlo's skin, there was only sense and need.

At the point when Finley advanced between Marlo's legs, her tongue tipped forward forcefully. Marlo gave a low, thundering snarl of endorsement; her clit was in effect affectionately lashed. Finley's ministrations were awesome: not very quick, nor excessively lethargic. Finley was ad-libbing decently well. However, she realized she was prevailing as Marlo's breath hitched and her sex expanded and pulsated. Oh my goodness, this is stunning... The two ladies were thinking something very similar as Finley's strokes heightened. Marlo quit having the option to think not long after Finley's fingers discovered their way inside her.

"Gracious!" Marlo's legs opened wantonly. Marlo had never given herself like this to sweethearts previously; however, her body was on auto-pilot, and her mind was flushed with want.

It normally took some time for Marlo to get off, yet Finley pitched her into insensibility, appearing to be little exertion.

Finley gazed in stunningness at Marlo, words ebbing and streaming in her mind happily: attractive, yummy, wonderful, provocative, orgasmic, mine, hers, affection, LOVE... love...

Marlo's grin was stifled immediately as she muttered, "You need to gimme a second..."

Finley set down close to Marlo and watched the blondie glide in the obscurity of her climax's luminosity, "Are you... was that... "

Marlo gestured her head, "Nobody's figured out how to do that to me before..."

"Liar," Finley cherished the commendation yet thought that it was difficult to accept.

Marlo apathetically followed a cross on her chest with her hand, "Vow to god. That is to say; I can scarcely move at present." Marlo opened one eye, "And you can do that all-out imperial power thing whenever you want..."

Finley reddened.

"That was stunning," Marlo smiled, "I have one request..."

"What?"

"Kindly absolutely never reveal to me where you figured out how to do that; I don't figure I could tolerate knowing."

Finley becomes flushed, "That was, uh, somewhat my first time doing that... You know, improvising."

"What?" Marlo's eyes enlarged, "You never... with...?"

Finley shook her head, "Not a chance. She, um, took care of me, and that was it..."

Marlo realized it was puerile. However, her heart made a little move of bliss. She set herself up on one elbow, "May I have your consent to approach, your highness?"

"It took you sufficiently long, Marlo..." Finley gestured. She opened her arms, and Marlo moved on top.

"Blessed shit..." Both ladies said together when their bodies adjusted.

"I'd prefer to 'take care of you' presently, the magnificence... furthermore, I mean to win your respect and outperform some other such attempts..."

Finley began chuckling. She halted immediately when Marlo started a hard and fast attack of Finley's faculties. "Good gracious, Marlo!" Finley screeched when Marlo's tongue and thumb discovered super soft spots at the same time. Marlo kept those two spots murmuring as her other hand meandered lower, her fingers cheerfully arriving on Finley's clit. Finley attempted to make sure to relax. Her cerebrum was struggling to find her sensitive spots. Also, the rude awakening Marlo was deftly giving against Finley's list of Marlo's sex dreams. At that point, her peak called, and it allured so legitimately that Finley figured she would be divided down the middle by it.

"Marlo... you will make me come to Marlo... inside... inside me... presently, Marlo, nectar, presently... please..."

Marlo complied, pushing her fingers inside. Marlo felt Finley's inside dividers grasp with persevering craving. It wasn't well before Finley came. She came so hard Marlo panted in wonder.

"Goodness," Marlo inhaled out.

Finley, in her trance, gone after Marlo and pulled her nearby. Both of them lay there, laced and savored, breathing each other in.
Finley wanted to grin, "It was you from the start... for what reason didn't you advise me?"

"I thought you were straight!" Marlo dissented, "If there was somebody who should do the advising, it was you!"

"You generally said I wasn't your sort!"

"I wasn't honest..." Marlo admitted, "Yet I didn't have a clue by what other method to avoid my affections for you."

Finley inclined in for a wonderfully attractive kiss, "And what sentiments do you have for me, Dr. Wright?"

Marlo laughed, "Goodness, the entire range of emotions... from degenerate sensations of bodily desire to the loftiest, knee-debilitating sensations of distraught enthusiastic love..."

"Love!" Finley howled, "I didn't have a clue about your mouth could say such a word."

"That word..." Marlo said discreetly, "was saved for you. I didn't think you'd at any point need to hear it from me."

Finley sneered, yet her heart was dissolving, "Ah, it's my shortcoming, right? I surmise I'll need to make it up to you..." She gave Marlo another kiss.

Marlo pulled back and took a gander at Finley briefly, "Your majesty..."

Finley's raised an eyebrow.

"Your highness, your modest subject solicitations credit for time served..."

"Marlo...?" Finley slanted her head curiously, "What are you ranting about?"

Marlo made a sound as if to speak, "Indeed, since it took us such a long time to sort this out, I'd like you to consent to time served... you know, we can skirt past the primary date, dating, occasions together bullshit..." Marlo took a full breath, "... to get to the 'if you don't mind, kindly wed me' part at this moment."

Finley was paralyzed. This was not what she anticipated. This was past what she anticipated. "Stand by. Are you proposing to me? You... Marlo 'there're-many-other-fish-in-the-ocean' Wright. Proposing to spend the remainder of your existence with me?"

Marlo's smile was irresistible.

Finley inclined forward, "You're truly genuine, right?"

Marlo gestured. For great measure, Marlo moved off the bed and stooped before Finley, "Genuinely. I love you. With each fiber of my being. Will you wed me?"

"Indeed," Finley gestured cheerfully, "Indeed, obviously... however, oh my goodness Marlo... this means..."

Marlo jumped back on the bed and began spoiling Finley's bosoms, "Yes... this implies that we will have an off-the-outlines gay-as anyone can imagine a wedding, and it will be astounding... yet, we don't need to consider that privilege now..." Marlo's hand-measured Finley's sex.

Finley murmured, "I can't help but concur... no reasoning this evening Marlo..."

"Your desire is my order," Marlo said as she dodged under the covers.

Different orgasmic hours after the fact, Finley got up to the sound of the french ways to the overhang being opened. Marlo's body was crushed up close to hers; her breathing was delicate and consistent. Who the hellfire is in my room! We bolted the entryway! At the point when Finley's eyes centered around the figure by the gallery entryways, she screamed, "Mother!"

Marlo sat straight up at Finley's outcry.

Juniper didn't turn away from her assignment, "Great morning, nectar. Greetings, Marlo. Paula's concocting your morning meal, yet I thought I'd come in first and ensure the room was somewhat less, um, stuffy..."

Finley pulled a bed sheet up to cover the two of them, "How could you get in here? We bolted the entryway!"

Juniper headed back towards the entryway and gave the two ladies a breezy look, "Yes - you bolted one entryway; however, this is a multi-room suite... with two entryways. Possibly now, you'll look at last consent to move into an appropriate house. With the main room... ideally one with soundproof dividers."

Juniper grinned when neither one of the women reacted, "Get yourselves at any rate mostly respectable. Paula will be in soon."

The two ladies gazed, surprised, as the more seasoned lady floated out of the room.

"Do you think she heard us?" Finley murmured.

"I couldn't care less if the entire city heard us," Marlo squirmed her eyebrows, "We were compensating for some recent setbacks."

Finley radiated with bliss and pulled up the covers around herself and Marlo minutes prior

Paula came in with the morning meal plate.

"Good day, ma'am... Dr. Wright," Paula said, "I'll return for these later. Ring if you need anything."

"Much appreciated, Paula," Finley said, attempting to marshal as much respect as possible. Paula gestured and took off of the room, yet not before she exclaimed, "I'm so glad for you both!"

The second the entryway shut, Finley quickly laid a kiss all the rage. Marlo transformed towards Finley and tunneled into her arms. Finley moaned cheerily as Marlo's tissue on hers shipped off a sparkle of excitement. This had happened a few times for the duration of the evening: Marlo or Finley would wake, and arms and hands would wind through the sheets with a sensual plan, every one of them hungry to discover better approaches for pleasuring the other.

"I could become accustomed to this..." Finley mumbled.

"What? Breakfast in bed?" Marlo asked mockingly.

"No, senseless. Having you for breakfast..." Finley murmured.

"Regular?" Marlo's heart was detonating.

"Each. Day." Finley said, accentuating each syllable with a kiss.

Explicit Erotic Sex Stories

Enticing KIARA

A spouse's lesbian enticers have the tables turned on them (Lesbian)

Pamela Vance

Jessica and Kiara

"I need you to focus, Lauren," Jessica pronounced, "On the off chance that you need to do this however much you guarantee, you need to realize the ideal approach. You can't simply be a tease a little, and afterward, give yourself wholeheartedly to her. Kiara has been willfully ignorant so long about her sexuality that she'll blow a gasket if you do. I will not have my kinship destroyed because you were messy and languid about tempting her. You need a decent strategy, and I will offer it to you."

Lauren moved on her stool and took a gander at her mom. Jessica Adams. The more seasoned lady may have been in her late forties, yet she was a beautiful example. Her long earthy-colored hair boiled down to simply over her shoulder bones. Her bangs floated down across her temple to simply over her hazel-hued eyes. She had a delightful grin that lit up her face at whatever point it showed up. Her body, however, thicker and more amble than Lauren's, had been very much kept up throughout the long term, something the nineteen-year-old could bear witness to. She had been lucky enough to test it more than once throughout the most recent year or something like that. Her mom had allured her into the delights of sapphic love soon after her eighteenth birthday celebration. The occasion had changed Lauren's life perpetually, and now she needed to do likewise for Kiara.

Kiara Settles was her mom's dearest companion. Lauren had discovered the fifty-year-old to be at the forefront of her thoughts increasingly throughout the previous year. Like Lauren's mom, Kiara was a delightful brunette with long wavy hair that finished in delicate twists. Lauren had started to see the lady's alarm earthy colored eyes on her habitually in the most recent year or more. These weren't casual looks by the same token. There appeared to be a yearning there. Lauren had gotten very skilled at getting on the signs ladies put off when they were keen on you. The light, coy contacts, and sweet commendations Kiara regularly gave her were predictable pointers of the MILF's longing.

Like her mom, Jessica, Lauren was sensibly certain that Kiara had next to zero consciousness of her emotions. It was likely her subliminal that was driving her to act how she did around Lauren. The delightful earthy colored looked at the young lady with long, light earthy colored hair was anxious to carry those sentiments to the cutting edge of Kiara's cognizance. She had developed so excited about having the option to taste the more seasoned lady's pussy, that she'd gone to her mom for help.

"I get, Mom. You know how I am about more seasoned ladies, however. I struggle not to get excessively excited about the possibility of being with another one. Also, the possibility of having Kiara's face between my legs energizes me continually." Lauren proclaimed.

Lauren had built up a preference for more established ladies soon after her enchantment. Even though her endeavors had been cumbersome, she'd, in any case, figured out how to lure and bed three ladies in their forties in the course of the most recent year. Lauren discovered each insight to be seriously elating. She got along with each of the three now and again still. Presently, however, she was eager for another victory. Kiara would be all the more a test. She was joyfully hitched to a man that adored her however much she cherished him. John was a fire fighter and an attractive person. Indeed, even somebody her age could comprehend the allure he held for Kiara. Lauren realized she wouldn't effectively give in the manner the others had.

Jessica grinned at her little girl. The hot youthful tart was a remarkable anxious purveyor of the possibility that each lady merited the experience of engaging in sexual relations with one more female eventually in her life. Lauren accepted that a lady on lady love experience shouldn't be denied any grown-up female like her mom.

Jessica was likewise exceptionally pulled in to Kiara and had frequently fantasized throughout the years about being with her closest companion. It was that kinship, however, that had held her back from acting. She esteemed their relationship an excessive amount to chance losing it.

Having Lauren step in and draw out Kiara's evident interest in lesbian love may end up being the solution to her supplications. If she could get the young lady to tune in and learn, she may before long have the option to appreciate snacking on Kiara's clit and delicate nipples. Kiara had once trusted that having them squeezed daintily and sucked on was sufficient to drive her into space. Jessica was anxious to test that hypothesis. She'd regularly fantasized about having the 3rd-grade instructor ride her hips while she tenderly bit on her companion's nipples. She could envision how Kiara would crush her wet pussy against her midriff accordingly. Jessica considered the thought heavenly.

"The way into a fruitful temptation of any straight lady is the abbreviation I.S.I.S," Jessica revealed to her girl.

Lauren grimaced and asked, "I trust you mean the Egyptian Goddess of ladies and kids and not the psychological militant association?"

Jessica grinned and said, "Truth be told. Be that as it may, for this situation, the name represents the four stages important to guarantee a fruitful enchantment."

Jessica tasted from her water bottle and said, "The primary letter, "I," means "Disconnecting your objective." You need to get her alone, so when you do any of the things important to tempt her, she doesn't need to stress over, according to other people. If there is any other person around, she will be excessively reluctant at any point to permit her body to respond how you need it to."

Jessica looked as Lauren recorded her recommendation in the scratch pad she generally had with her when chipping away at school work. She grinned at the possibility of the energetic, youthful temptress dealing with this experience like an intellectual exercise. It showed the youthful magnificence was viewing her craving appropriately.

"The other thing that Isolation permits you is conceivable deniability. On the occasion things go poorly, you can generally guarantee Kiara had fiercely misinterpreted your activities. By then, it's your assertion versus hers. I consider both of us concur that maintaining this side of ourselves mystery is the most intelligent strategy, so care should be taken," Jessica revealed to her little girl. She had no genuine stress over Kiara responding contrarily. However, it generally paid to play things securely.

"The subsequent letter, "S" means "Praise her excitedly," Jessica expressed. You must be disclosed to her how delightful her outfit is or how fabulous her hair and cosmetics look. Light addresses her arm or hands are fundamental while doing this. It helps partner the possibility of the nice sentiment she gets from your commendations, with the memory of honest yet private contacts from you. In the end, she will begin desiring closeness and consolation."

Lauren asked, "How far would it be advisable for me to push the contacts? Give me an illustration of what you mean."

Jessica went through a rundown of models showcasing each of her girls to show the more youthful lady how they should be utilized. " You never need the contact among you to overwhelm the endeavor to bond with her. So your contacts ought to be private yet unpretentious. You will likely give her goosebumps and not a feeling of caution."

Jessica looked as Lauren noticed her remark in her journal. At the point when the provocative young lady thought back up, Jessica said, "The following part is a significant one. It's a mental method called "Ingratiation." You use it to make yourself more amiable and alluring to the individual you're attempting to lure. It ordinarily requires doing a little report and schoolwork on the objective of your enchantment. Fortunately for you, you have me to fill in any of the spaces you may have on Kiara's preferences."

"So what," Lauren asked, "I profess to like her number one network show or her #1 food?"

Jessica grinned at her little girl and said, "That is essential for it. However, you must go further than that. It would help if you were prepared for the gorge that shows and become familiar with the personal insights concerning it. You need to peruse that book she loves and know its plot and character. You need to taste that food and the ability it's cooked and what its fixings are. As such, you must rat in your endeavors to guarantee she becomes tied up with the conviction that she's tracked down a close companion of sorts. If you effectively figure out how to do the initial three stages, all of you, however, guarantee you achievement in the fourth part."

"Which is?" Lauren asked as she turned upward from the notepad.

Her mom grinned back at her and replied, "All things considered, that would be "Enchantment," obviously. I have that underwear and sex toy party a month and a half from Friday. The air at those things is consistently a piece explicitly charged. A large portion of the ladies leave those gatherings half-alcoholic and already home and attack their spouses or sweethearts. That will be the perfect night for you to free Kiara's life up to its sexually unbiased potential."

"Ideas?" Lauren asked with a trace of fear in her voice.

An insidious grin ran over Jessica's lips as she said, "A few, however, I don't need you fixating on that piece of things. I need you zeroed in on the initial three stages. As we draw nearer to the seven days of the gathering, I'll fill you in on how I figure you should approach doing what needs to be done."

Lauren gestured her head and appeared to look ahead into the distance with simply a trace of a grin all over.

"What are you thinking about?" her mom asked with a curious smile.

Lauren becomes flushed a piece. In a guttural voice loaded up with excitement, she said, "I was envisioning how tasty it will be to have my face covered in Kiara's sweet pussy at last."

Connecting and stroking her little girl's cheek, Jessica said, "Indeed, why not follow me higher up to your room. That way, you can work on the pussy eating abilities you plan on utilizing on my closest companion."

Lauren stood and inclined in to kiss her mom's delicate lips. After a second, their tongues attacked each other's mouths and whipped to and fro against one another. The two ladies groaned, their excitement developing dramatically as time passes the kiss.

At the point when their lips at long last isolated, Lauren gazed toward her mom and said, "That sounds flavorful. However, you would do well to give back because considering having Kiara's pussy to participate in routinely has my underwear splashed."

"Me as well, Baby. Me as well," Jessica said as she snatched her girl's hand and anxiously started driving her to her room.

- - - - -

Kiara

Kiara Settles pulled up before her dearest companion's home and stopped behind a dark Nissan Pathfinder. She realized the vehicle had a place with Jessica's flawless girl Lauren and was somewhat astonished to see it there on a Friday night. Lauren was in her first year of school, and Kiara would have wagered cash. The young lady would have been perhaps the most searched out dates nearby. She was brilliant, expressive, and drawing in a young lady that even Kiara could concede was simple on the eyes.

Kiara had started to see the adjustments in the young lady not long after her eighteenth birthday celebration. Her initial high school's abnormal phase, a very long time with the supports, skin issues, and innocent figure, had offered a path to her turning into a delightful and agile young lady. Kiara had found herself gazing at the adjustments in the growing young lady on a few events. Lauren would regularly wear her hair up either in a pig tail or heaped on top of her head. Kiara started to respect the more youthful lady's long and elegant-looking neck. Lauren was such a staggering young lady that it was difficult to remove your eyes from her when she was in the room.

Kiara advanced up her companion's walkway and ventured up on her entryway patio. She discouraged the doorbell and held up as she heard the tolls reporting her appearance starting their tune.

The entryway opened, yet rather than it being Jessica, she was welcomed by the dazzling, youthful, and grinning face of Lauren. The young lady was wearing a short dark sweater dress that embraced her body like a glove. Kiara couldn't resist the opportunity to see how it formed itself to the young lady's B cup breasts and the flare of her hips. Kiara contemplated internally how blessed the more youthful lady was to have a beautiful, youthful body. That idea quickly made her redden. "Where did that come from," she couldn't resist the opportunity to ponder to herself.

Shaking off the humiliation of having gazed at her closest companion's girl in a particularly despicable manner, Kiara said, "Hello, Lauren, don't you look pretty. You should have a major date around evening time."

Lauren grinned back at Kiarabefore coming in and offering her an embrace. Kiara was immediately astonished at the cozy contact. She embraced her dearest companion's little girl back and couldn't resist the opportunity to feel the more youthful lady's breasts pound against hers. Kiara was wearing a ragged cotton shirt and no bra. That was one of the joys of being little breasted, having the option to abandon a bra. Not having that additional cushioning to secure her touchy nipples, she was currently attempting Kiara's inconvenience. She could feel the more youthful lady's breasts crushed against hers, and the subsequent stuns of joy flowing down her spine to Kiara's center carried a flush to her face and chest.

Lauren grinned back at Kiara; however, her eyes didn't meet Kiara's. Following her look, Kiara peered down and saw to her shock that both of her nipples projected from the flimsy cotton shirt. The brunette quickly becomes flushed and needed to battle the inclination to cover herself. Lauren saved her by turning and strolling back towards the kitchen as she said behind her, "Thank you, and indeed, I had a date. The jerk finally dropped because one of his fraternity siblings had a crisis. Would you be able to accept a particularly faltering reason? I've pretty much had it with men by and large."

Kiara followed behind the alluring young lady as she tuned in to her problem about her date. She wanted to see how the sweater dress embraced the rigid-looking bends of her nubile youthful hips. Kiara ended up nearly enchanted at how Lauren's can appear to sashay to and fro. It wasn't until they entered the kitchen and she saw Jessica remaining there pouring them both a glass of wine that Kiara figured out how to tear her eyes from Lauren's tight little rear.

"What's up with me," Kiara couldn't resist contemplating internally, "since when did I begin getting excited by ladies?"

The two old companions welcomed each other with a snappy embrace. Motioning towards her girl, Jessica said, "Lauren's date will be a flake-out, so I recommended she spend time with both of us on our young lady's evening."

The two ladies' Friday night social gatherings had become a practice of sorts. They had them at whatever point Kiara's significant other, John, was on the fire station's move toward the week's end. They would substitute the areas between their two homes. Whichever one of them was the visitor for that week would gather a short-term pack. Both of them would frequently keep awake until late talking or watching motion pictures while they devoured various jugs of wine. It was only from time to time that they had the chance to rest before a couple in the first part of the day.

Kiara came to take the glass of wine Jessica offered her and was shocked to feel sensitive hands hold onto her correct arm. Lauren's lovely face was there when she glanced over to one side. The dainty youthful excellence, who was scarcely five foot in tallness, gazed toward her and, with a great grin, said, "That is alright with you, isn't it, Mrs. Settles?"

Kiara felt herself gazing once more into the deep pools of those doe-like earthy colored eyes. She needed to shake off the impact the young lady was having on her to say, "Wha...Oh, it is. Assuming you can deal with several hours of your mom and my nonsensicalness, I don't perceive any reason why not."

Notwithstanding her case in case, Kiara felt tangled and conflicted concerning Lauren's quality. She appreciated the more youthful lady's conversation. Having watched her grow up into a maturing youthful magnificence, she felt near her.

In any case, of late, she'd ended up having messy musings about her Lauren. Thoughts and sensations of the sort she'd at no other time managed to have, regardless of whether it was brought about by laying by the pool with Jessica just to have Lauren go along with them in a tiny swimsuit. The sort suit that scarcely covered the young lady's nipples and vaginal region left her tight and tanned rump wholly uncovered. At that point, there was the time she'd watched from a higher up railing as Lauren and a high school companion had straightforwardly moved together down in the lounge of Jessica's home. Kiara had battled to tear her eyes away when she'd saw the two more established youngsters as they knock and ground their bodies together interestingly. As some hip bounce melody played over the theater setup's sound framework, Kiara had looked as Lauren held onto her companion's hips from behind and ground her pelvic locale against the denim-covered ass of her buddy. Their dance was highly sensual. That had been simply the first occasion when that Kiara had ended up pondering about Lauren's sexuality.

Lauren crushed her arm as though in much obliged and said, "I figure it will be fun, Mrs. Settles. You two consistently make me chuckle at whatever point you're together. Especially after you've had a glass or two."

Kiara could feel Lauren's left tit squeezed against her upper arm. As she gazed down into Lauren's grinning face to react, she couldn't resist the opportunity to see the more youthful lady's full base lip. Only briefly, she considered what it resembles to kiss and suck on those lips.

"Where the damnation did that come from?" She promptly thought when the prospect of kissing Lauren's had gone through her head. "She's my closest companion's girl, and what's more, I'm hitched and straight," Kiara contended inside her head.

"Are you OK?" Jessica asked, gazing at her with concern, "You looked somewhat bothered there briefly."

Kiara battled the desire to tear her arm away from the small yet enticing youthful brunette to one side. Acquiring her poise, she said, "I'm fine. It's simply been a difficult day, and I'm anticipating going through the whole evening unwinding."

Mysteriously, Kiara, at that point, peered down at Lauren and said, "And you're too old even to consider being calling me Mrs. Settles. Call me, Kiara."

Lauren's face appeared to illuminate as she was satisfied with Kiara's idea. She pressed her tit against Kiara's exposed right arm and said, "Alright, Kiara."

Kiara felt another shock of delight swell through her inner parts at the more youthful lady's response. As she pondered why she had proposed Lauren call her by her first name, the acknowledgment hit Kiara that her underwear was wet.

She moaned and took a somewhat significant beverage from her glass of wine; she wanted to think about what she'd found herself mixed up with and why she appeared to be unequipped for making it stop. Kiara wound up attracted to Lauren and, despite ongoing vows to herself in the previous months, was powerless to make it stop.

- - - - -

Jessica and Lauren

Lauren gazed upward from between her mom's thighs as she ran her tongue gradually and alluringly between the more seasoned lady's engorged lips. She could see the desire in her mom's eyes as she gazed back with a clear yearning.

359

"That is it, Baby. Lick mom's pussy," Jessica murmured as she gradually spun her hips against her little girl's eager mouth. She could feel her child young lady's tongue as it tested between her swollen labia before sliding into her around greased up the opening. She felt the youthful bi-sexuals lips structure a seal around her opening and start to suck at the good juices spilling from her office.

"Gracious, fuck," Jessica groaned, "that is it, Baby. Suck my pussy. I need to come everywhere on the provocative substance of yours."

Lauren groaned in pleasure and gradually hauled the thumb of her right hand up through her mom's split. At the point when she'd assembled enough of the more seasoned lady's juices to soak her opposable digit, she started to utilize it to make little circles against her sweetheart's clitoris.

Jessica came down and got a handle on the highest point of her little girl's head, pulling it significantly more solidly into contact with her hot pussy. She could feel her longing starting to peak and realized that she was going towards an incredible peak.

While she kept scouring her mom's stub with her thumb, Lauren solidified her tongue and started to screw the all-around soaked opening with her oral limb. The adjustment in incitement was barely enough to send Jessica over the edge. She came long and hard against her girl's face, content in the information that soon they could add Kiara to their rundown of female darlings.

Their Friday night had gone better compared to arranged. Her playful tease of a little girl had her closest companion silenced before she could even traverse the front entryway. The little tart had dressed as enticingly as conceivable with an end goal to have the most potent impact on Kiara. Her arranging hadn't gone unrewarded. The impact Lauren's appearance and coy nature had on the 3rd-grade instructor were evident the second she'd entered the kitchen. Kiara's touches had been at the full pole and contrasting the slim cotton top she'd worn. Jessica had nearly felt frustrated about her companion as she saw the impact Lauren was having on her.

Two glasses of wine for her and Kiara and a closet change had just raised Kiara and Lauren's lascivious conduct. The liquor had released Jessica's companion's commonly traditionalist lips significantly.

Lauren's decision of dozing clothing had been nearly just about as painstakingly chose as her unique outfit. She wore a chocolate-hued nightgown made of a heart-molded and transparent part of trim over her breasts and high-grade silk over the rest of the clothing piece. Her little breasts and conspicuous nipples were promptly evident underneath the ribbon.

She wore a dark pair of kid shorts-type underwear that seemed to have been shower painted on her lower half on her base. They were tight to the point that the parted of Lauren's young pussy was difficult to miss if you tried to look. Furthermore, as the night had gone on, Kiara had battled to tear her eyes away.

Lauren had selected the film they would watch. The solitary admonition they'd given her concerning her decisions was that it must be a sentiment. That was their typical daily schedule, so there was no motivation to transform it.

Jessica had realized what was coming early. She and Lauren had deliberately chosen the lesbian sentiment, "Desert Hearts," with the plan of stimulating Kiara significantly further. It was the narrative of a developed lady who came west to look for an impermanent home in Nevada with the end goal of a quick in and out separate. While there, she gets fascinated with and is lured by a lady in her mid-twenties.

Jessica had watched her companion's response to Lauren's decision of a film as the story unfurled. She made a note of Lauren's way and arranged herself against Kiara's right side, and clutched her correct arm as she inclined toward her clueless objective of temptation. It was difficult to make certain in the obscurity of the room. Yet, Kiara's breathing appeared to be shallow and speedy, especially during a portion of the more sexual pieces of the element.

While she'd clutched the more seasoned lady's arm, Lauren had guaranteed that her left breast was solidly squeezed into the delicate skin of Kiara's privileged rear arm muscle. Squeezing against the sheer trim of her top, Lauren realized the more established lady must have the option to feel her swollen nipple against her skin.

Lauren, feeling certain about herself in the last 50% of the film, had pushed things somewhat farther than she'd at first arranged. The two ladies were sharing a toss cover to keep warm. Lauren had taken her right hand that she'd recently been utilizing to stroke a finger all over the firm tissue of Kiara's correct arm and slid it under the cover. She'd let it stop with her palm on her thigh while her fingertips laid on Kiara's yoga pants-covered leg. Lauren had spent the following half-hour making delicate touches with her fingers on Lauren's flexible upper thigh.

Her mom's dearest companion had never opposed Lauren's advances. Despite what might be expected, Lauren was sensibly certain her enticement objective was excited in light of Kiara's breathing. Furthermore, when she'd delicately tickled at Kiara's upper thigh underneath the front of their toss cover, she'd felt the cougar shudder.

Another glass of wine following the film had delivered some somewhat ribald sexual chat between the three women. Lauren had driven the charge by relating the frustrating story of how she'd lost her virginity to her then-beau. The two more established ladies had giggled generously at Lauren's humorously realistic portrayal of her sweetheart's incompetent endeavors to fulfill her explicitly. At the point when she was through with her story, and they'd figured out how to quit chuckling, the two ladies guaranteed Lauren that there were to be sure men out there equipped for fulfilling a lady. Lauren had muttered to herself about how ladies didn't appear to battle to do it.

Jessica had then described the story of her first school sweetheart. Both of them had tormented her flatmate by repeatedly having intercourse on the opposite side of their common apartment. Jessica swore that by the third time she'd mounted the youthful stud, her stuffy flat mate had shown some signs of life. She said she could make out the young lady's outline as she fingered herself to the hints of their lovemaking.

Jessica left out the part where she'd tempted that equivalent flatmate later on that semester.

Indeed, even traditionalist Kiara had told the marginally naughty story of the first occasion when she'd jerked off. She'd been home alone and had discovered her parent's reserve of grown-up VHS tapes. In that general area sitting on her parent's bed, a more youthful Kiara had fingered herself to peak while watching a mid-eighties pornography called "SkinTight." She bashfully confessed to going through numerous an early evening time relaxing on her parent's bed, seeking after her fulfillment.

At the point when the three ladies had finally said goodnight, Lauren had given her mom a chaste kiss before going to Kiara. She'd grinned up at the taller lady and afterward positioned two hands on her cheeks and remained on her broken toes to kiss her goodbye. Lauren had kissed her as delicately as could be expected, permitting their lips to separate, and afterward united them back, both somewhat firmer and less virtuous. She'd finished the kiss by gradually sucking on Kiara's lower lip. The exact opposite thing she saw as she broke the kiss and immediately limited up the steps was Kiara frozen, remaining there in stun. Her lips were as yet pressed together as though in mid-kiss, and her eyes shut.

Lauren had more than once fingered herself to climax as she'd fantasized about what it resembles to finally allure Kiara. She realized that she would have the option to make the appealing cougar come more than once. Other than having the option to taste Kiara's pussy, at last, Lauren's number one dream was of being behind her mom's dearest companion, fingering her wet cunt. While she was doing as such, Kiara would lick and suck between her mom's legs. It would be heavenly once it at long last occurred. Lauren realized she would have to stay patient. It is destroying to surge things now and have Kiarabolt subsequently. No, Lauren had needed her mother's hot companion for a long time. She wouldn't chance to demolish things now.

- - - - -

Kiara

Kiara struggled to focus on her commute home the following morning. When she'd pulled out of her dearest companion's carport, she had become persuaded that Jessica's girl Lauren had been hitting on her since she'd addressed the entryway the earlier evening. Had it been guiltless and innocuous words or looks, Kiara wouldn't have been so disturbed by it. For hell's sake, she would have been complimented by it thinking about the source. Lauren was a genuinely lovely young lady who liked her. It would have been innocuous a few splendid glimmering cautioning lights.

One had been how her body had responded to the young lady's teases. When she'd said her goodnights and subsided into the sovereign estimated bed of the first-floor visitor room, Kiara's undies had been splashed. To such an extent that she'd been compelled to eliminate them and wash them out in the sink. She'd left them looming over the shower entryway in the wake of wringing them out. They'd in any case been too moist even to consider wearing today, so Kiara had slipped her pants on over her bare lower half and gone commando for breakfast. Her still, for the most part, wet undies had been discharged out in her suitcase.

As she'd slithered into bed the previous evening, her touchy nipples had still been erect. They'd been that path the greater part of the evening, at the point when youthful Lauren had started delicately touching her thigh underneath the sofa-bed. Kiara had gotten reluctant to let the upper portion of her body move. Kiara's nipples had gotten so delicate by that point, and the remainder of her body so stimulated, she'd been anxious about peaking had they brushed against her shirt.

In disgrace, the more established lady had been not able to withstand the allurement of slipping her hand between her thighs and running her fingers inside her pussies swollen lips. It was the thing that had been flowing through her brain as she played with herself that had been the second glaring admonition light.

The kiss.

Adequately genuine, it had been straightforward. However, Kiara could recall the absolute most sexual thing since her initial encounters with John. Lauren's lips had been so delicate and flexible as they'd touched hers that Kiara had gotten lost in those concise snapshots of arousing contact. Long after, the young lady had advanced up the steps and into her room. Kiara had ended up remaining there, wanting for only a couple more snapshots of that kiss.

It was that kiss she was considering when she slipped her ring and forefingers into her ravenous opening and started to finger herself with her right hand. As her palm quickly slapped against her clit, Kiara had started to daintily squeeze and roll the nipple of her left breast between her fingers. That kiss, that sweet kiss...

Her peak had come so unexpectedly that Kiara had been compelled to nibble at her base lip to hold back from shouting out. The climax rose and peaked as she envisioned Lauren's tongue entering her mouth. Flavorful spasms hustled through her center as she fantasized about holding onto the nubile youthful magnificence's tongue between her lips and sucking on it eagerly.

Kiara had made herself come three different occasions before she'd at long last had the option to sneak off into rest. And, after it's all said and done, she'd been spooky by dreams of Lauren doing unspeakably shrewd things to her body. Things that appeared to be considerably more significantly terrible and freak in the light of day. As unreasonable as her nighttime emanations had been, Kiara discovered considering them was making that natural shiver start to flow through her body.

As blameworthy as she felt for feeling how she did, there was no uncertainty that she considered the possibility of being with youthful Lauren in a lewd way fiercely energizing. At no other time had she genuinely thought to be sex with another lady. Presently she wound up fixating on her closest companion's girl. To say Kiara clashed would have been putting it mildly of scriptural extents.

She was soothed to see John's truck left in the carport of their home as she pulled in and left close to him. She accumulated her things and advanced into the house. After making a short outing into the pantry, where she tracked down a perfect pair of her underwear in the dryer, Kiara slipped on a shirt and advanced unobtrusively into her room.

It was John's propensity to sleep when he fell off the move. Kiara was reluctant to awaken him. Be that as it may, her need was exceptional and her blame so significant, she needed to have his rooster inside her immediately. Kiara expected to feel him somewhere inside her, beating away as he made her come. She frantically expected to feel his seed sprinkle her internal parts as he came on the off chance that just to wash away the two-timing contemplations of lesbian sex that had devoured her mind since the previous evening.

She quietly slipped into bed close to him and folded her left arm over his exposed midriff. Kiara kissed his neck as she came down and slid her hand into his fighters. Getting a handle on John's limp chicken, she started to delicately press and stroke it, believing it quickly solidify in her hold. Her significant other groaned in his rest as Kiara slid down the length of his body. Hauling his now bloated chicken out, she immediately slipped it between her lips and sucked at it as she gradually worked it as near the rear of her throat as she tried. Each time she worked her way back to the top, she would whirl her tongue around the head. Kiara took incredible consideration to give specific consideration to the frenulum on the underside of the head.

She felt her better half's enormous hand touch the rear of her neck. "Infant," he said, "did you miss me the previous evening?"

Kiara groaned accordingly and made an effort not to zero in on the genuine justification of the zeal she felt toward the beginning of today. All things being equal, allowing his cockerel to slide from underneath her lips with a pop, she sat up and rode his hips.

"I need you inside me, nectar," she implored him as she raised her hips and held onto his erection with her right hand. Focusing it between her lips and over her opening, Kiara gradually let her wet pussy down over his pounding part.

"Fuck," John groaned as Kiara reached as far down as possible on his chicken. She hung over and held onto his lips, kissing him with desire as she stirred her hips here and there his pulsating shaft gradually. Kiara groaned into John's mouth as she delighted in the sensation of him extending her opening. Even following thirty years, he could, in any case, work her into a furor when they were together.

"I don't have the foggiest idea what got into you earlier today," John shouted as he pushes up inside Kiara, "yet whatever it was, I like it." Kiara moaned so anyone can hear as she felt her significant other's balls slap against the underside of her opening. As he beat away, Kiara froze her hips set up mostly down his hard chicken. Doing so permitted its head to slide across her g-detect each time he pushes up inside her at the ideal point.

Kiara could feel her climax constructing and was more than substance to allow it to come at its speed. John, then again, evidently had different thoughts. He snatched both her hips and turned her over on her back. Kiara groaned in a fight when she felt him pull out his cockerel from her opening.

"Rollover on your stomach, Baby," he advised her. Frantically needing to feel him back inside her, Kiara did as he inquired. Sliding one hand under her stomach, John lifted her hips and slid a cushion up under her center. He, at that point, rode her legs and gradually started examining with the top of his rooster between her legs. Kiara profoundly moaned when she felt him finally hit his imprint.

When his chicken was again covered inside his better half, John started to pound away at her excited cunt with complete surrender. Kiara immediately felt her peak starting to develop. Hungry to be liberated from the messy musings that had penetrated her cognizant since the previous evening, Kiara worked both her hands underneath her breast. Pressing and moving her nipples between her fingers, she started to raise her hips to meet her better half's fast pushes. The two sweethearts came extremely close to each other. Kiara's peak held onto her body in its delightful grasp. Her vaginal muscles fixed down around John's inflexible rooster. The additional incitement was all it required to drive the fireman to the brink. He came profound inside his significant other, covering her internal parts with his seed.

At the point when the fire that had burned through the two of them started to fade away, John affectionately kissed the rear of his better half's neck. He could, in any case, feel small fits as they flowed through his significant other's pussy, touching his conditioning chicken.

"I love you," Kiara said as she washed in close contact with her significant other.

John slid out of her and painstakingly turned over on his side of the bed. Moving to his side, he inclined in and delicately kissed his better half's lips. "I love you as well," he answered.

Kiara shut her eyes and cuddled, facing her better half's warm body. Asking quietly that her fantasies would be lucid, she let rest guarantee her.

- - - - -

Jessica and Lauren

With the following woman's late evening being Kiara's chance to play have, the mother and girl combo battled to concoct an approach to remember Lauren for the celebrations by and by. It was the more youthful of the two ladies that surfaced with the answer for their concern.

Seeing it was her girl calling, Jessica got the telephone and said, "I trust you have a thought since I'm experiencing a mental blackout."

Lauren snickered into the mouthpiece on her end and said, "I figure I may have the thought recently. You two go out moving now and again, don't you?"

Getting a feeling of where her girl was going, Jessica replied, "No doubt, we ordinarily do it a couple of times each year. It's been almost five months since the last time. Allow me to figure; we will experience my little girl at the club, aren't we?"

"Bingo," Lauren replied, clearly pleased with her answer for their concern.

Jessica thought of her as a girl's thought. After a second, she could see a likely defect. "The lone issue I can see is the club we, as a rule, go to isn't the kind of spot you experience a lot of nineteen-year-olds," she disclosed to her little girl.

"I thought about that as well," Lauren answered, "If you can convince her to attempt another spot, I figure it will work. A few clubs have the correct combination of ages we need. They all oblige an enormous bit of gay customer base. However, that could work in support of ourselves as well."

"In what capacity?" Jessica asked her girl.

"Well," Lauren said, "Kiara must be pondering about my sexuality at this point. Imagine a scenario where you two were to go to one of these new clubs and detected your little girl out on the dance floor crushing against her exceptionally female date."

"Oooh, I see where you're going," Jessica shouted, "I could advise her by then how I'd presumed you may be sexually unbiased. I could even blame that to try how it truly was certainly not a serious deal. I'd had my trial stage in school as well."

"In school, after you were hitched last weekend..." Lauren prodded her mom.

"Ahem," Jessica said, "I'll have you know I'm done testing. I have my sexual openness consummated by this point throughout everyday life.

"Thus, you figure it will work?" Lauren asked her mom after they'd both quit giggling.

"I think it could very well," Jessica said, "Presently, I simply need to persuade her that it's an ideal opportunity to go out."

As it ended up, that didn't wind up being the assignment Jessica imagined it very well may be. Kiara appeared anxious to concur with her companion when Jessica disclosed that she gravely wanted to hit the dance floor. The two ladies were close to thrilled at the possibility of one of their dance journeys. Neither one of the women's better half felt like dancing, and the two of them disdained to go to clubs. The two ladies sometimes wanted to go out all alone and dance the night away while innocuously playing with the men they hit the dance floor with. Both delighted in the consideration they got from men they'd probably never see again.

Jessica realized that this evening would be extraordinary. She had battled to concoct a conceivable explanation regarding why they should stray from their ordinary everyday practice and club. Destiny had mediated for her sake when she found that their standard club was shut for redesigning.

As she maneuvered into Kiara's carport, she messaged her companion that she was holding up outside. Jessica felt ripples eject in her crotch the subsequent she spotted Kiara venture out her front entryway. The slender brunette was wearing a dark off-the-shoulder party dress. There was a cut running up her left thigh that featured the cougar's shapely legs impeccably. Kiara went to bolt her front entryway giving Jessica the ideal perspective on her heart-molded posterior. Jessica couldn't stand by until the second she could cover her tongue between those cheeks and taste her companion's juices. The nearer they went to that evening, the more grounded Jessica's longing was to get it going.

At the point when Kiara slid into the seat close to her, Jessica rushed to say, "Goodness, you look phenomenally hot in that dress, young lady. I don't know. I'll have the option to pull in any consideration with you wearing that outfit."

Kiara become flushed and shook her head at her companion's commendation. "With your bends and those eminent breasts, you never appear to need for dance accomplices."

As they went on to the freeway, Jessica reported the difference in setting from their typical club. "I don't figure it will be that huge a change. The group will probably be a smidgen more fluctuated in age and somewhat more diverse in style. However, that simply implies we will hit the dance floor with more youthful men than we typically do."

"Mmmh," Kiara groaned, "more youthful men can be a touch more forceful. We may get our rear ends snatched or get felt up."

"Nothing amiss with becoming hungry while moving," Jessica said wickedly, "as long as we eat off the menu at home."

The two ladies chuckled. Neither could at any point undermine their spouses with another man. The two of them adored their companions, yet a little innocuous being a tease wouldn't hurt them, principally if they never got some answers concerning it.

Things hushed up briefly as Jessica drove them towards their objective. At last, Kiara made some noise and said, "In this way, I guess Lauren had a hot date around evening time."

Jessica grinned and thought, "So she's at the forefront of your thoughts, huh?" To Kiara, she said, "Indeed, I conversed with her previous today. She assumed she might get fortunate around evening time."

Cutting her eyes to Kiara's direction, Jessica could see the more seasoned lady gazing out at the scenes passing by the traveler's window. Jessica needed to have the option to see her companion's response when she gave her the following piece of information.

"I figure my girl may be trying different things with her sexuality," Jessica expressed as though out of nowhere.

Kiara's head immediately jolted around towards her dearest companion. Jessica pondered internally, "That stood out enough to be noticed, huh."

"Wh...what makes you say that," Kiara faltered out.

Battling the desire to grin at her companion's overcompensation to her announcement, Jessica looked directly ahead of a street. "Indeed, she left her PC at home when she halted by an evening or two ago, and I may have done a little sneaking around."

"Furthermore, Kiara said, essentially inclining towards her companion in energetic expectation of an answer.

"All things considered, in her program history, I discovered she invests a lot of energy taking a gander at pornography in the nights. The greater part of the connections went to lesbian pornography recordings of a particular sort." Jessica said, attempting to sound somewhat undecided about what she'd found.

Jessica nearly chuckled when Kiara moved her right hand in dissatisfaction and said, "Go on."

"These scenes she favors watching are all of the young ladies her age engaging in sexual relations with more seasoned ladies. In a large portion of them, even the more youthful young ladies are inducing things. And afterward, there were connections to a wide range of lesbian erotica. Stories where more seasoned youngster young ladies tempt ladies as old as us or the other way around." Kiara said as though exasperated by the entire thing.

"Re?" Kiara asked before carefully adding, "How does that cause you to feel?"

Jessica impacted impeccably as she transformed into the club's passageway and started searching for a spot to stop. Moaning discernibly as though in acknowledgment, she said, "Indeed, at any rate, a lady won't get her pregnant. It could simply be a stage, or perhaps she's truly sexually unbiased. I don't have the foggiest idea. Dislike I can criticize her. I had my exploratory stage back in school as well."

Jessica chuckled at Kiara's response. Her companion snatched her arm as she killed the engine to the vehicle. With her eyes swelling at the news, Kiara asked, "And for what reason am I simply catching wind of this at this point?"

Jessica shrugged her shoulders as though attempting to shake her disclosure off and said, "It's not the sort of thing you simply proclaim, even to your best of companions. I wasn't attempting to shroud it. It never appeared natural to pronounce the amount I cherished sucking on a pussy back when I was in school. The subject just never appeared to come as of recently."

"You mean...you mean you loved it, being with another lady, I mean, "Kiara asked enthusiastically.

Gazing out her window at two appealing young ladies as they passed by the front of her vehicle, clasping hands, Jessica just grinned. "Kiara, understand me. I love sex with my

John. It's satisfying, and I love his cockerel, yet there's something else about being with a lady. They're gentler, smoother, and they don't have all that gross body hair. Their smell and their taste, indeed, men can't expect to think about similarly."

Going to take a gander at her closest companion and grasping her hand, Jessica pronounced, "And ladies, they simply realize how your body functions. They know all that makes you tick. I've never come so hard, or frequently, as I did when having intercourse with another lady."

Kiara sat back in her seat and gazed out the front window of the vehicle. It was as though, interestingly, she saw that they were at their objective. After a second, she asked, "So on the off chance that it was so acceptable, why to get hitched to a man."

Jessica chuckled and said, "Indeed, on the off chance that you'll recollect, things weren't totally, however open as they seem to be currently. Individuals of similar sex couldn't wed in those days. Additionally, there was pressure from my family to get hitched and have infants, and as I said, I truly love a hardened chicken."

"In this way, you never did it again after school?" Kiara inquired.

Jessica gave her companion a wily grin and hesitantly said, "I never said that."

Kiara sat ahead, holding Jessica's hand much tighter, and said, "You mean you do it? You go behind John's back with ladies?"

Acting somewhat irate, Jessica said, "Indeed, I still now and again engage in sexual relations with ladies. I don't consider it to be cheating, however. A lady can give me something John never could, a sweet wet pussy. Also, my occasional trysts with ladies simply appear to hoist my moxie, which John readily profits by."

Contracting away from her companion's response, Kiara said, "So... well..."

"Goodness, Kiara," Jessica said, "simply let it out."

Kiara appeared to pause for a minute to think of her as a question before taking a full breath and saying, "Along these lines, you truly like it actually, being with a lady."

Jessica grinned and said, "God, yes. The sex is mind-adjusting. Not better than sex with the man you love, yet incomprehensibly unique and energizing. I'll more than once come from my female sweethearts and afterward still be so wrapped up when I return home that I screw John's cerebrums out."

Jessica could perceive how turned on Kiara was. Her breathing was fast and shallow, her understudies enlarged completely, and she could smell the musk from her wet pussy here in the encased vehicle. She urgently needed to take her companion here and there, yet she'd guaranteed this enticement to Lauren. Her little girl was likely anticipating their appearance inside. She wouldn't allow her to down.

- - - - -

Kiara

Jessica grasped Kiara's hand as they crossed the parking area for the front passageway of the club. It wasn't the first occasion when they'd clasped delivers public. It wasn't that remarkable a thing for closest companions to do. It felt diverse, currently realizing that Jessica was sexually open. Kiara wound up pondering about the ladies that her companion was engaging in sexual relations with. Did she meet them at her work? Were

376

these female darlings clients of her inside enriching business? Why had Jessica never made advances on her? Didn't her companion track down her appeal?

It took Kiara a second to understand the inclination in her stomach was desire. She was envious of the idea Jessica wouldn't need her as her lesbian sweetheart. To begin with, Lauren and now Jessica. What had gotten into her?

Once inside, the two women tracked down an open stall and got comfortable to have a beverage or two preceding hitting the dance floor. If this new spot maintained structure, they would probably experience difficulty completing their first beverage before being drawn nearer by intrigued men needing to take them for a twist on the dance floor.

Kiara glanced around at the club. The group was certainly more youthful than the one they were accustomed to finding. There additionally appeared to be an extreme measure of same-sex couples moving together. Going to gaze toward the bar, Kiara noticed considerably more couples. By far, most had all the earmarks of being same-sex, and the greater part of those were ladies with ladies.

Had Jessica purposefully carried her to a gay move club?

Turning around to her companion, she discovered Jessica gazing at her. "I understand you're opinion, Kiara. I can see the wheels turning in your mind; yes, this club takes into account a group that is more liberal in their sexuality. That doesn't imply that this evening must be unique from any of our other dance outings. We have a couple of beverages, we dance together a few, we hit the dance floor with intrigued men, and afterward, we return home horny for our spouses. Alright, perhaps this evening I find the opportunity to hit the dance floor with another lady, other than that. However, nothing will be unique."

Kiara took in her companion's words and attempted to unwind to the new climate. She wasn't homophobic. She'd quite recently never been in an environment like this. Without a doubt, it was ordinary that there may be somewhat of a change period.

"It's always taking for the server to see us. I will make a beeline for the bar and get us both a gin and tonic. At the point when I get back, we can talk more. However, you need to attempt to unwind. You look firm as a board staying there. Who knows, perhaps if you slacken up somewhat after a beverage or three, you may appreciate hitting the dance floor with a lady as well." Jessica prodded her before leaving toward the bar.

Kiara zeroed in out on the dance floor as an approach to occupy the contemplations going through her mind. In contrast to their standard club, the moving going on here was significantly more sexual. Everywhere on the floor, couples ground and revolved their bodies against each other. It wasn't exceptional here for couples to make out on the dancefloor. Kiara could likewise see loads of open grabbing and stroking occurring.

Her eyes zeroed in on a blonde of medium stature. The lady's back was to her as she worked her hips to the music. The blonde's straight long hair influenced to and fro on schedule to the beat as the lady kissed her dance accomplice's neck from behind. Her accomplice was considerably more limited than her and had long earthy colored hair she wore in a twist. The hairdo uncovered her swan-like neck to the lips of the blonde. The brunette swung her head around, and as the two ladies started an enthusiastic kiss, Kiara's heartbeat rate accelerated as she understood she perceived the youthful brunette.

It was Jessica's little girl Lauren.

Kiara looked as the two eagerly kissed. Their lips were meeting up and isolating on different occasions as their tongues moved into one another's mouths. Their bodies turned as they proceeded to both dance and kiss. Kiara could see that both of the blondie's hands laid on Lauren's chest, stroking her tits from their base until the tips of her fingers held only the young lady's nipples.

Spellbound as she was by the thing she was watching and feeling a pounding starting to develop behind her clit, Kiara scarcely considered Jessica getting back with their beverages. It wasn't until she felt the glass against her hand that she figured out how to wake up from the fugue state Kiara ended up in.

"Earth to Kiara," Jessica shouted out absurdly as she snickered at her companion. "You seem as though you've seen a phantom,"

Kiara shook her head and, hollering, said, "Not an apparition, Lauren."

Jessica followed where Lauren pointed with her eyes, definitely understanding what she'd see exactly. She watched her little girl and the blonde she knew to be Grace Adler, Lauren's 11th grade English instructor. After Jessica had turned her little girl on to the delights of sapphic love, the young lady had searched her previous instructor out and tempted her. Effortlessness had been hitched for a very long time, and they had two sensibly small children. Jessica had no clue if the lady's significant other knew about what she was doing. The English educator was consistently anxious to connect with Lauren at whatever point she called.

Glancing back at Kiara, Jessica shrugged her shoulders and yelled, "I perceive that lady; she's one of Lauren's previous secondary teachers. My little girl truly is into more seasoned ladies."

All of a sudden, a lady who had all the earmarks of being in her late thirty's or mid-forties walked up to their table. She had short dark hair that boiled down to simply underneath her ears, a beautiful face, and a lean and athletic form. Notwithstanding her having unmistakable gentility about her, the lady had a butch quality. Maybe, it was her outfit, which comprised a tight pair of cowhide pants that shaped her body and a calfskin vest. That Kiara could recognize, the woman wore no shirt or underwear under the top. Her voice was also imposing and coarse sounding when she inclined down over their table and said, "Might both of you women want to move?"

Kiara grinned apprehensively up at the lady and afterward looked over at Jessica. Jessica gestured her head towards the lady as her eyes appeared to say pull out all the stops. Kiara ended up frozen. Unfit to move, she took a gander at Jessica, who appeared to moan before taking the other lady's hand and saying, "My companion may have a straight stick up her can. However, I'd love to hit the dance floor. With you."

The current melody playing had concluded, permitting Kiara to hear her companion's remark. Jessica stuck her tongue out at Kiara as she advanced out onto the dance floor with the woman in calfskin. A slow melody began playing, and Kiara curiously looked as Jessica set her arms around the calfskin woman's neck. The lovely dim headed woman with butch characteristics folded her arms over Jessica's midriff and pulled her in against her.

Kiara discovered her eyes, uncertain of where to look. To one side was Lauren, her back still went to her dance accomplice as the two ladies gradually influenced in the mood to the music. To one side was her long-term dearest companion, who seemed to have her mouth against the calfskin woman's ear. Regardless of whether she was kissing and snacking it or conversing with the lady, Kiara couldn't tell. She looked as Jessica and her accomplice shared a chuckle as they moved. She was then astonished to look as the two ladies' lips met up. This was certifiably not a short kiss as there was nothing virtuous about it. There was obvious enthusiasm required between the two ladies.

Kiara could feel the strap she'd worn starting to stick to the lips of her pussy underneath her dress. At no other time had she or Jessica occupied with any conduct as private during their dance evenings. She looked as the woman in calfskin ran her hands down over Jessica's round ass, measuring her cheeks and crushing as the two ladies kissed. What was it Jessica had said? It wasn't cheating because the ladies she dawdled with could offer her what her significant other proved unable, a sweet wet pussy..."

"Hello, you." Kiara heard in her ear. Looking into it, she saw Lauren grinning back at her. The little brunette mesh was pulled over her correct shoulder. She resembled a princess out of a Disney film between the interlace she wore and her large doe-like eyes. The young lady slid into the corner close to Kiara and inclined in, her ears brushing against Kiara's ear as she asked, "Where's my Mom?"

Kiara battled the shudder that ran down her spine from the contact with the young lady's flexible lips. She was incapable of talking; she called attention to the dance floor toward where Jessica hit the dance floor with the woman in calfskin. Kiara looked as Lauren's eyes looked out her mom. Peering down, she saw Lauren's lips and gotten herself by and by somewhere out in dreamland of their kiss.

Lauren turned and discovered her gazing. Giggling, the more youthful lady inclined in and said, "Mother consistently appeared to like her ladies with a dash of butch." Catching the vibe of shock all over, the delightful youthful brunette said, "What, she didn't reveal to you, I knew?" Kiara shook her head. Lauren shrugged her shoulders and said, "I'm certain she would have in the long run told." Then switching gears, she said, "Hello, my date consistently requires around a fifteen-minute smoke break partially as the night progressed. Would you come hit the dance floor with me, please?"

Kiara flushed at the possibility of hitting the dance floor with the young lady she hungered for to such an extent. She realized it wasn't right. She was a hitched lady and adored her better half. Despite Jessica's opinion, certainly, this wasn't right?

Notwithstanding the psychological fights, Kiara felt herself being pulled from the corner and to her feet despite what might be expected. Her body had abolished her mind's obstruction. As she permitted Lauren to lead her out onto the dance floor, she noticed Jessica and her dance accomplice as they fell through an entryway on the contrary side of the room. "Presently, where on earth is she off to?" Kiara quickly pondered.

Considerations of her companion finished as she felt Laurens' hands seize around her abdomen and attract her nearby. Habitually, Kiara slid her hands around the more diminutive lady's smooth neck and let her lead. Kiara was grateful for the second lethargic melody in succession. She attempted to envision herself doing a knock and pound with this youthful magnificence to a more cheery tune. Kiara felt one of Lauren's hands touch her back, sending an influx of joy racing to her middle. "God, how this young lady deals with me," she conceded to herself, "This is so off-base, I realize it is." But she did not endeavor to isolate herself from the choice feel of the body of her dearest companion's little girl. No, she realized she'd desired this contact since the evening of their kiss. She hadn't the will to leave it now.

Kiara felt Lauren's hand stop on the rear of her neck. It tenderly pulled her head down. Vulnerable to stop herself, Lauren thought she would indeed kiss this attractive heavenly messenger's delicate lips. She shut her eyes, hungry to feel the brush of Lauren's delicate kiss. However, it was her ear she felt the youthful excellence's lips brush against as the hot youthful brunette said, "Would you say you are alright, Kiara? You appear to be anxious."

Kiara felt chills hurry through her body. She could feel Lauren's warm breath against her neck, and its sensation was driving her to interruption. Had she at any point needed anything so gravely in her life? Simply being in Lauren's vicinity appeared to stir her and tangle her nerves in a heap of need, blame, desire, and want that the more seasoned lady felt powerless to stop.

Inclining down to Lauren's ear, Kiara permitted her lips to touch the more youthful lady's delicate flap tenderly. The vibe was enlightening, compelling Kiara to scrutinize her sexuality indeed effectively.

"I'm moderate hitting the dance floor with my closest companions delightful and sexually unbiased girl in a dance club that appears to provide food only to gay men and lesbians. I believe I'm doing affirm in light of everything."
Notwithstanding her nerves, Kiara ended up grinning down at Lauren as they held each other close. Investigating the more youthful lady's shoulder, she saw the blonde instructor Lauren had brought as her date. She remained at the bar, watching them intently. The melody finished, and Kiara constrained herself to relinquish Lauren hesitantly.

"Your date is over at the bar watching us. I don't believe she's satisfied." Kiara advised her.

Lauren shrugged and grasped Kiara's hand, driving her back to their table, and said, "Beauty will be alright. It's simply sex between us. She cherishes her better half. We simply attach at whatever point both of us needs a fix."

"A fix?" Kiara asked with a look of disarray all over.

Lauren grinned and came to across her own body to hold onto the upper arm of the hand she was holding. The motion made their contact considerably more close. Turning upward into Kiara's penniless eyes, she said, "Pussy. It very well may be irresistible. Like, Mom and Grace, I desire to meet a man and become hopelessly enamored one day, perhaps pop Mom out a grandbaby or two. In any case, I won't ever quit screwing ladies. Great, the sex with a lady is simply such a ton better."

Kiara gazed back at Lauren, speechless. Jessica had said something comparable. Could it be valid? Is it safe to say that she was passing up something by denying the craving she felt for this provocative youthful excellence?

When they arrived at the table, Kiara saw that Jessica was all the while missing. Inclining down to Lauren's ear, she said, "I don't have the foggiest idea where your Mom has made it off to."

Lauren grinned up at her and raised on her unstable toes, saying, "That lady she was hitting the dance floor with is Vicky; she's a section proprietor here. She likely took Mom to her private room in the back to screw her. Vicky continues to attempt to get me to return with her. However, I'm simply not pulled into that butch vibe. I like my ladies, excellent and female, similar to you." And with that, Lauren inclined up and delicately kissed Kiara's lips. Once, twice, multiple times. And afterward, very much like that, she was gone to get her date.

Kiara imploded once more into the corner. Coming up, she stroked her lips with her fingertips. They shivered with the memory of Lauren's touch. She gazed upward towards the bar and detected the youthful chestnut-haired excellence as she and her date held one another and burned through their beverages. She was all the while looking that way when development somewhere off to the side grabbed her eye. It was Jessica advancing across the dance floor alone. She was fixing her pullover and streamlining it as she spotted Kiara watching her.

"You're still staying here like a bunch on a log?" Jessica asked distrustfully, "Without a doubt, another lady has requested that you dance at this point."

Overlooking her dearest companion's subsequent remark, Kiara said, "Where would it be advisable for me to be, in Vicky's private reserved alcove letting her screw me?"

Jessica become flushed and gazed down into the lower part of her glass. Thinking back up, she said, "OK, you got me. Shoot me, Vicky is hot as fuck and has that vibe that does it for me. She revealed to me she frantically needed to have the option to peer down and see my face between her legs, and, guess what? I needed that as well."

The two ladies looked across the table at one another. At last, Kiara asked, "Anyway, how was it?"

Jessica let out a devilish grin and said, "It was tasty. I love it when a lady has a full bramble, and she was so delectable."

"TMI," Kiara said, scrunching up her face in shame, "And what was that remark about me having "a straight stick up my can."

Jessica grinned and shrugged her shoulders, "I call them as I see them. You are as yet staying here, all things considered."

Feeling somewhat irate, Kiara said, "I'll have you realize I hit the dance floor with a lovely young lady while you were no more. A slow dance at that."

That brought both of Jessica's eyebrows up. "Is that so? Also, how was it on the off chance that I can ask without you getting distraught."

Lauren feigned exacerbation and grinned, "I wasn't frantic. I was simply burnt out on feeling scorned because I'm not sexually open or lesbian."

Jessica raised one eyebrow at her as though she didn't exactly get her clarification however said nothing. She just continued hanging tight for her companion to address her inquiry.

"Fine," Kiara said, exasperated, "it was pleasant. Certainly not the same as hitting the dance floor with a man. Delicate yet firm as well. She smelled better compared to a man. It wasn't unusual like I figured it would be. Whenever felt better, normal."

"Which whore was she?" Jessica asked, watching out towards the dance floor.

Kiara roared with laughter and said, "I'm so happy you put it that way because the whore, was your girl."

"Lauren?" Jessica asked, and afterward, as though she was unable to accept what she was hearing, said, "My Lauren requested that you dance, and you said yes. Do I hear this right?"

Befuddled and somewhat dumbfounded at Jessica's response, Kiara asked, "And what's so unfathomable about that, Jessica? Am I not appealing enough?"

Jessica slid out of her seat and slid over close to her companion. She grasped Kiara's hand and said, "That isn't what I implied by any stretch of the imagination. You're dazzling, and I've generally discovered you hot. On the off chance that you hadn't been my dearest companion, I would have attempted to entice you myself quite a while past."

Kiara becomes flushed at her companion's attestation. Attempting to recuperate, she said, "I surmise I don't have that vibe that does it for you."

Jessica snickered and said, "Hello, I can't resist if a beautiful lady with a butch demeanor makes my pussy all gooey. However, ladylike can be sweet as well. But with regards to female ladies, I will, in general, be more assume responsibility than I am with ladies like Vicki."

"Alright," Kiara said, "however we've gotten diverted. For what reason did you discover it so difficult to trust Lauren would need to hit the dance floor with me."

Jessica shook her head and said, "It's not because I think that it's difficult to accept. It's the polar opposite. You are here quite hot, more seasoned lady who's hitched. On the off chance that she's keen on you, she will not release it until she has you. The issue is, I believe you're a little into her as well."

"No, no, no," Kiara said even though she realized she was deceiving her dearest companion. She was unquestionably into her little girl, regardless of whether she knew nothing could happen to it.

Jessica murmured and tapped her companion's shoulder. "Nectar, I saw how both of you clung to one another at our home. All the coquettish chitchat among you was clear regardless of whether I didn't think it was anything at that point. Has she kissed you yet?"

Kiara deflected her eyes and said nothing, successfully addressing Jessica's inquiry.

"Kiaraela Settles," Jessica said in a rebuking tone.

"What?" Kiara said protectively, "She kissed me goodnight that evening at your home and afterward again after we moved around evening time. I didn't search it out one or the other time."

"However, you didn't battle it by the same token. Did you." Jessica said.

At the point when Kiara wouldn't take a gander at her and would not answer, Jessica said, "Look, all I'm saying is you can't be so judgemental about me screwing ladies. Not when you have a few interests about Lauren. I don't care either way if you connect with my little girl. I truly don't. What I do mind is pietism. Pick a path and drive in it, young lady."

"Alright," Kiara said dejectedly, "and I don't have the foggiest idea what I'm feeling; your girl unquestionably affects me. I get all silenced around her, and she causes my body to respond in manners it shouldn't respond to another lady."

"Would I be able to ask you an inquiry?" Jessica said.

"Obviously," Kiara responded to her.

Watching out on the dance floor, Jessica said, "The day after that last women night at my home. After yours and Lauren's little tease fest, did you stroke off when you hit the sack, and did you return home and screw John the following day?"

Kiara moaned and said, "Do I need to address these inquiries."

Jessica grinned and said, "By posing that inquiry, you just sweet. Don't you see it? Lauren makes you sufficiently horny to need to get yourself off, and afterward, you return home and bounce John's bones. That is the way this works. The more pussy I get, the more pussy my better half appears to get. Screwing Lauren will just improve your relationship with John."

Not having any desire to manage the discussion any longer, Kiara said, "I need to pee. Would you be able to watch the table?"

When she sunk into the latrine slow down, Kiara considered everything both Jessica and Lauren had said around evening time. They'd both raved about how a lady could make you come such a ton harder and more frequently than a man. For Jessica's situation, even a man she appeared to adore definitely. Neither appeared to trust it was cheating to be with another lady. At that point, there was how Lauren influenced her. For hell's sake, in any event, seeing Jessica out on the dance floor with that Vicky lady had left her with sensations of desire.

The way to the slow down nearby to Kiara banged open, and she heard chuckling female voices as they shut the entryway behind them. "Lock it," Kiara tuned in to a recognizable voice say.

Kiara listened cautiously, attempting to put the voice. She heard the sound of a zipper being unfastened and saw a dark skirt drop to the floor. A ribbon pair of greenish-blue strap underwear dropped down similar legs with the lady rapidly venturing out of them.

"Screw indeed, Baby," a female voice murmured, "Lick my wedded pussy actually like that."

Kiara's carried a hand to her mouth, attempting to cover the wheeze of shock that got away from her. She was sensibly certain she presently perceived the first voice she'd heard.

It was Lauren, and she was in the following slow down going down on her wedded darling.

"Indeed, lick my clit, Baby. Actually, like that. Fuck, Lauren, I love your tongue. You will make my wedded pussy come so screwing hard."

Kiara recollected Jessica distinguishing the lady as Lauren's previous English instructor, Grace, something. Beauty Adler, that was it. Elegance appeared to be truly making the most of Lauren's oral abilities. Kiara wanted to think about what it would resemble her; Lauren was licking rather than her previous instructor.

"Screw indeed, Baby," Grace cooed, "suck my clit, Fuck, I'm coooommiiiiingggg."

Without speculation, Kiara had slid two fingers between her legs as she tuned in to the two ladies nearby. Her pussy was drenched as those fingers wound into her opening. She was unable to chance boisterously fingering herself with them directly nearby. She agreed to squirm her fingertips against her G-spot as she played her clit with her other hand.

"Your turn, Baby," Kiara heard Grace say, "I will suck your pussy and cause you to overlook your mom's companion."

Kiara halted, her heart hustling as she tuned indiscreetly.

"Stop, Grace," Lauren contended, "I disclosed to you I can't resist being pulled in to her. She's constantly been my unique pulverize the extent that more established ladies go. I need her, and I can't help that. I'm sorry I hit the dance floor with her, however, when I should be with you."

"You're such a skank for wedded more established pussy," Grace prodded Lauren, "I think about your companion Kinsey's mother and Professor Danvers at your school. Presently you need to add a fourth to the rundown of wedded pussies you love to suck. Is that it?"

Lauren didn't reply from the outset. There were clear sucking sounds and delicately groans coming from their bearing. Finally, Kiara heard Lauren say, "That is it, Mrs. Adler.

Suck my pussy. Does your better half know your such a prostitute for my cunt? Does he Mrs. Adler?"

Kiara was stunned to hear Lauren be so cold-blooded. She could tune in to the Grace lady uproariously, sucking away at the pussy that had become a fixation for Kiara. She stroked at her clit as she envisioned herself being down on her knees before her closest companion's little girl. It was her tongue between Lauren's legs. What might it suggest a flavor like? Would she have the option to make the female object of her longing groan how the two-faced English instructor was doing? What might Lauren's cum taste like?

"Oooh, that is it. Lick my pussy. Your wedded tongue is so screwing hot." Lauren groaned enticingly.

"On the off chance that it's so acceptable, for what reason do you need that other lady," Kiara heard Grace say.

Lauren groaned boisterously. "Fuck, that is acceptable, Grace. Furthermore, Kiara is special. I've been captivated by her for quite a long time. I've needed to have her as a darling for the most recent 18 months. Screw indeed, Baby. Not too far off. Suck on my clit..."

Kiara was close. She could feel her peak hustling towards the end goal. Kiara attempted to hold off. For reasons she couldn't comprehend, it was vital for Kiara that she climaxes simultaneously as Lauren. It very well may be her simple opportunity to do as such without really undermining John.

"That is it; you wedded whore, suck my pussy. I will come on that lovely face, Baby. Yesssssss, I'm coming," Lauren shouted out.

Sticking her fingers somewhere inside herself and against her G-spot, Kiara came hard. She held her breath as the spasms dashed through her body. Her thighs shuddered, and her pussy overwhelmed as her climax peaked.

At the point when Lauren and her date had left. Kiara tidied herself up and fixed up her garments. She, at that point, advanced out and across the dance floor. Moving toward her table, she saw Lauren and Grace staying there, pausing. However, there was no indication of Jessica.

Kiara advanced over to the bar. When she stood out enough to be noticed, she requested another gin and tonic. While she paused, she considered the dance floor and spotted Jessica hitting the dance floor with a lady who was significantly more Butch than Vicki had been. Her dance mate had spiky light hair and was thickly ripped, clearly a muscle head or weight lifter or some likeness. Kiara looked as the blondie stroked Jessica's butt and kissed her neck. Her companion appeared to be lost at the time and unconscious of what was happening around her. Kiara couldn't resist the opportunity to contemplate whether Jessica would allow this lady to screw her as well.

The barkeep gave her the gin and tonic. Kiara paid her and slipped a tip into the tip container. She, at that point, advanced over to the table where Lauren and her darling anticipated. A sensation of nervousness crawled through her as she moved toward the two ladies. Preparing her purpose, Kiara approached the table and slid in on the unfilled side.

"Hello," Lauren welcomed her with a grin, "Mother spotted us and inquired as to whether we could watch the table until you got back. She got the attention of another butch and needed to move."

Kiara grinned back at Lauren and said, "No doubt, I detected her out on the dance floor. It would appear that they're getting along very well. I'm contemplating whether she probably won't vanish with this one as well."

Lauren chuckled and afterward said, "Kiara, this is my date, Grace. Elegance, this is my Mom's dearest companion, Kiara."

Effortlessness contacted her hand across the table. Kiara noticed the commitment and wedding ring on the lady's hand as she shook it. At any rate, she wasn't concealing the reality. She was hitched.

"Ideal to meet you, Kiara," Grace said; however, her eyes recounted an alternate story, "I was considering what a straight, hitched lady pondered this." Grace spread her hands out, demonstrating the bar and dance floor.

Kiara saw Lauren harden. She grinned at Grace and said, "Even us straight, hitched ladies have been to move clubs previously. Furthermore, if you mean the gay and lesbian couples, that isn't too exceptional to me, all things considered."

"What's more, discovering your closest companion regularly has lesbian issues?" Grace snapped back without the fake grin.

"Elegance," Lauren snarled at the pretty blonde.

Kiara held up her hand at Lauren, flagging her that it was alright. "That would be her business. What's more, if it makes her cheerful and assists her with keeping her significant other upbeat, at that point, it's not my concern."

And afterward, as though to add an outcry highlight what she said, Kiara highlighted Grace's wedding ring. She added, "Very much like when you disregard your marital promises, that is your business."

Throwing back the rest of her beverage in one swallow, Kiara said, "Presently, if you women will pardon me. I need to go see a barkeep about another beverage."

Kiara cleared her path through the group and to the bar. The club appeared to be much more swarmed at such an inconvenient time than it had when they showed up. Remaining at the bar, Kiara looked as the melody that was at present playing finished. She noted Jessica and her weightlifter admirer as they advanced toward the table. Kiara chose to stick around at the bar. She truly didn't have any desire to return to the table with them four there. Despite what Kiara had said to Grace, she did, in reality, disapprove of what was happening. Indeed, she was pulled in to Lauren and, less significantly, perhaps even Jessica, yet she managed that. She hadn't given in the manner her companion or Grace had and ventured out on the man she'd submitted her life to.

Kiara was all the while remaining there at the bar fifteen minutes after the fact. She'd turned a few solicitations to move. She'd been complimented by the two ladies' advances and had discovered both appealing. Kiara was coming more to terms with the way that she, as well, may be sexually unbiased. Yet, she'd made a guarantee to John, and she planned to keep it.

A delicate touch on her correct arm made Kiara turn her head toward that path. She'd been anticipating that another invitation should move, or more. What she discovered was Lauren with a tragic grin all over.

"I'm grieved about Grace, Kiara. I sent her away and disclosed to her I would not like to see her any longer." Lauren said, truly. "If it's not too much trouble, return to the table with me. Mother and Alex, the butch lady she was hitting the dance floor with, they went out to Alex's vehicle to...well, you know." the little brunette said with a trace of humiliation.

"I heard you in the restroom," Kiara said to the more youthful lady as she gazed into her excellent earthy-colored eyes.

Lauren reddened once more, "Definitely; Mom revealed to us you were in there when she requested that we watch the table. I think realizing you were listening is the thing that encouraged Grace. I'm grieved, Kiara. I...I don't have the foggiest idea what else to say."

Flagging the barkeep to spruce up her beverage, Kiara said, "Why not go save our table. I'll be there in a moment, and we can talk."

Kiara watched Lauren clear her path through the group. She wanted to watch the ass of the small brunette as it squirmed its way across the room. Kiara felt another tickle of excitement clear its path through her center. Murmuring, she realized she needed to end this. It was hazardous to permit it to continue any further. Perilous to Kiara and possibly her marriage. She had practically no control around Lauren, and she knew it. If she didn't end things now, they could wind out of her control.

She advanced back to the table with her beverage close to the table, where she discovered Lauren looking out for her. There was still no indication of Jessica. Understanding the two ladies would have to talk without shouting across the table at each other, Kiara slid into the corner close to the hot youthful seductress.

"Still no indication of your Mom, I see," Kiara said, maybe a touch more disdainful than she proposed.

Lauren hurried nearer to her and said, "dislike she doesn't adore her better half, she does. She simply needs to satisfy this side of herself as well. She can't fulfill him if she is distraught. Haven't you at any point needed something so terrible it harmed? Something you knew would satisfy. How is it possible that you would perhaps satisfy John on the off chance that you made yourself hopeless because you denied yourself what you pined for the most."

Kiara tuned in to Lauren's rationale. The stunning piece of it was she appeared well and good. Kiara had spent such countless hours recently considering what it resembles to engage in sexual relations with Lauren. She'd even examined pornography locales taking a gander at lesbian pornography without precedent for her life. Far more atrocious, she'd discovered lesbian erotica that highlighted accounts of since a long time ago wedded spouses being enticed by a lot more youthful ladies. It had all sounded so delicious and enticing. When John was home, she would attack his body one moment and fussing at him the following. The circumstance Kiara wound up in was disappointing, and more terrible yet, it was influencing her marriage. That is the reason it was important to end things now.

"Lauren, this thing between us...it can't be," Kiara said, even as her brain battled against trusting it herself. "I'm hitched, and I love my significant other. Since I find myself...well, attracted to you, doesn't mean I need to follow up on it."

Kiara saw Lauren begin to contend back, yet held up her hand and said, "Pause, Lauren, kindly let me finish. I believe you're wonderful, and you cause me to feel things I've never felt for another female. Be that as it may, this needs to stop here. I'm heartbroken; it simply needs to stop."

Kiara looked as Lauren gazed back at her. There was no genuine response to what she said on the more youthful lady's face. At long last, Lauren said, "Kiara, do you know why I just have intercourse with hitched ladies?"

Lauren's inquiry tossed Kiara. It wasn't the kind of reaction she'd been anticipating. Realizing no alternate method to respond, she said, "No. Why?"

Lauren grasped her hand and kissed it, sending chills dashing down Kiara's spine. "Since I don't need to stress over them becoming hopelessly enamored with me. We both get what we need from the sex we have. At that point, we both go on about our lives. I can promise you that I can make you come like you never have. I can send you home from our time together completely satiated, and afterward, an hour after you get back, your so animated by the things we did that your significant other will receive the rewards. You're satisfied, loose, and persistently horny, all of which your marriage will profit by. The other wedded ladies I've tempted, they're more joyful than they've at any point been in their lives, and their marital associations are more grounded subsequently. If you prevent this from getting yourself, you will think twice about it."

"What are both of you up to?" Jessica said as she slid in inverse Kiara and her little girl.

Investigating at her dearest companion, Kiara said, "I'm all set." She didn't sit tight for a reaction. Remaining as she snatched her grip, Kiara said, "It was acceptable to see you, Lauren. You deal with yourself."

What's more, with that, Kiara advanced toward the exit.

Jessica and Lauren

Jessica, in a split second, realized they'd exaggerated their hand gravely. Taking a gander at her girl, she said, "Don't freeze; simply give the personal opportunity to fix this. Kiara's just responding this way since she understands now how terrible she needs this, and it conflicts with all that she's consistently known throughout everyday life. I must go, yet I'll call you when I get subsided into my room at her place."

Jessica discovered Kiara sitting in the vehicle, pausing for her. She slid into the driver's seat and continued to put on her safety belt. At last, she investigated at her companion and said, "I realize you're angry with me. Yet, I swear I didn't get ready for things to go along these lines. It had been a little while since I'd gotten out to this club, and I surmise I moved a piece diverted.

Jessica was just about as remorseful as could be expected. She felt embarrassed for having left her companion and irritated with herself for her absence of discretion. Jessica had permitted her to drive to double-cross her and Lauren's arrangements to open up an energizing new world for Kiara. She could never excuse herself if this reinforced Kiara's purpose and obstinate nature.

Kiara gazed eagerly out the traveler's side window. Jessica looked toward the path she was looking at and saw two alluring ladies occupied with a hefty make-out and petting meeting. A tall brunette with long hair was stuck to the vehicle as her blondie buddy kissed her enthusiastically. The blondie's left hand was behind the brunette's head on the rear of her neck. In the meantime, her right hand had slid under her buddy's dress. She had all the earmarks of being fingering the tall brunette irately.

Jessica took a gander at her dearest companion. The scene working out before them was affecting her. Her breath had revived, and if she knew it, she was wringing her hands as though in disappointment.

"You left me, not once, however, twice. You unloaded this on me about you and Lauren and afterward left me to get your stones off. Simultaneously, I sat alone in an odd club where individuals I'd at no other time needed to have interest in me continued harassing me to move." Kiara cried as she kept on watching the earthy-colored-headed young lady gets screwed by her date.

Jessica figured it was ideal for sitting discreetly as a mouse and permittingKiara to get everything out. Really at that time, could she attempt and fix the harm she'd done. Goodness, she'd got the part about Kiara "at no other time needing to have their advantage," yet she figured presently wasn't an ideal opportunity to bring it up.

"Furthermore, that shocking Grace, lady. The things she said... She had no privilege inferring the things she did." Kiara contended.

Jessica had no clue about the thing she was discussing. She gave careful consideration to ask Lauren what the insane low maintenance lesbian had rambled about.

"Also, those things Lauren said in the bathroom..." Kiara said, at long last dismissing her head from the lesbian sex that was, at last, slowing down somewhere out there. "I didn't request any of that. I can't help how she feels, and I can't help how my body responds to her, yet I can help what I do about it."

Jessica stayed there discreetly, pausing; she could see her companion wasn't done at this point. She was developing into something. That was plain to see.

"Jessica," Kiara said, grasping her hand, "How is it possible that you would do this to your John. He's a decent man and treats you so well. I've never heard you to such an extent as say a crossword regarding him. However, here you are on evenings he's away connecting with abnormal ladies. I can comprehend Lauren doing it. She's young and single. She hasn't made any guarantees or responsibilities to anybody. However, you and I have."

Jessica paused, and when it was apparent that Kiara was hanging tight for a reaction, she said, "Kiara, nectar, I do cherish John. He's an awesome spouse and a mindful darling. I need to develop old with him. However, that will not occur in case I'm troubled. I engaged in sexual relations with young ladies all through school, and if things had been how they are currently, I would have likely hitched a young lady. I love John's hard rooster, and I'd never go behind his back with another man, never. Yet, if I needed to abandon sex with a lady for an impressive measure of time, I'd be a hopeless bitch. I realize that I denied myself for reality because the initial quite a long while we were together. Things got so terrible; we were set out toward a separation."

Kiara tuned in to her eagerly. Jessica couldn't tell without a doubt if her words were breaking through to Kiara, yet in any event, she was by all accounts putting forth an attempt to take in the thing she was saying.

"In my marriage, it's a constant fight to set John up inwardly. You know how men can be. I feel like his mom, some of the time, ceaselessly attempting to console him. There's additionally the crucial factor consistently to look great—cosmetics, hair, shaving almost my whole damn body. At the point when I'm with a lady, it isn't that way. We simply appear to get one another. We're both there for some fast and easy friendship and spectacular climaxes. That second lady I was with around evening time made me come multiple times in less than a half-hour between her tongue and fingers. Who knows what she might have done on the off chance that she'd had a strapon, and we'd had the entire evening. Regardless of that, I'm so screwing horny right now from recalling that it that if John was home this evening and I wasn't dozing at your home, I'd return home and screw his cerebrums out."

Kiara just took a gander at her. Jessica could see the vibe of disarray all over. She could tell the lady was clashed ludicrous she was hearing.

"I've known for some time since Lauren liked you. Try not to misunderstand me; she doesn't consider you to be a potential heartfelt association. I'm talking more regarding an actual nature. I presumed she was into ladies for quite a while before she at any point affirmed it to me. Like mother, similar to girl, I presume. I've generally been skilled at spotting ladies who wanted that association with another lady. I saw it in her, and Kiara, I see it in you as well."

Jessica looked as tears went to Kiara's eyes. Her companion said, "Yet I don't need it, Jessica. I need to return to the status quo before I began feeling this stuff."

Jessica murmured and tenderly said, "I'm anxious about the possibility that that is beyond the realm of imagination, nectar. The genie is out of the container. There isn't any returning it. There's just allowing her to satisfy your most out of this world fantasies. What's more, you're deceiving yourself if you say you don't need it. I've seen the aching in your eyes. Also, you appreciated the consideration you got around evening time. Consideration from ladies who discovered you as hot and attractive as I do."

There, it was out, and there was no seriously concealing it. Jessica needed her dearest companion. She generally had. However, Kiara wasn't her typical sort. There was nothing butch about her, yet Jessica had always felt that in this present reality where she might have permitted herself to go gaga for a lady, it would have been Kiara.

Jessica saw it destroys fog Kiara's eyes. She didn't know which of her disclosures had caused the agony in her closest companion's eyes. Yet, she knew whether she could get her to see reason; all that hurt would break down the first run through Lauren's tongue sunk between her velvety folds.

Kiara hushed up the whole ride home. She gazed out her window, apparently somewhere down in idea. Jessica was starting to contemplate whether her companion probably won't lean toward her, drops her off, and afterward, head home.

Be that as it may, when they pulled up in Kiara's carport, all she said was, "I don't think about you, yet I could utilize a glass of wine."

At the point when they had both gotten into their nightclothes and gotten comfortable on the sofa, Kiara poured them both a full glass of an incredible red John had gotten from a companion who voyaged. They were both calm as though processing all that had happened that evening. It was Kiara who at long last ended the mass of quiet that lay between them.

"You were correct," she said. Jessica could advise it was a difficult confirmation for her to make.

Grinning and attempting to ease up the disposition, Jessica said, "You'll just be more explicit, Honey. I'm directly about to such an extent."

She looked as Kiara feigned exacerbation and took a beverage. In any case, with a stern look all over, she conceded, "About me, and ladies. Over the most recent few years, specifically, I've ended up seeing things about appealing ladies. Having contemplations, I had never suspected, in any event not deliberately. Recollecting now, I think there were consistently considerations there, yet how I was brought quieted them up in my mind."

Jessica watched her take another beverage. She stood by persistently for Kiara to continue, trusting that this would be the revelation she expected to make the last advance into a sexually unbiased way of life.

"I...I was in the washroom at the club when Lauren and Grace came in. They engaged in sexual relations in the slow down close to me, and that bitch Grace continued going on concerning why Lauren was keen on me. Lauren continued calling me her first genuine lady squash and saying how she'd needed me for so long..." Kiara halted there and reddened. Jessica could see the battle inside her.

Peering down in her lap as though unfit to connect, Kiara said, "I played with myself while tuning in to them engage in sexual relations. Hearing how Lauren needed me, hearing the awful things they were doing to one another, I think I came more enthusiastically than I at any point had in my life."

Kiara's tone showed no disgrace. She said it as though it involved reality, her voice practically droning as she talked.

"I'm apprehensive if I make this stride. I will not come out with something similar on the opposite side. I would prefer not to hurt John. I'm so frightened I will not have the option to categorize things like you, Lauren, and Grace." Kiara expressed.

At last, gazing toward Jessica, she admitted in just about a murmur, "I'm apprehensive I'll like it such a lot of that I will not have any desire to return to John, and I can't hazard that."

Also, with that, she brought down her wine and said goodnight.

Jessica messaged Lauren when she sunk into the bed in the guestroom.

Jessica: I surmise things could be more terrible. She's grappled with what's going on yet is reluctant to make that stride. She's concerned it will change her.

Lauren: What would I be able to do?

Jessica: Nothing. I think our best game-plan is to go radio-quiet regarding the matter, paving the way to the undergarments and sex toy party.

Lauren: Do you figure she will, in any case, appear for the gathering?

Jessica: I'll make sure. I will work on another point and attempt to hinder her apprehension. Give her another thing to zero in on totally.

Lauren: Okay, I confide in your judgment. However, she was harmed this evening, and I didn't care for seeing that. I would prefer not to hurt her any longer. Regardless of whether it implies I don't get what I need.

Jessica: Regarding the matter of disturbing Kiara. You genuinely need to quit seeing that simpleton, Grace. She's getting possessive, and that isn't acceptable.

Lauren: It's now done, and I can't help but concur. Kiara would make a substantially more delightful close friend at any rate. Significantly more helpful as well.

Jessica: For you and me both. I bet she tastes yummy.

- - - - -

Kiara

The following three weeks passed by gradually for Kiara. Even though she normally put two or three evenings every week with Jessica hanging out either openly or privately, she'd rationalized to evade her since the club's evening.

They chatted on the telephone a few times during the week and the two days of the end of the week. Kiara figured she would need to attempt to maintain a strategic distance from any conversation of the things that had occurred on their last woman's evening. Yet, Jessica never raised the subject, nor did she notice the obvious science among Kiara and her girl.

The alone time she referenced Lauren that first week was to say she hadn't seen or addressed her little girl since the dance club. She had called Lauren and left messages. However, she presently couldn't seem to hear back from her. She had addressed her flatmate, who said Lauren and been acting irritable and discouraged. Lauren hadn't had any desire to discuss what was disturbing her. However, the flatmate could tell she was crude over something.

By the Wednesday of the seven days of the gathering, Jessica hadn't referenced any of the untouchable subjects. Maybe they'd never occurred. It wasn't 'something very similar for Kiara, who contemplated the issue most of her days; however, clearly, the issue was finished for Jessica. It was Kiara who had at long last get some information about Lauren. She'd become worn out on trusting that Jessica will bring the subject up once more.

"I can tell she's been home while I'm busy working," Jessica had advised her. "Her cleaned and collapsed clothing is gone, and she's abandoned her filthy stuff. She did at last return one of my calls after I'd took steps to appear at her school. She would not like to discuss what had her vexed."

Kiara hadn't had any desire to bring the subject up. She'd been appreciative of Jessica's quietness on the matter. It made things less hard on Kiara in regards to the matter.

They'd been hard enough all alone.

Eventually, however, it just sneaked out. "Do you think whatever Lauren is vexed about had to do with me? You know, since I dismissed her and got so disturbed that evening at the bar."

Jessica had been no assistance on the matter. She'd essentially disclosed to Kiara that it wasn't for Kiara to stress over. She had done what she'd felt best for herself and her marriage. Jessica said that she would need to manage all alone whatever it was that had Lauren vexed.

Kiara had imagined that to some degree insensitive of Jessica and not at all like her companion. The entirety of the disclosures of the most recent few years to the side. She minded an incredible arrangement about Lauren having watched the youthful magnificence grow up. She despised the prospect of her being in torment.

Kiara didn't know the thing Jessica had said about her doing what was best for her, and her marriage was legitimate by the same token. Kiara had built up an undesirable fixation on the nights. John was working at the fire station watching lesbian pornography on the web while she jerked off. On the off chance that Kiara wasn't watching pornography, she was perusing lesbian stories on the erotica site she found. She was all the while having dreams of a sexual sort as well. One that included Lauren as well.

Because of her fixation, Kiara had grown to some degree a split character in her marriage. Brief, she would attack her better half and the following, closing him out or acting morose. John had repeatedly asked her what wasn't right, yet she didn't have a response for him. He'd at last quit asking her and started treating her with utter disdain.

Jessica had said about her marriage condition in the early years over and overplayed in Kiara's mind. She would not like to arrive at that point with John. She realized she needed to accomplish something, regardless of whether it was looking for treatment or some other type of help.

When the evening of the gathering at long last showed up, Kiara got herself apprehensive at the possibility of being at Jessica's once more. Her nervousness is based on a few parts of her present issue. She was both scared of the subject coming up and the prospect that it wouldn't be raised by any means. She realized she expected to discuss it with somebody, yet there was nobody she could trust. Jessica was her go-to individual when it came to things that she didn't feel good examining with John. Not having her to converse with about the upsetting her was an extreme impairment for her psychological steadiness.

She additionally realized the environment wouldn't be the most helpful for dependable choices of a sexual sort. The hot undergarments, sex toys, and free-streaming liquor at these gatherings typically prompted ribald and indecent talk from the regularly intoxicated ladies present. There had been more than one of these kinds of gatherings that had left Kiara feeling underhanded and horny when it was finished. Even though she could not see Jessica attempting to exploit the circumstance, she would never be certain. Her companion had clarified that last time they'd talked, how she felt about her explicitly. What's more, Kiara's fantasies of late had demonstrated those emotions weren't every one of the uneven.

At the point when she showed up at the gathering, there were at that point a few vehicles in the carport and more left along the road. Kiara had to stop out and about and walk a brief distance to the house. It was a direct result of this that she neglected to see Lauren's SUV sitting in the carport.

Jessica addressed the entryway, welcoming her closest companion with an embrace. Kiara was immediately given a glass of wine and got comfortable to join the spouses who were occupied with destroying their significant other's choices. The conversation didn't cause Kiara to feel terrible for the spouses. It caused her to feel terrible for their spouses.

After her first glass of wine, and similarly, as the host was preparing to begin, Kiara pardoned herself and headed into the kitchen to check whether Jessica required any assistance. She entered the kitchen, hoping to discover her companion. All things being equal, staying there in the morning meal alcove was a hopeless-looking Lauren. Kiara froze quickly, not realizing what to do. She saw the young lady held a half-full wine glass; a container of wine sat on the table before her.

"Hello Lauren," Kiara said, feeling both energized and uneasy about seeing the adolescent.

Lauren gazed toward Kiara and grinned a miserable grin. She tipped her wine glass toward Kiara and said, "I suppose I'm the last individual you needed to see around evening time."

Kiara drew a little nearer. God, what this young lady caused her to feel. The things she had fantasized and longed for doing to her. Kiara recalled only that morning when she had fingered herself to a heavenly climax. She'd been considering being between Lauren's legs interestingly, licking her pussy until the wonderful youthful brunette had come everywhere on her tongue. In the wake of peaking, Kiara had drawn the cream off her fingers her cunt had delivered from the distraught beating her digits had given her pussy. Her eyes shut; she'd envisioned it was Lauren's delectable squeezes and cream she was licking up.

Shaking off her unavoidable shrewd contemplations, Kiara said, "That is not so, Lauren. Needed nothing, however, for you to be glad. Your mother says that hasn't been the case recently."

At the point when Lauren wouldn't gaze toward her and didn't answer, Kiara strolled over to the stall. "Would I be able to go along with you briefly," she inquired.

Lauren didn't let out the slightest peep. She just hurried over. That is when Kiara saw the cases filling the seat on the contrary side of the morning meal niche.

Kiara knew declining to sit now would just serve to compound the situation. So quietly appealing to God for strength, she slipped into the seat close to the one individual she realized she came up short on the psychological grit to oppose at that point.

Kiara looked as Lauren turned up the glass of wine and brought down the rest of its substance. She, at that point, put the glass down and got the wine bottle. Kiara looked as she poured a full glass before inquiring about whether she'd like a top off.

When the two of them had full glasses, Kiara tasted and said, "Things being what they are, the reason have you been down of late?"

Lauren overlooked the inquiry, and going to Kiara, asked, "Have you considered what it resembles to be with me?"

Kiara felt her heart race. This was what she had been apprehensive about occurring. In any case, she attempted to act courageously and said, "You answer my inquiry, and I'll answer yours."

Lauren grinned unfortunately and said, "OK, assuming it's that significant for you to know, I'll advise you. Someone that I've minded an extraordinary arrangement about for some time presently discovered and dismissed me. They wouldn't be with me, notwithstanding me realizing that they need me as well, all since they're worried about the possibility that I will attempt to take them away from their significant other. I would prefer not to wed this individual; I simply need to bring them something I can see they frantically need; however they're simply excessively damn difficult to concede to it."

Hurt and disappointment came through in Lauren's voice.

After a second, Kiara said, "Yes."

With a confused look all over, Lauren said, "Indeed, what?"

Unfit to meet the more youthful lady's eyes, Kiara said, "Yes...I've considered what it resembles to be with you."

Lauren came to across her body with her left hand and held onto Kiara's right cheek, turning the more seasoned lady's face towards her. With her other hand, she delicately measured Kiara's left cheek and pulled her in until their lips met up.

For Kiara, it was an unadulterated delight. Lauren's lips were delicate, wet, and warm simultaneously. Her kiss was delicate but then anxious and pressing at the same time. It filled Kiara with an appetite that should have been taken care of and a need that should have been met. That yearning turned into an eager and unquenchable hunger when she felt Lauren's tongue slide between her lips. Kiara faltered just momentarily before permitting her tongue to meet Lauren's. The two stroked each other in a personal dance, similar to the one she'd imparted to Lauren on the dance floor. They knock, rotated, and twirled around one another in an arousing tango of sensuality.

Kiara groaned into the more youthful lady's mouth when she felt Lauren's right hand drop from her cheek and cup her left breast. Lauren crushed it, attracting her fingers to a highlight where they settled around her responsive nipple. Lauren squeezed and contorted at the bloated stub. Kiara felt a moving pressing factor working in her middle as floods of delight moved through her body because of Lauren's kiss and contact.

Kiara at long last broke their kiss, panting for air as she did. Her hustling heart asked for more oxygen as Lauren's lips slid to her neck and started to suck and snack along its surface. Lauren moved gradually up to the more seasoned lady's ear, sucking on the projection and running her tongue over its surface.

"I've needed you frantically for as far back as I can recollect. Sometime before you were ever mindful of my advantage, my pussy would become drenched at whatever point you approached visit with Mom." Lauren said in an imposing voice that without actual words discussed her craving. "I can hardly wait to taste you and suck your pussy. I will make you come again and again harder than you've at any point preceded. What's more, when you don't figure you can stand any longer, I will make you return once more."

Lauren's promise in her ear, her lips and tongue on Kiara's neck and lips, and those enchanted and tenacious fingers on her swollen nipple were a powerful enough blend to give Kiara her first genuine climax from lesbian sex. It moved through her body, pushing a delayed groan of endorsement from profound inside Kiara's chest. As she utilized one hand to grip the wrist associated with the fingers that were working her lengthened and delicate nipple. Kiara felt her thighs shudder. She could feel the dividers of her pussy shaking as her it overwhelmed in endorsement of what this alluring youthful seductress was causing her to feel.

All without at any point in any event contacting her pussy. What might it seem like when she did?

An explosion of loud giggling from the heading of the parlor burst the air pocket of isolation Kiara had cheated herself into accepting existed around them. A torrent of frenzy and blame hammered for her. Tearing her lips from their arid kiss and pushing against Lauren's shoulders, Kiara said, "No, Lauren. This isn't right. We need to stop." Kiara's arm snared Lauren's wine glass as she contorted in her seat, trying to move away from the youngster. The glass spilled, absorbing the front of Kiara's pullover red wine. Kiara stood and, without thinking back, ran from the kitchen rapidly. She'd not any more transformed the corner into the passage when she ran straightforwardly into Jessica.

Jessica saw her dearest companion's wine-doused shirt and terrified face and asked, "What the heck occurred, Kiara?"

Kiara was very nearly a fit of anxiety. Her heart was dashing, and her breathing hitched in her chest. Her developments caused minor peaks to keep on flowing through her doused cunt, double-crossing her cognizant craving for alarm. In her tangled expression, all Kiara could say in answer was, "Me...Lauren..."

That was all Jessica expected to hear. Jessica snatched Kiara's shoulders and said unobtrusively, however solidly, "Shhh, you need to quiet down, Honey. Go higher up to my restroom and wash your top in the sink before that wine stain sets in. I have a couple of sweatshirts in my base cabinet. Select yourself one, and you can wear it while your shirt washes. I'll get Lauren and ensure she's OK and come up in a piece to beware of you. Keep awake there until you've quieted yourself down."

- - - - -

Jessica and Lauren

"What the heck occurred?" Jessica said she discovered Lauren remaining against the kitchen island, a glass of wine in her grasp.

Lauren shrugged, looking bothered, and said, "We were talking, and she was by all accounts opening up, nearly playing with me. I began kissing her, and she was so into it. I was scouring her nipples while we kissed, and she got so animated from it she came. I mean hard as well, Mom. At that point, she heard everybody snickering in the lounge room and froze, pushing my wine over on herself."

"Fuck," Jessica moaned, "It's been two stages forward and one stage back the entire route with this arrangement. Tune in; you need to rush higher up and get her before she gets dressed. She's up there with her top off right presently washing it out. When you get her in my bed, I don't need her leaving my room until tomorrow first thing."

Lauren grinned and put her glass down. Kissing her mom on the lips, she immediately took off toward the flight of stairs.

At the point when Lauren unobtrusively went into the room, she bolted her mom's entryway. She realized her mom held the key to the lock sitting on the trim over the entryway. Lauren could hear water running in the washroom sink. She slid her top off and unfastened the skirt she wore, allowing it to slide to the floor off her tight hips. That left her wearing simply a silk greenish-blue strap and a couple of dark thigh highs. She sneaked off her heels and trusted that Kiara would open the restroom entryway.

When Kiara opened the entryway, she was peering down at her skirt as she streamlined the material. Lauren immediately pushed her in a tough spot. She snatched the more seasoned lady's wrists and constrained them to her side as her delicate lips braced down over Kiara's nipple. Lauren sucked in, permitting her lips to empty as she ran her tongue over the surface of the pink stub.

"Lauren...stop. I can't," Kiara said pleadingly. Her words clashed with her body's response to Lauren's advances. She moaned and angled her chest forward into Lauren's holding up

413

mouth as the more youthful lady's lips and tongue expertly worked her nipple. The young lady delivered Kiara's correct wrist and utilized her free hand to hold onto the other pink gumdrop-type nipple. She started to move it between her fingers generally.

Kiara groaned stronger and kept on curving her chest into the more youthful lady. Her free left hand came up and pushed pitifully at Lauren's correct shoulder as she said, "Please, Lauren. Stop."

Lauren knew by Kiara's incapable effort to drive her away from that her obstruction was practically gone. "No, Kiara," she answered after immediately delivering her grasp on Kiara's currently swollen breast. She quickly held onto the nipple between her teeth and pulled at it.

"Ohhh, fuck," Kiara groaned, her efforts to drive a lot more modest lady away debilitating significantly further. "Ppp...please stop, Lauren."

Lauren pushes her thigh between Kiara's leg and ground it into the more seasoned lady's pussy. Kiara groaned noisily in light of the additional sexual upgrades. She parted with one more weak effort to push Lauren as she asked, "Please, Lauren, stop."
Feeling positive about the heading this was going, Lauren delivered Kiara's other hand and pulled her mouth off Lauren's nipple. Her second hand supplanted it as she started squeezing and moving the two nipples all the while and smiled up at her victory, saying, "I said no, Kiara. Haven't you heard? At the point when a young lady says no, she implies no."

Lauren crushed the two nipples making Kiara's pussy hold as she came for the second time with negligible contact to her lower locale. Also, with that, all affectation on Kiara's part at opposition vanished. The hand she'd been utilizing to push at Lauren's shoulder pitifully slid behind the teenager's neck and pulled her in, pulverizing her lips against

Lauren's. The hot youthful brunette's mind cheered in triumph, understanding that Kiara was hers. Her perseverance had paid off, and she had the female darling she had pined over for practically the most recent two years.

Lauren groaned into Kiara's mouth as she felt her new lesbian sweetheart's tongue slide between her lips and start testing unavoidably for the youngsters.

Breaking their kiss, Lauren delivered Kiara's nipples and took her hands, saying, "Please, Baby. Go along with me on Mom's bed and allowed me to show you what genuine delight feels like."

Lauren pulled Sam toward the bed yet felt the more seasoned lady begin to stand up to. She delivered her hands, snared her arms around Kiara's neck, and was satisfied when she felt Kiara's hands tenderly stop on her midriff.

"What's up, infant," Lauren said as she fluttered her long eyelashes up at her new darling.

Kiara investigated the bed and said, "This is your Mom and Dad's bed. It would feel peculiar, and your Mom said she would come and beware of me. Imagine a scenario where she gets us."

Lauren snickered and raised on her toes, bringing her lips against Kiara's. She sucked on the more seasoned lady's base lip, nipping at it delicately. At the point when their kiss broke, Lauren said, "Infant, Mom understands what's going on up here. She's the one that sent me up here in the expectation I could free you up to an entirely different universe of sexual delight. She realizes how awful I've needed you for the most recent few years."

Lauren set her hands on Kiara's shoulders and delicately pushed the more established lady back towards the bed. At the point when the backs of Kiara's knees connected with the edge of the bed, she fell back onto its surface with a giggle.

Lauren came down and to the side of her skirt. She brought down the zipper and looked as Kiara raised her hips to permit her to slide the piece of clothing down her legs.

Taking a gander at the sight before her, Lauren felt her generally raised excitement to ascend into the stratosphere. Kiara wore the hottest pair of dark ribbon trendy person style undies made of a sheer, transparent sort of trim. Lauren could see her new sweetheart's pussy was shaven. Her legs were long and welcoming. Lauren couldn't stand by to feel them folded over her abdomen as she screwed the hot, more seasoned lady with her most loved strapon. She needed to have the option to hear her mom's hot companion shout in enchant as she carried her to deliver again and again.

"Fuck, you're so hot, Kiara," Lauren said, peering down thankfully. "I've needed you for such a long time. However, I didn't know it could at any point occur. You were so difficult I was apprehensive you could never surrender to what you needed thus clearly required."

Kiara gazed toward Lauren as she let her correct hand slide down and over her silk-covered focus. Lauren looked as the cougar sexually stroked between her thighs, pushing hard enough at the ribbon covering that it covered between her wet lips. Kiara groaned and said, "Please, Lauren, kindly screw me. I need to come so awful. I'm worn out on denying myself. I need to taste your pussy and lick you until you come everywhere on my tongue. If it's not too much trouble, show me what I've been feeling the loss of this time."

That was all the consolation Lauren required. She slid Kiara's underwear down her long and agile legs. Carrying them to her nose, she sniffed profoundly, breathing in the more seasoned lady's unmistakable scent, and discovered it to be mouthwateringly wonderful.

Sitting down on Kiara's lengthier edge, Lauren kissed and sucked at her nipples. Her mom's closest companion cooed in appreciation, her hands snatching the duvet and making clench hands as she squirmed underneath her dainty darling's body.

Lauren delivered Kiara's nipple with a discernible pop. Supplanting it with her fingers, she alluringly slid up the more seasoned lady's slender body and forcefully planted her lips against Kiara's. The two ladies tongues circumnavigated against each other in a fight for incomparability. Lauren felt Kiara's hands stop on her back and start to rub and touch her skin gradually as their lips and tongues kept on conflicting. The adolescent felt Kiara's hands slide down her back, where they discovered both her rear-end cheeks. The presently wanton cougar held both without a second thought and started to crush and grab them as she groaned into Lauren's mouth.

Needing more, Lauren broke their kiss and started to kiss her way down her new darling's body. She revered on both of Kiara's responsive pink little gumdrop nipples, drawing a groan of appreciation from the cougar. Lauren surrounded her tongue, the two stubs following her nipples and leaving a wet path as she hauled her tongue down Kiara's trim waist. Kiara squirmed and discharged a little snicker as Lauren dunked her tongue into her bellybutton.

Finally, she contacted her long-term objective of having her head between her mom's lovely dearest companion's legs. Lauren gazed upward and discovered Kiara gazing down at her with a look of only expectation all over. Lauren grinned back up at her as she hauled her tongue up the more seasoned lady's left internal thigh, leaving a little snack and wet kisses afterward.

"Fuck," Kiara moaned as she twisted under the ministrations of Lauren's lips and tongue. "Please, Lauren, please," Kiara asked.

She was holding her lips, a small part of an inch over the more established lady's engorged lips. Lauren looked up at her new darling with a wicked grin and asked, "Please, what, Kiara? Mention to me what it is that you need?"

Kiara's as of now flushed face and chest turned a more brilliant shade. She moaned and moved her head side to side as though opposing saying the words. In counter to the more seasoned lady's refusal of giving her what she needed, Lauren prodded her, further hauling her tongue all around the border of Kiara's sex. That drew out another moan of disappointment from her horny new sexually unbiased sweetheart.

"Try not to deny me, Kiara. I'm giving you the endowment of complete sexual satisfaction. Give me what I need, Baby,"

Kiara's hips came up off the bed as she groaned and said, "Please, Lauren, lick me. Lick my pussy, please."

Lauren shut her eyes and moaned. Hearing the words finally that she'd ached to hear for such a long time brought her a sensation of happiness. Thinking back up to see her sweetheart's appearance, Lauren brought down her tongue and planted it in Kiara's cut. She hauled it up gradually, feeling the more seasoned lady's juices coat her tongue. The tempting juices flooding her taste buds with the pith Lauren had been needing. The enthusiastic fever of anticipation she'd endured for the last just about two years satiated. The teenager brunette started permitting her cultivated tongue to tempt Kiara's shuddering cunt capably.

- - - - -

Kiara

Kiara had been up to speed in her little world when she'd made way for the washroom. Her top was likely destroyed, and she didn't know she hadn't effectively dedicated infidelity down in the kitchen with Lauren. On the off chance that John discovered, he would likely never completely pardon her. She'd be fortunate if it didn't end her marriage.

She scarcely possessed energy for her mind to enroll exposed feet and legs in the outskirts of her vision before Lauren's lips had arrived. The speed of the assault hadn't permitted Kiara's stun to enlist before she felt the divider against her back. Her wrists were abruptly bolted next to her inside the more youthful lady's protected hold as Lauren's tongue was promptly intruding against her nipple. The diligent youthful, sexually open's lips encompassed her aureola, shaping a seal, and started to suck forcefully.

The sensation was right away overpowering as the sensitive spots encompassing Kiara's solidifying nipple detonated with a bunch of pleasurable sensations. Notwithstanding the close orgasmic euphoria of how it felt, Kiara asked the youthful temptress to stop. There was no ideal opportunity to permit the conflict of clashing feelings in her mind to be settled as her body double-crossed her. She tracked down her back abruptly, angling into the vast mouth of the dainty yet strong youthful brunette.

Declining to consent to Kiara's interest, Lauren delivered her left hand and held onto her other nipple, moving it between her fingers. Heaving in amusement at the inclination, Kiara battled through the total confusion of her mind and carried her free hand to Lauren's shoulder. She needed to drive the young lady away. However, the consistent rushes of happiness moving through her body debilitated her determination. All that she could oversee was a powerless and inadequate endeavor that just served to extend her nipples. The additional incitement almost constrained a second peak from the debilitating Kiara.

She asked the youngster again to stop. Lauren delivered her nipple from between her lips and the hold on to her correct wrist. Trading her lips for the tips of her fingers, she started to wind and squeeze the swollen stubs. Lauren's disavowal was trailed by her sliding her thigh between Kiara's legs. The contact was perfect. Kiara's flimsy trim undies had become so immersed she felt her juices start to stream down her inward thighs.

Even though she felt no genuine solidarity to oppose, she carried two hands to Lauren's shoulders and again attempted to drive the more youthful lady away. Her will to reject Lauren practically gone, and realizing it was her last possibility not to turn out to be for all time lost in her cravings, Kiara begged the youngster once again.

Lauren prodded her about no significance no and dispatched what Kiara realized at that point would be the last attack she would require. As her teeth shut around Kiara's swollen nipple, the more established lady felt her pussy shake as she came for the second time in a brief period. All graciousness of Lauren's fixation on her delicate nipples.

With the inward mass of her pussy as yet spasming, Kiara acknowledged her new situation finally. She was sexually open and had a young female darling. There was not a single disgrace or humiliation insight in her acknowledgment of current realities. She'd had over a month to manage all that. Her blame for the sentiments she had, her judgment of Jessica's conduct, and hard respect for her conjugal pledges, every last bit of it. She was going to allow an exceptionally young lady to support her sexual necessities. She needed Lauren to suck her and screw her silly and utilize her for her pleasure. She was an adulteress and a poser.

Furthermore, interestingly, Kiara approved of that.

- - - - -

Jessica and Lauren

The youthful, sexually unbiased lady had gone through her collection of prodding strategies. She figured out how to stir Kiara up into a serious foam. The cougar's hips over and over angled off the bed as she supported Lauren's head between her hands. Lauren concluded the time had come to give the more established lady her delivery. She needed to taste her cum and charm her new sweetheart. Lauren needed there to be no danger of Kiara turning into a cushion princess. At the point when Lauren was through with her, the tender brunette would do anything for an encore.

At the point when Lauren's lips bolted around Kiara's clitoris, it resembled the neutron terminated at a center of fissionable material in a nuclear bomb. It set off a falling impact, and since Kiara's excitement was at that point at minimum amount, her peak detonated in a chain response of unadulterated joy.

Lauren got a handle on hold of the underside of Kiara's thighs and hung on like a bull rider as the more seasoned lady shook. The spasms flowing through her were supported by the flicking of Lauren's tongue against Kiara's clit.

At the point when the remainder of the spasms had passed, Lauren greased up three of her fingers by putting them in her mouth. At the point when they were doused, she eliminated them and situated them at Kiara's opening. Like the mindful sweetheart she was, Lauren slipped them into Kiara's smooth opening, hearing a speedy admission of breath from her new darling.

"Fuck," Kiara shouted as she got a handle on the duvet, grasping it as though she expected to slide off the bed. "How are you doing me?" she groaned as she started pushing her hips up to meet Lauren's pistoning fingers.

Lauren grinned, her eyes pools of her excitement said, "I'm screwing my new darling." The more youthful lady started to twist her fingers up and tap against Kiara's g-spot with each stroke.

"Ooooooooooooh, fuck. Soooo great," Kiara shouted out. Lauren looked as the cougar brought her hands up and started to squeeze and move her nipples. The more youthful lady brought down her head and started utilizing the harsh, level surface of her tongue on Kiara's profoundly charged little stub. Pivoting it around and around and setting as much pressing factor against the bloated stub as possible profoundly affected Kiara. The erogenous magistrate of the nipple, clit, and g-spot incitement all the while drove Kiara wild. Her hips erupted against Lauren's mouth and fingers, and she accompanied a delayed cry that made the more youthful lady's heart lift.

"We should see a man make you come that way," Lauren thought gladly to herself.

At the point when Kiara's quim at long last quit trembling, her breathing was all the while hustling. Lauren slid up close to her and said, "You should improve shape in case we continue to have intercourse."

At the point when the two quit giggling, Lauren inclined in and delicately took Kiara's lips. The two ladies' mouths opened, and their tongues compromised in a knot of delicate, wet substance. Kiara groaned into Lauren's mouth and gone after the more youthful lady's firm breasts. As she got a handle on a swollen nipple, Lauren broke their kiss and utilized a hand behind the more established lady's head to pull her in towards her chest.

"Suck on it, Baby," Lauren said, coordinating Kiara's mouth in towards her nipple. She felt warm wetness encompass her stub and aureola and felt the vibrations as she heard Kiara groan at the experience of sucking on her first female nipple.

"Ooooo, that is it, Baby," Lauren cooed as she stroked her fingers through her female sweetheart's hair. She felt Kiara's left hand slide down her body and to the swollen lips of her pussy. A finger slid into the wetness of her split and hauled upwards until it tracked down her engorged clitoris.

"Screw indeed, Baby. Play with my affection button. That feels so screwing great." Lauren said in recognition of Kiara's endeavors.

The more seasoned lady traded breasts and started to suck the opposite side mindfully while her fingers proceeded with a tireless assault on Lauren's little stub.

"I need you to suck on my pussy, child," Lauren said. "I need to come so terribly at present, and I need it to be on your tongue. I need to bless that lovely face of yours with my cum."

Kiara groaned accordingly and delivered the stranglehold her lips had on Lauren's nipple. She turned upward at Lauren. The high schooler could see the anxiety all over.

"Simply do the things you enjoyed when I went down on you. Focus on how my body reacts to what you do, and when you figure you've accomplished something I preferred, continue to do it. "

That appeared to facilitate a portion of the uncertainty in Kiara's eyes. She slid down and settled between Lauren's legs. The teenager spread her legs more extensively and drew her feet up until they were even with her base. This opened her pussy up like a blooming blossom so the cougar could look at target altogether.

Lauren noticed Kiara and realized this was the second that the more seasoned lady could always remember. Her first sweet taste of pussy would everlastingly be scratched in her brain, and it would be Lauren that she would consider when she reviewed it.

- - - - -

Kiara

Kiara analyzed the sight before her taking everything incautiously. Lauren's excitement was obvious to her. Her external labia were puffy and articulated. Her inward labia shimmered with wetness. The crinkled lines of her clitoral hood peered down over everything. What's more, simply looking out from under, she could perceive what John in every case coarsely called, "the little man in the boat."

The smell of Lauren's excitement was without a doubt engaging. It was a rich and gritty smell, not overwhelming, however welcoming. There was none of the suspiciousness she had consistently heard more adolescent guys partner with the smell.

Kiara utilized the fingers of her right hand to marginally spread the high schooler's lips separated, giving her full admittance to the fortunes inside. She warily brought down her head and hauled her tongue up one side of Lauren's labia and afterward back down the other. Kiara paused for a minute to step her tongue once again into her mouth and permit the taste to enroll in her cerebrum. It was not normal for anything she had anticipated. It was sweet and tart simultaneously with simply a trace of salt. She brought down her tongue once more into the wrinkle and licked straightforwardly up the center, halting short of Lauren's clit. Kiara, at that point, turned around bearing and hauled her tongue down to the young lady's opening. There she went here and there aimlessly around the opening, taking in a portion of the new squeezes that leaked from the inside.

Kiara groaned, concluding that she preferred the flavor of Lauren's pussy without question. More enthused and less uncertain of herself, Kiara folded her lips over one of Lauren's external labia and sucked eagerly on it. The more youthful lady groaned in endorsement, giving Kiara a reference point for later on. She rehashed the interaction on the opposite side, drawing another groan of endorsement. Pulling out all the stops, Kiara slid down and stuffed her tongue as profound into Lauren's tight opening as could be expected. She sucked at the young lady's wonderful honeypot taking in however much of her shamefully delicious nectar as could reasonably be expected.

"Screw, that feels so great," Lauren said as she revolved her hips against Kiara's energetic mouth. "I think after I please your tongue, I must reward you by getting my strapon and screwing your sweet pussy until you beseech me to stop."

Kiara moaned at Lauren's words. She could, as of now, feel the shivers of excitement returning in her center. Her young darling's guarantees sounded enticingly tasty. Since Kiara's sexually open cravings had bloomed, and her tease with Lauren had started. She'd gone to her better half consistently for sexual alleviation, and he'd generally planned to please. Kiara needed to concede; however, taking Lauren's strapon was especially welcoming. John was a fragile living creature and blood. When he came, he was down and out for some time. One thing she'd gained from the lesbian pornography she'd become dependent on was that a strapon had no recuperation time. It was, in every case, hard.

She was utilizing that idea as inspiration. Kiara turned her consideration up towards the youthful ladies clit and started to Kiaraper it with her tongue. She folded her lips over the young lady's hood and sucked at it while turning the tip of her tongue against Lauren's stub.

Lauren got a handle on the cougar's long hair as she pulled her mouth in more tight against her hot cunt. Kiara could tell the more youthful lady was close. Her breathing and

425

groans gave each sign of an approaching climax. The prospect of at last tasting her cum extended the giganticness existing apart from everything else for Kiara.

"Screw Baby, here it comes. Ohhhhhh, Yesssssssss," Lauren murmured as she ground her spasming cunt against Kiara's mouth. Kiara felt a sprinkle of wetness coat her jaw and neck as her young sweetheart spurted with every fit. Lauren had guaranteed the more seasoned lady that she would bless her, and she had conveyed.

At the point when her pussy and breathing had at long last quieted down. Lauren peered down to discover Kiara lapping up the bounteous measure of juices that clung to her lips and thighs.

"For someone that was so speculative about licking their first pussy, you sure appear to appreciate the taste," Lauren prodded her mom's closest companion. "It is safe to say that you are a skank for the flavor of my cum now?"

Kiara becomes flushed at the inquiry however didn't avoid responding to it. "God, indeed, I don't know what I was expecting, but rather I venerate the flavor of your pussy." And as though to underscore her words, she hauled her tongue up Lauren's middle and over her clit before adding, "And your cum is screwing tasty."

A shy grin all over, Lauren said, "You know, I believe there's more where that came from in case you're feeling hungry."

Lauren's solicitation to her new darling was anxiously acknowledged. No verbal affirmation was given. However, none was required. Kiara covered her tongue into the more youthful lady's spilling channel and started to lick away with vigorous enthusiasm.

- - - - -

Jessica and Lauren

Jessica had been horny to the place of interruption as she'd engaged her visitors. The other eleven ladies present were just as randy as her between the free-streaming liquor and all the sex talk. Jessica had started to think she'd need to open a window to air the room out from the musky smell that had started to penetrate the limits. Luckily, before that became fundamental, the gathering began to separate, and her visitors started leaving. Some left their vehicles left in the city and require a Uber or Lyft to get them home. They were smashed to think about driving.

At the point when the remainder of her visitors had said their farewells, Jessica immediately headed up the steps. Cleanup of the wreck would need to stand by until tomorrow around lunchtime. Her mind had been unable to leave considerations of what was going on between her girl and closest companion. What's more, presently, she frantically needed to go along with them. Tasting Kiara's sweet pussy had been available in her relentless dreams since not long after the two ladies had met. At long last, on account of her girl, she would have the option to experience those fantasies.

Jessica shed her garments as she climbed the steps attempting to be just about as calm as expected. She needed to have the option to astound her sweet and provocative companion, if conceivable.

She deliberately attempted the entryway however discovered it bolted. Recovering the key, she quietly embedded it into the lock and turned it feeling the hook give way. She swung the entryway open as tenderly as could be expected and took in the sights and sounds before her.

Her girl lay on her back, her head set up on cushions, and her legs attracted and spread wide. Kiara was between her legs with her head covered in the more youthful lady's pussy.

According to the sounds radiating from her throat as she lapped away at Lauren's delicious quim, Kiara was especially having a ball. The more established lady was on her knees and had them spread wide to lower herself down nearer to her sweetheart.

The view mixed something in Jessica. Her more predominant butch darlings consistently prefer to drive Jessica to lick and test their butt heads with her tongue. She generally went about as though it would be an attack against her inclination to do as such, however, covertly delighted in the demonstration and the corruption of having them compel her to perform it.

Kiara's pink little sphincter appeared to wink at her, nearly beseeching her to intrigue it. She felt her mouth water in light of spreading those rigid cheeks much further separated and covering her tongue into her attractive companion's tight ass.

Detecting what her mom was attempting to do, Lauren expanded her moans and flailing the bed uncontrollably. She was attempting to give her mom the cover expected to make it onto the bed and behind Kiara without being recognized. She watched Kiara for signs that she'd saw her dearest companion climb onto the bed. The cougar was lost in the rapture of feasting on her delicious treat. On the off chance that she identified the development behind her, she gave no sign.

All that changed when her mom brought her mouth down to Kiara's rear while getting a handle on her can cheek and spreading them separated. The more seasoned lady's eyes enlarged in shock and afterward folded once more into her head as she attempted to raise. Lauren held her head solidly set up until she settled back in and continued eating her pussy as though she were eager.

"That is your closest companion, who I accept is right now licking your butt nugget," Lauren prodded. "Vicki disclosed to me once in the certainty that Mother can be a

428

remarkable compliant skank when she is with her butch darlings. Challenges! I surmise I let that slip."

Jessica felt her face flush and her pussy spout at Lauren's embarrassing words. She had no clue that Vicki had imparted data of their affairs to her little girl. She was unable to help, can't help thinking about what all the excellent butch had told Lauren.

"You need to be an accommodating whore for your dearest companion?" Lauren prodded her mom.

Jessica moaned and felt her pussy release much more, yet raised and said, "Nectar, please don't..."

"Get that tongue back in her butt nugget at present," Lauren raged at her in a decided tone. She'd never addressed her mom in a particularly bold voice previously. Overwhelming a sweetheart was not her thing. Lauren had just done so because drawing out her mother's more agreeable side with Kiara being available was delightful. In any case, she needed to concede to a specific degree of hunger in the manner her mom immediately sunk her tongue back between Kiara's cheeks.

Lauren wanted to push things considerably further. "Who might have figured my bossy and honestly, some of the time, the obnoxious mother might want to have another lady hit her rear end cherry red. Vicki says it makes her pussy pour whenever she trains her for being an insidious prostitute. Is that valid, Mommy? Is it true that you are an accommodating little agony whore?"

Jessica moaned into Kiara's can yet didn't react. She felt powerless, both needing to beseech her little girl to stop and needing the embarrassment to proceed.

"Kiara, why not check whether you can get your companion to quit being a mischievous skank and answer my inquiry," Lauren said.

She delivered her grasp on the more established lady's head and was both shocked and excited when her head returned up to and went to towards her companion and said, "Answer your girl, skank." She, at that point, covered her face again in Lauren's steaming grab decisively.

Jessica moaned, feeling both loss and happiness at being dealt with so discourteously by the pair. Shame and embarrassment poured through her as she raised and said, "Y...yes, Honey. I can't resist, yet it's actual." Then to both conceal her disgrace, and because it energized her to do as such, she covered her tongue once more into Kiara's jerking butt nugget.

Kiara moaned uproariously into Lauren's cunt, sending scrumptious shudders of joy flowing through the youngster's body. She could feel the compel starting to assemble again and realized that it was nearly an ideal opportunity to blessing her new darling with a greater amount of her cum. "I'm so close, Baby. Make me please that talented tongue of yours."

Anxious to do precisely that, Kiara sunk two fingers into Lauren's tight cunt and started examining them against the top of her internal dividers. At the point when the hot high schooler felt the more seasoned lady's fingers hit the correct spot, she said, "Indeed, Baby, not too far off. Tap in that general area. Fuck, yes!" Lauren uproariously shouted as she felt herself peak the slope and fall over into blankness.

She felt Kiara's mouth enlarge as her pussy started to fit, and the wondrous spasms flowed through her center. She indeed spurted, this time, straightforwardly out from the dark mouth of the wanton cougar devouring her products. She saw Kiara's cheeks attract

430

as the hot, more seasoned lady breastfed at her emitting pussy. Not a drop got away from her lips, her eyes folding once more into her head in amusement.

Jessica understood what Kiara was as of now encountering. She'd frequently discovered pleasure in the manner her little girl came and cherished the flavor of her delightful ambrosia. Considering it made her can't help thinking about what her closest companions cum would resemble. Needing to acquire firsthand information, she supplanted her tongue with her thumb and started to squeeze it against Kiara's rose bloom. She felt it give somewhat, and the tip of her opposable digit slip in the past the main ring.

"Fuck!" Kiara shouted out as Jessica infiltrated her further, permitting her thumb to slip right, taking all things together with the path to the knuckle. Her companion appeared to freeze completely still, unsure of the new sensation Jessica's attacking digit was causing. Jessica sat down on her back as she gradually kept on working her thumb all through Kiara's rosebud in small augmentations. Facilitating under Kiara, Jessica carried her mouth to her companions, dribbling cunt, hearing Kiara coo accordingly.

Feeling her companion's tight sphincter unwind around her digit, at last, Jessica covered the rest of it inside her can. She started to screw her new darlings can gradually, nearly pulling out it all together each time before once again introducing it into her profundities. Kiara moaned in uneasiness with each stroke inside her butt-centric depression. Yet, Jessica realized the agony would relax. When it did, she anticipated being the primary individual at any point to furnish Kiara with the vibe of a butt-centric climax.

Jessica slid her lips up Kiara's split, gathering the deviant flavorful juices that had amassed there. At the point when she arrived at Kiara's clit, she started to work it earnestly. She desired the taste she would be reimbursed with once her attractive companion came and trusted their future would hold bunches of little playdates this way.

"I think my prostitute mom needs to taste your cum, infant," Lauren said as she is truly making the most of her job as an abuser of her mom. "Might you want to come on her hot and scandalous face?"

"Gracious, God, yes," Kiara groaned. Lauren saw the more seasoned lady had started to shake once more into the strokes her mom was pushing into her butt. The sensitive spots and delight focus so regularly disregarded there had clearly at last defeated the sensations of distress. Kiara's groan got persistent as she pushes once more into Jessica's attacking thumb before bringing her mouth down to Lauren's clit.

Feeling insatiable, Lauren invited the more seasoned lady's voracious tongue back between her legs by pushing her hips up to welcome it. The vibrations of Kiara's groans passing from her lips and tongue and into Lauren's swollen stub were quickly assembling her towards another peak.

Kiara brought her mouth up and nearly murmured out the words, "Indeed, skank. Screw me and suck my cunt. I will come so screwing hard. Fuck, fuck, fuck..."

Jessica felt Kiara's juices course down over her mouth and jaw. She eagerly started lapping away to get the valuable arrival of tasty discharges. She discovered delectation in Kiara's quintessence and realized she wouldn't have the option to manage without it later. Regardless, the two ladies' relationship had changed. Jessica would do whatever she could to ensure it was to improve things.

"Mother, in case you're finished tidying up what ought to be your companion's all-around fulfilled cunt, could you come up here and give mine some consideration. Watching both of you truly made me go." Lauren said unassumingly.

At the point when her mom just laid there, gradually proceeding to lick at Kiara's twat, Lauren poked at and recuperating Kiara and gestured toward her mom.

Kiara grinned back at her and came to down, jabbing at Jessica, "Whore, get up here and suck your girl's pussy until she comes." Taking a second to consider what she'd recently said, "Pause, I can't accept that I recently said that."

Lauren giggled and said, "No doubt, the thought took some becoming acclimated to for me as well. Yet, it was Mom who was my first. She allured me; however, frankly, I truly didn't avoid her all that amount."

Jessica slid out from underneath Kiara and crept up to her little girl who's smile embarrassed her considerably. She should end this. However, the pulsating in her clit and the great delight she got from hearing Kiara be controlling and belittling to her provided her the opportunity to stop and think. Having butch young ladies domme her had been her private and mystery fixation. In any event, she thought it had. So much for having the option to believe that bitch Vicki.

At no other time, however, had a genuine femme had that impact on her. It may have been the great emotions she'd generally had for her dearest companion. She'd constrained herself to divert them into their companionship. Without that support in the manner and with her little girl's curious nature, that not, at this point, appeared to be a choice.

Her disappointment with her little girl vanished as she settled between her legs. The young lady truly had a lovely pussy and a delicious one as well. Being an accommodating prostitute when it came to ladies had its benefits. Jessica couldn't deny herself when she requested somebody she needed to be overwhelmed by, including Kiara.

Lauren groaned as her mom sucked at her clit. She felt Kiara get comfortable close to her and murmured as the more established lady started to kiss her. In contrast to their past kisses, this one was listless and more erotic. All in all, too agreeable for Lauren's solace.

She had a "no getting genuinely included" rule when it went to the more seasoned ladies she had lesbian undertakings with. It was the central motivation behind why she generally picked joyfully wedded ladies to entice. They didn't require the enthusiastic association and were content just to appreciate the sex.

Until Grace, it had gone easily, and afterward, her previous instructor had gotten possessive. She'd just be more cautious in the ladies she picked. I couldn't have one of them going lethal fascination on her.

Kiara was extraordinary, however. There was a novel thing about her. Possibly it was having grown up so near the attractive brunette, or maybe it was how long she had desired to be with her mom's closest companion.

Whatever it was, she felt it is not difficult to get snared on Kiara and fall for her, and that just would not do. Lauren had taken extremely numerous precautionary measures to guarantee something to that effect didn't occur. She realized she would have to proceed with caution.

Lauren had deceived Kiara and her mom about having engaged in sexual relations with men. The story she'd advised had been identified with her by a secondary school sweetheart. She had made a cursory effort of having associations with young men in secondary school. In any case, Lauren had never been truly pulled into any of them. She'd had careless makeout meetings with those folks while they pawed at her. Lauren had given back, giving a few handjobs, yet had would not go any further.

She realized where it counts that she was only pulled into ladies, especially more seasoned ladies. Yet, Lauren held out trust that she could meet a man that stimulated her. It would be a more normal life and make having a kid a lot more straightforward. Lauren needed to be a mother, and the complexities and added cost of doing that in an equivalent sex relationship appeared to be overwhelming. Like her mom, Lauren realized she could have her female sweethearts as an afterthought. There were in every case explicitly unfulfilled ladies out there that longed to be truly delighted, and Lauren was only the lady to do it.

A ringing cell intruded on her kiss with Kiara. It wasn't a ring that Lauren perceived. "That would be John checking in with me," said Kiara as she bounced up and advanced over to her tote. Lauren watched her rear end as it squirmed its way into the bathroom and contemplated whether Kiara would feel any blame when conversing with her significant other. "I surmise we'll know when she emerges from the restroom," she thought before directing her concentration toward her prostitute mother.

"You are getting a charge out of that pussy, aren't you whore?" she prodded her mom.

Jessica gazed toward her, not under any condition feeling the surge she felt when Lauren had done likewise around Kiara. All things being equal, she just felt aggravated.

"You know, you can stow that crap, or you can diddle your self to finish," she cautioned her little girl.

Lauren chuckled and said, "Intriguing."

"What?" Jessica said with disturbance before returning to licking her little girl's clit. However bothered as she seemed to be with the young lady, Kiara had advised her to do it, and damn her compliant nature, she would not like to baffle her new darling.

"Gracious, it just happened to me that you were normally accommodating with your closest companion, however with her not here, you're back to your bossy old self," Lauren said with a chuckle. "You need her to rule you, don't you?"

In just about a frenzy, Jessica raised and said, "Shhhhh! Try not to allow her to hear you."

"At that point, answer the inquiry," Lauren said in a loud voice that made her mom wince.

"Indeed, alright," Jessica conceded in a loud murmur, "It was surprising, and I realize you were simply prodding me, regardless. Be that as it may, the embarrassment of her understanding what Vicki said and afterward how she took to bossing me around. It hit home for me."

"Hit it up, skank. I think better when my pussy is eaten, and possibly I can think about an approach to get it going." Lauren said with a grin.

Jessica gave her the finger yet returned to sucking at the young lady's clit. Hello, she cherished eating pussy, and Kiara had advised her to. What was a compliant skank expected to do?

She heard the restroom entryway open. Lauren admired see Kiara leave the washroom happily. She slid back up on the bed close to Lauren and rapidly shover her tongue in the more youthful lady's mouth. "I surmise that addresses that question," Lauren pondered internally.

At the point when their lips isolated, Lauren asked, "So how was John?" She needed to get Kiara's feedback and check whether there was any lament.

"Goodness, he was incredible. They had a few calls around evening time, and he'd recently returned from one and planned to scrub down and attempt to get some rest. He needed to hear I love him before he set down." Kiara said with a major grin that talked about the amount she adored the man.

Peering down at Jessica, Kiara said, "I see your skank mother hasn't gotten you off. What is by all accounts the issue?"

Lauren could tell that Kiara was clever. Her mom couldn't as she felt her tongue kick into overdrive. Feeling somewhat the rascal and needing to perceive what both of them would do, Lauren said, "Possibly she didn't take your interest to make me come true. Vicki said agreeable whores like her should be focused when they don't care about their domme. Possibly you need to hit her."

Kiara smiled naughtily and bounced up enthusiastically, sliding over behind her dearest companion. The more seasoned lady winked at Lauren and accepted an incredible way about herself.

"Whore, when I advise you to eat your girl's pussy and make her come, I anticipate that you should take care of business conveniently." and with that, she smacked Jessica's butt hard.

Jessica moaned and felt her pussy spout before the sting of the blow at any point enlisted in her cerebrum. She could not trust her body was responding to Kiara's emulating of a somehow it was. Jessica realized her companion was just doing it since she was up to speed in the zeal of the evening. That, and she speculated Kiara was somewhat fascinated with her girl at this moment and would follow all her ideas. A reality filled her agreeable little soul with desire; however, she realized that Kiara was simply one more sexual close companion to Lauren.

The subsequent explode sent shudders to her spine. The third made them moan so anyone can hear, and the fourth had beads of cunt juice splattering within her thigh. Is it accurate to say that they were getting more earnestly? She could swear they were, and the delightful consume in her butt cheeks sent her excitement soaring. The fifth and 6th blow was certainly harder, to such an extent that she became mindful she had quit licking Lauren's clit. The seventh and eighth fixed her as she came hard, essentially laying her cheek against her little girl's pussy as her thighs shuddered, and she groaned like the skank she was.

For Lauren, it was a twofold shock. For one, she didn't anticipate that Kiara should be so overflowing about her hitting obligations. However, when the imagined domme got moving, she went at it with energy. By the fifth and 6th blow, she was truly laying the wood to her mom, affecting the compliant. Her mother had quit licking, and her eyes had gone smooth. When she peaked with the following arrangement of blows, Lauren didn't know who was more amazed, Kiara or her mom.

- - - - -

Kiara

"Did she just come?" Kiara pondered, peering down at Jessica as the lady's thighs shook, and evident spasms appeared to race through her hips.

Peering down at the red effects she'd had on her dearest companions round and stout behind, Kiara felt a little shiver start between her legs. What wasn't right with her? Kiara had just been playing in the first place, yet the more she'd down-poured her give over on Jessica's round ass, the energizing she'd felt. The sexually open novice couldn't resist the opportunity to consider the thing that was said about her.

Made up for lost time at the time, Kiara permitted her fingers to touch over her closest companion's shapely ass and slide down between her legs. "Fuck," Kiara thought as she felt the wetness between Jessica's legs. Peering down, Kiara could see the sparkly wetness covering the lady's thighs. "She appreciates being dealt with like this," Kiara contemplated to herself, "so for what reason would it be a good idea for me to feel regretful about receiving a little happiness in return as well?"

Kiara gazed toward Lauren, who smiled back at her, gesturing her head with her eyes wide. Kiara hadn't envisioned it. Jessica had certainly come from being hit, and Lauren knew it as well.

Lauren winked at her and, in an exasperated way, said, "Incredible, you punish the prostitute for not making me come, and she speaks. Perhaps you should show her the legitimate method to make a lady come."

Kiara felt a surge that Lauren would pick her tongue over her mom's. Feeling awful for Jessica right currently appeared to be a misuse of feeling as she appreciated being dealt with along these lines. Kiara adored her companion and couldn't resist the opportunity to show it even in her false control of the lady.

She stroked Jessica's red ass cheeks, and getting a handle on the lady's shoulder, pulled up while saying, "Sit up, sweetheart."

Jessica did as she was asked. However, Kiara saw her companion appeared to be not able to meet her eyes. The lady was humiliated by the facts that had been uncovered concerning her sexual nature. Kiara could comprehend that completely. She'd managed a great deal of those equivalent sentiments over the most recent few months.

Highlighting a spot, Kiara said, "Lay on your back with your head here and your feet towards the entryway."

Kiara saw that Jessica didn't spare a moment to do as she inquired. This wasn't her companion's typical character. Jessica could be out and out domineering now and again with her better half and stubborn with others. She, for a reality, realized the lady maintained her business with a consistent hand. She was inclined to micromanage her representatives and never surrendered control of anything pertinent to one of her colleagues.

Indeed, even with Kiara, Jessica was inclined to pushing her plan under normal conditions. So the revelation of her dearest companion's calm nature with ladies was taking a psychological change on Kiara's part. It wasn't that she was deciding on her companion. Not in the wake of being so condemning of her for having undermined her significant other. That had just been a distraction to cover her own emotions; Kiara presently figured it out.

What's more, the fact of the matter was Kiara sort of got a shiver at bossing around Jessica. Her companions here and their shrill nature appeared to vanish out and out when Kiara had bossed her around this evening—furthermore, beating her. She had begun to do it to satisfy Lauren; however, fuck, whenever she'd gotten rolling, Kiara had truly wound up getting into it.

Riding her dearest companion's head, Kiara said, "I will ride your face while I eat your girl's pussy, whore. You'd damn well better make me precede she does. Assuming you don't, Lauren and I will attach you to that seat in the corner, and you'll need to watch us make each other come throughout the evening." Reaching behind herself, Kiara got a nipple and bent it generally. She astounded herself in how brutal she was and in the little rush it gave her. Jessica's moan of joy at howKiaratreated her supported her and expanded the sensation it caused Kiara to feel.

"Do you get me, whore?" Kiara requested.

"Indeed, Kiara, "Jessica said, "I comprehend."

Kiara settled her pussy down all over and brought her mouth down to Lauren's cunt afterward. She started to run her fingers through Kiara's hair as she sucked and snack at Lauren's lips while every so often utilizing her tongue to prod the adolescent's clit. Kiara needed to get her thoroughly stirred again before sucking her sweet little love bud once more into her mouth.

"Ooooh, indeed, child," Lauren cooed as she scoured her tits. "That feels so screwing great. I love how you eat my pussy. I can hardly wait to come on your tongue once more."

Kiara cherished hearing her satisfying words, and Jessica had appeared to acknowledge her danger truly. She was truly working over Kiara's clit. The cougar couldn't resist the opportunity to start to spin her hips, touching her pussy in little circles all over. Kiara had effectively forgotten about the occasions she'd come this evening. However, she realized she'd add another to the absolute soon.

"Fuck, infant," Lauren cooed, "I believe you will make me come soon. That skank eating your pussy should be working it truly hard. Since I can feel my structure."

Jessica, who had effectively been greatly working Kiara's clit, heard her girl's driving words. She slid two of her fingers into Kiara's steaming opening accordingly and started to screw her. The cougar had almost contacted her pinnacle. Kiara truly didn't have any desire to attach her companion to the seat for the evening. In this way, she dialed down her assault on Lauren's clit, barely enough to permit herself to arrive at a peak first, however scarcely.

"Mmmmm," Kiara groaned into Lauren's pussy as she came and could feel her juices as they overwhelmed Jessica's face. Only seconds after the fact, Lauren started to peak too.

"Fuck, Baby, Yessssssssssssss!" she almost snarled as she also came. Kiara brought her mouth down to cover Lauren's pussy and get her compensation for a job done the right way while she scoured Lauren's clit with two fingers. She got a good portion of her to come and gulped it all eagerly. For the second time that evening, Kiara proved unable' help yet intellectually kick me for holding up until this late in life to experience something like this.

Kiara raised her hips off of Jessica's cum covered face and inclined down to kiss Lauren. The high schooler kissed Kiara's lips and licked her juices off the cougar's face. A demonstration Kiara discovered especially sensual. Not having any desire to fail to remember Jessica, Kiara broke their kiss and went to see her dearest companion licking white cream off her fingers. Kiara flushed when she understood it was hers. John was always prodding her about how Kiara would cream his cockerel when he screwed her. Seeing her in a charming fog as she inspected her closest companion's treats with a look of complete desire in her eyes amazed Kiara.

It additionally energized her, which revealed to Kiara exactly how far gone she was with this new side of herself.

Taking a gander at her two new darlings and old companions, Kiara said, "I don't think about both of you, yet I could utilize a beverage and a bite. Such a lot of peaking has truly removed it from me."

Kiara slid off the bed and snatched Jessica's hand, saying, "Please whore. Help me with the tidbits and drink." Kiara was speaking the truth about requiring the food. In any case, what she truly required was a second alone with her dearest companion. She expected to ensure they were OK.

- - - - -

442

Jessica and Lauren

Lauren was happy for the second alone. She required a touch of time to think. There had been a great deal going on of late in her life. Lauren felt she had a few choices to make. Choices that could influence her folks, her own life, and her future whenever they were made.

She was beginning to presume that she was gay. Lauren had dated many folks somewhat recently. These folks were the best of the best in her school. Lauren realized she was something other than a beautiful face and a hot body. She was keen and had desired. There was no justification for her to need to settle, so her principles were high.

The issue was, she immediately found every one of the folks needing. It wasn't that they had any obvious blemishes. She'd quite recently felt no flash of fascination with any of them, notwithstanding them being folks that each young lady nearby craved. In any event, the straight and sexually unbiased young ladies. For her situation, she'd felt nothing.

The equivalent couldn't be said for her flatmate's closest companion, Alana. She'd been acquainted with the excellent youthful individual of two or multiple times. She had quickly considered what her pussy would suggest a flavor like; however, that was the extent that it had gone. As of late, however, she'd had the chance to spend time with the two companions and had been sickened when she'd got herself unfit to get the young lady off her mind. Interestingly, she'd permitted herself to get seduced by somebody single and her age. She'd endeavored to dodge such confusions.

There was no genuine motivation to get concerned. Alana was straight. Lauren knew because she'd heard her flatmate notice a few times that the two were twofold dating. She'd even met part of the gang, a b-ball player on the school crew.

All that had changed when her companionship with Alana had arrived at the point that the young lady felt agreeable enough to impart her mysterious to Lauren. It turned that the attractive dark coed was gay and was just dating the person as cover. The "beau" was gay as well. The two were each other's whiskers.

In this way, Lauren had been staying away from her new companion for the most recent week. She didn't confide in herself around the young lady. She feared what may occur if she invested any energy with her.

Issue two was her mother. The lady had started to invest more energy at the club they'd taken Kiara to. Lauren knew from conversing with Vicki that her mom had gotten fascinated with the butch blonde muscle head that she'd engaged in sexual relations with that evening at the club. Vicki said she'd appeared at the club to meet the lady the entire father's last excursion for work.

It was her Mom who had encouraged her never to restrict herself to one individual to forestall getting entrapped in anything heartfelt with a lady. However, here she was, making time with this domme.

Things had deteriorated over the most recent few weeks. Her mom had rationalized work issues to venture out from home on two events and didn't return until nearly noon. Lauren had taken in of that reality from her dad during a visit to her parent's home. When on a third event, she referenced a night out with the young ladies, Lauren's dad had said nothing, yet she could tell he was frantic. Lauren had been visiting to do clothing when her mom left. After an hour, Lauren had caught her dad call Kiara's better half John and the fire station and casually inquire about whether Kiara had gone out with his significant other around evening time. He hadn't loved it when he discovered that John had recently conversed with Kiara, and the lady had appreciated a calm night at home.

From that point forward, Kiara had discovered things had been unsettled between her folks. They'd battled when her mom had gotten back from her alleged young lady's night out. Lauren didn't have the foggiest idea about the subtleties. However, her mom had disclosed to her things had gotten very warm.

Seeing her mom's response to Kiara around evening time gave her expectation. Kiara was able to keep furnishing her with the vital control the lady unmistakably longed for; maybe her parent's marriage could be saved. She realized her dad could never reconsider scrutinizing her investing energy with Kiara. Until the occasions of the most recent half a month, the two were in every case together at any rate.

Lauren concluded she would simply need to disclose the circumstance to Kiara. It was clear to her that the cougar had appreciated ruling her mom. It was especially obvious when she'd punished her. It would be great if Lauren could persuade Kiara that this was the awesome the two of them.

Kiara may likewise be the perfect individual for her to converse with about her concern. She unquestionably wouldn't pass judgment on her for being gay and might have some solid counsel. Lauren just couldn't address her mom about it. She'd attempted, however, had never fully had the option to suggest the topic. Lauren would need to figure out some time alone with Kiara.

On the first floor, the two more seasoned ladies worked next to making them three a tidbit. Jessica couldn't meet her companion's eyes and wanted to contemplate whether the lady was passing judgment on her.

"Are you OK, Jessica?" Kiara inquired.

Jessica gestured her head and said, "Sure." She needed to take a gander at Kiara yet thought it was hard because of her dearest companion's disgrace and embarrassment, discovering exactly how accommodating she was. What was more terrible was she could feel her pussy releasing and a consistent vacillate in her clit. A similar disgrace and embarrassment were driving her excitement. It was an endless loop.

"Alright, stop," requested Kiara as she got Jessica's hand, taking the blade she'd been utilizing to cleave vegetables away. "Take a gander at me, Jessica, at present."

Jessica felt the heartbeat in her clitoris accelerate. God, how she cherished how Kiara was so assuming responsibility. The things it did to her! She'd played with being overwhelmed by butch ladies her entire grown-up life. In school, she'd had a butch sweetheart that had acquainted her with the way of life, and she'd been a major enthusiast of it from that point onward. After meeting John and getting hitched, she'd needed to save all that. She'd, in any case, had intercourse with ladies, yet being ruled was something that raised the stakes for her, as it were. It filled a need she had and permitted her not to get focused on everyday life.

Yet, having a domme was a responsibility, and they would, in general, be possessive. A domme couldn't have cared less if your better half expected you home at a specific time. She didn't mind that your child required you or was debilitated. She anticipated that you should be available to her when she called.

So Jessica had recently been content with the sex she had with John and the incredible sex she had with her female sweethearts. Jessica kept her toe in the nearby D/s scene, however. When the everyday pressure arrived at the point she could not deal with it; she would associate with one of the neighborhood domme's and permit them to mitigate that pressure by ruling her.

In the course of the most recent couple of years, her business had taken off incredibly. She was busier than at any other time and had gotten herself increasingly relying upon a few of the neighborhood domme's to own her. A large portion of them, Jessica, met at the club. There were a few others that she at times would slip away with during the week's worth of work and permit them to overwhelm her.

The most recent couple of months had been horrendous. Jessica's business was battling, and the constrain had driven her to invest much more energy than was normal, easing pressure at the party club. Vicki was accepting of assisting her with a trip with no surprises. She knew Jessica's circumstance and regarded it.

Her new companion Alex wasn't exactly something very similar. She'd met the blonde muscle head the night she and Kiara had gone to the club. The butch had come up the table she was sitting at with Lauren and Grace. Jessica was looking out for Kiara to get back from the bathroom when the lady strolled up, hanging over the table. Her short, spikey light hair and amazing physical make-up had engaged Jessica, as had her butch character. Simply seeing her had Jessica wet. The prospect of how she could deal with her with all that strength made her thighs tremble.

From the start, Jessica had been going reveal to her she was unable to move around evening time however trusted they could do so one more evening. She would make a unique excursion only for this lady. Alex had just gotten her hand and made it plain that they planned to move now. Jessica had not been able to stand up.

While moving, Alex had pulled her in close and touched her tits and ass as though they were the solitary individuals present. She'd given up to the lady's lips with a moan of happiness, returning her kiss with just as much warmth as the domme gave. At the point when Alex had said into her ear that she planned to take her out to her vehicle and screw her silly, Jessica couldn't get to the vehicle adequately quick. Had the lady disclosed to her that she was taking her home, at last, she would have left Kiara abandoned.

After some underlying kissing, Alex had educated Jessica to hang over the secondary lounge. At the point when Jessica agreed, Alex had pulled her spruce up over her hips and her undies down to her knees. She'd, at that point, continued to finger screw the cougar to a few amazing peaks. Alex had then covered her long tongue in Jessica's grab and ate her to a few more. Jessica, at that point, spent the following half-hour sucking the butch domme's wet pussy and an enormous clit. She'd given nearly as numerous as she got carrying Alex to climax in any event multiple times. She'd at that point tongued the butch's butt nugget while fingering her to a fourth.

Alex had educated her then that she comprehended the circumstance with her companion yet that she expected Jessica back on Tuesday night. Jessica had been so up to speed in the experience that she'd promptly concurred. They'd traded telephone numbers, and afterward, she'd returned inside to discover Kiara.

She'd deceived John Tuesday evening about a work crisis and afterward met Alex at her place. The domme had screwed her for almost four hours, making Jessica come multiple times. She'd returned home that evening and scrubbed down before sliding into bed close to John. He'd awoken and taken a gander at the clock before turning his back to her without saying a word.

There was an explanation she didn't engage with these dommes. It generally caused issues like this in her marriage. Be that as it may, Alex was simply so screwing hot with how she could make Jessica's body react. Indeed, even in the manner in which her enormous, solid hands punished Jessica. That first night she'd return home with her butt cheeks still scrumptiously consuming.

She disclosed to herself that she wouldn't see the domme once more. She was unable to face the challenge of demolishing her relationship with John. She adored him to an extreme.

Be that as it may, when Alex had messaged her again on Friday, she'd been too powerless to even think about standing up to. She detested herself right to the domme's home. Once there, however, she immediately had failed to remember her blame. Alex had caught her getting through the entryway and constrained her to strip exposed. Stripped, that is, except her wedding ring, which she over and again spat on while sitting all over.

The sad thing was, it had made Jessica hot when she'd done it.

The following Monday night, another content from Alex had constrained her to come up with one more work crisis. She realized that pardon wouldn't hold up any longer after that evening. However, she soothed herself that she'd stress over sometime later.

This opportunity she'd get back home with indentations on the two breasts. Alex had called it "denoting her property," and at that point, Jessica had cherished it. When she'd returned home and seen the teeth checks and slight wounding, she'd felt unique. If John had seen them, the gig would have been up. She'd be exceptionally cautious about uncovering herself around them until they mended. That had implied no sex, which just appeared to worsen the couple's relationship issues.

Thus the circle went. Jessica got pushed at work and over her marriage. She proceeded to have Alex rule and screw her. Which just prompted more pressure in her marriage. That pressure prompted her being not able to amass at work. It was simply the actual quintessence of the term dangerous conduct.

The last bit of trouble that will be tolerated for John had been when Alex had requested Jessica meet her on a Wednesday night. She'd revealed to John that she was meeting a portion of her female workers for a woman's evening. Jessica clarified that she'd been working them so hard. Jessica felt she expected to reimburse them a piece. In transit there, the idea happened to Jessica that maybe she should call Kiara and request that her companion cover for her. Be that as it may, after how Kiara had responded to her decisions about the club, Jessica had selected not to.

That had ended up being a helpless decision. At the point when Jessica got back from another orgasmic experience with Alex, John had been hanging tight for her.

Their battle had been dreadful. John had blamed her for undermining him and swore that he would separate from her on the off chance that he could demonstrate it. She had denied everything. That had left her without a plan of action to the extent that is seeing ladies went other than Lauren.

In any case, Kiara tolerating her sexually open side and turning out to be important for the condition conceivably opened new entryways for Jessica altogether. Her better half never scrutinized the time the two ladies spent together. It gave her the ideal female sexual accomplice and the one Jessica had consistently desired.

Yet, presently she was frightened. HowKiara had treated her this evening and how Jessica's body had reacted was a blessing from heaven. On the off chance that solitary, her dearest companion, truly appreciated doing it, Jessica could have it both ways. She was worried about the possibility that her companion was just doing it to satisfy Lauren and got no genuine delight out of the demonstration. The prospect of asking Kiara to domme her and have this lady she appreciated oddball her was startling.

"I need to understand what the issue is, and I need to know now," Kiara advised her undoubtedly.

Jessica moaned and said, "I'm simply embarrassed that you discovered how agreeable I am; that's it in a nutshell." She asked Kiara would get her misleading statement.

"Nectar, I realize I passed judgment on you for going behind John's back with ladies. What's more, I feel like a major misleading jerk for that at this point. It was so unreasonable of me to pass judgment on you when I needed to do something very similar so gravely. I simply didn't try to do it since I didn't have the mental fortitude. You and Lauren saved me from my ineptitude. I was unable to be more excited with how things have gone, and that incorporates getting some answers concerning you."

Jessica gazed at her inclination, a scramble of expectation in her heart. "So you don't believe I'm some sort of monstrosity?" she inquired.

Kiara grinned and touched Jessica's cheek. "No, nectar. I love you an excessive amount of at any point to imagine that of you." Flushing a smidgen, she added, "And to be straightforward. I tracked down the entire thing sort of hot."

Jessica was so glad she inclined in and kissed her companion. The delicate kiss before long transformed into an enthusiastic kiss with the two ladies' tongues investigating the other's mouth. After a period, Kiara severed the kiss and said, "Hello, quiet down whore. I a few containers of water and a few snacks before things get to sexual once more."

Jessica grinned at her companion and said half-tongue in cheek, "Indeed, Mistress." Kiara smacked her solidly on the butt and gave her the blade back, advising her to get to cleaving.

After renewing themselves with Jessica and Kiara's snacks and arranged, they held up as Lauren left the room, saying she needed to get something. The high schooler got back with a rucksack that she immediately opened and recovered a strap-on tackle from. Pulling an enormous dildo from inside the pack, Lauren gave both to Kiara.

"I think you need to screw your prostitute. Mother made you precede you could make me peak, so you should compensate her for being a decent pet." Lauren said with a grin. She, at that point, saw her mom and teasingly said, "That is the correct term, isn't it, Mom?"

Jessica didn't reply; she just stuck her tongue out at her girl.

"Well, actually, isn't she both our prostitute?' Kiara asked, positioning one eyebrow.

"No," said Lauren, "She's my mother, so I'm apprehensive she has a place with you, and you're left with her."

Kiara grinned and said, "I surmise there are undeniably less pleasurable obligations. In any case, you must show me how this thing functions. I'm as yet in the center of my Lesbian 101 course, all things considered."

Lauren told her the best way to associate the dildo. It was ten creeps long and fatter than some other cockerel Lauren claimed. She helped Kiara into the harness and got it solidly to her ideal hips.

Taking a gander at Jessica, Kiara said, "On the bed whore so I can screw that sweet pussy of yours until you beseech me to stop." She, at that point, went to Lauren and said, "Would you be able to ensure she's acceptable and wet for me while I lube this beast up?"

"Obviously," Lauren murmured as she advanced excitedly between her mom's legs. The high schooler was eager to see Kiara by taking to the predominant job with her mom. Possibly she would have the option to rescue her parent's relationship yet.

Jessica looked as her girl gazed toward her as she anxiously licked all over her pussy. The more seasoned lady realized she was at that point wet from her conversation with Kiara first floor and the makeout meeting the two ladies had shared. At that point, to have Lauren serve her up on a plate to be screwed by Kiara with that huge strapon, there was no chance she was unable to be doused.

Jessica understood what her girl was doing. She was subtlely pushing Kiara towards being her domme, and she cherished Lauren for it much like never before. Her girl probably knew about the pressure in her home actually like Jessica was certain Lauren understood what she'd been up to recently. The lesbian and sexually open local area around was developing. However, it was still little sufficient that word got around. There was a minimal possibility that Alex had stayed silent about ruling her. She could undoubtedly see the news finding its way back to Lauren from somebody at the club.

"Your whore is acceptable and wet. Presently all Mom needs is her Mistress to screw her truly hard." Lauren is detailed.

Kiara took a gander at her companion and said, "I need you up down on the ground. I need to watch that round ass of yours shake while I screw you, a prostitute."

Jessica murmured happily and turned over, ascending on her knees. She curved her back and said, "Is this acceptable, Mistress?"

Lauren grabbed Kiara's eye and several words to her. It required her a second. However, the accidental domme at last comprehended. Getting comfortable behind her agreeable companion, Kiara snatched an ass cheek and crushed it, saying, "Great young lady."

Jessica groaned at Kiara's reaction. She'd generally wanted to hear acclaim from the ladies that ruled her. Yet, it was particularly satisfying coming from her closest companion. Their nearby bond just made the endorsement seriously tempting.

Lauren looked as Kiara got a handle on the cockerel and tested at the opening to her mom's pussy. When she thought that it was, the teenager saw the cougar gradually start caring for the large cockerel into her new prostitute. Lauren acknowledged if the two ladies knew it, they required one another. Together they were the ideal circumstance. The two of them could address each other's issues in a perfect illustration of lesbian advantageous interaction.

When she had the fat chicken mostly inside Jessica, Kiara started to screw her companion in short strokes. Everyone covered the cockerel more profound into Jessica's extended vaginal waterway.

"Goodness, Goddamn, Kiara. That is so screwing acceptable." Jessica moaned.

Lauren got a grin from Kiara just before she smacked Jessica's right ass cheek hard and asked, "What did you call me?"

Her companion's head came up as her hips push back to meet Kiara's strokes. The gel rooster was extending her opening so great and was covered inside her. The lady would have screwed her she felt nearest to on the planet. No, right that. She would have been overwhelmed by the lady she was going gaga for.

"I'm heartbroken, Mistress," Jessica apologized. "I guarantee it will not occur once more."

Kiara smacked her accommodating's other cheek similarly as she reached as far down as possible in the curvy brunette. "Is it accurate to say that you are fit to be screwed now, skank?"

"Indeed, please, Mistress," Jessica asked.

"Please, what?" Kiara requested.

"Kindly screw me, Mistress. Make my pussy yours. Make a case for it, and I'm yours until the end of time."

Lauren had started to finger herself as she watched the two ladies. It was a particularly suggestive sight, and she realized this was the second that could save her parent's marriage. Lauren required Kiara to venture up to her and do comparably her sub had asked. She expected to make a case for her mom with the goal that Jessica would disregard the wide range of different dommes in and out of town. Principally that, Alex bitch.

Jessica was in a condition of unadulterated euphoria when Kiara started to screw her hard as she hit her can cheeks. The lady substituted each side to coordinate with the beating she was giving.

"Who's pussy? Am I screwing?" Kiara requested to know.

Jessica's answer came rapidly. "Itttssssyooouuurs, Mistress," The cougar proclaimed as she pushes back to meet each stroke. She could feel her peak assembling and could advise it would have been a major one.

Recollecting a sexual lesbian story she'd read that elaborate a prevailing lady enticing a lot more youthful lady, Kiara said, "Don't you come until I advise you to."

Lauren could feel herself drawing near to coming. This was screwing hot watching these two hot mothers screw one another. What amazed her, however, was Kiara's abrupt knowledge of D/s vernacular. It was simply something more she would need to get some information about when they talked alone later.

"Soooo close," Jessica sang as her moans arrived at a top in both recurrence and volume. "Would I be able to come, Mistress?" Jessica asked.

Kiara brought her to give over on Jessica's butt with evil power and said, "Come for your, Mistress whore. Come for me now!"

"Ahhhhyesssss, fuck, fuck, fuck!" Jessica pronounced as the peak to end all peaks hammered into her like a tsunami. Kiara proceeded to cylinder into her as though she'd hadn't yet come. The lady's endurance was mind-boggling, and Jessica realized that she would allow this lady to screw her anyplace and whenever.

Pointing at Lauren, Kiara said in a requesting tone, "Slide up under your mom and lick her clit until she comes back once more."

"I'm not agreeable. For what reason is Kiara bossing me around?" Lauren pondered internally. Yet, she ended up getting in line. The high schooler attempted to persuade herself that she was just doing it for an opportunity to taste her mom's cum. Yet, where it counts inside, there was this little pestering sort of stimulation that disclosed to her it wasn't the specific truth.

Jessica had recently had the Mount Everest of peaks; however, as of now could feel another privilege behind it. At the point when Lauren's tongue started to stimulate her clit, the cougar started to groan uproariously once more. She realized she was simply minutes from one more astounding climax graciousness of her new darling and Mistress. Jessica attempted to get the mist free from the happiness that obfuscated her reasoning. She knew there was something she expected to do; it was only there in her mind. In any case, the nearer her peak got, the harder it was to see.

A sharp smack to Jessica's rear end cheek almost sent the agreeable over the edge. In any case, it cleared the brain haze barely enough for Jessica to recall what she expected to do.

"Please, Mistress, would I be able to come?" the accommodating cougar asked.

"Is my pet's pussy prepared to take care of her whore girl some cum?" Kiara prodded both the mother and girl.

"Indeed, Mistress," Kiara shouted out.

"I will tally down from five. At the point when I arrive at nothing, you may come and not before at that point." the domme requested.

"Five," Kiara said as she beat the cockerel in so hard the head beat against Jessica's cervix, drawing a loud moan from the sub.

"Four," she said as she released another persistent push.

"Three," Kiara called out as her push again struck Jessica's cervix and made the lady figure she wouldn't make it.

"Two," Kiara shouted before adding, "Suck her clit hard little girl skank."

"One." Jessica had started to howl, a sound that indicated something important.

"Zero, come for your Mistress, whore!" Kiara requested in a firm voice sending Jessica into blankness.

Jessica wasn't a squirter. She would cream everywhere on a cockerel or fingers that screwed her truly well, yet she won't ever spurt. She did now, however, and intensely. Lauren got a facial storm as her mom's body discharged many spouts. Lauren attempted to get however much of the sweet nectar as expected yet discovered face and hair covered in new cum.

Jessica fell over on her side, laying alongside her little girl. Kiara cuddled up close to her companion and kissed her gently, mentioning to her what a decent young lady she was.

The domme then pointed at Lauren and said, "Take a gander at what a wreck you made of your whore girl's face. You'll have to tidy that up for her privilege after you come here and tidies up my cockerel."

Lauren took a gander at Kiara with an odd demeanor all over.

"I provided you a request prostitute, and I anticipate that you should follow it. Presently!" Kiara shouted, making both Lauren and Jessica bounce. Jessica felt her depleted pussy return to life at the presentation of strength her new domme showed over her little girl.

Lauren, however, was stunned by how the conventionally delicate Kiara verbally confronted her. She wasn't agreeable and didn't get off on very similar things her mom did. She didn't know why the change in Kiara towards her was going on.

She was all the while thinking these things when she understood she had her lips folded over the top of the huge cockerel taking in her mom's cum. She hadn't known about sitting up and creeping over to the cougar. Was that right? Had she truly slithered like...a pet?

Lauren worked her mouth around the base, licking and drawing the cream off the outside of the gel rooster. The youngster needed to concede, her mom's cream was delectable. Lauren did whatever it takes not to consider her responses towards Kiara's new tyrannical character and why she would subliminally submit to the lady's solicitations. No, that wasn't precise, they were requests, and she felt constrained not to allow the lady to down. She needed to satisfy how her mom did.

"Come here, pet. I need my pussy licked, and I need to come on your beautiful face." Lauren heard Kiara say. It took her a second to understand the cougar was conversing with her. She watched Kiara and her mom as they lay one next to the other. Their tongues investigated each other's mouths. Also, when their lips would isolate, Lauren could hear Kiara murmuring to her mom. She could not make out the thing the domme was saying; however, she could reveal to it satisfied her mom.

She realized she ought to educate Kiara that she wasn't agreeable and, like this, couldn't be a pet. She should simply get up and leave the two to play their games. She'd prevailing with regards to getting her mom a domme that she could have without destroying her marriage. Kiara currently had a completely satisfying sexual coexistence and sexuality. Notwithstanding the fantastic sexual coexistence she imparted to her significant other, no longer would she need to feel fragmented and could be a shockingly better spouse for John.

She realized she should simply leave.

All things being equal, she crept over where Kiara and her mom were snuggling and settled her head between the domme's legs. She felt an odd feeling of euphoria, and a shiver goes through her clitoris when Kiara stroked her head and said, "Great young lady."

- - - - -

Kiara

Kiara couldn't accept that how this night had wound up happening. She had been apprehensive about seeing Jessica again and eased in, realizing that Lauren wouldn't be at home. Presently here she was with her closest companion snuggled bare in her arms while her little girl's head was between her legs. Kiara groaned her endorsement as the accomplished teenager lesbian lapped away at her all-around very much satisfied pussy. She was unable to get enough of these two. However much Kiara cherished it when John screwed her and made her come. There was something to be said for having two unquenchable skanks willing to satisfy your enthusiastic moxie persistently.

During Kiara's introduction to the universe of web lesbian pornography, she had inquisitively seen a progression of recordings regarding the matter of D/s connections. She did it trying to see better what Jessica escaped the hookups she'd as of late become so fixated on. Simultaneously, a portion of the video's more sadomasochist parts wasn't to the cougar's taste. Seeing one lady overwhelming another did strangely tantalize her excitement. While the sex between the two ladies was energizing, it was the information that both were getting what they required that most engaged Kiara.

Another hunt of the subject had driven her to a progression of stories on a site called Literotica. They managed separation from their mother, who perceived her eighteen-year-old sitter as bicurious and compliant. She begins tempting the young lady and transforming her into her pet. Kiara had considered the thought peculiarly thrilling. The point of view of the domme addressed something inside Kiara. The lady was uncompromising with her charge yet adoring. She supported the young lady and tried to fill the high schooler's dreams and wants.

While Jessica's accommodation was a known amount, Kiara likewise saw indications of a similar sort in her little girl. The adolescent had consistently appeared to be anxious to satisfy everyone around her. However, she had never shown up completely content herself. Maybe she was looking for something yet didn't know what it was. Kiara's effort to overwhelm the young lady was more a guess out of nowhere that appeared to have struck its planned imprint.

Lauren professed to date men. However, Kiara had seen no indications of it since her secondary school days. And still, at the end of the day, it had appeared to be easygoing. Kiara knew from Jessica that Lauren went through a large portion of her end-of-the-week evenings at a similar dance club that they'd taken Kiara to. Her weeknights were loaded up with school work, and that left the cougar to contemplate whether the high schooler probably won't be a lesbian.

Peering down, the exquisite youngster gazed back at her with a look of satisfaction all over as she nursed at Kiara's sex. She grinned at the doe-looked at adolescent and said, "You're a particularly perfect minimal lesbian pet. Do you like sucking your Mistress' pussy?" Kiara realized the high schooler was puzzled about how she had been attracted to respond to Kiara's orders. She could see the contention present on the young lady's face and contemplated whether Lauren would have the option to deny what she was feeling.

Finally, the high schooler gestured as she proceeded to lick and suck at Kiara's engorged clitoris.

Knowing from her perusing that she expected to build up firm limits to solidify the chain of command inside their relationship, Kiara said, "Utilize your words, pet."

Kiara thought a little dread immediately appeared in the high schooler's eyes. Be that as it may, it blurred as she appeared to acknowledge her destiny. "Indeed, Mistress," Lauren reacted before bringing her mouth down to Kiara's sex and sucking her delicate clit back into her mouth as she groaned happily.

The new domme utilized the following two hours to imbue Lauren's brain the young lady's acknowledgment of their new relationship. She had Lauren wear the strapon while Kiara rode the huge part to a few pivotal peaks. As the gel cockerel filled every one of the little hiding spots in her very much fulfilled sex, Jessica rode her girl's face as Lauren fanatically sucked away at her mom's juices.

Kiara discovered she couldn't completely portray a portion of the ideas about dommes she'd read in the narratives on Literotica. In those, the dommes would finger or fuck their dommes with strapons yet would infrequently go down on them. That wasn't worth it to Kiara. She cherished the flavor of pussy decidedly an excessive amount to denying herself this new delight. She licked both her new darlings to various climaxes and satisfied her new dependence on female cum without limit.

They finished the night with another of Lauren's toys. A long twofold finished dildo. After them, three alternated, screwing each other to fruition. Kiara utilized every lady's bountiful juices to grease up the rosebud of every lady. She, at that point, had them slide the long part into their butt-centric cavities and screw each other as she alternated sucking and licking at their clits.

Watching how the two prostitutes came uproariously, Kiara got herself curious concerning how it would feel. She had attempted butt-centric sex with John yet had always been unable to loosen up enough to appreciate the demonstration. Even though it had been John's thought, Kiara got herself too unsure about his opinion about her being willing to accomplish something so devious.

Needing to attempt once more, she had Lauren edge her sphincter and coat it with her finger. The new compliant tenderly scoured her mischievous spot before permitting it to crawl into Kiara's lower area like a snake cautiously. As when Jessica had entered her before with a thumb, it was awkward from the start. It wasn't long, however, before she felt herself unwind.

As Jessica kissed her and scoured her clitoris, Lauren slid a second finger into her opening and held it there until Kiara loose. At the point when the domme disclosed to her, it was OK, Lauren started to saw her fingers in and out while contorting them to and fro like a wine tool.

At the point when the adolescent astounded her by adding a third finger, Kiara shouted out. "Fuck, that consumes. Go, a lethargic prostitute. Allow me to become accustomed to it."

Lauren continued bending her fingers when finally she was prepared, loosening up the domme's unpracticed butt-centric opening. Jessica had supplanted the enormous cockerel on the strapon with a lot more slender seven-inch assortment in the interim.

At the point when she felt prepared, Kiara laid back with her head level on the bed and drew her knees up, and pulled them back as near her head as could be expected. It was JessicaKiarawho had trained to wear the outfit. She had Lauren stoop close by and rub her puffy clit while Jessica slid the silicone staff into her holding up the ass.

It was awkward from the outset. Kiara felt full, and there was consuming regardless of Lauren having released her up.

"Go sluggish, my pet," Kiara said as she attempted to constrain her butt-centric musculature to unwind around the firm rooster. Jessica started to stroke the cockerel in a sluggish and shifted pistoning movement. Inside a moment, Kiara's moans of inconvenience started to change into more pleasing sounds. Lauren's control of her swollen clit positively diverted Kiara until it appeared to be the sensitive spots in her butt-centric waterway woke up. They started to transmit a glow of pleasurable sentiments all through her center.

"Screw my butt, whore," Kiara requested the agreeable mother, "Fuck, that feels so great."

Jessica obliged her request and started to stroke the rooster in a snappier style. Lauren's right hand had become a haze on her clit as three fingers on her left hand slid into the hot, smooth profundities of the dommes pussy.

"Indeed, pet. Goodness, fuck, screw fuck, that is acceptable. I will come so hard. Fuck, " Kiara shouted out as she felt a pressing factor starting inside her. It seemed like a bladder of air gradually being filled inside her body. Furthermore, when it at last popped, she found that rather than air, it had been loaded up with plenty of euphoric mind synthetic compounds that flowed through her body at Mach speeds.

At the point when her gigantic peak at last dwelled, Kiara felt as loose and depleted as she had any time in her life. The three ladies cuddled themselves under the sheet and cover in the wake of eliminating the duvet canvassed in their juices and cum. Each of the three enjoyed a hearty chuckle over the prospect of Jessica taking the costly bed blanket to the laundry and their opinion about the scents exuding from it.

Kiara lay in her two sweethearts with Lauren cuddled against one breast and Jessica cuddled against the other. She nodded off, feeling ecstatically content and thinking about what the future held.

- - - - -

Epilog

Kiara sat in her kitchen, drinking some espresso. Sitting in the seat inverse her was Alana, a lovely dark coed and Lauren's first sweetheart. On her knees and between Kiara's legs stooped Jessica. The agreeable mother groaned as she wantonly sucked and snacked at Kiara's augmented labia. The cougar was dressed for work and was stooping on a cushion. She had one hand up her short skirt as she fingered her pussy.

On the opposite side of the table, Alana stroked Lauren's head and guided the now twenty-year-old mouth to her clit. Lauren could consider the to be stub as it jabbed its head out from underneath its dim hood. Lauren wanted to nurse at Alana's pussy. The taste was superb, and she adored how she could make her Mistress shout with joy. Simply a week ago, she had conceded her adoration to Alana, and to her heart's enjoyment, the sentiments had been returned.

"Along these lines, what are both of you youthful darlings up to this evening?" Kiara asked Alana. She truly loved this young lady and trusted that she and Lauren made it the distance. Lauren was in her second year of school, with Alana being lesser. At the point when she and Kiara had talked alone the day after Kiara's lesbian despoiling, the young brunette's affirmations had come at nothing unexpected.

Kiara had urged the young lady to act naturally and guaranteed her that her folks would be cheerful. Kiara realized that as long as Lauren's choices drove her down a solid way, Jessica and her John would consistently uphold her.

Her story about what Jessica had been up to had additionally not come as a tremendous astonishment. Lauren had disclosed how her mom required her as a companion, yet perhaps more critically, as a lasting Mistress. Lauren's clarified how their spouses could never be dubious of the time the two spent together. That would permit them plentiful freedom for sweet D/s play.

Kiara had effectively been offering thought to her future relationship with the pair that morning. On the off chance that the previous night's brilliant illustration of lesbian lewdness was an illustration of what she could expect, Kiara realized she needed a long period of it.

The most recent year had been perhaps the awesome Kiara's life. Explicitly it was indeed at the first spot on her list. Her marriage with John was the best it had at any point been. From the start, he appeared to be somewhat confused about the progressions of his significant other. She was greedy for his rooster and appeared to need it each time she could get him up, which with the assistance of present-day synthetic compounds, ended up being a considerable amount. She had, as of late, gotten him into watching pornography. He essentially appeared to like lesbian pornography. That gave Kiara trust that she wouldn't need to live covertly for the remainder of their coexistences.

Another addition was the sentiment that had gotten back to their relationship. On occasion, it felt like John was attempting to court her once more.

"We truly didn't have any plans past perhaps visiting the club," Alana said before peering down at Lauren, who affectionately gazed back at her. Alana added, "My young switch her likes getting her pet to play with. We've been keeping watch yet haven't yet discovered the perfect lady."

"Allow me to figure," Kiara said with a chuckle, "She needs to tempt a more seasoned wedded lady to turn into her whore."

Alana contacted the tip of her nose as she snickered alongside her domme friend. Lauren just groaned as the prospect of having the option to have another agreeable darling that she could present to her Mistress enticed her mind.

"Furthermore, both of you women?" Alana said before delivering a loud groan as her thighs trembled and afterward shut around Lauren's head. Kiara was directly behind her as she peaked, sprinkling her warm young lady cum everywhere on Jessica's beautiful face.

"Discussing exchanging," Alana said, "Care to?"

Kiara grinned over at her young companion and said, "I thought you'd never inquire."

The two submissives traded places and indeed started to entertain themselves with their number one tidbit.

"Neither of us wants to battle the group at the club around evening time. I figured I might arrange Lissy and Bridget over this evening for a little lesbian bash." Kiara said as she scoured Lauren's head as the youthful skank flicked her tongue against her clit. She winked down at the young lady. Melissa, Lissy, was an eighteen-year-old young lady that Kiara had found working at a neighborhood dress store. Lissy was at that point out as a lesbian. However, Kiara could recognize a compliant nature about the young lady. She'd allured her in the changing area and had been going about as domme for the adolescent from that point forward.

Bridget was Lissy's mother. At the point when she'd discovered that her little girl was having what she saw as an illegal lesbian undertaking with a lady a lot more established than her, she'd been resentful. She had visited Kiara at home. While they talked in the receiving area of Kiara's home, Jessica had entered and, at a snap of Kiara's finger, had dropped to her knees and slithered between Kiara's legs.

Bridget had appeared to be stunned from the start to see a lady ten years more established than her do something like this. In any case, as Kiara watched Lissy's mom, she could see that she was unable to remove her eyes from the sight before her. Kiara deliberately stripped back Jessica's hair and held it to her side to give Bridget a superior perspective on the thing that was going on.

At the point when Kiara saw Bridget licking her lower lip, her eyes spacey with obvious longing, she had made her play. She inquired as to whether she had at any point been with a lady. Bridget had simply had the option to shake her head no. Kiara followed that up by inquiring as to whether she'd at any point considered the big picture. Bridget appeared to fight in her mind concerning whether she should reply. At the point when Bridget at long last gestured her head, Kiara disclosed to her that the domme would permit Bridget to supplant her pet between her legs. However, to do that, she would need to drop to her knees and creep across the room and give her assertion that she needed to turn into Kiara's new compliant close by her girl enthusiastically. The fight inside the accommodating mother seethed for almost two minutes as she watched the sapphic love occurring before her.

At the point when she dropped to her knees and started to slither towards her new Mistress, Kiara tapped Jessica's head and had her hurry to the side. It took one taste of Kiara's pussy and a covering of her young lady cum before Bridget had submitted and completely promised herself as a pet.

"You know," Kiara said, "I've truly got everything I can deal with among John and Jessica. Lissy will be disappearing from school in only a couple of months. I can deal with her up to that point. Possibly both of you should remain here and play with us around evening time. If you build up jumping at the chance to Bridget, maybe Lauren would consider turning into her all-day domme."

Peering down at her pet, Alana asked, "Does that seem like something you'd prefer to do? You provocative little prostitute."

Lauren gestured her head in endorsement and afterward returned to licking Kiara's sweet pussy.

Indeed, life was, in fact, acceptable.

CPSIA information can be obtained
at www.ICGtesting.com
Printed in the USA
LVHW060712300421
686057LV00006B/357

9 781802 355215